W9-BIM-495

Praise for John Grisham
and his legal thriller *The Confession*

"Grisham is an adept ringmaster.... He channels his zeal and his legal expertise into a story that his fans will appreciate." —*St. Louis Post-Dispatch*

"Grisham is the master of the legal thriller. Readers who share his views as well as those sitting on the fence will find much to love and lament in the tragic story of Donté Drumm." —*USA Today*

"A superb work of social criticism in the literary troublemaker tradition of Upton Sinclair's *The Jungle*." —*The Washington Post*

*

"Never let it be said this man doesn't know how to spin a good yarn." —*Entertainment Weekly*

"There's no doubt that Grisham has his finger on the pulse of America." —*Orlando Sentinel*

"John Grisham may well be the best American storyteller writing today." —*The Philadelphia Inquirer*

"Grisham keeps you turning those pages."
—San Francisco *Examiner*

"Grisham knows how to tell a story."
—*The Denver Post*

BOOKS BY JOHN GRISHAM

JOHN
GRISHAM

DELL | NEW YORK

THE CONFESSION

A NOVEL

Sale of this book without a front cover may be unauthorized. If this book is coverless, it may have been reported to the publisher as "unsold or destroyed" and neither the author nor the publisher may have received payment for it.

The Confession is a work of fiction. Names, characters, places, and incidents either are the product of the author's imagination or are used fictitiously. Any resemblance to actual persons, living or dead, events, or locales is entirely coincidental.

2011 Dell Export Mass Market Edition

Copyright © 2010 by Belfry Holdings, Inc.

All rights reserved.

Published in the United States by Dell, an imprint of
The Random House Publishing Group,
a division of Random House, Inc., New York.

DELL is a registered trademark of Random House, Inc., and the colophon is a trademark of Random House, Inc.

Originally published in hardcover in the United States by Doubleday, a division of Random House, Inc., in 2010.

ISBN 978-0-440-42295-2
eBook ISBN 978-0-385-53413-0

Cover photograph: © Fry Design Ltd./Getty Images
Cover design: John Fontana

Printed in the United States of America

www.bantamdell.com

2 4 6 8 9 7 5 3

THE CONFESSION

PART ONE

THE CRIME

1

The custodian at St. Mark's had just scraped three inches of snow off the sidewalks when the man with the cane appeared. The sun was up, but the winds were howling; the temperature was stuck at the freezing mark. The man wore only a pair of thin dungarees, a summer shirt, well-worn hiking boots, and a light Windbreaker that stood little chance against the chill. But he did not appear to be uncomfortable, nor was he in a hurry. He was on foot, walking with a limp and a slight tilt to his left, the side aided by the cane. He shuffled along the sidewalk near the chapel and stopped at a side door with the word "Office" painted in dark red. He did not knock and the door was not locked. He stepped inside just as another gust of wind hit him in the back.

The room was a reception area with the cluttered, dusty look one would expect to find in an old church. In the center was a desk with a nameplate that announced the presence of Charlotte Junger, who sat not far behind her name. She said with a smile, "Good morning."

"Good morning," the man said. A pause. "It's very cold out there."

"It is indeed," she said as she quickly sized him up. The obvious problem was that he had no coat and nothing on his hands or head.

"I assume you're Ms. Junger," he said, staring at her name.

"No, Ms. Junger is out today. The flu. I'm Dana Schroeder, the minister's wife, just filling in. What can we do for you?"

There was one empty chair and the man looked hopefully at it. "May I?"

"Of course," she said. He carefully sat down, as if all movements needed forethought.

"Is the minister in?" he asked as he looked at a large, closed door off to the left.

"Yes, but he's in a meeting. What can we do for you?" She was petite, with a nice chest, tight sweater. He couldn't see anything below the waist, under the desk. He had always preferred the smaller ones. Cute face, big blue eyes, high cheekbones, a wholesome pretty girl, the perfect little minister's wife.

It had been so long since he'd touched a woman.

"I need to see Reverend Schroeder," he said as he folded his hands together prayerfully. "I was in church yesterday, listened to his sermon, and, well, I need some guidance."

"He's very busy today," she said with a smile. Really nice teeth.

"I'm in a rather urgent situation," he said.

Dana had been married to Keith Schroeder long enough to know that no one had ever been sent away from his office, appointment or not. Besides, it was a frigid Monday morning and Keith wasn't really that busy. A few phone calls, one consultation with a young couple in the process of retreating from a wedding, under way at that very moment, then the usual visits to the hospitals. She fussed around the desk, found the simple questionnaire she was looking for, and said, "Okay, I'll take some basic information and we'll see what can be done." Her pen was ready.

"Thank you," he said, bowing slightly.

"Name?"

"Travis Boyette." He instinctively spelled his last name for her. "Date of birth, October 10, 1963. Place, Joplin, Missouri. Age, forty-four. Single, divorced, no children. No address. No place of employment. No prospects."

Dana absorbed this as her pen frantically searched for the proper blanks to be filled. His response created far more questions than her little form was designed to accommodate. "Okay, about the address," she said, still writing. "Where are you staying these days?"

"These days I'm the property of the Kansas Department of Corrections. I'm assigned to a halfway house on Seventeenth Street, a few blocks from here. I'm in the process of being released, 'reentry,' as they like to call it. A few months in the halfway house here in Topeka, then I'm a free man with nothing to look forward to but parole for the rest of my life."

The pen stopped moving, but Dana stared at it anyway. Her interest in the inquiry had suddenly lost steam. She was hesitant to ask anything more. However, since she had started the interrogation, she felt compelled to press on. What else were they supposed to do while they waited on the minister?

"Would you like some coffee?" she asked, certain that the question was harmless.

There was a pause, much too long, as if he couldn't decide. "Yes, thanks. Just black with a little sugar."

Dana scurried from the room and went to find coffee. He watched her leave, watched everything about her, noticed the nice round backside under the everyday slacks, the slender legs, the athletic shoulders, even the ponytail. Five feet three, maybe four, 110 pounds max.

She took her time, and when she returned Travis Boyette was right where she'd left him, still sitting monklike, the fingertips of his right hand gently tapping those of his left, his black wooden cane across his thighs, his eyes gazing forlornly at nothing on the far wall. His head was completely shaved, small, and perfectly round and shiny, and as she handed him the cup, she pondered the frivolous question of whether he'd gone bald at an early age or simply preferred the skinned look. There was a sinister tattoo creeping up the left side of his neck.

He took the coffee and thanked her for it. She resumed her position with the desk between them.

"Are you Lutheran?" she asked, again with the pen.

"I doubt it. I'm nothing really. Never saw the need for church."

"But you were here yesterday. Why?"

Boyette held the cup with both hands at his chin, like a mouse nibbling on a morsel. If a simple question about coffee took a full ten seconds, then one about church attendance might require an hour. He sipped, licked his lips. "How long do you think it'll be before I can see the reverend?" he finally asked.

Not soon enough, Dana thought, anxious now to pass this one along to her husband. She glanced at a clock on the wall and said, "Any minute now."

"Would it be possible just to sit here in silence as we wait?" he asked, with complete politeness.

Dana absorbed the stiff-arm and quickly decided that silence wasn't a bad idea. Then her curiosity returned. "Sure, but one last question." She was looking at the questionnaire as if it required one last question. "How long were you in prison?" she asked.

"Half my life," Boyette said with no hesitation, as if he fielded that one five times a day.

Dana scribbled something, and then the desktop keyboard caught her attention. She pecked away with a flourish as if suddenly facing a deadline. Her e-mail to Keith read: "There's a convicted felon out here who says he must see you. Not leaving until. Seems nice enough. Having coffee. Let's wrap things up back there."

Five minutes later the pastor's door opened and a young woman escaped through it. She was wiping her eyes. She was followed by her ex-fiancé, who managed both a frown and a smile at the same time. Neither spoke to Dana. Neither noticed Travis Boyette. They disappeared.

When the door slammed shut, Dana said to Boyette, "Just a minute." She hustled into her husband's office for a quick briefing.

The Reverend Keith Schroeder was thirty-five years old, happily married to Dana for ten years now, the father of three boys, all born separately within the span of twenty months. He'd been the senior pastor at St. Mark's for two years; before that, at a church in Kansas City. His father was a retired Lutheran minister, and Keith had never dreamed of being anything else. He was raised in a small town near St. Louis, educated in schools not far from there, and, except for a class trip to New York and a honeymoon in Florida, had never left the Midwest. He was generally admired by his congregation, though there had been issues. The biggest row occurred when he opened up the church's basement to shelter some homeless folks during a blizzard the previous winter. After the snow melted, some of the homeless were reluctant to leave. The city issued a citation for unauthorized use, and there was a slightly embarrassing story in the newspaper.

The topic of his sermon the day before had been forgiveness—God's infinite and overwhelming power to forgive our sins, regardless of how heinous they might be. Travis Boyette's sins were atrocious, unbelievable, horrific. His crimes against humanity would surely condemn him to eternal suffering and death. At this point in his miserable life, Travis was convinced he could never be forgiven. But he was curious.

"We've had several men from the halfway house," Keith was saying. "I've even held services there." They were in a corner of his office, away from the desk, two new friends having a chat in saggy canvas chairs. Nearby, fake logs burned in a fake fireplace.

"Not a bad place," Boyette said. "Sure beats prison." He was a frail man, with the pale skin of one confined to unlit places. His bony knees were touching, and the black cane rested across them.

"And where was prison?" Keith held a mug of steaming tea.

"Here and there. Last six years at Lansing."

"And you were convicted of what?" he asked, anxious to know about the crimes so he would know much more about the man. Violence? Drugs? Probably. On the other hand, maybe Travis here was an embezzler or a tax cheat. He certainly didn't seem to be the type to hurt anyone.

"Lot of bad stuff, Pastor. I can't remember it all." He preferred to avoid eye contact. The rug below them kept his attention. Keith sipped his tea, watched the man carefully, and then noticed the tic. Every few seconds, his entire head dipped slightly to his left. It was a quick nod, followed by a more radical corrective jerk back into position.

After a period of absolute quiet, Keith said, "What would you like to talk about, Travis?"

"I have a brain tumor, Pastor. Malignant, deadly, basically untreatable. If I had some money, I could fight it—radiation, chemo, the usual routine—which might give me ten months, maybe a year. But it's glioblastoma, grade four, and that means I'm a dead man. Half a year, a whole year, it really doesn't matter. I'll be gone in a few months." As if on cue, the tumor said hello. Boyette grimaced and leaned forward and began massaging his temples. His breathing was heavy, labored, and his entire body seemed to ache.

"I'm very sorry," Keith said, realizing full well how inadequate he sounded.

"Damned headaches," Boyette said, his eyes still tightly closed. He fought the pain for a few minutes as nothing was said. Keith watched helplessly, biting his tongue to keep from saying something stupid like, "Can I get you some Tylenol?" Then the suffering eased, and Boyette relaxed. "Sorry," he said.

"When was this diagnosed?" Keith asked.

"I don't know. A month ago. The headaches started at Lansing, back in the summer. You can imagine the quality of health care there, so I got no help. Once I was released and sent here, they took me to St. Francis Hospital, ran tests, did the scans, found a nice little egg in the middle of my head, right between the ears, too deep for surgery." He took a deep breath, exhaled, and managed his first smile. There was a tooth missing on the upper left side and the gap was prominent. Keith suspected the dental care in prison left something to be desired.

"I suppose you've seen people like me before," Boyette said. "People facing death."

"From time to time. It goes with the territory."

"And I suppose these folks tend to get real serious about God and heaven and hell and all that stuff."

"They do indeed. It's human nature. When faced with our own mortality, we think about the afterlife. What about you, Travis? Do you believe in God?"

"Some days I do, some days I don't. But even when I do, I'm still pretty skeptical. It's easy for you to believe in God because you've had an easy life. Different story for me."

"You want to tell me your story?"

"Not really."

"Then why are you here, Travis?"

The tic. When his head was still again, his eyes looked around the room, then settled on those of the pastor. They stared at each other for a long time, neither blinking. Finally, Boyette said, "Pastor, I've done some bad things. Hurt some innocent people. I'm not sure I want to take all of it to my grave."

Now we're getting somewhere, Keith thought. The

burden of unconfessed sin. The shame of buried guilt. "It would be helpful if you told me about these bad things. Confession is the best place to start."

"And this is confidential?"

"For the most part, yes, but there are exceptions."

"What exceptions?"

"If you confide in me and I believe you're a danger to yourself or to someone else, then the confidentiality is waived. I can take reasonable steps to protect you or the other person. In other words, I can go get help."

"Sounds complicated."

"Not really."

"Look, Pastor, I've done some terrible things, but this one has nagged at me for many years now. I gotta talk to someone, and I got no place else to go. If I told you about a terrible crime that I committed years ago, you can't tell anyone?"

Dana went straight to the Web site for the Kansas Department of Corrections and within seconds plunged into the wretched life of Travis Dale Boyette. Sentenced in 2001 to ten years for attempted sexual assault. Current status: incarcerated.

"Current status is in my husband's office," she mumbled as she continued hitting keys.

Sentenced in 1991 to twelve years for aggravated sexual battery in Oklahoma. Paroled in 1998.

Sentenced in 1987 to eight years for attempted sexual battery in Missouri. Paroled in 1990.

Sentenced in 1979 to twenty years for aggravated sexual battery in Arkansas. Paroled in 1985.

Boyette was a registered sex offender in Kansas, Missouri, Arkansas, and Oklahoma.

"A monster," she said to herself. His file photo was that of a much heavier and much younger man with dark, thinning hair. She quickly summarized his record and sent an e-mail to Keith's desktop. She wasn't worried about her husband's safety, but she wanted this creep out of the building.

After half an hour of strained conversation and little progress, Keith was beginning to tire of the meeting. Boyette showed no interest in God, and since God was Keith's area of expertise, there seemed little for him to do. He wasn't a brain surgeon. He had no jobs to offer.

A message arrived on his computer, its appearance made known by the distant sound of an old-fashioned doorbell. Two chimes meant anyone might be checking in. But three chimes signaled a message from the front desk. He pretended to ignore it.

"What's with the cane?" he asked pleasantly.

"Prison's a rough place," Boyette said. "Got in one fight too many. A head injury. Probably led to the tumor." He thought that was funny and laughed at his own humor.

Keith obliged with a chuckle of his own, then stood, walked to his desk, and said, "Well, let me give you one of my cards. Feel free to call anytime. You're always welcome here, Travis." He picked up a card and glanced at his monitor. Four, count 'em, four convictions, all related to sexual assault. He walked back to the chair, handed Travis a card, and sat down.

"Prison's especially rough for rapists, isn't it, Travis?" Keith said.

You move to a new town; you're required to hustle down to the police station or the courthouse and register as a sex offender. After twenty years of this, you just assume that everybody knows. Everybody's watching. Boyette did not seem surprised. "Very rough," he agreed. "I can't remember the times I've been attacked."

"Travis, look, I'm not keen on discussing this subject. I have some appointments. If you'd like to visit again, fine, just call ahead. And I welcome you back to our services this Sunday." Keith wasn't sure he meant that, but he sounded sincere.

From a pocket of his Windbreaker, Boyette removed a folded sheet of paper. "You ever hear of the case of Donté Drumm?" he asked as he handed the paper to Keith.

"No."

"Black kid, small town in East Texas, convicted of murder in 1999. Said he killed a high school cheerleader, white girl, body's never been found."

Keith unfolded the sheet of paper. It was a copy of a brief article in the Topeka newspaper, dated Sunday, the day before. Keith read it quickly and looked at the mug shot of Donté Drumm. There was nothing remarkable about the story, just another routine execution in Texas involving another defendant claiming to be innocent. "The execution is set for this Thursday," Keith said, looking up.

"I'll tell you something, Pastor. They got the wrong guy. That kid had nothing to do with her murder."

"And how do you know this?"

"There's no evidence. Not one piece of evidence. The cops decided he did it, beat a confession out of him, and now they're going to kill him. It's wrong, Pastor. So wrong."

"How do you know so much?"

Boyette leaned in closer, as if he might whisper something he'd never uttered before. Keith's pulse was increasing by the second. No words came, though. Another long pause as the two men stared at each other.

"It says the body was never found," Keith said. Make him talk.

"Right. They concocted this wild tale about the boy grabbing the girl, raping her, choking her, and then throwing her body off a bridge into the Red River. Total fabrication."

"So you know where the body is?"

Boyette sat straight up and crossed his arms over his chest. He began to nod. The tic. Then another tic. They happened quicker when he was under pressure.

"Did you kill her, Travis?" Keith asked, stunned by his own question. Not five minutes earlier, he was making a mental list of all the church members he needed to visit in the hospitals. He was thinking of ways to ease Travis out of the building. Now they were dancing around a murder and a hidden body.

"I don't know what to do," Boyette said as another wave of pain hit hard. He bent over as if to throw up and then began pressing both palms against his head. "I'm dying, okay? I'll be dead in a few months. Why should that kid have to die too? He didn't do anything." His eyes were wet, his face contorted.

Keith watched him as he trembled. He handed him a Kleenex and watched as Travis wiped his face. "The tumor is growing," he said. "Each day it puts more pressure on the skull."

"Do you have medications?"

"Some. They don't work. I need to go."

"I don't think we're finished."

"Yes we are."

"Where's the body, Travis?"

"You don't want to know."

"Yes I do. Maybe we can stop the execution."

Boyette laughed. "Oh, really? Fat chance in Texas." He slowly stood and tapped his cane on the rug. "Thank you, Pastor."

Keith did not stand. Instead, he watched Boyette shuffle quickly out of his office.

Dana was staring at the door, refusing a smile. She managed a weak "Good-bye" after he said "Thanks." Then he was gone, back on the street without a coat and gloves, and she really didn't care.

Her husband hadn't moved. He was still slouched in his chair, dazed, staring blankly at a wall and holding the copy of the newspaper article. "You all right?" she asked. Keith handed her the article and she read it.

"I'm not connecting the dots here," she said when she finished.

"Travis Boyette knows where the body is buried. He knows because he killed her."

"Did he admit he killed her?"

"Almost. He says he has an inoperable brain tumor and will be dead in a few months. He says Donté Drumm had nothing to do with the murder. He strongly implied that he knows where the body is."

Dana fell onto the sofa and sank amid the pillows and throws. "And you believe him?"

"He's a career criminal, Dana, a con man. He'd rather lie than tell the truth. You can't believe a word he says."

"Do you believe him?"

"I think so."

"How can you believe him? Why?"

"He's suffering, Dana. And not just from the tumor. He knows something about the murder, and the body. He knows a lot, and he's genuinely disturbed by the fact that an innocent man is facing an execution."

For a man who spent much of his time listening to the delicate problems of others, and offering advice and counsel that they relied on, Keith had become a wise and astute observer. And he was seldom wrong. Dana was much quicker on the draw, much more likely to criticize and judge and be wrong about it. "So what are you thinking, Pastor?" she asked.

"Let's take the next hour and do nothing but research. Let's verify a few things: Is he really on parole? If so, who is his parole officer? Is he being treated at St. Francis? Does he have a brain tumor? If so, is it terminal?"

"It will be impossible to get his medical records without his consent."

"Sure, but let's see how much we can verify. Call Dr. Herzlich—was he in church yesterday?"

"Yes."

"I thought so. Call him and fish around. He should be making rounds this morning at St. Francis. Call the parole board and see how far you can dig."

"And what might you be doing while I'm burning up the phones?"

"I'll go online, see what I can find about the murder, the trial, the defendant, everything that happened down there."

They both stood, in a hurry now. Dana said, "And

what if it's all true, Keith? What if we convince ourselves that this creep is telling the truth?"

"Then we have to do something."

"Such as?"

"I have no earthly idea."

2

Robbie Flak's father purchased the old train station in downtown Slone in 1972, while Robbie was still in high school and just before the city was about to tear it down. Mr. Flak Sr. had made some money suing drilling companies and needed to spend a little of it. He and his partners renovated the station and reestablished themselves there, and for the next twenty years prospered nicely. They certainly weren't rich, not by Texas standards anyway, but they were successful lawyers and the small firm was well regarded in town.

Then along came Robbie. He began working at the firm when he was a teenager, and it was soon evident to the other lawyers there that he was different. He showed little interest in profits but was consumed with social injustice. He urged his father to take on civil-rights cases, age- and sex-discrimination cases, unfair-housing cases, police-brutality cases, the type of work that can get one ostracized in a small southern town. Brilliant and brash, Robbie finished college up north, in three years, and sailed through law school at the University of Texas at Austin. He never interviewed for a job, never thought about working anywhere but the train station in downtown Slone. There were so many people there he wanted to sue, so many mistreated and downtrodden clients who needed him.

He and his father fought from day one. The other lawyers either retired or moved on. In 1990, at the age of thirty-five, Robbie sued the City of Tyler, Texas, for housing discrimination. The trial, in Tyler, lasted for a month, and at one point Robbie was forced to hire bodyguards when the death threats became too credible. When the jury returned a verdict for $90 million, Robbie Flak became a legend, a wealthy man, and an unrestrained radical lawyer now with the money to raise more hell than he could ever imagine. To get out of his way, his father retired to a golf course. Robbie's first wife took a small cut and hurried back to St. Paul.

The Flak Law Firm became the destination for those who considered themselves even remotely slighted by society. The abused, the accused, the mistreated, the injured, they eventually sought out Mr. Flak. To screen the cases, Robbie hired young associates and paralegals by the boatload. He picked through the net each day, took the good catches, and tossed the rest away. The firm grew, then it imploded. It grew again, then it broke up in another meltdown. Lawyers came and went. He sued them, they sued him. The money evaporated, then Robbie won big in another case. The lowest point of his colorful career happened when he caught his bookkeeper embezzling and beat him with a briefcase. He escaped serious punishment by negotiating a thirty-day misdemeanor jail sentence. It was a front-page story, and

Slone hung on every word. Robbie, who, not surprisingly, craved publicity, was bothered more by the bad press than by the incarceration. The state bar association issued a public reprimand and a ninety-day suspension of his license. It was his third entanglement with the ethics panel. He vowed it would not be his last. Wife No. 2 eventually left, with a nice check.

His life, like his personality, was chaotic, outrageous, and in constant conflict with itself and those around him, but it was never dull. Behind his back, he was often referred to as "Robbie Flake." And as his drinking grew worse, "Robbie Flask" was born. But regardless of the turmoil, of the hangovers and crazy women and feuding partners and shaky finances and lost causes and scorn of those in power, Robbie Flak arrived at the train station early each morning with a fierce determination to spend the day fighting for the little people. And he did not always wait for them to find him. If Robbie got wind of an injustice, he often jumped in his car and went searching for it. This relentless zeal led him to the most notorious case of his career.

In 1998, Slone was stunned by the most sensational crime in its history. A seventeen-year-old senior at Slone High, Nicole Yarber, vanished and was never seen again, dead or alive. For two weeks, the town stood still as thousands of volunteers combed the alleys and fields and ditches and abandoned buildings. The search was futile.

Nicole was a popular girl, a B student, a member of the usual clubs, church on Sunday at First Baptist, where she sometimes sang in the youth choir. Her most important achievement, though, was that of being a cheerleader at Slone High. By her senior year, she had become the captain of the squad, perhaps the most envied position in school, at least for girls. She was on and off with a boyfriend, a football player with big dreams but limited talent. The night she disappeared, she had just spoken to her mother by cell and promised to be home before midnight. It was a Friday in early December. Football was over for the Slone Warriors, and life had returned to normal. Her mother would later state, and the phone records bore this out, that she and Nicole spoke by cell phone at least six times a day. They also averaged four text messages. They were in touch, and the idea that Nicole would simply run away without a word to her mom was inconceivable.

Nicole had no history of emotional problems, eating disorders, erratic behavior, psychiatric care, or drug use. She simply vanished. No witnesses. No explanations. Nothing. Prayer vigils in churches and schools ran nonstop. A hotline was established and calls flooded in, but none proved credible. A Web site was created to monitor the search and filter the gossip. Experts, both real and fake, came to town to give advice. A psychic appeared, unsolicited, but left town when no one offered to pay. As the search dragged on, the gossip seethed nonstop as the town talked of little else. A police car was parked in front of her home twenty-four hours a day, ostensibly to make the family feel better. Slone's only television station hired another rookie reporter to get to the bottom of things. Volunteers scoured the earth as the search spread throughout the countryside. Doors and windows were bolted. Fathers slept with their guns on their nightstands. Little children were watched closely by their parents and babysitters. Preachers reworked their sermons to beef up their slant against evil. The police gave daily briefings for the first week, but when they realized they had nothing to say, they began skipping days. They waited and waited, hoping for the lead, the unexpected phone call, the snitch looking for the reward money. They prayed for a break.

It finally came sixteen days after Nicole disappeared. At 4:33 a.m., the home phone of Detective Drew Kerber rang twice before he grabbed it. Though exhausted, he had not been sleeping well. Instinctively, he flipped a switch to record what was about to be said. The recording, later played a thousand times, ran:

> *Kerber: "Hello."*
> *Voice: "Is this Detective Kerber?"*
> *Kerber: "It is. Who's calling?"*
> *Voice: "That's not important. What's important is that I know who killed her."*
> *Kerber: "I need your name."*
> *Voice: "Forget it, Kerber. You wanna talk about the girl?"*
> *Kerber: "Go ahead."*
> *Voice: "She was seeing Donté Drumm. A big secret. She was trying to break it off, but he wouldn't go away."*
> *Kerber: "Who's Donté Drumm?"*
> *Voice: "Come on, Detective. Everybody knows Drumm. He's your killer. He grabbed her outside the mall, tossed her over the bridge on Route 244. She's at the bottom of the Red River."*

The line went dead. The call was traced to a pay phone at an all-night convenience store in Slone, and there the trail ended.

Detective Kerber had heard the hushed rumors of Nicole seeing a black football player, but no one had been able to verify this. Her boyfriend adamantly denied it. He claimed that they had dated on and off for a year, and he was certain that Nicole was not yet sexually active. But like many rumors too salacious to leave alone, it persisted. It was so repulsive and so potentially explosive that Kerber had thus far been unwilling to discuss it with Nicole's parents.

Kerber stared at the phone, then removed the tape. He drove to the Slone Police Department, made a pot of coffee, and listened to the tape again. He was elated and couldn't wait to share the news with his investigative team. Everything fit now: the teenage love affair—black on white, still very much taboo in East Texas—the attempted breakup by Nicole, the bad reaction from her scorned lover. It made perfect sense.

They had their man.

Two days later, Donté Drumm was arrested and charged with the abduction, aggravated rape, and murder of Nicole Yarber. He confessed to the crime and admitted that he'd tossed her body into the Red River.

Robbie Flak and Detective Kerber had a history that had almost been violent. They had clashed several times in criminal cases over the years. Kerber loathed the lawyer as much as he loathed the other lowlifes who represented criminals. Flak considered Kerber an abusive thug, a rogue cop, a dangerous man with a badge and gun who would do anything to get a conviction. In one memorable exchange, in front of a jury, Flak caught Kerber in an outright lie and, to underscore the obvious, yelled at the witness, "You're just a lying son of a bitch, aren't you, Kerber?"

Robbie was admonished, held in contempt, required to apologize to Kerber and the jurors, and fined $500. But his client was found not guilty, and nothing else mattered. In the history of the Chester County Bar Association, no lawyer had ever been held in contempt as often as Robbie Flak. It was a record he was quite proud of.

As soon as he heard the news about Donté Drumm's arrest, Robbie made a few frantic phone calls, then took off to the black section of Slone, a neighborhood he knew well. He was accompanied by Aaron Rey, a former gang member who'd served time for drug distribution and was now gainfully employed by the Flak Law Firm as a bodyguard, runner, driver, investigator, and anything else Robbie might need. Rey carried at least two guns on his person and two more in a satchel, all legal because Mr. Flak had gotten his rights restored and now he could even vote. Around Slone, Robbie Flak had more than his share of enemies. However, all of these enemies knew about Mr. Aaron Rey.

Drumm's mother worked at the hospital, and his father drove a truck for a lumber mill south of town. They lived with their four children in a small whiteframed house with Christmas lights around the windows and garland on the door. Their minister arrived not long after Robbie. They talked for hours. The parents were confused, devastated, furious, and frightened beyond reason. They were also grateful that Mr. Flak would come and see them. They had no idea what to do.

"I can get myself appointed to handle the case," Robbie said, and they agreed.

Nine years later, he was still handling it.

Robbie arrived at the station early on Monday morning, November 5. He had worked on Saturday and Sunday and did not feel at all rested from the weekend. His mood was gloomy, even foul. The next four days would be a chaotic mess, a frenzy of events, some anticipated and others wholly unexpected, and when the dust settled at 6:00 p.m. on Thursday, Robbie knew that in all likelihood, he would be standing in a cramped witness room at the Huntsville prison, holding hands with Roberta Drumm as the State of Texas injected her son with enough chemicals to kill a horse.

He'd been there once before.

He turned off the engine of his BMW but could not unfasten his seat belt. His hands clutched the steering wheel as he looked through the windshield and saw nothing.

For nine years, he had fought for Donté Drumm. He had waged war as he had never done before. He had fought like a madman at the ridiculous trial in which Donté was convicted of the murder. He had abused the appellate courts during his appeals. He had danced around ethics and skirted the law. He had written grating articles declaring his client's innocence. He had paid experts to concoct novel theories that no one bought. He had pestered the governor to the point that his calls were no longer returned, not even by lowly staffers. He had lobbied politicians, innocence groups, religious groups, bar associations, civil-rights advocates, the ACLU, Amnesty International, death-penalty abolitionists, anybody and everybody who might possibly be able to do something to save his client. Yet the clock had not stopped. It was still ticking, louder and louder.

In the process, Robbie Flak had spent all his money, burned every bridge, alienated almost every friend, and driven himself to the point of exhaustion and instability. He had blown the trumpet for so long that no one heard it anymore. To most observers, he was just another loudmouthed lawyer screaming about his innocent client, not exactly an unusual sight.

The case had pushed him over the edge, and when it was over, when the State of Texas finally succeeded in executing Donté, Robbie seriously doubted if he could go on. He planned to move, to sell his real estate, retire, tell Slone and Texas to kiss his ass, and go live in the mountains somewhere, probably in Vermont, where the summers are cool and the state does not kill people.

The lights came on in the conference room. Someone else was already there, opening up the place, preparing for the week from hell. Robbie finally left his car and went inside. He spoke to Carlos, one of his longtime paralegals, and they spent a few minutes over coffee. The talk soon turned to football.

"You watch the Cowboys?" Carlos asked.

"No, I couldn't. I heard Preston had a big day."

"Over two hundred yards. Three touchdowns."

"I'm not a Cowboys fan anymore."

"Me neither."

A month earlier, Rahmad Preston had been right there, in the conference room, signing autographs and posing for photos. Rahmad had a distant cousin who'd been executed in Georgia ten years earlier, and he had taken up the cause of Donté Drumm with big plans to enlist other Cowboys and NFL heavyweights to help wave the flag. He would meet with the governor, the parole board, big business boys, politicians, a couple of rappers he claimed to know well, maybe even some Hollywood types. He would lead a parade so noisy that the state would be forced to back down. Rahmad, though, proved to be all talk. He suddenly went silent, went into "seclusion," according to his agent, who also explained that the cause was too distracting for the great running back. Robbie, always on the conspiracy trail, suspected that the Cowboys organization and its network of corporate sponsors somehow pressured Rahmad.

By 8:30, the entire firm had assembled in the conference room, and Robbie called the meeting to order. At the moment he had no partners—the last had left in a feud that was still tied up in litigation—but there were two associates, two paralegals, three secretaries, and Aaron Rey, who was always close by. After fifteen years with Robbie, Aaron knew more law than most seasoned paralegals. Also present was a lawyer from Amnesty Now, a London-based human rights group that had donated thousands of skilled hours to the Drumm appeals. Participating by teleconference was a lawyer in Austin, an appellate advocate furnished by the Texas Capital Defender Group.

Robbie ran through the plans for the week. Duties

were defined, tasks distributed, responsibilities clari-
fied. He tried to appear upbeat, hopeful, confident
that a miracle was on the way.

The miracle was slowly coming together, some
four hundred miles due north, in Topeka, Kansas.

3

A few of the details were confirmed with little effort. Dana, calling from St. Mark's Lutheran and just going about her business of following up on those kind enough to visit their church, chatted with the supervisor at Anchor House, who said that Boyette had been there for three weeks. His "stay" was scheduled for ninety days, and if all went well, he would then be a free man, subject, of course, to some rather stringent parole requirements. The facility currently had twenty-two male residents, no females, and it was operated under the jurisdiction of the Department of Corrections. Boyette, like the others, was expected to leave each morning at 8:00 and return each evening at 6:00, in time for dinner. Employment was encouraged, and the supervisor usually kept the men busy in janitorial work and odd, part-time jobs. Boyette was working four hours a day, at $7 an hour, watching security cameras in the basement of a government office building. He was reliable and neat, said little, and had yet to cause trouble. As a general rule, the men were very well behaved because a broken rule or an ugly incident could send them back to prison. They could see, feel, and smell freedom, and they didn't want to screw up.

About the cane, the supervisor knew little. Boyette was using it the day he arrived. However, among a group of bored criminals there is little privacy and an avalanche of gossip, and the rumor was that Boyette had been severely beaten in prison. Yes, everybody knew he had a nasty record, and they gave him plenty of room. He was weird, kept to himself, and slept alone in a small room behind the kitchen while the rest bunked down in the main room. "But we get all types in here," the supervisor said. "From murderers to pickpockets. We don't ask too many questions."

Fudging a bit, or perhaps a lot, Dana breezily mentioned a medical concern that Boyette noted on the visitor's card he'd been kind enough to fill out. A prayer request. There was no card, and Dana asked for forgiveness with a quick petition to the Almighty. She justified the small and harmless lie with what was at stake here. Yes, the supervisor said, they'd hauled him to the hospital when he wouldn't shut up about his headaches. These guys love medical treatment. At St. Francis, they ran a bunch of tests, but the supervisor knew nothing more. Boyette had some prescriptions, but they were his business. It was a medical matter and off-limits.

Dana thanked him and reminded him that St. Mark's welcomed everyone, including the men from Anchor House.

She then called Dr. Herzlich, who was a thoracic surgeon at St. Francis and a longtime member of St. Mark's. She had no plans to inquire into the medical status of Travis Boyette, since such nosiness was far out of bounds and certain to go nowhere. She would let her husband chat with the doctor, with his door shut, and in their veiled and professional voices they might find common ground. The call went straight to voice mail, and Dana left a request for Herzlich to phone her husband.

While she worked the phone, Keith was glued to his computer, lost in the case of Donté Drumm. The Web site was extensive. Click here for a factual summary, 10 pages long. Click here for a complete trial transcript, 1,830 pages long. Click farther down for the appellate briefs, with exhibits and affidavits, another 1,600 or so pages. A case history ran for 340 pages and included the rulings from the appeals courts. There was a tab for the Death Penalty in Texas, and one for Donté's Photo Gallery, Donté on Death Row, the Donté Drumm Defense Fund, How You Can Help, Press Coverage and Editorials, Wrongful Convictions and False Confessions, and the last one was for Robbie Flak, Attorney-at-Law.

Keith began with the factual summary. It read:

The town of Slone, Texas, population forty thousand, once cheered wildly when Donté Drumm roamed the field as a fearless linebacker, but now it nervously awaits his execution.

Donté Drumm was born in Marshall, Texas, in 1980, the third child of Roberta and Riley Drumm. A fourth child arrived four years later, not long after the family moved to Slone, where Riley found a job with a drainage contractor. The family joined the Bethel African Methodist Church and are still active members. Donté was baptized in the church at the age of eight. He attended the public schools in Slone, and by the age of twelve was being noticed as an athlete. With good size and exceptional speed, Donté became a force on the football field, and at the age of fourteen, as a freshman, was starting linebacker for the varsity at Slone High

School. He was named all-conference as a sophomore and junior, and had verbally committed to play for North Texas State before a severe ankle injury ended his career during the first quarter of the first game of his senior year. Surgery was successful, but the damage was done. The scholarship offer was withdrawn. He did not finish high school, because he was incarcerated. His father, Riley, died of heart disease in 2002, while Donté was on death row.

When Donté was fifteen years old, he was arrested and charged with assault. It was alleged that he and two black friends beat another black youth behind the gymnasium at the high school. The case was handled through juvenile court. Donté eventually pleaded guilty and was given probation. When he was sixteen, he was arrested for simple possession of marijuana. By then, he was an all-conference linebacker and well-known in town. The charges were later dismissed.

Donté was nineteen years old when he was convicted in 1999 for the abduction, rape, and murder of a high school cheerleader named Nicole Yarber. Drumm and Yarber were seniors at Slone High School. They were friends and had grown up together in Slone, though Nicole, or "Nikki," as she was often called, lived in the suburbs while Donté lived in Hazel Park, an older section of town that is primarily black middle-class. Slone is one-third black, and while the schools are integrated, the churches and civic clubs and neighborhoods are not.

Nicole Yarber was born in Slone in 1981, the first and only child of Reeva and Cliff Yarber, who divorced when she was two years old. Reeva remarried, and Nicole was raised by her mother and stepfather, Wallis Pike. Mr. and Mrs. Pike had two additional children. Aside from the divorce, Nicole's upbringing was typical and unremarkable. She attended public elementary and middle schools and in 1995 enrolled as a freshman at Slone High. (Slone has only one high school.

Aside from the usual church schools for kindergartners, the town has no private schools.) Nicole was a B student who seemed to frustrate her teachers with a noted lack of motivation. She should have been an A student, according to several summaries. She was well liked, popular, very social, with no record of bad behavior or trouble with the law. She was an active member of the First Baptist Church of Slone. She enjoyed yoga, water-skiing, and country music. She applied to two colleges: Baylor in Waco and Trinity in San Antonio, Texas.

After the divorce, her father, Cliff Yarber, left Slone and moved to Dallas, where he made a fortune in strip malls. As an absentee father, he apparently tried to compensate through expensive gifts. For her sixteenth birthday, Nicole received a bright red convertible BMW Roadster, undoubtedly the nicest car in the parking lot at Slone High. The gifts were a source of friction between the divorced parents. The stepfather, Wallis Pike, ran a feed store and did well financially, but he couldn't compete with Cliff Yarber.

In the year or so before her disappearance, Nicole dated a classmate by the name of Joey Gamble, one of the more popular boys in school. Indeed, in the tenth and eleventh grades, Nicole and Joey were voted most popular and posed together for the school yearbook. Joey was one of three captains of the football team. He later played briefly at a junior college. He would become a key witness at the trial of Donté Drumm.

Since her disappearance, and since the subsequent trial, there has been much speculation about the relationship between Nicole Yarber and Donté Drumm. Nothing definite has been learned or confirmed. Donté has always maintained that the two were nothing more than casual acquaintances, just two kids who'd grown up in the same town and were members of a graduating class of over five hundred. He denied at trial, under oath, and he has denied ever since, that he had a sexual relationship with Nicole. Her friends have always believed this too. Skeptics, however, point out that Donté would be foolish to admit an intimate relationship with a woman he was accused of murdering. Several of his friends allegedly said that the two had just begun an affair when she disappeared. Much speculation centers upon the actions of Joey Gamble. Gamble testified at trial that he saw a green Ford van moving slowly and "suspiciously" through the parking lot where Nicole's BMW was parked at the time she disappeared. Donté Drumm often drove such a van, one owned by his parents. Gamble's testimony was attacked at trial and should have been discredited. The theory is that Gamble knew of Nicole's affair with Donté, and as the odd man out he became so enraged that he helped the police frame their story against Donté Drumm.

Three years after the trial, a voice analysis expert hired by defense lawyers determined that the anonymous man who called Detective Kerber with the tip that Donté was the killer was, in fact, Joey Gamble. Gamble vehemently denies this. If it is true, then Gamble played a significant role in the arrest, prosecution, and conviction of Donté Drumm.

A voice jolted him from another world. "Keith, it's Dr. Herzlich," Dana said through the phone's intercom.

Keith said, "Thanks," and paused for a moment to clear his mind. Then he picked up the phone. He began with the usual pleasantries, but knowing the doctor was a busy man, he quickly got down to business. "Look, Dr. Herzlich, I need a little favor, and if it's too sticky, just say so. We had a guest during the worship service yesterday, a convict in the process of being paroled, spending a few months at a halfway house, and he's really a troubled soul. He stopped by this morning, just left actually, and he claims to have some rather severe medical problems. He's been seen at St. Francis."

"What's the favor, Keith?" Dr. Herzlich asked, as if he were staring at his wristwatch.

"If you're in a rush, we can talk later."

"No, go ahead."

"Anyway, he claims to have been diagnosed with a brain tumor, a bad one, glioblastoma. Says it's fatal, says he'll be dead soon. I'm wondering how much of this you can verify. I'm not asking for confidential info, you understand? I know he's not your patient, and I don't want anyone to violate procedures here. That's not what I'm asking. You know me better than that."

"Why do you doubt him? Why would anyone claim to have a brain tumor when he really doesn't?"

"He's a career criminal, Doctor. A lifetime behind bars and all that, probably not sure where the truth is. And I'm not saying I doubt him. He had two episodes of severe headaches in my office, and they were painful to watch. I'd just like to confirm what he's already said. That's all."

A pause, as if the doctor were looking around for eavesdroppers. "I can't pry too deep, Keith. Any idea who the doc is here?"

"No."

"All right. Give me a name."

"Travis Boyette."

"Got it. Give me a couple of hours."

"Thanks, Doctor."

Keith hung up quickly and returned to Texas. He continued with the factual summary:

Nicole disappeared on Friday night, December 4, 1998. She had spent the evening with girlfriends at a cinema in the only mall in Slone. After the movie, the girls—four of them—ate pizza at a restaurant that was also in the mall. Entering the restaurant, the girls chatted briefly with two boys, one of whom was Joey Gamble. Over pizza, the girls decided to meet at the home of Ashley Verica to watch late-night television. As the four girls left the restaurant, Nicole excused herself to use the ladies' room. Her three friends never saw her again. She called her mother and promised to be home by midnight, her curfew. Then she vanished. An hour later, her friends were concerned and were making calls. Two hours later, her red BMW was found where she'd left it in a parking lot at the mall. It was locked. There was no sign of a struggle, no sign of anything wrong, no sign of Nicole. Her family and friends panicked, and the search began.

The police immediately suspected foul play and organized a massive effort to find Nicole. Thousands volunteered, and through the days and weeks that followed, the city and county were scoured as never before. Nothing was found. Surveillance cameras at the mall were too far away, out of focus, and of no benefit. No one reported seeing Nicole leave the mall and walk to her car. Cliff Yarber offered a reward of $100,000 for information, and when this sum proved ineffective, he raised it to $250,000.

The first break in the case came on December 16, twelve days after her disappearance. Two brothers were fishing on a sandbar in the Red River near a landing known as Rush Point, when one of them stepped on a piece of plastic. It was Nicole's gym membership card. They poked through the mud and sand and found another card—her student ID issued by Slone High. One of the brothers recognized the name, and they immediately drove to the police station in Slone.

Rush Point is thirty-eight miles due north of the city limits.

The police investigators, led by Detective Drew Kerber,

made the decision to sit on the news about the gym membership and ID cards. They reasoned that the better strategy was to find the body first. They conducted an exhaustive, though futile, search of the river for miles east and west of Rush Point. The state police assisted with teams of divers. Nothing else was found. Authorities as far away as a hundred miles downriver were notified and asked to be on the alert.

While the search of the river was under way, Detective Kerber received an anonymous tip implicating Donté Drumm. He wasted little time. Two days later, he and his partner, Detective Jim Morrissey, approached Donté as he was leaving a health club. Several hours later, two other detectives approached a young man named Torrey Pickett, a close friend of Donté's. Pickett agreed to go to the police station and answer a few questions. He knew nothing about the disappearance of Nicole and was not concerned, though he was nervous about going to the police station.

"Keith, it's the auditor. Line two," Dana announced through the intercom. Keith glanced at his watch—10:50 a.m.—and shook his head. The last voice he wanted to hear at the moment was that of the church's auditor.

"Is the printer full of paper?" he asked.

"I don't know," she fired back. "I'll check."

"Please load it up."

"Yes, sir."

Keith reluctantly hit line two and began a dull but not extended discussion of the church's finances through October 31. As he listened to the numbers, he pecked away at his keyboard. He printed the ten-page factual summary, thirty pages of news articles and editorials, a summary of the death penalty as practiced in Texas, Donté's account of life on death row, and when informed that the printer was out of paper, he clicked on Donté's Photo Gallery and looked at the faces. Donté as a child with parents, two older brothers, one younger sister; Donté as a small boy wearing a choir robe in church; various poses of Donté the linebacker; a mug shot, front page of the *Slone Daily News*; Donté being led in handcuffs into the courthouse; more photos from the trial; and the annual file photos from prison, beginning in 1999 with a cocky glare at the camera and ending in 2007 with a thin-faced, aging man of twenty-seven.

When the auditor was done, Keith walked to the outer room and sat down across from his wife. She was sorting through the copies he'd printed, scanning them as she went. "Did you read this?" she asked, waving a stack of papers.

"Read what? There are hundreds of pages."

"Listen," she said, and began to read: "The body of Nicole Yarber has never been found, and while this might thwart prosecutions in some jurisdictions, it did not slow things in Texas. In fact, Texas is one of several states with a well-developed case law allowing prosecutions in murder cases where there is no definitive proof that a murder has indeed taken place. A dead body is not always required."

"No, I did not get that far," he said.

"Can you believe it?"

"I'm not sure what to believe."

The phone rang. Dana snatched it and abruptly informed the caller that the minister was unavailable. When she hung up, she said, "Okay, Pastor. What's the plan?"

"There is no plan. The next step, the only step I

can think of right now, is to have another talk with Travis Boyette. If he admits he knows where the body is, or was, then I'll press him to admit the murder."

"And if he does? What then?"

"I have no idea."

4

The investigator trailed Joey Gamble for three days before he made contact. Gamble wasn't hiding, nor was he hard to find. He was an assistant manager at a mammoth auto parts discount warehouse in the Houston suburb of Mission Bend, his third job in the past four years. He had one divorce under his belt and perhaps another on the way. He and his second wife were not living together and had retreated to neutral corners where the lawyers were waiting. There wasn't much to fight over, at least not in assets. There was one child, a little boy with autism, and neither parent truly wanted custody. So they fought anyway.

The file on Gamble was as old as the case itself, and the investigator knew it by heart. After high school, the kid played one year of football at a junior college, then dropped out. He hung around Slone for a few years working at various jobs and spending most of his spare time in the gym, where he ate steroids and built himself into a hulking specimen. He boasted of becoming a professional bodybuilder, but eventually grew tired of the work. He married a local girl, divorced her, moved to Dallas, and then drifted to Houston. According to the high school yearbook, Class of 1999, he planned to own a cattle ranch if the NFL thing didn't work out.

It did not, nor did the ranch, and Joey was holding a clipboard and frowning at a display of windshield wipers when the investigator made his move. The long aisle was empty. It was almost noon, a Monday, and the store was practically empty.

"Are you Joey?" the investigator asked with a tight smile just under a thick mustache.

Joey glanced down at the plastic name badge pinned above his shirt pocket. "That's me." He tried to return the smile. This was, after all, retail, and the customer must be adored. However, this guy did not appear to be a customer.

"My name's Fred Pryor." The right hand shot out like a boxing punch bound for the gut. "I'm a private investigator." Joey grabbed it, almost in self-defense, and they shook hands for a few awkward seconds. "Nice to meet you."

"A pleasure," Joey said, his radar at full alert. Mr. Pryor was about fifty years old, thick in the chest, with a round tough face topped with gray hair that required work each morning. He wore a standard navy blazer, tan polyester slacks that were straining at the waist, and, of course, a pair of well-shined, pointed-toe boots.

"What kind of investigator?" Joey asked.

"I'm not a cop, Joey. I'm a private investigator, duly licensed by the State of Texas."

"You got a gun?"

"Yep." Pryor flung open his blazer to reveal a 9-millimeter Glock strapped under his left armpit. "You wanna see the permit?" he asked.

"No. Who are you working for?"

"Donté Drumm's defense team."

The shoulders sagged a bit, the eyes rolled, the air escaped in one quick sigh of frustration, as if to say, "Not that again." But Pryor expected this and moved in quickly. "I'll buy you lunch, Joey. We can't talk here. There's a Mexican place around the corner. Meet me there. Give me thirty minutes, okay? That's all I ask. You get lunch. I get some face time. Then maybe you'll never see me again."

The Monday special was quesadillas, all you can eat for $6.50. The doctor told him to lose some weight, but he craved Mexican food, especially the greased-up, flash-fried, American version.

"What do you want?" he asked.

Pryor glanced around as if others were listening. "Thirty minutes. Look, Joey, I'm not a cop. I have no authority, no warrant, no right to ask for anything. But you know the history better than me."

Pryor would later report to Robbie Flak that at that point the kid lost his edge, stopped smiling, and his eyes half closed in a look of submission and sadness. It was as if he knew this day would eventually arrive. At that moment, Pryor was certain they would catch a break.

Joey glanced at his watch and said, "I'll be there in twenty minutes. Order me one of their house margaritas."

"You got it." Pryor thought that drinking at lunch could be problematic, at least for Joey. But then, the alcohol might help.

The house margarita was served in a clear, bowl-shaped pitcher of some sort and was enough of a beverage for several thirsty men. As the minutes passed, condensation formed on the glass and the ice began to melt. Pryor sipped iced tea with lemon and sent a message to Flak: "Meeting JG for lunch now. Later."

Joey arrived on time and managed to squeeze his sizable frame into the booth. He slid the glass over, took the straw, and inhaled an impressive quantity of the booze. Pryor made some small talk until the waiter took their orders and disappeared, then he moved in closer and got to the point.

"Donté will be executed Thursday. Did you know that?"

Joey nodded slowly. Affirmative. "I saw it in the paper. Plus, I talked to my mother last night and she said the town is buzzing."

The mother was still in Slone. The father was working in Oklahoma, maybe separated. An older brother was in Slone. A younger sister had moved to California.

"We're trying to stop the execution, Joey, and we need your help."

"Who's we?"

"I'm working for Robbie Flak."

Joey almost spit. "Is that nut still around?"

"Of course he is. He'll always be around. He's represented Donté from day one, and I'm sure he'll be in Huntsville Thursday night at the bitter end. That is, if we can't stop the execution."

"The paper said the appeals have run out. There's nothing left to do."

"Maybe, but you never quit. A man's life is at stake, how can you quit?"

Another pull on the straw. Pryor hoped the guy was one of those passive drunks who take the booze and sort of melt into the furnishings, as opposed to the hell-raisers who knock back two drinks and try to clear out the bar.

Joey smacked his lips and said, "I guess you're convinced he's innocent, right?"

"I am. Always have been."

"Based on what?"

"Based on the complete lack of physical evidence; based on the fact that he had an alibi, he was somewhere else; based on the fact that his confession is as bogus as a three-dollar bill; based on the fact that he's passed at least four polygraph tests; based on the fact that he has always denied any involvement. And, Joey, for purposes of this discussion, based on the fact that your testimony at trial was completely unbelievable. You didn't see a green van in the parking lot in the vicinity of Nicole's car. It was impossible. You left the mall through the entrance to the cinema. She was parked on the west side, on the other side of the mall. You fabricated the testimony to help the cops nail their suspect."

There was no eruption, no anger. He took it well, much like a child caught red-handed with a stolen coin and unable to utter words.

"Keep going," Joey said.

"You want to hear it?"

"I'm sure I've heard it before."

"Indeed you have. You heard it at trial, eight years ago. Mr. Flak explained it to the jury. You were crazy about Nicole, but she wasn't crazy about you. Typical high school drama. You dated off and on, no sex, a rather stormy relationship, and at some point you suspected that she was seeing someone else. Turned out this was Donté Drumm, which, of course, in Slone and in a lot of other small towns, could lead to real problems. No one knew for sure, but the gossip was out of control. Maybe she tried to break it off with him. He denies this. He denies everything. Then she disappeared, and you saw the opportunity to nail the guy. Nail him you did. You sent him to death row, and now you're about to be responsible for killing him."

"So, I'm gettin' all the blame here?"

"Yes, sir. Your testimony placed him at the scene of the crime, or at least the jury thought so. It was almost laughable because it was so inconsistent, but the jury was anxious to believe you. You didn't see a green van. You lied. You fabricated. You also called Detective Kerber with the anonymous tip, and the rest is history."

"I did not call Kerber."

"Of course you did. We have the experts to prove it. You didn't even try to disguise your voice. According to our analysis, you had been drinking but weren't drunk. There was a slight slur in a few of your words. You want to see the report?"

"No. It was never admitted in court."

"That's because we didn't know about your phone call until after the trial, and that's because the cops and prosecutors concealed it, which should have led to a reversal, which, of course, is pretty rare here in Texas."

The waitress arrived with a platter of sizzling quesadillas, all for Joey. Pryor took his taco salad and asked for more tea. After a few generous bites, Joey said, "So who killed her?"

"Who knows? There's no proof she's even dead."

"They found her gym card and student ID."

"Yeah, but they didn't find her body. She could be alive for all we know."

"You don't believe that." A gulp of the margarita to wash things down.

"No, I don't. I'm sure she's dead. Right now it

doesn't matter. We're racing against time here, Joey, and we need your help."

"What am I supposed to do?"

"Recant, recant, recant. Sign an affidavit telling the truth. Tell us what you really saw that night, which was nothing."

"I saw a green van."

"Your friend didn't see a green van, and he walked out of the mall with you. You didn't mention anything to him. In fact, you didn't say anything to anybody for over two weeks, then you heard the rumor that her gym card and student ID had been found in the river. That's when you put together your fiction, Joey, that's when you decided to nail Donté. You were outraged because she would prefer a black guy to you. You called Kerber with the anonymous tip, and all hell broke loose. The cops were desperate and stupid and couldn't wait to pursue your fiction. It worked perfectly. They beat a confession out of him, only took them fifteen hours, and, bingo! it's front-page news—'Donté Drumm Confesses.' Then your memory works a miracle. You suddenly remember that you saw a green van, just like the Drumms', moving suspiciously around the mall that night. What was it, Joey, three weeks later when you finally told the cops about the van?"

"I saw a green van."

"Was it a Ford, Joey, or did you just decide it was a Ford because that's what the Drumms owned? Did you really see a black guy driving it, or was that just your imagination?"

To keep from responding, Joey stuffed half a quesadilla into his mouth and chewed slowly. As he did so, he watched the other diners, unable or unwilling to make eye contact. Pryor took a bite, then pressed on. His thirty minutes would be gone soon enough.

"Look, Joey," he said in a much softer tone, "we can argue the case for hours. I'm not here to do that. I'm here to talk about Donté. You guys were friends, you grew up together, you were teammates for, what, five years? You spent hours together on the football field. You won together; you lost together. Hell, you were co-captains your senior year. Think of his family, his mother and brothers and sister. Think of the town, Joey, think how bad things will get if he's executed. You gotta help us, Joey. Donté didn't kill anybody. He's been railroaded from the beginning."

"Didn't realize I had this much power."

"Oh, it's a long shot. Appeals courts are not too impressed with witnesses who suddenly change their minds years after the trial and hours before the execution. You give us the affidavit, we'll run to court and scream as loud as possible, but the odds are against us. We gotta try, though. At this point, we'll try anything."

Joey stirred his drink with the straw, then took a sip. He rubbed his mouth with a paper napkin and said, "You know, this is not the first time I've had this conversation. Mr. Flak called me years ago, asked me to stop by his office. This was long after the trial. I think he was working on the appeals. He begged me to change my story, tell his version of the truth. Told him to go to hell."

"I know. I've been working on the case for a long time."

After demolishing half of the quesadillas, Joey suddenly lost interest in lunch. He shoved the platter away and pulled the drink in front of him. He stirred it slowly and watched the liquid spin around the glass.

"Things are a lot different now, Joey," Pryor said softly, pressing. "It's late in the fourth quarter, the game's almost over for Donté."

The thick maroon fountain pen clipped inside Pryor's shirt pocket was in fact a microphone. It was entirely visible, and next to it was a real pen with ink and a ballpoint in case writing was required. A tiny, hidden wire ran from Pryor's shirt pocket to the left front pocket of his slacks, where he kept his cell phone.

Two hundred miles away, Robbie was listening. He was in his office with the door locked, alone, on a speakerphone that also recorded everything.

"You ever see him play football?" Joey asked.

"No," Pryor answered. Their voices were clear.

"He was something. He roamed the field like Lawrence Taylor. Fast, fearless, he could wreck an offense all by himself. We won ten games when we were sophomores and juniors, but we could never beat Marshall."

"Why didn't the bigger schools recruit him?" Pryor asked. Keep him talking, Robbie said to himself.

"Size. He stopped growing in the tenth grade, and he could never get his weight above 220. That's not big enough for the Longhorns."

"You should see him now," Pryor said without missing a beat. "He weighs about 150, gaunt and skinny, shaves his head, and he's locked up in a tiny cell twenty-three hours a day. I think he's lost his marbles."

"He wrote me a couple of letters, did you know that?"

"No."

Robbie leaned closer to the speakerphone. He'd never heard this.

"Not long after he was sent away, when I was still living in Slone, he wrote to me. Two, maybe three letters. Long ones. He went on about death row and how awful it is—the food, the noise, the heat, the isolation, and so on. He swore he never touched Nikki, never got involved with her. He swore he was nowhere near the mall when she disappeared. He begged me to tell the truth, to help him win his appeal and get out of prison. I never wrote him back."

"You still have the letters?" Pryor asked.

Joey shook his head. "No, I've moved around so much."

The waitress appeared and removed the platter. "Another margarita?" she asked, but Joey waved her off. Pryor leaned forward on his elbows until their faces were two feet apart. He began, "You know, Joey, I've worked on this case for years. Spent thousands of hours, not only working, but thinking, trying to figure out what happened. Here's my theory. You went nuts over Nikki, and why not? She was cute as hell, popular, hot, the kind of girl you want to put in your pocket and take home forever. But she broke your heart, and nothing is more painful for a seventeen-year-old. You were devastated, crushed. Then she disappeared. The entire town was shocked, but you and those who loved her were especially horrified. Everyone wanted to find her. Everyone wanted to help. How could she simply vanish? Who snatched her?

Who could harm Nikki? Maybe you believed Donté was involved, maybe not. But you were a wreck emotionally, and in that state you decided to get involved. You called Detective Kerber with the anonymous tip, and from there everything snowballed. At that moment, the investigation took a wrong turn and no one could stop it. When you heard the news that he'd confessed, you figured you'd done the right thing. Got the right guy. Then you decided that you wanted a little piece of the action. You concocted the story about the green van, and suddenly you're the star witness. You became the hero to all those wonderful people who loved and adored Nicole Yarber. You took the stand at the trial, raised your right hand, told something that was not the whole truth, but it didn't matter. You were there, helping your beloved Nikki. Donté was led away in shackles, taken straight to death row. Maybe you understood that he would one day be executed, maybe you didn't. I suspect that way back then, when you were still a teenager, you could not appreciate the gravity of what's happening now."

"He confessed."

"Yes, and his confession is about as reliable as your testimony. For many reasons, people say things that aren't true, don't they, Joey?"

There was a long gap in the conversation as both men considered what to say next. In Slone, Robbie waited patiently, though he had never been known for his patience or quiet moments of self-reflection.

Joey spoke next. "This affidavit, what goes in it?"

"The truth. You state, under oath, that your testimony at trial was not accurate, and so on. Our office will prepare it. We can have it done in less than an hour."

"Not so fast. So, I would say, basically, that I lied during the trial?"

"We can dress up the language, but that's the gist of it. We'd also like to settle the matter about the anonymous tip."

"And the affidavit would be filed in court and end up in the newspapers?"

"Sure. The press is following the case. Any last-minute motions and appeals will be reported."

"So, my mother will read in the newspaper that I'm now saying I lied at trial. I'll be admitting that I'm a liar, that right?"

"Yes, but what's more important here, Joey? Your reputation or Donté's life?"

"But you said it's a long shot, right? So, chances are I'll admit to being a liar and he still gets the needle. Who wins that one?"

"He damn sure doesn't."

"I don't think so. Look, I gotta get back to work."

"Come on, Joey."

"Thanks for lunch. Nice meetin' you." And with that, he slid out of the booth and hurried out of the restaurant.

Pryor took a deep breath and stared at the table in disbelief. They were talking about the affidavit, then the conversation ended. He slowly pulled out his cell phone and talked to his boss. "Did you get all that?"

"Yep, every word," Robbie said.

"Anything we can use?"

"No. Nothing. Not even close, really."

"I didn't think so. Sorry, Robbie. I thought at one point he was ready to snap."

"You did all you could, Fred. Nice job. He's got your card, right?"

"Yes."

"Call him after work, say hello, just remind him you're there and ready to talk."

"I'll try to meet him for a drink. Something tells me he tends to overindulge. Maybe I can get him drunk and he'll say something."

"Just make sure it's being recorded."

"Will do."

5

On the third floor of St. Francis Hospital, Mrs. Aurelia Lindmar was recovering from gallbladder surgery and doing well. Keith spent twenty minutes with her, ate two pieces of cheap, stale chocolate mailed in by a niece, and managed to make a graceful departure when a nurse popped in with a syringe. On the fourth floor, he huddled in the hallway with the soon-to-be widow of Mr. Charles Cooper, a stalwart member of St. Mark's whose bad heart was finally giving out. There were three other patients Keith needed to see, but their conditions were stable and they would live until tomorrow, when he would have more time. On the second floor, he tracked down Dr. Herzlich, who was eating a cold sandwich from a machine and reading a dense text as he sat alone in a small cafeteria.

"Have you had lunch?" Kyle Herzlich asked politely as he offered a chair to his minister. Keith sat down, looked at the puny sandwich—white bread with a thin slice of some brutally processed meat in the middle—and said, "Thanks. I had a late breakfast."

"Fine. Look, Keith, I've managed to snoop a bit,

got as far as I can go, actually, you do understand these things?"

"Of course I do: And I did not intend for you to pry into private matters."

"Never. Can't do it. But I've asked around, and, well, there are ways of gleaning some of the facts. Your man has been here at least twice in the past month, lots of tests, and the tumor thing checks out. Not a pretty prognosis."

"Thanks, Doctor." Keith was not surprised to learn that Travis Boyette was telling the truth, at least about his brain tumor.

"Can't say any more than that." The doctor managed to eat, read, and talk at the same time.

"Sure, no problem."

"What's his crime?"

You don't want to know, Keith thought. "A nasty one. Career boy, long record."

"Why's he hanging around St. Mark's?"

"We're open to the public, Doctor. We're supposed to serve all God's people, even those with criminal records."

"I suppose. Anything to worry about?"

"No. He's harmless." Just hide the women and girls, and perhaps the little boys too. Keith thanked him again and excused himself.

"See you Sunday," the doctor said, his eyes glued to a medical report.

Anchor House was a square, boxlike building of red brick and painted windows, the type of structure that could be used for anything, and probably had been since it was hastily constructed forty years earlier. Whoever built it had been pressed for time and saw no need for involving the architects. At 7:00 on Monday evening, Keith entered from the sidewalk off Seventeenth Street and stopped at a makeshift front desk where an ex-con was monitoring things. "Yes, sir," he said without a trace of warmth.

"I need to see Travis Boyette," Keith said.

The monitor looked to his left, to a large open room where a dozen or so men were sitting in various stages of relaxation and gazing at a very loud, large television, enthralled with *Wheel of Fortune*. Then he looked to his right, to another large open room where a dozen or so men were either reading battered paperbacks or playing checkers and chess. Boyette was in a wicker rocker, in a corner, partially hidden behind a newspaper. "Over there," the man said, nodding. "Sign here."

Keith signed in and walked to the corner. When Boyette saw him approach, he grabbed his cane and scrambled to his feet. "Didn't expect you," he said, obviously surprised.

"I was in the neighborhood. Got a few minutes to talk?"

The other men were taking casual note of Keith. The checkers and chess went on without interruption.

"Sure," Boyette said, glancing around. "Let's go to the mess hall." Keith followed him, watching the left leg as it paused slightly with each step, causing the shuffle. The cane jabbed the floor as they clicked along. How awful would it be, Keith asked himself, to live each minute with a grade-four tumor between your ears, growing and growing until your skull seems ready to crack? As miserable a person as he was, Keith couldn't help but feel sorry for him. A dead man.

The mess hall was a small room with four long

folding tables and a wide opening at the far end that gave way to the kitchen. The cleanup crew was making a racket back there, slinging pots and pans and laughing. Rap music came from a radio. It was the perfect cover for a hushed conversation.

"We can talk here," Boyette said, nodding at a table. Crumbs of food were scattered about. The thick smell of cooking oil hung in the air. They sat down across from each other. Since they had nothing in common but the weather, Keith decided not to waste time.

"Would you like some coffee?" Boyette asked politely.

"No, thanks."

"Smart move. Worst coffee in Kansas. Worse than prison."

"Travis, after you left this morning, I went online, found the Web site for Donté Drumm, and spent the rest of the day lost in that world. It's fascinating, and heartbreaking. There are serious doubts about his guilt."

"Serious?" Boyette said with a laugh. "There should be serious doubts. The boy had nothing to do with what happened to Nikki."

"What happened to Nikki?"

A startled look, like a deer in headlights. Silence. Boyette wrapped his hands around his head and massaged his scalp. His shoulders began to shake. The tic came and went and came back again. Keith watched him and could almost feel the agony. The rap music thumped mindlessly from the kitchen.

Keith slowly reached into his coat pocket and removed a folded sheet of paper. He unfolded it and slid it across the table. "Recognize this girl?" he asked. It was a copy of a black-and-white photo printed from the Web site, a photo of Nicole Yarber, posing in her cheerleader outfit, holding a pom-pom, smiling with all the innocence of a sweet seventeen-year-old.

At first, Boyette did not react. He looked at Nikki as if he'd never seen her before. He stared at her for a long time, then the tears came without warning. No gasps, no sobs, no apologies, just a flood of moisture that ran down his cheeks and dripped off his chin. He made no effort to wipe his face. He looked at Keith, and the two men stared at each other as the tears continued. The photo was getting wet.

Boyette grunted, cleared his throat, and said, "I really want to die."

Keith came back from the kitchen with two cups of black coffee in paper cups, along with some paper towels. Boyette took one, wiped his face and chin, and said, "Thanks."

Keith resumed his seat and said, "What happened to Nikki?"

Boyette seemed to count to ten before saying, "I've still got her."

Keith thought he was prepared for every possible answer, but in fact he was not. Could she be alive? No. He'd spent the past six years in prison. How could he keep her locked up somewhere? He's crazy.

"Where is she?" Keith asked firmly.

"Buried."

"Where?"

"Missouri."

"Look, Travis, these one-word answers will keep us here forever. You came to my office this morning for one reason, and that was to finally confess. But you couldn't muster the courage, so here I am. Let's hear it."

"Why do you care?"

"That's pretty obvious, isn't it? An innocent man is about to be executed for something you did. Maybe there's time to save him."

"I doubt it."

"Did you kill Nicole Yarber?"

"Is this confidential, Pastor?"

"Do you want it to be?"

"Yes."

"Why? Why not confess, then make a full admission, then try to help Donté Drumm? That's what you should do, Travis. Your days are numbered, according to what you said this morning."

"Confidential or not?"

Keith took a breath, then made the mistake of taking a sip of coffee. Travis was right.

"If you want it to be confidential, Travis, then it is."

A smile, a tic. He glanced around, though they had yet to be noticed by anyone else. He began to nod. "I did it, Pastor. I don't know why. I never know why."

"You grabbed her in the parking lot?"

The tumor expanded, the headaches hit like lightning. He grabbed his head again and weathered the storm. His jaws clenched in a determined effort to keep going. "I grabbed her, took her away. I had a gun, she didn't fight much. We left town. I kept her a few days. We had sex. We—"

"You didn't have sex. You raped her."

"Yes, over and over. Then I did it, and buried her."

"You killed her?"

"Yes."

"How?"

"Strangled her with her belt. It's still there, around her neck."

"And you buried her?"

"Yes." Boyette looked at the photo, and Keith could almost see a smile.

"Where?"

"South of Joplin, where I grew up. Lots of hills, valleys, hollows, logging trails, dead-end roads. She'll never be found. They never got close."

A long pause as the sickening reality settled in. Of course, there was a chance he was lying, but Keith could not force himself to believe that. What could he possibly gain by lying, especially at this stage in his miserable life?

The kitchen lights went out and the radio was turned off. Three burly black men made their exit and walked through the mess hall. They nodded and spoke politely to Keith, but only glanced at Travis. They closed the door behind themselves.

Keith took the copy of the photo and turned it over. He uncapped his pen and wrote something on it. "How about a little background, Travis?" he said.

"Sure. I have nothing else to do."

"What were you doing in Slone, Texas?"

"Working for a company called R. S. McGuire and Sons, out of Fort Smith. Construction. They had a contract to build a warehouse for Monsanto, just west of Slone. I hired on as a laborer, just a grunt, crappy work, but it's all I could find. They paid me less than minimum wage, in cash, off the books, same as the Mexicans. Sixty hours a week, flat rate, no insurance, no skill, no nothing. It won't be worth your time to check with the company, because I was never officially employed. I was renting a room in an old motel west of town, called the Rebel Motor Inn. It's probably still there. Check it out. Forty bucks a week. The job lasted five or six months. One Friday night I saw the lights, found the field behind the high school, bought a ticket, and sat with the crowd. Didn't know a soul. They were watching football. Me, I was watching the cheerleaders. Always loved the cheerleaders. Cute little butts, short skirts, dark tights on underneath. They bounce and flip and throw each other around and you see so much of them. They want you to see. That's when I fell in love with Nicole. She was there for me, showing it all. I knew from the first moment that she was the one."

"The next one."

"Right, the next one. Every other Friday, I'd go to the games. I never sat in the same place twice, never wore the same clothes. Used different caps. You learn these things when you're tracking someone. She became my whole world, and I could feel the urges getting stronger and stronger. I knew what was about to happen, but I couldn't stop it. I can never stop it. Never." He took a sip of coffee and grimaced.

"Did you see Donté Drumm play?" Keith asked.

"Maybe, I don't remember. I never watched the games, didn't notice anything but Nicole. Then, suddenly, no more Nicole. The season was over. I got desperate. She drove this hot little red BMW, the only one in town, so she was not too hard to find, if you knew where to look. She liked the usual hangouts. I saw her car parked at the mall that night, figured she was at the movies. I waited and waited. I'm very patient when I have to be. When the parking space next to her car became vacant, I backed into it."

"What were you driving?"

"An old Chevrolet pickup, stole it in Arkansas. Stole the tags in Texas. I backed into the parking space so my door was next to hers. When she walked into the trap, I jumped her. I had a gun and a roll of duct tape, and that's all I ever needed. Not a sound."

He rattled off the details with an unaffected detachment, as if describing a scene from a movie. This is what happened. This is how I did it. Don't expect me to make sense of it.

The tears were long gone. "It was a bad weekend for Nikki. I almost felt sorry for her."

"I don't really want those details," Keith said, interrupting. "How long did you stay in Slone after you killed her?"

"A few weeks, I guess. Through Christmas, into January. I was reading the local paper, watching the late-night news. The town was in a frenzy over the girl. Saw her mom cry on television. Real sad. Every day there was another search party, with a television news crew chasing after it. Fools. Nikki was two hundred miles away, sleeping with the angels." He actually chuckled at the memory.

"Surely, you don't think this is funny."

"Sorry, Pastor."

"How did you hear about the arrest of Donté Drumm?"

"There was a little greasy spoon near the motel, and I liked to go there for coffee early in the morning. I heard 'em talking, said a football player had confessed, a black boy. I bought a newspaper, sat in my truck, read the story, and thought, What a bunch of idiots! I was stunned. Couldn't believe it. There was a mug shot of Drumm, nice-looking kid, and I remember staring at his face and thinking that he must've had a screw loose. Why else would he confess to my crime? Kinda pissed me off. The boy had to be crazy. Then the next day his lawyer came out strong in the paper, yelling about how the confession was bogus, how the cops tricked the kid, overwhelmed him, broke him down, wouldn't let him out of the room for fifteen hours. That made sense to me. I've never met a cop I could trust. The town almost blew up. The whites wanted to string him up on Main Street. The blacks felt pretty strongly the boy was getting railroaded. Things were tense. Lots of fights at the high school. Then I got fired and moved on."

"Why were you fired?"

"Stupid. Stayed too long in a bar one night. The cops busted me for drunk driving, then they realized the truck and tags were stolen. I spent a week in jail."

"In Slone?"

"Yep. Check it out. January 1999. Charged with grand larceny, drunk driving, and whatever else they could throw at me."

"Was Drumm in the same jail?"

"Never saw him, but there was a lot of talk. Rumor was they'd moved him to another county for safety reasons. I couldn't help but laugh. The cops had the real killer, they just didn't know it."

Keith made notes, but had trouble believing what he was actually writing. He asked, "How'd you get out?"

"They assigned me a lawyer. He got my bond lowered. I bailed out, skipped town, and never went back. I drifted here and there and then got arrested in Wichita."

"Do you remember the lawyer's name?"

"You still fact-checking, Pastor?"

"Yes."

"You think I'm lying?"

"No, but it doesn't hurt to check the facts."

"No, I don't remember his name. I've had a lot of lawyers in my life. Never paid 'em a dime."

"The arrest in Wichita was for attempted rape, right?"

"Sort of. Attempted sexual battery, plus kidnapping. There was no sex, didn't make it that far. The girl knew karate. Things didn't go the way I planned. She kicked me in the balls and I puked for two days."

"I believe your sentence was ten years. You served six, now you're here."

"Nice job, Pastor. You've done your homework."

"Did you keep up with the Drumm case?"

"Oh, I thought about it off and on for a few years. I figured the lawyers and courts would eventually realize they had the wrong boy. I mean, hell, even in Texas they have higher courts to review cases and such. Surely, somebody along the way would wake up and see the obvious. Over time, I guess I forgot about it. Had my own problems. When you're in max security, you don't spend a lot of time worrying about other people."

"What about Nikki? You spend time thinking about her?"

Boyette did not respond, and as the seconds limped along, it became obvious that he would not answer the question. Keith kept scribbling, making notes to himself about what to do next. Nothing was certain.

"Do you have any sympathy for her family?"

"I was raped when I was eight years old. I don't recall a single word of sympathy from anyone. In fact, no one raised a hand to stop it. It went on. You've seen my record, Pastor, I've had several victims. I couldn't stop. Not sure I can stop now. Obviously, sympathy is not something I waste time with."

Keith shook his head with a look of disgust.

"Don't get me wrong, Pastor. I have a lot of regrets. I wish I hadn't done all those terrible things. I've wished a million times that I could be normal. My whole life I've wanted to stop hurting people, to somehow straighten up, stay out of prison, get a job, and all that. I didn't choose to be like this."

Keith deliberately folded the sheet of paper and tucked it into his coat pocket. He screwed the cap onto his pen. He folded his arms across his chest and stared at Boyette. "I guess you're willing to sit by and let things run their course down in Texas."

"No, I'm troubled by it. I'm just not sure what to do."

"What if they found the body? You tell me where she's buried, and I'll try to contact the right people down there."

"You sure you want to get involved?"

"No, but I can't ignore it either."

Boyette bent forward and began pawing at his head again. "It's impossible for anybody else to find her," he said, his voice breaking up. A moment passed, and the pain eased. "I'm not sure I could now. It's been so long."

"It's been nine years."

"Not that long. I went back to see her a few times after she died."

Keith showed him both palms and said, "I don't want to hear it. Suppose I call Drumm's lawyer and tell him about the body. I won't give your name, but at least someone down there knows the truth."

"Then what?"

"I don't know. I'm not a lawyer. Maybe I can convince someone. I'm willing to try."

"The only person who can possibly find her is me,

and I can't leave the state of Kansas. Hell, I can't leave this county. If I do, they'll bust me for parole violations and send me back to prison. Pastor, I ain't going back to prison."

"What difference does it make, Travis? You'll be dead in a few months, according to your own words."

Boyette became very calm and still and began tapping his fingertips together. He stared at Keith with hard, dry, unblinking eyes. He spoke softly but firmly. "Pastor, I can't admit to a murder."

"Why not? You have at least four felony convictions, all related to sexual assault. You've spent most of your adult life in prison. You have an inoperable brain tumor. You actually committed the murder. Why not have the courage to admit it and save an innocent man's life?"

"My mother is still alive."

"Where does she live?"

"Joplin, Missouri."

"And her name?"

"You gonna give her a call, Pastor?"

"No. I won't bother her. What's her name?"

"Susan Boyette."

"And she lived on Trotter Street, right?"

"How'd you—?"

"Your mother died three years ago, Travis."

"How'd you—?"

"Google, took about ten minutes."

"What's Google?"

"An Internet search company. What else are you lying about? How many lies have you told me today, Travis?"

"If I'm lying, then why are you here?"

"I don't know. That's an excellent question. You

tell a good story and you have a bad record, but you can't prove anything."

Boyette shrugged as if he didn't care, but his cheeks turned red and his eyes narrowed. "I don't have to prove anything. I'm not the accused, for a change."

"Her gym card and student ID were found on a sandbar in the Red River. How does that fit into your story?"

"Her phone was in her purse. As soon as I got her, the damned thing started ringing and wouldn't stop. Finally, I got mad, grabbed the purse, and threw it off the bridge. I kept the girl, though. I needed her. She reminds me of your wife, very cute."

"Shut up, Travis," Keith said instinctively, before he could stop himself. He took a deep breath and patiently said, "Let's keep my wife out of this."

"Sorry, Pastor." Boyette removed a thin chain from around his neck. "You want proof, Pastor. Take a look at this." A gold class ring with a blue stone was attached to the chain. Boyette unsnapped the chain and handed the ring to Keith. It was narrow and small, obviously worn by a female. "That's ANY on one side," Boyette said with a smile. "Alicia Nicole Yarber. On the other side, you have SHS 1999. Dear old Slone High."

Keith squeezed the ring between his thumb and his forefinger, and stared at it in disbelief.

"Show that to her mother and watch her weep," Boyette said. "The only other proof I have, Pastor, is Nicole herself, and the more I think about her, the more I'm convinced that we should just leave her alone."

Keith placed the ring on the table and Boyette took it. He suddenly kicked his chair back, grabbed his cane, and stood. "I don't like being called a liar, Pastor. Go home and have fun with your wife."

"Liar, rapist, murderer, and you're also a coward, Travis. Why don't you do something good for once in your life? And quick, before it's too late."

"Just leave me alone." Boyette opened the door, then slammed it behind him.

6

The prosecution's theory of guilt had been based in part on the desperate hope that one day, someone, somewhere would find Nicole's body. It couldn't stay submerged forever, could it? The Red River would eventually give it up, and a fisherman or a boat captain or maybe a kid wading in the backwater would discover it and call for help. After the remains were identified, the puzzle's final piece would fit perfectly. All loose ends would be tied up. No more questions, no more doubts. The police and prosecutors could quietly, smugly close the book.

The conviction, without the body, was not that difficult to obtain. The prosecution attacked Donté Drumm from all angles, and while it pushed relentlessly for a trial, it also banked heavily on the appearance of a corpse. But nine years had passed and the river had not cooperated. The hopes and prayers, the dreams in some cases, had vanished long ago. And while this caused doubts in the minds of some observers, it did nothing to dampen the convictions of those responsible for Donté's death sentence. After years of rigid tunnel vision, and with so much at stake, they were certain beyond all doubt that they had nailed her killer. They had invested far too much to question their own theories and actions.

The district attorney was a man named Paul Koffee, a tough career prosecutor who'd been elected and reelected without serious opposition for over twenty years. He was an ex-Marine who enjoyed a fight and usually won. His high conviction rate was splashed across his Web site and, during elections, trumpeted in gaudy advertisements sent by direct mail. Sympathy for the accused was rarely shown. And, like the routines of most small-town district attorneys, the grind of chasing meth addicts and car thieves was broken only by a sensational murder and/or rape. Much to his well-guarded frustration, Koffee had prosecuted only two capital murders in his career, a paltry record in Texas. Nicole Yarber's was the first and the most notorious. Three years later, in 2002, Koffee had won an easier death verdict in a case involving a botched drug deal that left bodies all over a country road.

And two was all he would get. Because of a scandal, Koffee was leaving office. He'd promised the public that he would not seek reelection in two years. His wife of twenty-two years had left him in a rather swift and noisy exit. The Drumm execution would be a final moment of glory.

His sidekick was Drew Kerber, who, after his exemplary work in the Drumm case, had been promoted to chief detective, Slone PD, a position he still proudly held. Kerber was pushing forty-six, ten years younger than the prosecutor, and though they often worked closely together, they ran in different social circles. Kerber was a cop. Koffee was a lawyer. The lines were clear in Slone, as in most small southern towns.

At various times, each had promised Donté Drumm that he would be there when he "got the needle." Kerber did so first, during the brutal interrogation that produced the confession. Kerber, when he wasn't jabbing the kid in the chest and calling him every name in the book, promised him over and over that he would get the needle, and that he, Detective Kerber, would be there to witness it.

For Koffee, the conversation had been much briefer. During a break in the trial, while Robbie Flak was not around, Koffee had arranged a quick and secret meeting with Donté Drumm under a stairwell just outside the courtroom. He offered a deal—plead guilty and take life, no parole. Otherwise, you'll get death. Donté declined and again said he was innocent, at which Koffee cursed him and assured him he would watch him die. Moments later, Koffee denied the encounter when Flak verbally assaulted him.

The two men had lived with the Yarber case for nine years, and for various reasons they had often seen the need to "go see Reeva." It was not always a pleasant visit, not always something they looked forward to, but she was such an important part of the case that she could never be neglected.

Reeva Pike was Nicole's mother, a stout, boisterous woman who had embraced victimhood with an enthusiasm that often bordered on the ridiculous. Her involvement in the case was long, colorful, and often contentious. Now that the story was entering its final act, many in Slone wondered what she would do with herself when it was over.

Reeva had badgered Kerber and the police for two weeks as they frantically searched for Nicole. She had wailed for the cameras and publicly berated all elected officials, from her city alderman to the governor, because they had not found her daughter. After the arrest and alleged confession of Donté Drumm, she made herself readily available for lengthy interviews in which she showed no patience with the presumption of innocence and demanded the death penalty, and the sooner the better. For many years, she had taught the Ladies' Bible Class at the First Baptist Church and, armed with scripture, could practically preach on the subject of God's approval of state-sponsored retribution. She repeatedly referred to Donté as "that boy," which riled up the blacks in Slone. She had other names for him too, with "monster" and "cold-blooded killer" being two favorites. During the trial, she sat with her husband, Wallis, and their two children in the front row directly behind the prosecution, with other relatives and friends wedged closely around them. Two armed deputies were always close by, separating Reeva and her clan from the family and supporters of Donté Drumm. Tense words were exchanged during recesses. Violence could have erupted at any moment. When the jury announced its death sentence, Reeva jumped to her feet and said, "Praise be to God!" The judge called her down immediately and threatened to remove her. As Donté was led away in handcuffs, she could not restrain herself. She screamed, "You murdered my baby! I'll be there when you take your last breath!"

On the first anniversary of Nicole's disappearance, and presumably her death, Reeva organized an elaborate vigil at Rush Point on the Red River, near the sandbar where the gym card and student ID were found. Someone built a white cross and stuck it in the ground. Flowers and large photos of Nikki were packed around it. Their preacher led a memorial service and thanked God for the "just and true verdict" that had just been handed down by the jury. Candles were burned, hymns were sung, prayers were offered. The vigil became an annual event on that date, and Reeva was always there, often with a news crew in tow.

She joined a victims' group and was soon attending conferences and giving speeches. She compiled a long list of complaints with the judicial system, the primary one being that of the "endless, painful delays," and she became adept at pleasing a crowd with her new theories. She wrote vicious letters to Robbie Flak and even tried writing to Donté Drumm.

Reeva created a Web site, WeMissYouNikki.com, and loaded it with a thousand photos of the girl. She blogged incessantly about her daughter and the case, often pecking away throughout the night. Twice, Robbie Flak threatened to sue her for libelous material she published, but he knew it was wiser to leave her alone. She hounded Nikki's friends to post their favorite memories and stories, and held grudges against the kids who lost interest.

Her behavior was often bizarre. Periodically, she took long drives downriver in search of her daughter. She was often seen standing on bridges, gazing at the water, lost in another world. The Red River bisects Shreveport, Louisiana, 120 miles south and east of Slone. Reeva became fixated on Shreveport. She found a hotel downtown with a view of the river, and this became her refuge. She spent many nights and days there, roaming the city, loitering around shopping malls, cinemas, and any of the other places where teenagers liked to gather. She knew it was irrational. She knew it was inconceivable that Nikki could have survived and was alive and hiding from her. Nonetheless, she kept driving to Shreveport and watching the faces. She couldn't quit. She had to do something.

Several times, Reeva dashed off to other states where teenage girls went missing. She was the expert with wisdom to share. "You can survive this" was her motto, her effort to soothe and comfort the families, though many back home wondered how well she was surviving.

Now, as the final countdown was under way, she was in a frenzy with the details of the execution. The reporters were back, and she had plenty to say. After nine long and bitter years, justice was finally at hand.

Early Monday evening, Paul Koffee and Drew Kerber decided it was time to go see Reeva.

She met them at the front door with a smile, even quick hugs. They never knew which Reeva they would find. She could be charming, and she could be frightening. But with Donté's death so close, she was gracious and vibrant. They walked through the comfortable suburban split-level to a large room behind the garage, an add-on that had become Reeva's war room over the years. Half was an office with filing cabinets, the other half a shrine to her daughter. There were large framed color blowups, portraits done posthumously by admirers, trophies, ribbons, plaques, and an award from the eighth-grade science fair. Most of Nikki's life could be traced through the displays.

Wallis, her second husband and Nicole's stepfather, was not at home. He had been seen less and less over the years, and it was rumored that he simply couldn't take much more of his wife's constant mourning and griping. She served them iced tea as they sat around a coffee table. After a few pleasantries, the conversation moved to the execution.

"You have five slots in the witness room," Koffee said. "Who gets them?"

"Wallis and I, of course. Chad and Marie are undecided, but will probably be there." She threw out the names of Nicole's half brother and half sister as if they couldn't decide to go to the game or not. "The last place will probably be Brother Ronnie. He doesn't want to watch an execution, but he feels the need to be there for us."

Brother Ronnie was the current pastor of the First Baptist Church. He'd been in Slone for about three years, had obviously never met Nicole, but was convinced of Drumm's guilt and afraid to cross Reeva.

They talked for a few minutes about the protocol on death row, the rules regarding witnesses, the timeline, and so on.

"Reeva, could we talk about tomorrow?" Koffee asked.

"Of course we can."

"Are you still doing the Fordyce thing?"

"Yes. He's in town now and we'll film at ten in the morning, right here. Why do you ask?"

"I'm not sure it's such a good idea," Koffee said, and Kerber nodded his agreement.

"Oh, really. And why not?"

"He's such an inflammatory character, Reeva. We are very concerned about the aftershocks Thursday night. You know how upset the blacks are."

"We are expecting trouble, Reeva," Kerber added.

"If the blacks start trouble, then arrest them," she said.

"It's exactly the kind of situation Fordyce loves to pounce on. He's an agitator, Reeva. He wants to start trouble so he can get in the middle of it. Helps his ratings."

"It's all about ratings," Kerber added.

"Well, well. Aren't we nervous," she chided.

Sean Fordyce was a New York–based talk-show host who'd found a niche on cable sensationalizing murder cases. His slant was unapologetically from the right side of the street, always in support of the latest execution, or gun rights, or the rounding up of illegal immigrants, a group he loved to attack because they were much easier targets than others with dark skin. It was hardly original programming, but Fordyce struck gold when he began filming the families of victims as they prepared to watch the executions. He became famous when his tech crew managed to successfully hide a tiny camera in the frame of a pair of eyeglasses worn by the father of a young boy who was murdered in Alabama. For the first time, the world saw an execution, and Sean Fordyce owned the footage. He played it and played it and, with each showing, commented on how simple it was, how peaceful and painless and much too easy for such a violent killer.

He was indicted in Alabama, sued by the dead man's family, and threatened with death and censure, but he survived it. The charges didn't stick—they couldn't nail down a specific crime. The lawsuit was thrown out. Three years after the stunt, he was not only standing but standing at the top of the cable garbage heap. Now he was in Slone, preparing for another episode. Rumor was that he'd paid Reeva $50,000 for the exclusive.

"Please reconsider, Reeva," Koffee said.

"No, Paul. The answer is no. I'm doing it for Nicole, for my family, and for the other victims out there. The world needs to see what this monster has done to us."

"What's the benefit?" Koffee said. Both he and Kerber had ignored phone calls from Fordyce's production team.

"Maybe the laws can be changed."

"But the laws are working here, Reeva. Sure, it's taken longer than we wanted, but in the scheme of things nine years is not bad."

"Oh my God, Paul, I can't believe you just said that. You haven't lived our nightmare for the past nine years."

"No, I haven't, and I don't pretend to understand what you've been through. But the nightmare won't end Thursday night." And it certainly would not, not if Reeva had anything to do with it.

"You have no idea, Paul. I can't believe this. The answer is no. No, no, no. I'm doing the interview and the show will run. The world will see what it's like."

They had not expected to be successful, so they were not surprised. When Reeva Pike made up her mind, the conversation was over. They shifted gears.

"So be it," Koffee said. "Do you and Wallis feel safe?"

She smiled, and almost chuckled. "Of course, Paul. We got a houseful of guns and the neighbors are on high alert. Every car that comes down this street is watched through rifle scopes. We are not expecting trouble."

"There were phone calls at the station today," Kerber said. "The usual anonymous stuff, vague threats about this and that if the boy is executed."

"I'm sure you guys can deal with it," she said with

no concern whatsoever. After waging such a relentless war of her own, Reeva had forgotten how to be afraid.

"I think we should have a patrol car parked outside for the rest of the week," Kerber said.

"Do as you wish. It doesn't matter to me. If the blacks start trouble, they won't do it over here. Don't they normally burn their own buildings first?"

Both men shrugged. They'd had no experience with riots. Slone had an unremarkable history with race relations. What little they knew had been learned from the television news. Yes, it did seem as if the riots were confined to the ghettos.

They talked about this for a few minutes, then it was time to leave. They hugged again at the front door and promised to see each other after the execution. What a great moment it would be. The end of the ordeal. Justice at last.

Robbie Flak parked at the curb in front of the Drumm home and braced himself for another meeting.

"How many times have you been here?" his passenger asked.

"I don't know. Dozens and dozens." He opened the door, climbed out, and she did the same.

Her name was Martha Handler. She was an investigative journalist, a freelancer who worked for no one but was paid occasionally by the big magazines. She had first visited Slone two years earlier when the Paul Koffee scandal broke and after that had developed a fascination with the Drumm case. She and Robbie had spent hours together, professionally, and things might have degenerated from there, but for the fact that Robbie was committed to his current live-in, a woman twenty years his junior. Martha no longer believed in commitment and gave mixed signals as to whether the door was open or not. There was sexual tension between the two, as if they were both fighting the urge to say yes. So far, they had been successful.

At first, she claimed to be writing a book about the Drumm case. Then it was a lengthy article for *Vanity Fair*. Then it was one for the *New Yorker*. Then it was a screenplay for a movie to be produced by one of her ex-husbands in L.A. In Robbie's opinion, she was a passable writer, with a brilliant recall of the facts, but a disaster with organization and planning. Whatever the final product, he had complete veto power, and if her project ever earned a dime, he and the Drumm family would get a share. After two years with her, he was not counting on any payoff. He liked her, though. She was wickedly funny, irreverent, a total zealot to the cause, and she had developed a fierce hatred for almost every person she'd met in Texas. Plus, she could guzzle bourbon and play poker far past midnight.

The small living room was crowded. Roberta Drumm sat on the piano bench, her usual position. Two of her brothers stood by the door to the kitchen. Her son Cedric, Donté's oldest brother, was on the sofa holding a toddler who was asleep. Her daughter, Andrea, Donté's younger sister, had one chair. Her preacher, Reverend Canty, had another. Robbie and Martha sat close to each other in flimsy, shaky chairs brought in from the kitchen. Martha had been there many times, and had even cooked for Roberta when she had the flu.

After the usual hellos and hugs and instant coffee, Robbie began talking. "Nothing happened today, which is not good news. First thing tomorrow, the parole board will issue its decision. They don't meet, they just circulate the case and everybody votes. We don't expect a recommendation for clemency. That rarely happens. We expect a denial, which we will then appeal to the governor's office and ask for a reprieve. The governor has the right to grant one thirty-day reprieve. It's unlikely we'll get one, but we have to pray for a miracle." Robbie Flak was not a man of prayer, but in the staunch Bible Belt of East Texas, he could certainly talk the talk. And he was in a room full of people who prayed around the clock, Martha Handler being the exception.

"On the positive side, we made contact today with Joey Gamble, found him outside of Houston, a place called Mission Bend. Our investigator had lunch with him, confronted him with the truth, impressed upon him the urgency of the situation, and so on. He is following the case and knows what's at stake. We invited him to sign an affidavit recanting the lies he told at trial, and he declined. However, we won't give up. He was not decisive. He seemed to waver, to be troubled by what's happening to Donté."

"What if he signs the affidavit and tells the truth?" Cedric asked.

"Well, we suddenly have some ammunition, a bullet or two, something to take to court and make some noise. The problem, though, is that when liars start recanting their testimony, everybody gets real suspicious, especially judges hearing appeals. When does the lying stop? Is he lying now, or was he lying then? It's a long shot, frankly, but right now everything is a long shot." Robbie had always been blunt, especially when dealing with the families of his criminal clients.

And at this stage in Donté's case, it made little sense to raise hopes.

Roberta sat stoically with her hands wedged under her legs. She was fifty-six years old, but looked much older. Since the death of her husband, Riley, five years earlier, she had stopped coloring her hair and stopped eating. She was gray and gaunt and said little, but then she never had said much. Riley had been the big talker, the boaster, the bruiser, with Roberta in the role as the fixer who eased behind her husband and patched up the rifts he created. In the past few days, she had slowly accepted reality, and seemed overwhelmed by it. Neither she nor Riley, nor any member of the family, had ever questioned Donté's innocence. He had once tried to maim ballcarriers and quarterbacks, and he could adequately defend himself when necessary on the playground or in the streets. But Donté was really a pushover, a sensitive kid who would never harm an innocent person.

"Martha and I are going to Polunsky tomorrow to see Donté," Robbie was saying. "I can take any mail you might have for him."

"I have a meeting with the mayor at 10:00 a.m. tomorrow," Reverend Canty announced. "I'll be joined by several other pastors. We intend to convey our concerns about what might happen in Slone if Donté is executed."

"It'll be ugly," said an uncle.

"You got that right," Cedric added. "Folks on this side are fired up."

"The execution is still set for 6:00 p.m. on Thursday, right?" asked Andrea.

"Yes," Robbie said.

"Well, when will you know for sure that it'll be carried out?" she asked.

"These things usually go down to the wire, primarily because the lawyers fight to the last minute."

Andrea looked uneasily at Cedric, then said, "Well, I'll just tell you, Robbie, a lot of people on this side of town plan to get outta here when it happens. There's gonna be trouble, and I understand why. But once it starts, things might get out of control."

"The whole town better look out," Cedric said.

"That's what we'll tell the mayor," Canty said. "He'd better do something."

"All he can do is react," Robbie said. "He has nothing to do with the execution."

"Can't he call the governor?"

"Sure, but don't assume the mayor is against the execution. If he got through to the governor, he'd probably lobby against a reprieve. The mayor is a good old Texas boy. He loves the death penalty."

No one in the room was fond of the mayor, or the governor for that matter. Robbie moved the discussion away from the prospect of violence. There were important details to be discussed. "According to the rules from the Department of Corrections, the last family visit will take place at 8:00 a.m. on Thursday morning, at the Polunsky Unit, before Donté is transferred to Huntsville." Robbie continued, "I know you'll be anxious to see him, and he's desperate to see you. But don't be surprised when you get there. It will be just like a regular visit. He'll be on one side of a sheet of Plexiglas, you'll have to stay on the other. You talk by phone. It's ridiculous, but then this is Texas."

"No hugs, no kisses?" Andrea said.

"No. They have their rules."

Roberta began crying, quiet sniffles with big tears. "I can't hug my baby," she said. One of her brothers handed her a tissue and patted her shoulder. After a minute or so, she pulled herself together and said, "I'm sorry."

"Don't be sorry, Roberta," Robbie said. "You're the mother, and your son is about to be executed for something he didn't do. You have the right to cry. Me, I'd be bawling and screaming and shooting at people. Still might do it."

Andrea asked, "What about the execution itself? Who's supposed to be there?"

"The witness room is divided by a wall to separate the victim's family from the inmate's family. All witnesses stand. There are no seats. They get five slots, you get five slots. The rest are given to the lawyers, prison officials, members of the press, and a few others. I'll be there. Roberta, I know you plan to be a witness, but Donté is adamant that he doesn't want you there. Your name is on his list, but he doesn't want you to watch."

"I'm sorry, Robbie," she said, wiping her nose. "We've had this discussion. I was there when he was born and I'll be there when he dies. He may not know it, but he'll need me. I will be a witness."

Robbie wasn't about to argue. He promised to return the following evening.

7

Long after the boys were asleep, Keith and Dana Schroeder were in the kitchen of their modest, church-owned parsonage in central Topeka. They sat directly across from each other, each with a laptop, notepads, and decaf coffee. The table was littered with materials found on the Internet and printed in the church office. Dinner had been quick, macaroni and cheese, because the boys had homework and the parents were preoccupied.

Checking online sources, Dana had been unable to confirm Boyette's claim that he had been arrested and jailed in Slone in January 1999. The town's old court records were not available. The bar directory listed 131 lawyers in Slone. She picked ten at random, called them, said she was with the parole office in Kansas and was checking the background of a Mr. Travis Boyette. Did you ever represent a man by that name? No. Then sorry to disturb you. She did not have the time to call every lawyer, and it seemed futile anyway. She planned to call the city court clerk's office first thing Tuesday morning.

After holding Nicole's class ring, Keith had little

doubt that Boyette was telling the truth. What if the ring had been stolen before she disappeared? Dana asked. And fenced at a pawnshop? What if? It seemed unlikely Boyette would purchase such a ring from a pawnshop, didn't it? Back and forth they went for hours, each questioning every idea the other had.

Much of the material scattered around the table came from two Web sites, WeMissYouNikki.com and FreeDonteDrumm.com. Donté's Web site was maintained by the law offices of Mr. Robbie Flak and was far more extensive, active, and professionally done. Nikki's Web site was run by her mother. Neither made the slightest effort at neutrality.

From Donté's, under the tab for Case History, Keith scrolled down to the heart of the prosecution's case, The Confession. The narrative began by explaining that it was based on two very different accounts of what happened. The interrogation, which took place over a period of fifteen hours and twelve minutes, proceeded with few interruptions. Donté was allowed to use the restroom three times, and was twice escorted down the hall to another room for polygraph exams. Otherwise, he never left the room, which had the in-house nickname "The Choir Room." Sooner or later, the cops liked to say, the suspects start singing.

The first version was based on the official police report. This consisted of notes taken throughout the interrogation by Detective Jim Morrissey. During one three-hour stretch, while Morrissey took a nap on a cot in the locker room, the notes were taken by a Detective Nick Needham. The notes were typed into a neat fourteen-page report, which Detectives Kerber, Morrissey, and Needham swore to be the truth, and nothing but. Not a single word in the report suggests the use of threats, lies, promises, trickery, intimidation, physical abuse, or violations of constitutional rights. Indeed, all of the above were denied repeatedly in court by the detectives.

The second version contrasted sharply with the first. The day after his arrest, while Donté was alone in a jail cell, charged with kidnapping, aggravated rape, and capital murder, and while he was slowly recuperating from the psychological trauma of the interrogation, he recanted his confession. He explained to his lawyer, Robbie Flak, what had happened. Under Flak's direction, Donté began writing his account of the interrogation. When it was finished two days later, it was typed by one of Mr. Flak's legal secretaries. Donté's version was forty-three pages long.

Thus, a summary of the two accounts, with some analysis thrown in.

THE CONFESSION

On December 22, 1998, eighteen days after the disappearance of Nicole Yarber, Detectives Drew Kerber and Jim Morrissey of the Slone Police Department drove to the South Side Health Club looking for Donté. The club is frequented by the more serious athletes in the area. Donté worked out there almost every afternoon, after school. He lifted weights and was rehabbing his ankle. He was in superb physical condition and was planning to enroll at Sam Houston State University next summer, then try out for the football team as a walk-on.

At approximately 5:00 p.m., as Donté was leaving the club alone, he was approached by Kerber and Morrissey, who introduced themselves in a friendly manner and asked Donté if he would talk to them about Nicole Yarber. Donté agreed, and Kerber suggested they meet at the police station, where they could relax and be more comfortable. Donté was nervous about this, but he also wanted to cooperate fully. He knew Nicole—he'd helped search for her—but knew nothing about her disappearance, and thought that the meeting at the station would take just a few minutes. He drove himself, in the family's well-used green Ford van, to the police station and parked in a visitor's slot. As he walked into the station, he had no idea that he was taking his last steps as a free man. He was eighteen years old, had never been in serious trouble, and had never been subjected to a prolonged police interrogation.

He was checked in at the front desk. His cell phone, wallet, and car keys were taken and put in a locked drawer for "security reasons."

The detectives led him to an interrogation room in the basement of the building. Other officers were around. One, a black policeman in uniform, recognized Donté and said something about football. Once inside the interrogation room, Morrissey offered him something to drink. Donté declined. There was a small rectangular table in the center of the room. Donté sat on one side, both detectives on the other. The room was well lit with no windows. In one corner, a tripod held a video camera, but it was not directed at Donté, as far as he could tell, nor did it appear to be turned on.

Morrissey produced a sheet of paper and explained that Donté needed to understand his *Miranda* rights. Donté asked if he was a witness or a suspect. The detective explained their procedures required that all persons interrogated be informed of their rights. No big deal. Just a formality.

Donté began to feel uncomfortable. He read every word on the paper, and since he had nothing to hide, signed his name, thus waiving his right to remain silent and his right to an attorney. It was a fateful, tragic decision.

Innocent people are much likelier to waive their rights during an interrogation. They know they are innocent, and they want to cooperate with the police to prove their innocence. Guilty suspects are more inclined not to cooperate. Seasoned criminals laugh at the police and clam up.

Morrissey took notes, beginning with the time the "suspect" entered the room—5:25 p.m.

Kerber did most of the talking. The discussion began with a long summary of the football season, the wins, the losses, what went wrong in the play-offs, a coaching change that was the hot rumor. Kerber seemed truly interested in his future and hoped his ankle healed so he could play in college. Donté expressed confidence that this would happen.

Kerber seemed especially interested in Donté's current weight-lifting program, and asked specific questions about how much he could bench-press, curl, squat, and deadlift.

There were a lot of questions about him and his family, his academic progress, his work experience, his brief run-in with the law on that marijuana thing when he was sixteen, and after what seemed like an hour, they finally got around to Nicole. The tone changed. The smiles were gone. The questions became more pointed. How long had he known her? How many classes together? Mutual friends? Whom did he date? Who were his girlfriends? Whom did she date? Did he ever date Nicole? No. Did he ever try to date her? No. Did he want to date her? He wanted to date a lot of girls. White girls? Sure, he wanted to, but he didn't. Never dated a white girl? No. Rumor has it that you and Nicole were seeing each other, trying to keep it quiet. Nope. Never met her privately. Never touched her. But you admit you wanted to date her? I said I wanted to date a lot of girls, white and black, even a couple of Hispanic. So, you love all girls? A lot of them, yes, but not all.

Kerber asked if Donté had participated in any of the

searches for Nicole. Yes, Donté and the entire senior class had spent hours looking for her.

They talked about Joey Gamble and some of the other boys Nicole had dated through high school. Kerber repeatedly asked if Donté dated her, or was seeing her on the sly. His questions were more like accusations, and Donté began to worry.

Roberta Drumm served dinner each night at 7:00, and if for some reason Donté wasn't there, he was expected to call. At 7:00 p.m., Donté asked the detectives if he could leave. Just a few more questions, Kerber said. Donté asked if he could call his mother. No, cell phones were not permitted inside the police station.

After two hours in the room, Kerber finally dropped a bomb. He informed Donté that they had a witness willing to testify that Nicole had confided to her close friends that she was seeing Donté and there was a lot of sex involved. But she had to keep it quiet. Her parents would never approve. Her rich father in Dallas would cut off his support and disinherit her. Her church would be scornful. And so on.

There was no such witness, but police are permitted to lie at will during an interrogation.

Donté strongly denied any relationship with Nicole.

And, Kerber went on with his tale, this witness had told them that Nicole was becoming increasingly worried about the affair. She wanted to end it, but that he, Donté, refused to leave her alone. She thought she was being stalked. She thought Donté had become obsessed with her.

Donté vehemently denied all of this. He demanded to know the identity of this witness, but Kerber said it was all confidential. Your witness is lying, Donté said over and over.

As with all interrogations, the detectives knew the direction their questions were headed. Donté did not. Abruptly, Kerber changed subjects and grilled Donté about the green Ford van, and how often he drove it, and where, and so on. It had been in the family for years, and it was shared by the Drumm children.   ·

Kerber asked how often Donté drove it to school, to the gym, to the mall, and to several other places frequented by high school students. Did Donté drive it to the mall on the night of December 4, a Friday, the night Nicole disappeared?

No. On the night Nicole disappeared, Donté was at home with his younger sister. His parents were in Dallas at a weekend church convention. Donté was babysitting. They ate frozen pizza and watched television in the den, something his mother did not usually allow. Yes, the green van was parked in the driveway. His parents had taken the family's Buick to Dallas. Neighbors testified that the green van was where he said it was. No one saw it leave during the night. His sister testified that he was with her throughout the night, that he did not leave.

Kerber informed the suspect that they had a witness who saw a green Ford van in the mall parking lot around the time Nicole disappeared. Donté said there was probably more than one such van in Slone. He began asking the detectives if he was a suspect. Do you think I took Nicole? he asked over and over. When it became evident that they did, he grew extremely agitated. He was also frightened at the thought of being suspected.

Around 9:00 p.m., Roberta Drumm was concerned. Donté rarely missed dinner, and he usually kept his cell phone in his pocket. Her calls to him were going straight to voice mail. She began calling his friends, none of whom knew his whereabouts.

Kerber asked Donté straight-out if he had killed Nicole and disposed of her body. Donté angrily denied this, denied any involvement whatsoever. Kerber said he didn't believe Donté. The exchanges between the two became tense and the language deteriorated. Accusations, denials, accusations, denials. At 9:45 p.m., Kerber kicked back his chair and stormed out of the room. Morrissey put down his pen and apologized for Kerber's behavior. He said the guy was under a lot of stress because he was the lead detective and everybody wanted to know what happened to Nicole. There was a chance she was still alive. Plus, Kerber was a hothead who could be overbearing.

It was the classic good-cop, bad-cop routine, and Donté knew exactly what was going on. But since Morrissey was being polite, Donté chatted with him. They did not discuss the case. Donté asked for a soft drink and something to eat, and Morrissey went to get it.

Donté had a good friend by the name of Torrey Pickett. They had played football together since the seventh grade, but Torrey had some legal problems the summer before his junior year. He was caught in a crack-selling sting and sent away. He did not finish high school and was currently working at a grocery store in Slone. The police knew that Torrey clocked out each weeknight at 10:00, when the store closed. Two uniformed officers were waiting. They asked him if he would voluntarily come down to the station and answer some questions about the Nicole Yarber case. He hesitated, and this made the police suspicious. They told him that his buddy Donté was already down there and needed his help. Torrey decided to go see for himself. He rode in the backseat of a police car. At the station, Torrey was placed in a room two doors down from Donté. The room had a large window with one-way glass so that officers could look in but the suspect could not see them. It was also wired so that the interrogation could be heard on a speaker in the hall. Detective Needham worked alone and asked the usual generic, noninvasive questions. Torrey quickly waived his *Miranda* rights. Needham soon got to the topic of girls, and who was dating whom and who was fooling around when they were not supposed to be. Torrey claimed he barely knew Nicole, hadn't seen her in years. He scoffed at the idea that his pal Donté was seeing the girl. After thirty minutes of questioning, Needham left the room. Torrey sat at a table and waited.

Meanwhile, in "The Choir Room," Donté was getting another jolt. Kerber informed him they had a witness who was willing to testify that Donté and Torrey Pickett grabbed the girl, raped her in the back of the green van, then tossed her body off a bridge over the Red River. Donté actually laughed at this lunacy, and his laughter rankled Detective Kerber. Donté explained that he was laughing not about a dead girl but at the fantasy that Kerber was putting together. If Kerber really had a witness, then he, Kerber, was foolish for believing the lying idiot. The two men called each other liars, among other things. A bad situation became even uglier.

Suddenly Needham opened the door and informed Kerber and Morrissey that they had Torrey Pickett "in custody." This news was so exciting that Kerber jumped to his feet and left the room again.

Moments later he was back. He resumed the same line of questioning and accused Donté of the murder. When Donté denied everything, Kerber accused him of lying. He claimed to know for a fact that Donté and Torrey Pickett raped and killed the girl, and if Donté wanted to prove his innocence, then they should start with a polygraph. A lie-detector test. It was foolproof, clear evidence, admissible in court, and so on. Donté was immediately suspicious of the test, but at the same time thought it might be a good idea, a quick way to end this foolishness. He knew he was innocent. He knew he could pass the test, and in doing so, he could get Kerber off his back before things got worse. He agreed to an exam.

Under the stress of police questioning, innocent people are far likelier to agree to a polygraph. They have nothing to hide and they're desperate to prove it. Guilty suspects rarely consent to the exams, and for obvious reasons.

Donté was led to another room and introduced to a Detective Ferguson, who'd been at home asleep an hour earlier when Detective Needham called. Ferguson was the department's polygraph expert, and he insisted that Kerber, Morrissey, and Needham leave the room. Ferguson was extremely polite, soft-spoken, even apologetic for putting Donté through the process. He explained everything, ran through the paperwork, rigged up the machine, and began asking Donté about his involvement in the Nicole Yarber matter. This went on for about an hour.

When Ferguson finished, he explained that it would be a few minutes before he could digest the results. Donté was taken back to "The Choir Room."

The results clearly showed that Donté was telling the truth. However, the law, as decided by the U.S. Supreme Court, permits the police to engage in a wide range of deceptive practices during interrogations. They can lie at will.

When Kerber returned to "The Choir Room," he was holding the graph paper from the test. He threw it at Donté, hitting him in the face, and called him a "lyin' son of a bitch!" Now they had proof that he was lying! They had clear evidence that he snatched his ex-lover, raped her, killed her in a fit of rage, and threw her off a bridge. Kerber picked up the graph paper, shook it in Donté's face, and promised him that when the jury saw the results of the test, they would find him guilty and give him death. You're looking at the needle, Kerber said over and over.

Another lie. Polygraphs are so famously unreliable that their results are never admitted in court.

Donté was stunned. He felt faint. He was bewildered and struggled to find words. Kerber relaxed and took his seat across the table. He said that in many cases involving horrible crimes, especially those committed by good, decent folks—noncriminals—the killer subconsciously erases the act from his memory. He just "blocks it out." This is quite common, and he, Detective Kerber, because of his extensive training and vast experience, had seen this many times. He suspected that Donté was quite fond of Nicole, maybe even in love, and did not plan to harm her. Things got out of control. She was dead before he realized it. Then he was in shock at what he'd done, and the guilt was crushing. So he tried to block it out.

Donté continued to deny everything. He was exhausted and laid his head on the table. Kerber slapped the table violently, startling his suspect. He again accused Donté of the crime, said they had the witnesses and the proof, and that he would be dead within five years. Texas prosecutors know how to streamline the system so that the executions are not delayed.

Kerber asked Donté to just imagine his mother, sitting in the witness room, waving at him for the last time, crying her eyes out, as they strapped him down and adjusted the chemicals. You're a dead man, he said more than once. But there was an option. If Donté would come clean, tell them what happened, make a full confession, then he, Kerber, would guarantee that the state would not seek the death penalty. Donté would get life with no parole, which was no piece of cake, but at least he could write letters to his mom and see her twice a month.

Such threats of death and promises of leniency are unconstitutional, and the police know it. Both Kerber and Morrissey denied using these tactics. Not surprisingly, Morrissey's notes make no reference to threats or promises. Nor do they accurately record the time and sequence of events. Donté did not have access to a pen and paper and, after five hours of interrogation, lost track of time.

Around midnight, Detective Needham opened the door and announced, "Pickett's talking." Kerber smiled at Morrissey, then left in another dramatic exit.

Pickett was alone in his locked room, fuming because he'd been forgotten. He had not seen or spoken to anyone in over an hour.

Riley Drumm found his green van parked at the city jail. He'd been driving the streets and was relieved to find the van. He was also concerned about his son and what kind of trouble he was in. The Slone City Jail is next door, and attached, to the police department. Riley went to the jail first and, after some confusion, was told that his son was not behind bars. He had not been processed. There were sixty-two prisoners back there, none by the name of Donté Drumm. The jailer, a younger white officer, recognized Donté's name and was as helpful as possible. He suggested that Mr. Drumm check next door with the police department. This he did, and it too proved confusing and frustrating. It was 12:40 a.m. and the front door was locked. Riley called his wife with an update, then he pondered how to get inside the building. After a few minutes, a patrol car parked nearby, and two uniformed officers emerged. They spoke to Riley Drumm, who explained why he was there. He followed them inside and took a seat in the lobby. The two officers left in search of his son. Half an hour passed before they reappeared and said that Donté was being questioned. About what? Why? The officers did not know. Riley began waiting. At least the boy was safe.

The first crack occurred when Kerber produced a color eight-by-ten photo of Nicole. Weary, alone, frightened, uncertain, and overwhelmed, Donté took one look at her pretty face and began crying. Kerber and Morrissey exchanged confident smiles.

Donté wept for several minutes, then asked to use the restroom. They escorted him down the hall, stopping at the window so he could see Torrey Pickett sitting at a table, holding a pen, writing on a legal pad. Donté stared in disbelief, even shook his head and mumbled something to himself.

Torrey wrote a one-page summary in which he denied knowing anything about Nicole Yarber's disappearance. The summary was somehow misplaced by the Slone Police Department and has never been seen.

Back in "The Choir Room," Kerber informed Donté that his pal Torrey had signed a statement in which he swore, under oath, that Donté was seeing Nicole, that he was crazy about her, but she was worried about the consequences and trying to break up. Donté was desperate and stalking the girl. Torrey was afraid he might hurt her.

As Kerber delivered this latest series of lies, he read from a sheet of paper, as if it were Torrey's statement. Donté closed his eyes, shook his head, and tried to understand what was happening. But his thoughts were much slower now, his reaction time deadened by fatigue and fear.

He asked if he could leave, and Kerber yelled at him. The detective cursed him and said no, he could not leave, because he was their prime suspect. He was their man. They had the proof. Donté asked if he needed a lawyer, and Kerber said of course not. A lawyer can't change the facts. A lawyer can't bring back Nicole. A lawyer can't save your life, Donté, but we can.

Morrissey's notes make no reference to the discussion about lawyers.

At 2:20 a.m., Torrey Pickett was allowed to leave. Detective Needham led him through a side door so he would not bump into Mr. Drumm in the lobby. The detectives in the basement had been warned that the defendant's father was in the building and wanted to see him. This was denied under oath at several hearings.

Morrissey began to fade and was replaced by Needham. For the next three hours, while Morrissey napped, Needham took notes. Kerber showed no signs of slowing down. As he hammered away at the suspect, he seemed to energize himself. He was about to break the suspect, solve the case, and become the hero. He offered Donté another crack at the polygraph, this one to be limited solely to the question of his whereabouts on Friday, December 4, at approximately 10:00 p.m. Donté's first reaction was to say no, to distrust the machine, but such wisdom was overridden by the desire to get out of the room. Just get away from Kerber. Anything to get the psycho out of his face.

Detective Ferguson hooked him up to the machine again and asked a few questions. The polygraph made its noises, its graph paper slowly rolled out. Donté stared at it without a clue, but something told him the results would not be good.

Again, the results proved he was telling the truth. He was at home that Friday, babysitting, and he never left.

But the truth was not important. While he was away, Kerber moved his chair to a corner, as far from the door as possible. When Donté returned, he took his place and Kerber pulled his chair close so that their knees were practically touching. He began cursing Donté again, telling him he had not only flunked the second polygraph but "severely flunked" it. For the first time, he touched Donté, by jabbing his right index finger into his chest. Donté slapped his hand away and was ready to fight, when Needham stepped forward with a Taser. The detective seemed anxious to give it a try, but did not. Both cops cursed and threatened Donté.

The jabbing continued, along with the nonstop accusations and threats. Donté realized he would not be allowed to leave until he gave the cops what they wanted. And maybe they were right after all. They seemed so certain about what happened. They were convinced beyond any doubt that he was involved. His own friend was saying that he and Nicole were involved in a relationship. And the polygraphs—what would the jury think when they learned that he had lied? Donté was doubting himself and his own memory. What if he had blacked out and erased the terrible deed? And he really didn't want to die, not then, not five or ten years down the road.

At 4:00 a.m., Riley Drumm left the police station and went home. He tried to sleep but could not. Roberta made coffee and they worried and waited for sunrise, as if things would clear up then.

Kerber and Needham took a break at 4:30 a.m. When they were alone in the hallway, Kerber said, "He's ready."

A few minutes later, Needham opened the door quietly and peeked in. Donté was lying on the floor, sobbing.

They took him a doughnut and a soft drink and resumed the interrogation. A revelation slowly came over Donté. Since he could not leave until he gave them their story, and since he would, at that moment, confess to killing his own mother, why not play along? Nicole would turn up soon enough, dead or alive, and this would solve the mystery. The police would look like fools for verbally beating a confession out of him. Some farmer or hunter would stumble over her remains, and these clowns would be exposed. Donté would be vindicated, freed, and everyone would feel sorry for him.

Twelve hours after the interrogation began, he looked at Kerber and said, "Give me a few minutes, and I'll tell you everything."

After the break, Kerber helped him fill in the blanks. He had sneaked out of the house after his sister was asleep. He was desperate to see Nicole because she was pushing him away, trying to break off their affair. He knew Nicole was at the movies with friends. He drove there, alone, in the green Ford van. He confronted her in the parking lot near her car. She agreed to get in. They drove around Slone, then into the countryside. He wanted sex, she said no. They were finished. He tried to force himself on her and she fought back. He forced her into sex, but it wasn't enjoyable. She scratched him, even drew blood. The attack turned ugly. He flew into a rage, began to choke her, and he couldn't stop, didn't stop until it was too late. Then he panicked. He had to do something with her. He yelled at her back in the rear of the van, but she never responded. He drove north, toward Oklahoma. He'd lost track of time, then realized that dawn was approaching. He had to get home. He had to get rid of her body. On the Route 244 bridge over the Red River, at approximately 6:00, on the morning of December 5, he stopped the van. It was still dark, she was still very dead. He tossed her over and waited until he heard the sickening splash below. He cried all the way back to Slone.

For three hours, Kerber coached him, prodded him, corrected him, cursed him, reminded him to tell the truth. The details had to be perfect, Kerber kept saying. At 8:21 a.m., the video camera was finally turned on. A wiped-out, stone-faced Donté Drumm sat at the table with a fresh soft drink and doughnut in front of him, visible so that their hospitality could be shown.

The video ran for seventeen minutes, and would send him to death row.

Donté was charged with abduction, aggravated rape, and capital murder. He was taken to a cell where he promptly fell asleep.

At 9:00 a.m., the chief of police, along with the district attorney, Mr. Paul Koffee, held a press conference to announce the Nicole Yarber case had been solved. Sadly, one of Slone's former football heroes, Donté Drumm, had confessed to the murder. Other witnesses verified his involvement. Sympathies to her family.

The confession was attacked immediately. Donté recanted and his attorney, Robbie Flak, went public with a scathing condemnation of the police and their tactics. Months later, the defense lawyers filed motions to suppress the confession, and the suppression hearing lasted for a week. Kerber, Morrissey, and Needham testified at length, and their testimony was hotly challenged by the defense. They steadfastly denied using threats, promises, or intimidation. They specifically denied using the death penalty as a means to frighten Donté into cooperating. They denied verbally abusing the suspect or pushing him to the point of exhaustion and collapse. They denied that Donté had ever mentioned a lawyer, or that he wanted to terminate the interrogation and go home. They denied any knowledge of his father's presence at the station and his desire to see his son. They denied the fact that their own polygraph tests showed clear evidence of truthfulness, but instead testified that the results were "inconclusive," in their opinions. They denied any trickery with the alleged statement of Torrey Pickett. Pickett testified on Donté's behalf and denied telling the police anything about an affair between Donté and Nicole.

The trial judge expressed grave concerns about the confession, but not grave enough to exclude it from the trial. She refused to suppress it, and it was later shown to the jury. Donté watched it as if he were watching a different person. No one has ever seriously questioned the fact that it guaranteed his conviction.

The confession was attacked again on appeal, but the Texas Court of Criminal Appeals unanimously affirmed the conviction and death sentence.

When Keith was finished, he left the table and went to the bathroom. He had the feeling that he had just been interrogated. It was well after midnight. Sleep would be impossible.

8

By 7:00 on Tuesday morning, the Flak Law Firm was bustling with a frantic, nervous energy one might expect from a group of people fighting both the clock and some very long odds to save a man's life. Tension was palpable. There were no smiles, none of the usual smart-ass remarks from people who worked together each day with the absolute freedom of saying anything to anyone at any time. Most of those present had been around six years earlier when Lamar Billups got the needle at Huntsville, and the finality of his death had been a shock. And Billups had been a nasty character. His favorite pastime had been beating up people in bar fights, preferably with pool cue sticks and broken bottles, and the state finally got fed up with him. On his deathbed, his last words were "See you in hell" and away he went. He was guilty, and never made a serious claim otherwise. His murder had been in a small town sixty miles away, hardly noticed by the citizens of Slone. He had no family, no one for the firm to be acquainted with. Robbie disliked him immensely, but clung rigidly to the belief that the state had no right to kill him.

The State of Texas versus Donté Drumm was a far different matter. Now they were fighting for an innocent man, and his family was their family.

The long table in the main conference room was the center of the storm. Fred Pryor, who was still in Houston, was on the speakerphone, giving a quick update on his efforts to flip Joey Gamble. The two had spoken by phone late Monday night, and Gamble was even less cooperative.

"He kept asking about perjury and how serious a crime it is," Pryor said, his voice at full volume.

"Koffee's threatening him," Robbie said, as if he knew it to be true. "Did you ask him if he's talking to the district attorney?"

"No, but I thought about it," Pryor replied. "I didn't, because I figured he would not divulge that."

"Koffee knows he lied at trial, and he's told the kid that we'll make a last-minute run at him," Robbie said. "He's threatened him with a prosecution for perjury if he changes his story now. Wanna bet on that, Fred?"

"No. Sounds about right."

"Tell Joey the statute of limitations has run on perjury. Koffee can't touch him."

"You got it."

The speakerphone was switched off. A platter of pastries hit the table and attracted a crowd. Robbie's two associates, both women, were reviewing a request for a reprieve from the governor. Martha Handler sat at one end of the table, lost in the world of trial transcripts. Aaron Rey, with his jacket off and both pistols visible and strapped to his shirt, sipped coffee from a paper cup as he scanned the morning newspaper. Bonnie, a paralegal, worked at a laptop.

"Let's assume Gamble comes through," Robbie

said to his senior associate, a prim lady of undetermined age. Robbie had sued her first plastic surgeon twenty years earlier when a face-lift produced a result that was less than desirable. But she had not given up on the corrective work; she had simply changed surgeons. Her name was Samantha Thomas, or Sammie, and when she wasn't working on Robbie's cases, she was suing doctors for malpractice and employers for age and race discrimination. "Get the petition ready, just in case," he said.

"I'm almost finished with it," Sammie said.

The receptionist, Fanta, a tall, slender black woman who had starred in basketball at Slone High and would have graduated, under different circumstances, with both Nicole Yarber and Donté Drumm, entered the room with a handful of phone messages. "A reporter from *The Washington Post* called and wants to talk," she said to Robbie, who immediately focused on her legs.

"Is it someone we know?"

"Never seen the name before."

"Then ignore."

"A reporter from the *Houston Chronicle* left a message at 10:30 last night."

"It's not Spinney is it?"

"It is."

"Tell him to go to hell."

"I don't use that language."

"Then ignore."

"Greta has called three times."

"Is she still in Germany?"

"Yes, she can't afford a plane ticket. She wants to know if she and Donté can get married through the Internet?"

"And what did you tell her?"

"I said no, it's not possible."

"Did you explain that Donté has become one of the most eligible bachelors in the world? That he's had at least five marriage proposals in the past week, all from Europe? All kinds of women, young, old, fat, skinny, the only trait they share is that they are ugly? And stupid? Did you explain that Donté is rather particular about whom he marries and so he's taking his time?"

"I didn't talk to her. She left a voice mail."

"Good. Ignore."

"The last one is from a minister from a Lutheran church in Topeka, Kansas. Called ten minutes ago. Said he might have information about who killed Nicole, but is not sure what to do about it."

"Great, another nut. How many of those did we have last week?"

"I've lost count."

"Ignore. It's amazing how many fruitcakes show up at the last minute."

She placed the messages amid the pile of debris in front of Robbie and left the room. Robbie watched every step of her exit, but did not gawk as usual.

Martha Handler said, "I don't mind calling the fruitcakes."

"You're just looking for material," Robbie shot back. "It's a waste of valuable time."

"Morning news," Carlos, the paralegal, said loudly and reached for the remote control. He aimed it at a wide-screen television hanging in a corner, and the chatter stopped. The reporter was standing in front of the Chester County Courthouse, as if something dramatic might happen there at any minute. He gushed:

"City officials are mum on their plans to deal with potential unrest here in Slone in the wake of the scheduled execution of Donté Drumm. Drumm, as you know, was convicted in 1999 of the aggravated rape and murder of Nicole Yarber and, pending a last-minute stay or reprieve, will be executed at the prison in Huntsville at 6:00 Thursday evening. Drumm has maintained his innocence, and many here in Slone do not believe he is guilty. From the beginning, the case has had racial overtones, and to say the town is divided is quite an understatement. I'm here with Police Chief Joe Radford."

The camera pulled back to reveal the rotund figure of the chief, in uniform.

"Chief, what can we expect if the execution is carried out?"
"Well, I guess we can expect justice to be served."
"Do you anticipate trouble?"
"Not at all. Folks have got to understand that the judicial system works and that the verdict of the jury must be carried out."
"So, you don't foresee any problems Thursday night?"
"No, but we'll be out in full force. We'll be ready."
"Thanks for your time."

The camera zoomed in, cutting out the chief.

"Organizers are planning a protest tomorrow at noon, right here in front of the courthouse.

*Sources confirmed that a permit for a rally has
been issued by city hall. More on that later."*

The reporter signed off and the paralegal pushed
the mute button. No comment from Robbie, and
everybody went back to work.

The Texas Board of Pardons and Paroles has seven
members, all appointed by the governor. An inmate
desiring clemency must petition the board for relief. A
petition may be as simple as a one-page request, or as
thorough as a voluminous filing with exhibits, affidavits, and letters from around the world. The one
filed by Robbie Flak on behalf of Donté Drumm was
one of the most exhaustive in the board's history.
Clemency is rarely granted. If denied, an appeal can
be made to the governor, who cannot grant clemency
on his own initiative but is allowed to issue one
thirty-day reprieve. On those rare occasions when the
board grants clemency, the governor has the right to
overrule it and the state proceeds with the execution.

For a condemned prisoner facing death, the board
usually makes its decision two days before the execution. The board doesn't actually meet to take a vote,
but instead circulates a ballot by fax. Death by Fax,
as it is known.

For Donté Drumm, news of his Death by Fax came
at 8:15 on Tuesday morning. Robbie read the decision aloud to his team. No one was remotely surprised. They had lost so many rounds by now that a
victory was not something they expected.

"So, let's ask the governor for a reprieve," Robbie
said with a smile. "I'm sure he'll be happy to hear
from us again." Of the truckload of motions and pe-

titions and requests that his firm had filed in the last month, and would continue to churn out until his client was dead, a request for a reprieve from the governor of Texas was undoubtedly the biggest waste of paper. Twice in the past year the governor had ignored clemency approvals from his parole board and allowed the executions. He loved the death penalty, especially when seeking votes. One of his campaigns featured the slogan "Tough Texas Justice" and included his promise to "empty death row." And he was not talking about early parole.

"Let's go see Donté," Robbie announced.

The drive from Slone to the Polunsky Unit near Livingston, Texas, was a hard three-hour grind on two-lane roads. Robbie had made it a hundred times. A few years earlier, when he had three clients on death row—Donté, Lamar Billups, and a man named Cole Taylor—he grew weary of speeding tickets and rural drivers and near misses because he was on the phone. He bought a van, a long, heavy one with plenty of room, and he took it to a high-end custom shop in Fort Worth where they installed phones, televisions, and every gadget on the market, along with plush carpet, fine leather captain's chairs that both swiveled and reclined, a sofa in the rear, if Robbie needed a nap, and a bar in case he became thirsty. Aaron Rey was named the designated driver. Bonnie, the other paralegal, usually sat in the front passenger seat, ready to jump when Mr. Flak barked. The trips became much more productive as Robbie worked the phone and laptop or read briefs on the way to Polunsky and back, traveling comfortably in the portable office.

His chair was directly behind the driver's. Next to him was Martha Handler. Up front with Aaron was Bonnie. They left Slone at 8:30 a.m. and were soon winding through the hills of East Texas.

The fifth member of the team was a new one. Her name was Dr. Kristina Hinze, or Kristi, as she was called around the Flak office, where no one was presumptuous enough to wear a title and most first names were shortened. She was the latest in a series of experts Robbie had burned cash on in his efforts to save Donté. She was a clinical psychiatrist who'd studied prisoners and prison conditions, and she'd written a book that argued, among other things, that solitary confinement is one of the worst forms of torture. For $10,000, she was expected to meet with Donté, evaluate him, then prepare (quickly) a report in which she would describe his deteriorated mental condition and declare that (1) he had been driven crazy by eight years of solitary and (2) such confinement constitutes cruel and unusual punishment.

In 1986, the U.S. Supreme Court stopped the execution of insane people. Robbie's final thrust would be to portray Donté as a psychotic schizoid who understood nothing.

The argument was a long shot. Kristi Hinze was only thirty-two years old, not far removed from the classroom, with a résumé that included no experience in court. Robbie was not concerned. He only hoped she got the chance to testify in a hearing on mental competency, months down the road. She had the rear sofa, papers spread everywhere, hard at work like everyone else.

When Robbie finished a phone call, Martha Handler said, "Can we talk?" This had become her standard opening when she had questions.

"Sure," he said.

She clicked on one of her many tape recorders and slid it in front of him. "On the subject of money, you were appointed by the judge to represent Donté, who qualified as in indigent defendant, but—"

"Yep, Texas has no public defender system to speak of," he interrupted. After months together, Martha had learned that she should never expect to finish a sentence. He went on, "So the local judges appoint their buddies or drag in some poor schmuck when the case is so bad no one wants it. Me, I went to the judge and volunteered. She was happy to give it to me. No other lawyer in town would get near it."

"But the Drumms are not exactly poor. They both—?"

"Sure, but here's how it works. Only a rich person can afford to pay a lawyer for a capital defense, and there are no rich people on death row. I could've squeezed five or ten thousand bucks out of the family, made 'em mortgage their house again, something like that. But why bother? The fine folks of Chester County would pay. This is one of the great ironies of the death penalty. The people want the death penalty—something like 70 percent in this state—yet they have no idea how much they're paying for it."

"How much have they paid?" she asked, deftly inserting the question before he could start talking again.

"Oh, I don't know. A lot. Bonnie, how much have we been paid so far?"

With no hesitation and hardly a glance over her shoulder, Bonnie said, "Almost $400,000."

Robbie went on, barely skipping a beat, "That includes attorney's fees, at the rate of $125 an hour, plus expenses, primarily for investigators, and then a nice chunk for expert witnesses."

"That's a lot of money," Martha said.

"It is and it isn't. When a law firm is working for $125 an hour, it's losing serious money. I'll never do it again. I can't afford it. Neither can the taxpayers, but at least I know I'm losing my ass. They do not. Ask the average Joe on Main Street in Slone how much he and his fellow citizens have paid to prosecute Donté Drumm, and you know what he'll say?"

"How am I supposed to—"

"He'll say he doesn't have a clue. Have you heard about the Tooley boys in West Texas? It's a famous case."

"I'm sorry, I must've missed—"

"These two brothers, the Tooleys, a couple of idiots, somewhere out in West Texas. What county, Bonnie?"

"Mingo."

"Mingo County. Very rural. A great story, listen. These two thugs are robbing convenience stores and gas stations. Very sophisticated stuff. One night, something goes wrong, and a young female clerk gets shot. Sawed-off shotgun, really nasty. They catch the Tooley brothers because the boys forgot about all of the video cameras. The town is outraged. The police are strutting. The prosecutor is promising swift justice. Everybody wants a quick trial and quick execution. There's not much crime in Mingo County, and no jury there has ever sent a man to death row. Now, there are many ways to feel neglected in Texas, but living in a community that's been left out of the execution business is downright embarrassing. What do the kinfolks in Houston think? These Mingo people see their opportunity. They want blood. The boys refuse to plea-bargain because the prosecutor insists on death. Why plead to death? So they try them, together. Quick convictions and, finally, death. On appeal, the court finds all manner of error. The prosecutor really butchered the case. The convictions are thrown out. The case is sent back for separate trials. Two trials, not one. Are you taking notes?"

"No, I'm searching for some relevance here."

"It's a great story."

"That's all that matters."

"A year or so passes. The boys are tried separately. Two new guilty verdicts, two more trips to death row. The appeals court sees more problems. I mean, glaring problems. The prosecutor was a moron. Reversals, sent back for two new trials. The third time, one jury convicts the gunman of murder and he gets life. The other jury convicts the one who didn't fire the gun of murder and he gets death. Go figure. It's Texas. So one brother is serving life. The other went to death row, where he committed suicide a few months later. Somehow he got a razor and slashed himself."

"And your point is?"

"Here's the point. From start to finish, the case cost Mingo County $3 million. They were forced to raise property taxes several times, and this led to an uprising. There were drastic budget cuts in schools, road maintenance, and health services. They closed their only library. The county was near bankruptcy for years. And all of it could have been prevented if the prosecutor had allowed the boys to plead guilty and take life without parole. I've heard that the death penalty is not that popular in Mingo County now."

"I was more interested in—"

"From soup to nuts, it takes about two million bucks to legally kill a man in Texas. Compare that with the $30,000 it costs per year to keep one on death row."

"I've heard this before," Martha said, and indeed she had. Robbie never shied away from his soapbox, especially when the subject was the death penalty, one of his many favorites.

"But what the hell. We have plenty of money in Texas."

"Can we talk about Donté Drumm's case?"

"Oh, why not?"

"The defense fund. You—"

"Established a few years back, a certified nonprofit governed by all relevant code sections set forth by the Internal Revenue Service. Administered jointly by my office and Andrea Bolton, younger sister of Donté Drumm. Receipts so far total how much, Bonnie?"

"Ninety-five thousand dollars."

"Ninety-five thousand dollars. And how much is on hand?"

"Zero."

"That's what I figured. Would you like a break-down of where the money went?"

"Maybe. Where did it go?"

"Litigation expenses, law firm expenses, expert witnesses, a few bucks to the family to travel back and forth to see Donté. Not exactly a high-powered nonprofit. All moneys have been raised through the Internet. Frankly, we haven't had the time or man-power to pursue fund-raising."

"Who are the donors?"

"Mostly Brits and Europeans. The average dona-tion is something like twenty bucks."

"Eighteen fifty," Bonnie said.

"It's very hard to raise money for a convicted mur-derer, regardless of his story."

"How much are you out of pocket?" Martha asked.

There was no rapid response. Bonnie, finally stumped, gave a slight shrug from the front seat. "I don't know," Robbie said. "If I had to guess, it would be at least $50,000, maybe a hundred. Maybe I should've spent more."

Phones were buzzing throughout the van. Sammie at the office had a question for the boss. Kristi Hinze was talking to another psychiatrist. Aaron was listening to someone as he drove.

The party began early with sweet potato biscuits straight from Reeva's oven. She loved to cook them, and eat them, and when Sean Fordyce admitted he'd never eaten one, she feigned disbelief. By the time he arrived, with his hairdresser, makeup girl, appointment secretary, and publicist all hustling around him, the home of Reeva and Wallis Pike was crammed with neighbors and friends. The thick smell of fried country ham wafted out the front door. Two long trucks were backed into the driveway, and even the crew members were chomping on biscuits.

Fordyce, an Irish ass from Long Island, was slightly irritated by the crowd, but put on his game face and signed autographs. He was the star. These were his fans. They bought his books, watched his show, and gave him his ratings. He posed for a few photographs, ate a biscuit with ham, and seemed to like it. He was pudgy, with a doughy face, not exactly the traditional looks of a star, but that didn't matter anymore. He wore dark suits and funky eyeglasses that made him appear far more intelligent than he acted.

The set was in Reeva's room, the large addition stuck to the rear of the house like a cancerous growth. Reeva and Wallis were situated on a sofa, with color blowups of Nicole as the backdrop. Wallis wore a tie and looked as if he'd just been ordered out of his bedroom, which in fact he had. Reeva was heavily made up, her hair freshly colored and permed, and she wore her finest black dress. Fordyce sat in a chair, close to them. He was tended to by his handlers, who sprayed his hair and powdered his forehead. The crew fussed with the lighting. Sound checks were done. Monitors were adjusted. The neighbors were packed in tight behind the cameras with stern instructions not to make a sound.

The producer said, "Quiet! We're rolling."

Close-up on Fordyce as he welcomed his audience to another episode. He explained where he was, whom he was interviewing, and the basics of the crime, the confession, and the conviction. "If all goes as expected," he said gravely, "Mr. Drumm will be executed the day after tomorrow."

He introduced the mother and the stepfather and, of course, passed along his condolences for this tragedy. He thanked them for opening their home so that the world, through his cameras, could witness the suffering. He began with Nicole. "Tell us about her," he almost pleaded.

Wallis made no effort to speak, something he would do throughout the interview. This was Reeva's show. She was excited and overstimulated and after just a few words began crying. But she had cried in public for so long that she could now chatter away while the tears flowed. She went on and on about her daughter.

"Do you miss her?" Fordyce asked, one of his

patented inane questions designed only to elicit more emotion.

Reeva gave it to him. He handed her the white handkerchief from his coat pocket. Linen. The man oozed compassion.

He finally got around to the execution, which was the thrust of his program. "Do you still plan to be there?" he asked, certain of the answer.

"Oh yes," she said, and Wallis managed to nod.

"Why? What will it mean to you?"

"It means so much," she said. The thought of revenge dried the tears. "This animal took my daughter's life. He deserves to die and I want to be there, to stare him in the eyes when he takes his last breath."

"Do you think he'll look at you?"

"I doubt it. He's a coward. Any human who could do what he did to my precious little girl, I doubt he'll be man enough to look at me."

"What about his last words? Do you want an apology?"

"Yes, but I'm not expecting one. He has never taken responsibility for what he did."

"He confessed."

"Yes, but then he changed his mind and he's denied it ever since. I expect he'll deny it when they strap him down and he says good-bye."

"Anticipate for us, Reeva. Tell us how you think you'll feel when he's pronounced dead."

Just the thought made her smile, but she quickly caught herself. "Relief, sadness, I don't know. It'll be the closing of another chapter in a long, sad story. But it won't be the end."

Wallis frowned slightly upon learning this.

"What's the final chapter here, Reeva?"

"When you lose a child, Sean, especially one taken in such a violent way, there is no end."

"There is no end," he repeated somberly, then turned to the camera, and, with every effort at great drama, said again, "There is no end."

They took a quick break, moved some cameras, and added more spray to Fordyce's hair. And when they rolled again, he managed to get a few grunts from Wallis, stuff that wouldn't last ten seconds in editing.

The filming was over in less than an hour. Fordyce made a quick exit—he was also working on an execution in Florida. He made sure everyone knew there was a jet waiting to take him there. One of his camera crews would hang around Slone for the next two days, hoping for violence.

Fordyce would be in Huntsville on Thursday night, looking for drama, praying the execution would not be put off. His favorite part of his show was the post-execution interview when he got the victim's family fresh from the prison. They were usually emotional wrecks, and he knew that Reeva would light up the screen.

9

It took Dana almost two hours of persistent calling and cajoling to find the right deputy clerk willing to dig through the right record logs to determine that, yes, in fact, one Travis Boyette was arrested for drunk driving in Slone, Texas, on January 6, 1999. After he was jailed, more serious charges were added. He had posted bond, then skipped town. The charges were dismissed and the file was closed when Mr. Boyette was arrested and sentenced to ten years in prison in Kansas. The clerk explained the procedure in Slone was to dispose of cases that would not or could not be pursued. There were no outstanding warrants on him, at least not in Slone and Chester County.

Keith, who'd been unable to sleep and brewed the first pot of coffee at 3:30 a.m., called Mr. Flak's office the first time at 7:30 a.m. He was not entirely certain what he would say to the lawyer if he got him on the phone, but he and Dana had decided they could not sit by and do nothing. When he was stiff-armed by Flak's receptionist, he called another lawyer.

Matthew Burns was an assistant prosecutor and an active member of St. Mark's. He and Keith were the same age and had coached their sons' T-ball teams together. Luckily, Burns was not in trial Tuesday morning, but was still quite busy in court with first appearances and other routine matters. Keith found the right courtroom, one of several in the courthouse, and from a seat in the back row watched the flow of justice. After an hour, he was fidgeting and ready to leave, though he wasn't sure where to go. Burns finished another appearance before the judge, stuffed his paperwork into his briefcase, and headed for the door. He nodded at Keith, who followed. They found a quiet place in the bustling corridors, a well-used wooden bench near a stairwell.

"You look like hell," Burns began pleasantly.

"Thanks. I'm not sure that's a nice way to greet your minister. I couldn't sleep last night, Matthew. Not one minute. Did you look at the Web site?"

"Yes, for about ten minutes at the office. I'd never heard of Drumm, but then these cases tend to run together now. They're pretty routine down there."

"Drumm's innocent, Matthew," Keith said with a certainty that surprised his friend.

"Well, that's what the Web site says. But he's not the first killer who claimed to be innocent."

The two had rarely talked about the law or any issue related to the death penalty. Keith assumed that, as a prosecutor, Matthew supported it. "The killer is here in Topeka, Matthew. He was in church Sunday morning, probably in a pew not far from you and your family."

"You have my attention."

"He's just been paroled, spending ninety days at the halfway house, and he's dying of a brain tumor. He stopped by the office yesterday for counseling. He has a long history of sexual assaults. I've talked to him twice, and he's admitted, in confidence of course, he raped and killed the girl. He knows where the body is buried. He doesn't want Drumm to be executed, but he doesn't want to come forward either. He's a mess, Matthew, a real sick psycho who'll be dead himself in a few months."

Matthew exhaled and shook his head as if he'd been slapped. "May I ask why you're in the middle of this?"

"I don't know. I just am. I know the truth. The question is, how does one go about stopping an execution?"

"Good God, Keith."

"Yes, I've talked to Him too and I'm still waiting on His guidance. But until it comes, I need some from you. I've called the defense lawyer's office in Texas, but that went nowhere."

"Don't you have to keep these matters in confidence?"

"Yes. And I will. But what if the murderer decides to come clean, to tell the truth, to try to save this man from being executed? What then? How do we go about it?"

"We? Not so fast, buddy."

"Help me here, Matthew. I don't understand the law. I've read the Web site until I'm cross-eyed, and the more I read, the more confused I become. How do you convict a man of murder when there is no dead body? How do you believe a confession that was so obviously coerced by the police? Why are jailhouse snitches allowed to testify in return for lighter sentences? How can a black defendant get an all-white jury? How can the jurors be so blind? Where are the appellate courts? I have a long list of questions."

"And I can't answer all of them, Keith. Seems,

though, that the only important one is the first—how do you stop the execution?"

"I'm asking you, pal, you're the lawyer."

"Okay, okay. Let me think for a minute. You need some coffee, don't you?"

"Yes. I've only had a gallon."

They walked down a flight of stairs to a small canteen where they found a table in a corner. Keith bought the coffee, and when he sat down, Matthew said, "You gotta have the body. If your man can produce the body, then Drumm's lawyers could probably get a stay from the courts. If not, the governor might delay the execution. I'm not sure how the mechanics work down there. Every state is different. Without the body, though, your man will sound like just another quack that shows up looking for attention. Keep in mind, Keith, that there will be the usual last-minute filings. These death-penalty lawyers know how to play the system, and a lot of executions get delayed. You may have more time than you think."

"Texas is pretty efficient."

"Good point."

"Two years ago, Drumm came within a week of execution. Something clicked in a federal court filing, don't ask me what. I read it last night and I'm still confused. Anyway, according to the Web site, a last-minute miracle is unlikely now. Drumm's had his miracle. His luck has run out."

"Finding the body is crucial. That's the only clear proof that your man is telling the truth. Do you know where it is? If you do, don't tell me. Just tell me if you know."

"No. He's told me the state, the nearby town, the general location, but he's also said that he hid it so well he may have trouble finding it."

"Is it in Texas?"

"Missouri."

Matthew shook his head. He took a long drink and said, "What if this guy is just another lying con, Keith? I see a dozen a day. They lie about everything. They lie out of habit. They lie when the truth would be of far greater help to themselves. They lie on the witness stand and they lie to their own lawyers. And the longer they stay in prison, the more they lie."

"He has her class ring, Matthew. Wears it on a cheap little chain around his neck. He stalked the girl; he was obsessed with her. He showed me the ring. I held it and inspected it."

"You're sure it's real?"

"If you saw it, you would say it's real."

Another long drink. Matthew glanced at his watch.

"You gotta go?"

"Five minutes. Is this guy willing to go to Texas and proclaim the truth?"

"I don't know. He says that if he leaves this jurisdiction, he violates his parole."

"He's not lying about that. But if he's dying, why does he really care?"

"I asked him that. His answer was vague. Plus, the guy has no money, no way to get down there. He has zero credibility. No one will give him the time of day."

"Why did you call the lawyer?"

"Because I'm desperate, Matthew. I believe this guy, and I believe Drumm's innocent. Maybe Drumm's lawyer will know what to do. I don't know."

There was a gap in the conversation. Matthew

nodded and spoke to two other lawyers at the next table. He glanced at his watch again.

"One last question," Keith said. "Just a hypothetical one. What if I convinced this guy to hustle down to Texas, as soon as possible, and start telling his story?"

"You just said he can't get there."

"Yes, but what if I take him?"

"No, hell no, Keith. You'd be aiding in the violation of his parole agreement. Absolutely not."

"How serious is that?"

"I'm not sure, but it could get you embarrassed, maybe even defrocked for all you know. I doubt if you would serve time, but it would be painful enough."

"How is he supposed to get down there?"

"I thought you said he hasn't decided to go."

"But if he does?"

"Take it one step at a time, Keith." The third glance at his watch. "Look, I gotta run. Let's meet somewhere for a quick lunch and finish this conversation."

"Good idea."

"There's a deli down the street at the corner of Seventh. It's called Eppie's. We can get a booth in the back and have a quiet chat."

"I know the place."

"See you at noon."

The same ex-con with the permanent scowl was working the front desk at Anchor House. He was quite busy with a crossword and did not appreciate the interruption. Boyette was not there, he said curtly. Keith pressed gently. "Is he at work?"

"He's at the hospital. Took him in last night."

"What happened?"

"Fits and seizures is all I know. Dude's really messed up, in more ways than one."

"Which hospital?"

"I didn't drive the ambulance." And with that, he returned to his crossword and the conversation was over.

Keith found his patient on the third floor of St. Francis Hospital, in a semiprivate room next to the window. A flimsy curtain separated the two beds. As a minister making his rounds, and a familiar face at that, Keith told the nurse that Mr. Boyette had visited his church and needed to see him. Nothing more was needed.

Boyette was awake and had an IV tube taped to his left hand. He smiled when he saw Keith and offered a limp right hand for a quick shake. "Thanks for coming, Pastor," he said with a weak, scratchy voice.

"How do you feel, Travis?"

Five seconds passed. He raised his left hand slightly and said, "Some pretty good drugs. I feel better."

"What happened?" Keith asked, though he thought he knew.

Boyette looked at the window, though he could see nothing but a gray sky. Ten seconds passed. "After you left, Pastor, I got real upset. The headaches hit hard and wouldn't go away. Then I blacked out, and they brought me here. Said I was shaking and jerking."

"I'm sorry, Travis."

"Most of it's your fault, Pastor. You did it. You got me all stressed-out."

"I'm very sorry, but please remember that you

came to see me, Travis. You wanted my help. You told me about Donté Drumm and Nicole Yarber, two people I'd never heard of. You said what you said. I didn't initiate our contact."

"True." He closed his eyes. His breathing was heavy and labored.

There was a long pause. Keith leaned over, and almost in a whisper said, "Are you there, Travis?"

"Yes."

"Then listen to me. I have a plan. You want to hear it?"

"Sure."

"First, we make a video of you telling your story. You admit what you did to Nicole. You explain that Donté had nothing to do with her abduction and death. You tell everything, Travis. And you tell where she's buried. Give as much detail as possible so that, with some luck, they might be able to find her. We do the video now. Here in the hospital. And once I have it, I'll zip it down to Texas, to Donté's lawyers, to the prosecutor, the judge, the police, the appeals courts, the governor, and every newspaper and television station down there so they will know. Everybody will know. I'll do this electronically so they'll have it in a matter of minutes. Then, for the second part of my plan, you give me the ring. I'll photograph it and send the pictures to all the folks I just mentioned, also by Internet. I'll send the ring by overnight delivery to Donté's lawyers and they'll have the physical evidence. What about it, Travis? You can tell your story and never leave this hospital bed."

The eyes never opened.

"Are you there, Travis?"

A grunt. "Uh-huh."

"It'll work, Travis. We can't waste any more time."

"It is a waste of time."

"What is there to lose? Just the life of an innocent man."

"You called me a liar last night."

"That's because you lied."

"Did you find my arrest record in Slone?"

"We did."

"So I wasn't lying."

"Not about that. And you're not lying about Donté Drumm."

"Thank you. I'm going to sleep now."

"Come on, Travis. It'll take less than fifteen minutes to make the video. I can even do it now with my cell phone, if you want."

"You're hurting my head again, Pastor. I feel a seizure. You need to leave now, and please don't come back."

Keith stood straight and took a deep breath. To make sure things were clear, Boyette repeated himself, but much louder. "You need to leave, Pastor. And please don't come back."

In the rear of Eppie's, the two settled over large bowls of beef stew. Matthew pulled some notes out of a pocket and spoke with a mouthful. "There's no code section directly on point, but you would probably be charged with obstruction of justice. Don't even think about taking that guy to Texas."

"I just talked to our man. He is—"

"Our man? I didn't realize I'd been drafted."

"He's in the hospital. Had seizures last night. The tumor is quickly killing him. He's lost his desire to help the cause. He's a creep, a psychopath, probably crazy before the tumor took over his brain."

"Why did he come to church?"

"Probably to get out of the halfway house for a few hours. No, I shouldn't say that. I've seen real emotion from this guy, real guilt, and a fleeting desire to do what's right. Dana found one of his former parole officers in Arkansas. The officer talked a little and said that our man was a member of some white supremacist gang in prison. Donté Drumm, of course, is black, and so I'm questioning how much sympathy is really there."

"You're not eating," Matthew said as he took a bite.

"I'm not hungry. I have another idea."

"You are not going to Texas. They would probably shoot you down there."

"Okay, okay. Here's the idea. What if you call the lawyer for Donté Drumm? I couldn't get past the receptionist. I'm just a humble servant of the Lord, but you're a lawyer, a prosecutor, and you speak their language."

"And what might I say to him?"

"You could say that you have reason to believe that the real killer is here in Topeka."

Matthew chewed a mouthful and waited. He said, "Is that all? Just like that. This lawyer gets a weird phone call from me. I say what I say, which isn't much, and that's supposed to give the lawyer new ammunition to file in court and stop the execution? Am I right here, Keith?"

"I know you can be more persuasive than that."

"Try this scenario. This creep is your typical pathological liar who's about to die—poor guy. And he decides to go out with a bang, decides to get one last shot of revenge at a system that's beaten him up. He learns of this case in Texas, does his research, realizes that the body has never been found, and, presto, he's got his story. He finds the Web site and becomes fluent in the facts, and now he's toying with you. Can you imagine the attention this guy would get? But his health won't cooperate. Leave it alone, Keith. He's probably a fake."

"How would he hear about the case?"

"It's been in the newspapers."

"How would he find the Web site?"

"You ever hear of Google?"

"He does not have access to computers. He's been at Lansing for the past six years. Prisoners do not have access to the Internet. You should know that. Can you imagine what would happen if they did? Access, plus all that idle time. No software in the world would be safe. He does not have access to a computer at the halfway house. This guy is forty-four years old, Matthew, and has spent most of his adult life in prison. He's probably terrified of computers."

"What about Drumm's confession? That doesn't bother you?"

"Of course it does, but according to his Web site—"

"Keith, come on. That Web site is run by his lawyers. Talk about slanted. It's so one-sided it loses credibility."

"What about the ring?"

"It's a high school ring, one of a billion. Not exactly difficult to produce or replicate."

Keith's shoulders sagged and slumped and he was suddenly very tired. He lacked the energy to keep arguing.

"You need some sleep, my friend," Matthew said. "And you need to forget this case."

"Maybe you're right."

"I think I am. And if the execution happens Thursday, don't beat yourself up. The odds are heavy that they have the right guy."

"Spoken like a true prosecutor."

"Who just happens to be a friend."

10

On October 29, 1999, two weeks after he was convicted, Donté Drumm arrived on death row at the Ellis Unit at the prison in Huntsville, a town of thirty-five thousand, about ninety miles north of downtown Houston. He was processed and issued the standard wardrobe of two sets of white shirts and pants, two white jumpsuits, four pairs of boxers, two white T-shirts, one pair of rubber shower shoes, one thin blanket, and one small pillow. He was also given a toothbrush, a tube of toothpaste, a plastic comb, and one roll of toilet paper. He was assigned to a small cell with one concrete bunk, and a stainless steel toilet and sink. He became one of 452 male inmates on death row. There were twenty-two condemned women housed at another prison near Gatesville, Texas.

Because he had no record of bad behavior in prison, he was classified as a Level I. As such, he was allowed a few extra privileges. He could work up to four hours a day in the garment factory on death row. He could spend his exercise time in a yard with a few other inmates. He could shower once a day, alone without supervision. He could participate in religious services, craft workshops, and educational programs. He could receive a maximum of $75 a month from the outside. He could purchase a television, a radio, writing supplies, and some food from the commissary. And he was allowed visitors twice a week. Those who violated the rules were demoted to Level II, where the privileges were curtailed. The bad boys were reduced to Level III, where all goodies were taken away.

Though he had been in a county jail for almost a year, the shock of death row was overwhelming. The noise was relentless—loud radios and televisions, the constant banter of the other inmates, the shouts from the guards, the whistling and gurgling from the old plumbing pipes, and the banging of the cell doors being opened and closed. In one letter to his mother, he wrote: "The racket never stops. Never. I try to ignore it, and for an hour or so I can, but then someone will scream or start singing badly and a guard will yell and everybody will laugh. This goes on at all hours. The radios and televisions are turned off at ten at night, and that's when the loudmouths start their foolishness. Living like an animal in a cage is bad enough, but the noise is driving me crazy."

But he soon learned that he could endure the confinement and the rituals. He wasn't sure, though, if he could live without his family and friends. He missed his brothers and sister and father, but the thought of being permanently separated from his mother was enough to make him weep. He cried for hours, always with his face down, in the dark, and very quietly.

Death row is a nightmare for serial killers and ax murderers. For an innocent man, it's a life of mental torture that the human spirit is not equipped to survive.

His sentence of death took on a new meaning on November 16 when Desmond Jennings was executed for killing two people during a bad drug deal. The following day, John Lamb was executed for the murder of a traveling salesman, the day after Lamb had been paroled from prison. The next day, November 18, Jose Gutierrez was executed for an armed robbery and murder he committed with his brother. The brother had been executed five years earlier. Jennings had been on death row for four years, Lamb sixteen, Gutierrez ten. A guard told Donté that the average stay on death row before execution was ten years, which, he said proudly, was the shortest in the nation. Once again, Texas was number one. "But don't worry," the guard said. "It's the longest ten years of your life, and, of course, the last." Ha, ha.

Three weeks later, on December 8, David Long was executed for the hatchet slayings of three women in a Dallas suburb. During his trial, Long told the jury he would kill again if not given the death penalty. The jury obliged. On December 9, James Beathard was executed for another triple homicide. Five days later, Robert Atworth was executed, after only three years on death row. The following day, Sammie Felder was executed after a twenty-three-year wait.

After Felder's death Donté wrote a letter to Robbie Flak in which he said, "Hey, man, these dudes are serious around here. Seven killings in four weeks. Sammie was number 199 since they got the green light a few years back. He's also number 35 for this year, and they've got 50 scheduled for next year. You got to do something, man."

Living conditions went from bad to worse. Administrators within the Texas Department of Criminal Justice (TDCJ) were in the process of moving

death row from Huntsville to the Polunsky Unit near
the town of Livingston, forty miles away. Though no
official reason was given, the move came after an unsuccessful escape attempt by five condemned prisoners. Four were captured within the prison. The fifth
one was found floating in a river, cause of death unknown. Not long thereafter, the decision was made to
tighten security and move the men to Polunsky. After
four months in Huntsville, Donté was shackled and
put on a bus with twenty others.

At the new place, he was assigned to a cell that
measured six feet by ten feet. There were no windows. The door was solid metal, with a small square
opening so the guards could look in. Below it was a
narrow slot for a food tray. The cell was enclosed, no
bars to look through, no way to see another human.
It was a cramped bunker of concrete and steel.

The people who ran the prison decided that a
twenty-three-hour-a-day lockup was the proper way
to control the prisoners and prevent escape and violence. Virtually all forms of inmate contact were elim-
inated. No work programs, religious services, group
recreation, nothing that would allow human interac-
tion. Televisions were banned. For one hour each day,
Donté was led to a "day room," a small, enclosed, in-
door space not much larger than his cell. There, alone
and watched by a guard, he was supposed to enjoy
whatever recreation he could fabricate in his mind.
Twice a week, weather permitting, he was taken outside to a small, semi-grassy area known as the "dog
kennel." For an hour, he could look at the sky.

Remarkably, he soon found himself longing for the
nonstop noise he had so despised at Huntsville.

After a month in Polunsky, in a letter to Robbie
Flak, he wrote: "For twenty-three hours a day, I'm

locked in this closet. The only time I speak to another person is when the guards bring food, or what they call food around here. So all I see is guards, not the kinds of people I'd choose. I'm surrounded by murderers, real murderers, and I'd rather talk to them than talk to the guards. Everything in here is designed to make life as bad as possible. Take mealtime. They feed us breakfast at three in the morning. Why? Nobody knows, and nobody asks. They wake us up to feed us crap that most dogs would run from. Lunch is at three in the afternoon. Supper is at ten at night. Cold eggs and white bread for breakfast, sometimes applesauce and pancakes. Peanut butter sandwiches for lunch. Sometimes baloney, bad baloney. Rubber chicken and instant mashed potatoes for supper. Some judge somewhere said that we're entitled to twenty-two hundred calories a day—I'm sure you know this—and if they figure they're a little short, they just pile on some more white bread. It's always stale. Yesterday for lunch I got five slices of white bread, cold pork and beans, and a chunk of moldy cheddar cheese. Can we sue over the food? Probably already been done. But I can take the food. I can take the searches at all hours. I think I can handle anything, Robbie, but I'm not sure about the solitary confinement. Please do something."

He became even more depressed and despondent, and was sleeping twelve hours a day. To fight boredom, he replayed every football game of his high school career. He pretended to be a radio announcer, calling the action, adding the color, always with the great Donté Drumm as the star. He rattled off the names of his teammates, everyone but Joey Gamble, and gave fictitious names to his opponents. Twelve games for his sophomore season, thirteen for his junior, and whereas Marshall had beaten Slone both years in the play-offs, Donté would have none of it in prison. The Slone Warriors won those games, and advanced until they slaughtered Odessa Permian in the championship game, in Cowboys Stadium, in front of seventy-five thousand fans. Donté was the Most Valuable Player. Mr. Texas Football for both years, something that had never been done before.

After the games, after he'd signed off his broadcasts, Donté wrote letters. His goal each day was to write at least five. He read his Bible for hours and memorized verses of scripture. When Robbie filed another thick brief in another court, Donté read every word. And to prove it, he wrote long, grateful letters to his lawyer.

But after a year in isolation, he began to fear that he was losing his memory. The scores of his old games slipped away. Names of teammates were forgotten. He couldn't rattle off the twenty-seven books of the New Testament. He was lethargic and couldn't shake his depression. His mind was disintegrating. He was sleeping sixteen hours a day and eating half the food they brought him.

On March 14, 2001, two events almost pushed him over the edge. The first was a letter from his mother. It was three pages long, in the handwriting that he treasured, and after he read the first page, he quit. He could not finish reading a letter. He wanted to and he knew that he should, but his eyes would not focus and his mind would not process her words. Two hours later, he received the news that the Texas Court of Criminal Appeals had affirmed his conviction. He wept for a long time, then stretched out on his bunk and stared at the ceiling in a semi-catatonic fog. He didn't move for hours. He refused lunch.

In the last game of his junior year, in the play-offs against Marshall, his left hand had been stepped on by a three-hundred-pound offensive tackle. Three fingers were crushed and broken. The pain was instant and so intense that he almost passed out. A trainer taped the fingers together, and on the next series Donté was back in the game. For almost the entire second half, he played like a wild man. The pain made him crazy. Between plays, he stood stoically and watched the offensive huddle, never once shaking his hand, never touching it, in no way acknowledging the pain that made his eyes water. From somewhere, he found the iron will and the incredible toughness to finish the game.

Though he'd forgotten that score too, he vowed to reach down again, reach into the depths of his gut and the subconscious layers of a brain that was failing him, and find the will to stop his slide into insanity. He managed to pull himself off the bed. He fell to the floor and did twenty push-ups. Then he did sit-ups until his abdomen ached. He ran in place until he could no longer lift his feet. Squats, leg lifts, more push-ups and sit-ups. When he was covered in sweat, he sat down and made a schedule. At five each morning, he would begin a precise series of exercises and work nonstop for sixty minutes. At 6:30 a.m., he would write two letters. At 7:00 a.m., he would memorize a new verse of scripture. And so on. His goal was a thousand push-ups and sit-ups a day. He would write ten letters, and not just to his family and close friends. He would find some new pen pals. He would read at least one book a day. He would cut his sleep in half. He would begin a journal.

These goals were printed neatly, labeled "The Routine," and stuck to the wall beside his metal mir-

ror. Donté found the enthusiasm to stick to his regi-
men. He attacked it each morning. After a month, he
was doing twelve hundred push-ups and sit-ups a day,
and the hard muscles felt good. The exercise brought
the blood back to his brain. The reading and writing
opened new worlds. A young girl in New Zealand
wrote him a letter, and he shot one right back. Her
name was Millie. She was fifteen years old, and her
parents approved the correspondence, but they monitored his letters. When she sent a small photo of herself, Donté fell in love. He was soon doing two
thousand push-ups and sit-ups, spurred on by the
dream of one day meeting Millie. His journal was
filled with graphic, erotic scenes of the couple as they
traveled the world. She wrote him once a month, and
for every letter she mailed, she got at least three in return.

Roberta Drumm made the decision not to tell
Donté his father was dying of heart disease. And
when, during one of her many routine visits, she told
him his father was dead, Donté's fragile world began
to crack again. The knowledge that his father had
died before he could walk out of prison fully exonerated proved too much. He allowed himself to break
his rigid routine. He skipped a day, then a second. He
couldn't stop crying and trembling.

Then Millie dropped him. Her letters arrived
around the fifteenth of each month, every month for
over two years, plus cards for his birthday and
Christmas. For a reason Donté would never know,
they stopped. He sent her letter after letter and received nothing in return. He accused the prison
guards of tampering with his mail and even convinced Robbie to make some threats. Gradually,
though, he accepted the fact that she was gone. He

fell into a dark and long depression, with no interest in The Routine. He began a hunger strike, didn't eat for ten days, but gave it up when no one seemed to care. He went weeks with no exercise, no reading, no journal entries, and letters only to his mother and Robbie. Before long, he'd forgotten the old football scores again and could only recall a few of the more famous scripture verses. He would stare at the ceiling for hours, mumbling over and over, "Jesus, I'm losing my mind."

The Visitors' Room at Polunsky is a large, open area with plenty of tables and chairs and vending machines along the walls. In the center, there is a long row of booths, all divided by glass. The inmates sit on one side, their visitors on the other, and all conversations are by phone. Behind the inmates, guards are always looming, watching. To one side, there are three booths used for attorney visits. They, too, are divided by glass, and all consultations are by phone.

In the early years, Donté was thrilled at the sight of Robbie Flak sitting at the narrow counter on the other side of the glass. Robbie was his lawyer, his friend, his fierce defender, and Robbie was the man who would right this incredible wrong. Robbie was fighting hard and loud and threatening hellfire for those who were mistreating his client. So many of the condemned had bad lawyers on the outside or no lawyers at all. Their appeals had run, the system was finished with them. No one out there was advocating on their behalf. But Donté had Mr. Robbie Flak, and he knew at some moment in each day his lawyer was thinking about him and scheming a new way to get him out.

But after eight years on death row, Donté had lost hope. He had not lost faith in Robbie; he'd simply realized that the Texas systems were much more powerful than one lawyer. Absent a miracle, this wrong would run its course. Robbie had explained that they would file motions until the very end, but he was also realistic.

They spoke through the phone, each happy to see the other. Robbie brought greetings from the entire Drumm family. He'd visited their home the night before, and gave all the details. Donté listened with a smile, but said little. His conversational skills had deteriorated along with everything else. Physically, he was a skinny, stooped, aging man of twenty-seven. Mentally, he was a mess. He could not keep up with time, never knew if it was night or day, often skipped meals, showers, and his daily hour of recreation. He refused to say a word to the guards and often had trouble following their most basic commands. They were somewhat sympathetic because they knew he was not a threat. He sometimes slept eighteen to twenty hours a day and when he wasn't asleep, he was unable to do anything. He had not exercised in years. He never read and managed to write a letter or two each week, but only to his family and Robbie. The letters were short, often incoherent, and filled with misspelled words and glaring grammatical errors. The writing was so sloppy that it was disheartening. A letter from Donté was not a pleasant envelope to open.

Dr. Kristi Hinze had read and analyzed hundreds of letters he'd written during his eight years on death row. She had already formed the opinion that the solitary confinement had driven him far from reality. He was depressed, lethargic, delusional, paranoid, schizophrenic, and suicidal. He was hearing voices, those of his late father and his high school football coach. In layman's terms, his brain had shut down. He was insane.

After a few minutes of summarizing where they were with the last-minute appeals, and covering the events scheduled for the next two days, Robbie introduced Dr. Hinze. She took the seat and the phone and said hello. Robbie stood close behind her with a legal pad and pen. For over an hour, she asked questions about his daily routine, his habits, dreams, thoughts, desires, and feelings about death. He surprised her by saying that 213 men had been executed while he had been on death row. Robbie confirmed the number to be accurate. But there were no more surprises, no more specifics. She quizzed him at length about the reasons he was there, and why he was to be executed. He did not know, did not understand why they were doing this to him. Yes, he was certain that he was about to be executed. Just look at the other 213.

One hour was enough for Dr. Hinze. She handed the phone back to Robbie, who sat down and began talking about the details for Thursday. He told Donté that his mother was determined to watch the execution, and this upset him. He began crying and finally put the phone down to wipe his face. He refused to pick it up, and when he stopped crying, he locked his arms across his chest and stared at the floor. Finally, he stood and walked to the door behind him.

The rest of the team waited outside in the van, a guard nearby, casually watching them. When Robbie and Dr. Hinze returned to the van, Aaron waved at the guard and drove away. They stopped at a pizza place on the edge of town and had a quick lunch. They had just settled back in the van and were leaving Livingston when the phone rang. It was Fred Pryor. Joey Gamble had called and wanted to meet for a drink after work.

11

In a normal week, Reverend Schroeder would spend most of Tuesday afternoon locked in his office with the phones on hold as he searched for his next sermon's topic. He looked at current events, thought about the needs of his flock, prayed a lot, and, if nothing happened, would go to the files and look at old sermons. When the idea finally hit, he would write a quick outline and then begin the full text. At that point, the pressure was off, and he could practice and rehearse until Sunday. Few things felt worse, though, than waking up on Wednesday morning with no idea what he would say on Sunday.

But with Travis Boyette on his mind, he could concentrate on nothing else. He took a long nap after lunch Tuesday and felt thickheaded, almost groggy when it was over. Dana had left the office to tend to the children, and Keith puttered around the church, unable to do anything productive. He finally left. He thought about driving to the hospital and checking on Boyette, in hopes that perhaps the tumor had shifted and the man had changed his mind. But that was unlikely.

While Dana cooked dinner and the boys were busy with homework, Keith found solitude in the garage. His latest project was to organize it, paint it, and then plan to keep it shipshape forever. He usually enjoyed the mindless cleaning, but Boyette managed to ruin even that. After half an hour, he gave up and took his laptop to their bedroom and locked the door. The Drumm Web site was like a magnet, a thick juicy novel, with so much he had not yet read.

THE KOFFEE-GRALE SCANDAL

The prosecution of Donté Drumm was led by Paul Koffee, the district attorney for Slone and Chester County. The presiding judge at Donté's trial was Vivian Grale. Both Koffee and Grale were elected officials. At the time of the trial, Koffee had been in office for thirteen years. Grale had been on the bench for five. Koffee was married to his wife, Sara, and they had, and still have, three children. Grale was married to her husband, Frank, and they had, and still have, two children.

The Koffees are now divorced, as are the Grales.

The only significant motion filed by the defense that was granted by Judge Grale was a request to change the venue of the trial. Given its sensational nature and extensive coverage in the media, a fair trial was impossible in Slone. Attorneys for Donté wanted to move it far away, and they suggested either Amarillo or Lubbock, each about five hundred miles from Slone. Judge Grale granted the request—experts agree that she really had no choice; to have the trial in Slone would have been to create certain reversible error—and she decided to hold it in Paris, Texas. The courthouse in Paris is exactly forty-nine miles from the courthouse in Slone. After the conviction, attorneys for Donté argued vehemently on appeal that trying the case in Paris was no different from trying it in Slone. Indeed, during the jury selection process, over half of the prospective jurors admitted they had heard something about the case.

Other than the change of venue, Judge Grale showed no patience with the defense. Her most crucial ruling was to allow Donté's coerced confession. Without it, the prosecution had no case, no evidence, nothing. The confession was their case.

But other rulings were almost as damaging. The police and prosecutors used a favorite tactic when they produced a jailhouse snitch by the name of Ricky Stone. Stone was in jail on drug charges and agreed to cooperate with Detective Kerber and the Slone police. He was placed in a cell with Donté Drumm for four days, then removed. Donté never saw him again until the trial. Stone testified that Donté talked openly about the rape and murder of Nicole and said that he went crazy after she broke up with him. They had been dating secretly for several months, they were in love, but she became frightened and worried that her wealthy father would cut off the money if he knew she was seeing a black guy. Stone testified that he had been promised nothing by the prosecutor in return for his testimony. Two months after Donté was convicted, Stone pleaded guilty to a misdemeanor and walked out of jail.

Stone had an extensive criminal record and zero credibility. He was a classic jailhouse snitch, fabricating testimony in return for a lighter sentence. Judge Grale allowed him to testify.

Stone later recanted and said he'd been pressured by Detective Kerber and Paul Koffee to lie.

Judge Grale also permitted testimony that had been discredited for many years in many jurisdictions. During the search for Nicole, the police used bloodhounds to sniff around for clues. The dogs were given a scent from Nicole's car and some articles in it, and turned loose. The trails led nowhere, that is, until Donté was arrested. The police then allowed the bloodhounds to sniff through the green Ford van owned by the Drumm family. According to the dogs' handler, the dogs became excited, agitated, and showed every sign of picking up Nicole's scent in the van. This unreliable testimony was first played out in a pretrial hearing. Attorneys for Donté were incredulous and demanded to know how they were supposed to cross-examine a bloodhound. Attorney Robbie Flak was so outraged that he called one of the dogs, a bloodhound named Yogi, a "stupid son of a bitch." Judge Grale held him in contempt and fined him $100. Remarkably, the dogs' principal handler was still allowed to testify at trial, and stated to the jury that after thirty years of experience with bloodhounds, he was "absolutely certain" that Yogi had picked up Nicole's scent in the green van. He was eviscerated on cross-examination by Robbie Flak, who at one point demanded to have the dog brought to the courtroom, sworn in, and put in the witness chair.

Judge Grale exhibited animosity toward the defense lawyers, especially Robbie Flak. She was much more agreeable with Paul Koffee.

And with good reason. Six years after the trial, it became known that the judge and the prosecutor were involved in a long-running illicit romance. The affair came to light when a disgruntled ex-secretary in Mr. Koffee's office filed a claim for sexual harassment and produced e-mails, phone records, and even phone recordings that revealed her ex-boss's involvement with Judge Grale. Lawsuits followed, as did divorces.

Judge Grale resigned from the bench in disgrace and left Slone while her divorce was pending. Paul Koffee was reelected without opposition in 2006, but only after promising to quit when the term was over.

Attorneys for Donté sought relief because of the obvious conflict of interest between the judge and the prosecutor. The Texas Court of Criminal Appeals said that while the affair was "unfortunate" and "could possibly give the appearance of impropriety," it did not violate the defendant's right to a fair trial. Relief in the federal courts was just as elusive.

In 2005, Paul Koffee filed a defamation suit against Robbie Flak for statements Flak made in an interview about Koffee's intimate involvement with his trial judge. Flak countersued Koffee for a myriad of offenses. The litigation is still pending.

Hours later, when the lights were off and the house was quiet, Keith and Dana stared at the ceiling and debated whether they should go look for the sleeping pills. Both were exhausted, but sleep seemed impossible. They were tired of reading about the case, discussing it, tired of worrying about a young black man on death row whom they had never heard of until the day before, and they were especially frustrated with the newest person in their lives, one Travis Boyette. Keith was certain he was telling the truth. Dana was leaning that way but was still skeptical because of his disgusting criminal record. They were tired of arguing about it.

If Boyette was telling the truth, could they be the only people in the world who knew for certain that Texas was about to execute the wrong man? If so, what could they do? How could they do anything if Boyette refused to admit the truth? And if he changed his mind and decided to admit the truth, what were they supposed to do about it? Slone was four hundred miles away, and they didn't know anyone there. Why should they? They'd never heard of the place until yesterday.

The questions raged through the night, and the answers were nowhere to be found. They decided to watch the digital clock until midnight, and, if still awake, go find the pills.

At 11:04 p.m., the phone rang and startled them. Dana hit a light switch. The caller ID read, "St. Fran. Hospital."

"It's him," she said. Keith picked up the receiver and said, "Hello."

"Sorry to call so late, Pastor," Boyette said in a low, strained voice.

"It's okay, Travis. We were not asleep."

"How's your cute little wife?"

"Fine. Look, Travis, I'm sure you're calling for a reason."

"Yes, sorry, Pastor. I really want to see the girl again, you know what I mean?"

Keith held the receiver so Dana could squeeze in with her left ear. He did not want to repeat everything afterward. "I'm not sure what you mean, Travis," he said.

"The girl, Nicole, my little Nikki. I'm not long for this world, Pastor. I'm still in the hospital, an IV in my arm, all kinds of dope in my blood, and the doctors are telling me that it won't be long. I'm half-dead now, Pastor, and I don't like the thought of kicking the bucket without one last visit with Nikki."

"She's been dead for nine years."

"No shit. I was there, remember. It was awful, what I did to her was just awful, and I've apologized before, several times, face-to-face. But I gotta go again, tell her just once more how sorry I am about what happened. You know what I mean, Pastor?"

"No, Travis, I have no idea what you mean."

"She's still there, okay? She's where I left her."

"You said you probably couldn't find her now."

There was a long pause as Travis seemed to recall this. "I know where she is," he said.

"Great, Travis. Then go find her. Go dig her up and look at her bones and tell her you're sorry. Then what? You'll feel better about yourself? Meanwhile, an innocent man gets the needle for your crime. I have an idea, Travis. After you tell Nicole you're sorry one last time, why don't you go to Slone and stop by the cemetery, find Donté's grave, and tell him you're sorry too?"

Dana turned and frowned at her husband. Travis took another pause, and then said, "I don't want that boy to die, Pastor."

"That's really hard to believe, Travis. You've kept quiet for nine years while he's been accused and persecuted. You've wasted yesterday and today, and if you keep flip-flopping, the time will run out and he'll be dead."

"I can't stop it."

"You can try. You can go to Slone and tell the authorities where the body is buried. You can admit the truth, show them the ring, make plenty of noise. I'm sure the reporters and cameras would love you. Who knows, maybe a judge or the governor will take notice. I don't have a lot of experience in these matters, Travis, but it seems to me that they might find it difficult to execute Donté Drumm when you're on television claiming you killed Nicole and you acted alone."

"I don't have a car."

"Rent one."

"I haven't had a driver's license in ten years."

"Take a bus."

"I don't have the money for a bus ticket, Pastor."

"I'll loan you the money. No, I'll give you the money for a one-way bus ticket to Slone."

"What if I have a seizure on the bus, or black out? Hell, they might kick me off in Podunk, Oklahoma."

"You're playing games, Travis."

"You gotta take me, Reverend. Just me and you. If you'll drive me down there, I'll tell the truth about what really happened. I'll take them to the body. We can stop the execution, but you gotta go with me."

"Why me?"

"Ain't nobody else around right now, Pastor."

"I have a better idea. Tomorrow morning, let's go downtown to the prosecutor's office. I have a friend there. You tell him the story. Maybe we can convince him to call the prosecutor in Slone, as well as the police chief and defense lawyer and, I don't know, maybe even a judge somewhere. They'll listen to him a lot quicker than they'll listen to a Lutheran minister who knows nothing about the criminal justice system. We can video your statement, send it immediately to the authorities in Texas, send it to the newspapers too. How about it, Travis? You won't violate parole. I won't get in trouble by helping you."

Dana was nodding her approval. Five seconds. Ten seconds. Finally, Travis said, "Maybe it'll work, Pastor. Maybe we can stop the execution, but there's no way they're finding her. I have to be there for that."

"Let's concentrate on stopping it."

"They're discharging me tomorrow morning at nine."

"I'll be there, Travis. The prosecutor's office is not far away."

Five seconds, ten seconds. "I like it, Pastor. Let's do it."

*   *   *

At 1:00 a.m., Dana found the bottle of over-the-counter sleeping aids, but an hour later they were still awake. The trip to Texas occupied them. They had discussed it briefly once before, but were so afraid of it they had not pursued the conversation. The idea was ludicrous—Keith in Slone with a serial sex offender of dubious credibility, trying to get someone to listen to a bizarre tale while the town counted down the final hours of Donté Drumm. The unlikely pair would be ridiculed, maybe even shot. And upon his return to Kansas, the Reverend Keith Schroeder could find himself accused of a crime for which there would be no defense. His job and career could hang in the balance. All because of a lowlife like Travis Boyette.

12

Wednesday morning. Six hours after leaving his office just after midnight, Robbie was back in the conference room preparing for another frantic day. The night had not gone well. The drinking session with Fred Pryor and Joey Gamble produced nothing, except an admission by Gamble that Mr. Koffee had indeed called and reminded him of the penalties for perjury. Robbie had listened to the entire session. Pryor, who over the years had become masterful with his recording devices, had used the same pen mike and passed along their conversation through a cell phone. The sound quality was remarkable. Robbie had enjoyed a few drinks along with them, in his office, with Martha Handler sipping bourbon and Carlos, the paralegal, drinking beer and monitoring the speakerphone. They all had enjoyed their booze for almost two hours, Joey and Fred in a fake saloon somewhere outside of Houston, and the Flak Law Firm hard at work at the office in the old train station. After two hours, though, Joey had had enough—even beers— and said he was tired of being pressured. He could not accept the reality that a last-minute affidavit signed by him would repudiate his testimony at trial. He did not want to call himself a liar, though he stopped short of admitting he'd lied.

"Donté should not have confessed," he said several times, as if uttering a false confession were grounds enough for a death sentence.

But Pryor would shadow him throughout Wednesday and Thursday, if necessary. He believed there was still a slight chance, one that increased as the hours went by.

At 7:00 a.m., the firm gathered in the conference room for the daily briefing. All were present, all bleary-eyed and fatigued and ready for the final push. Dr. Kristi Hinze had worked through the night and finished her report. She summarized it briefly while everyone ate pastries and gulped coffee. The report was forty-five pages long, more than the court would want to read, but maybe enough to get someone's attention. Her findings surprised no one, at least no one within the Flak Law Firm. She described her examination of Donté Drumm. She had reviewed his medical and psychological history while in prison. She had read 260 letters he had written over the eight years he'd been on death row. He was schizophrenic, psychotic, delusional, and depressed and did not understand what was happening to him. She went on to condemn solitary confinement as a means of incarceration and again labeled it as a cruel form of torture.

Robbie instructed Sammie Thomas to file their petition for relief with Dr. Hinze's report attached in full to the firm's co-counsel in Austin. Throughout the appellate process, all eight years of it, Robbie's firm had been assisted by the Texas Capital Defender Group, commonly referred to as the Defender Group, a non-profit that represented about 25 percent of the inmates on death row. The Defender Group did nothing but capital appeals, and did so with great expertise and diligence. Sammie would send the petition and report electronically, and at 9:00 a.m. the Defender Group would file hard copies with the Court of Criminal Appeals.

With an execution looming, the court was on alert and prepared to quickly address the last-minute filings. If they were denied, which they usually were, Robbie and the Defender Group could then run to federal court and fight their way up the mountain, hoping for a miracle at some point.

He discussed these strategies and made certain everyone knew what was to be done. Carlos would be in charge of the Drumm family the following day, though he would remain in Slone. He was to make sure they arrived at Polunsky on time for their final visit. Robbie would be there to make the final walk with his client and to witness the execution. Sammie Thomas and the other associate would remain at the office and coordinate the filings with the Defender Group. Bonnie, the paralegal, would stay in touch with the offices of the governor and the attorney general.

The request for a reprieve had been filed with the governor's office, and its denial was being awaited. The Kristi Hinze petition was ready to go. Unless and until Joey Gamble had a change of heart, there was no new evidence to make a fuss about. As the meeting dragged on, it became evident that there was little of substance left to do. The conversation waned. The frenzy was beginning to subside. Everyone was suddenly tired. The waiting had begun.

*   *   *

When Vivian Grale was elected to the bench in 1994, her campaign had been about high moral standards, putting the laws of God first, putting criminals in prison for even longer periods of time, and, of course, more efficient use of the death chamber down at Huntsville. She won by thirty votes. She defeated a wise and experienced judge by the name of Elias Henry, and she did so by cherry-picking several criminal cases in which Judge Henry had dared to show compassion for the accused. She splashed these around in ads that made him look like a coddler of pedophiles.

After her affair with Paul Koffee was exposed, after her divorce, and after she resigned and left Slone in disgrace, the voters repented and returned to Judge Henry. He was reelected without opposition. He was now eighty-one years old and in declining health. There were rumors that he might not be able to finish his term.

Judge Henry had been a close friend of Robbie's father, who died in 2001. Because of this friendship, he was one of the few judges in East Texas whose blood pressure did not spike when Robbie Flak walked into the courtroom. Elias Henry was about the only judge Robbie trusted. At Judge Henry's invitation, Robbie agreed to meet in his chambers at 9:00 a.m. Wednesday morning. The purpose of the meeting was not discussed on the phone.

"This case bothers me a great deal," Judge Henry said after a few pleasantries were out of the way. They were alone, in an old office that had changed little in the forty years Robbie had visited it. The courtroom was next door and empty.

"As well it should." They both had unopened bottles of water in front of them on a worktable. The judge, as always, wore a dark suit with an orange tie. He was having a good day, his eyes fierce and intense. There were no smiles.

"I've read the transcript, Robbie," he said. "I started last week and I've read it all, and most of the appellate briefs as well. Taking a view from the bench, I can't believe Judge Grale allowed that confession into evidence. It was coerced and blatantly unconstitutional."

"It was, Judge, and it is. I won't defend her, but she had little choice. There was no other credible evidence. If she tossed the confession, then Koffee had nowhere to go. No conviction, no defendant, no suspect, no dead body. Donté would have walked out of jail, which would have been front-page news. As you well know, Judge Grale had to face the voters, and judges don't get reelected in East Texas if they keep the law above politics."

"Tell me about it."

"Once he knew the confession would go to the jury, Koffee was able to piece together other evidence. He stomped and strutted and convinced the jury that Donté was the killer. He pointed fingers at him, and then he cried at the very mention of Nicole's name. Quite a performance. What's the old saying, Judge? 'If you don't have the facts, yell'—and he did a lot of yelling. The jury was more than willing to believe him. He won."

"You fought like hell, Robbie."

"Should've fought harder."

"And you're convinced he's innocent? No doubt in your mind?"

"Why are we having this discussion, Judge? It seems rather moot at this point."

"Because I'm going to call the governor and ask

for a reprieve. Maybe he'll listen, I don't know. I wasn't the trial judge. I was, as we know, retired at the time. But I have a cousin in Texarkana who gave the governor a ton of money. It's a long shot, but what's there to lose? What's wrong with delaying things another thirty days?"

"Nothing. You're having doubts about his guilt, Judge?"

"Serious doubts. I would not have admitted the confession. I would have thrown the snitch in jail for lying. I would have excluded that clown with his bloodhounds. And the boy, what's his name—"

"Joey Gamble."

"Right, the white boyfriend. His testimony would probably go to the jury, but it was too inconsistent to carry weight. You said it best in one of your briefs, Robbie. This conviction is based on a bogus confession, a dog named Yogi, a lying snitch who later recanted, and a jilted lover bent on revenge. We can't convict people with garbage such as this. Judge Grale was biased—I guess we know why. Paul Koffee was blinded by his own tunnel vision and the fear he might be wrong. It's a terrible case, Robbie."

"Thank you, Judge. I've lived it for nine years."

"And it's dangerous. I met with two black lawyers yesterday, good guys, you know them. They're angry with the system, but they're also afraid of the backlash. They expect trouble if Drumm is executed."

"That's what I hear."

"What can be done, Robbie? Is there a way to stop this? I'm not a death-penalty lawyer, and I don't know where your appeals are right now."

"The tank is almost empty, Judge. We're filing an insanity petition now."

"And your chances?"

"Slim. Donté has no record of mental illness until now. We're alleging that eight years on death row have driven him insane. As you know, the appeals courts usually frown on theories that are hatched at the last minute."

"Is the boy crazy?"

"He has severe problems, but I suspect he knows what's happening."

"So you're not optimistic."

"I'm a criminal defense lawyer, Judge. Optimism is not in my DNA."

Judge Henry finally unscrewed the cap off the plastic bottle of water and took a sip. His eyes never left Robbie. "Very well, I'll call the governor," he said, as if his phone call would save the day. It would not. The governor was getting lots of calls right now. Robbie and his team were generating plenty.

"Thanks, Judge, but don't expect much. This governor has never stopped an execution. In fact, he wants to speed them up. He has his eye on a Senate seat, and he counts votes before he chooses what to eat for breakfast. He's a two-faced, cutthroat, dirt-dumb, chickenshit, slimy little bastard with a bright future in politics."

"So you didn't vote for him?"

"I did not. But please give him a call."

"I will. I'm meeting with Paul Koffee in half an hour to discuss this with him. I don't want him to be surprised. I'll also chat with the fellow over at the newspaper. I want to be on record in opposition to this execution."

"Thanks, Judge, but why now? We could've had this conversation a year ago, or five. It's awfully late to get involved."

"A year ago, few people were thinking about Donté

Drumm. There was no execution looming. There was a chance he would find relief in a federal court. Maybe a reversal, a new trial. I don't know, Robbie. Maybe I should've been more involved, but this is not my case. I was busy with my own matters."

"I understand, Judge."

They shook hands and offered their farewells. Robbie took the back stairs so he wouldn't bump into some lawyer or clerk who wanted to chat. As he hurried along the empty corridor, he tried to think of another elected official in Slone or in Chester County who had voiced support for Donté Drumm. One came to mind, the only black city councilman in Slone.

For nine years, he had fought a long and lonely battle. And he was about to lose. A phone call from the cousin of a big donor would never be enough to stop an execution in Texas. The machinery was well-oiled and efficient. It was in motion, and there was no way to stop it.

On the front lawn of the courthouse, city workers were assembling a makeshift podium. A few policemen loitered about, chatting nervously as they watched the first church bus unload. A dozen or so black folks got off and made their way across the lawn and past the war memorials. They found their spot, unfolded chairs, and began to wait. The rally, or protest, or whatever it was to be called, was scheduled for noon.

Robbie had been asked to speak, but declined. He couldn't think of anything to say that would not be inflammatory, and he did not want to be accused of inciting the crowd. There would be enough trouble-makers.

According to Carlos, who was charged with monitoring the Web site, the comments, and the blogs, the traffic was increasing dramatically. Protests were being planned for Thursday in Austin, Huntsville, and Slone and on the campuses of at least two of the black universities in Texas.

Give 'em hell, Robbie thought as he drove away.

13

Keith arrived early at the hospital and made his rounds. St. Mark's Lutheran currently had half a dozen members in various stages of treatment or recuperation. He said hello to all six, shared a quick word of comfort, held their hands in prayer, then was off to get Mr. Boyette for what promised to be an eventful day.

Eventful in unexpected ways. Mr. Boyette was already gone. According to a nurse, when they checked on him at 6:00 a.m., they found his bed empty and neatly made up, his hospital gown folded next to his pillow, and the IV wrapped carefully around the portable stand next to his bed. An hour later, someone from Anchor House called with the message that Travis Boyette was back home and wanted his doctor to know all was well. Keith drove to Anchor House, but Boyette was not there. According to a supervisor, he was not scheduled to work on Wednesdays. No one had any idea where he was or when he might return. As Keith was driving to St. Mark's, he told himself not to worry, not to panic, Boyette would show. Then he called himself an idiot for placing even the remotest bit of confidence in a confessed murderer, a serial rapist, and a compulsive liar. Because he habitually tried to see the good in every person he knew and met, he realized, as he began to panic, that he had been much too gentle with Boyette. He had tried too hard to be understanding, even compassionate. Hell, the man had murdered a seventeen-year-old girl just to satisfy his lust and was now seemingly content to watch another man die for the crime. God only knew how many other women he'd raped.

Keith was angry when he entered the church office. Charlotte Junger, back from the flu, greeted him with a cheery "Good morning, Pastor," and Keith was barely civil.

"I'm locked in my office, okay? No calls, unless it's a man named Travis Boyette."

"Yes, sir."

He closed his door, ripped off his coat, and called Dana with the latest news. "He's loose on the streets?" she asked.

"Well, yes, he's in the process of getting paroled. He's served his time, and he's about to be a free man. I guess you could say he's loose."

"Thank God for the tumor."

"I can't believe you said that."

"Sorry. I can't either. What's the plan?"

"There's nothing to do but wait. Maybe he'll show up."

"Keep me posted."

Keith called Matthew Burns in the prosecutor's office and told him there was a delay. Matthew had first been cool to the idea of meeting Boyette and videoing his statement, but he came around. He had agreed to make a call or two to Texas after he heard Boyette's story, if, in fact, he believed what he heard. He was disappointed to hear the man was missing.

Keith checked the Drumm Web site for an update, something he'd done almost every waking hour since Monday morning. He went to the filing cabinets and pulled out folders with old sermons. He called Dana again, but she was having coffee with the girls.

At exactly 10:30 a.m., he called the law office of Robbie Flak. The young lady who answered the phone explained that Mr. Flak was unavailable. Keith said he understood this and said that he'd called yesterday, Tuesday, left his phone numbers, but had not heard from anyone. "I have information about the murder of Nicole Yarber," he said.

"What type of information?" she asked.

"I need to speak to Mr. Flak," Keith said firmly.

"I will give him the message," she said, just as firmly.

"Please, I'm not some wacko. This is very important."

"Yes, sir. Thank you."

He decided to violate the vow of confidentiality. There were two possible consequences. First, Boyette could sue him for damages, but Keith was no longer worried about this. The brain tumor would take care of any future litigation. And if for some reason Boyette survived, he would be required to prove that Keith's breach of confidence had caused him damages. Though Keith knew little about the law, he found it difficult to believe that a judge or jury anywhere would have sympathy for such a miserable person.

The second consequence was that of a possible disciplinary action by the church. But in light of the facts, and especially in light of the liberal leanings of the synod, he could not imagine anything more than a slap on the wrist.

Screw it, he said to himself. I'm talking.

He typed an e-mail for Robbie Flak. He described himself, leaving all possible phone numbers and addresses along the way. He described his encounter with an unnamed parolee who once lived in Slone, and did so at the time Nicole disappeared. This parolee has a lengthy criminal record, a violent one, and was once arrested and jailed in Slone. Keith had verified this. The man confessed to the rape and murder of Nicole Yarber and gave plenty of details. Her body was buried deep in the hills south of Joplin, Missouri, where this parolee grew up. The only person who can find the body is the parolee himself. Please call. Keith Schroeder.

An hour later, Keith left his office and drove back to Anchor House. No one had seen Boyette. He drove downtown and had another quick lunch with Matthew Burns. After some debate, and a bit of cajoling, Matthew pulled out his cell phone and called Flak's office. Keith heard him say, "Yes, hello, my name is Matthew Burns, and I am a prosecutor in Topeka, Kansas. I would like to speak to Mr. Robbie Flak." Mr. Flak was unavailable.

"I have some information about the Donté Drumm case, specifically the identity of the real killer." Mr. Flak was still unavailable. Matthew then gave his phone numbers, cell and office, and invited the receptionist to visit the Web site for the City of Topeka, Office of the City Attorney, to verify his legitimacy. She said she would do this.

"I'm not some nut, okay? Please have Mr. Flak call me as soon as possible. Thank you."

They finished lunch and agreed to alert each other

if a call came from Texas. Driving back to the office, Keith was relieved to have a friend, an attorney at that, willing to lend a hand.

By noon, the streets of downtown Slone had been blocked and barricaded, and routine traffic had been diverted elsewhere. Dozens of church buses and vans were double-parked around the courthouse, but the police were not writing tickets. Their orders were to maintain a presence, keep the peace, and, by all means, do nothing to provoke anyone. Emotions were high. The situation was tense. Most of the merchants closed their shops, and most of the white folks disappeared.

The crowd, all black, continued to grow. Hundreds of students from Slone High School skipped out and arrived in packs, already rowdy and anxious to be heard. Factory workers brought their lunch boxes and ate while they milled around the courthouse lawn. Reporters took photos and scribbled notes. Camera crews from Slone and Tyler bunched together near the podium on the front steps of the courthouse. At 12:15 p.m., Mr. Oscar Betts, president of the local NAACP chapter, stepped to the microphones, thanked everyone for coming, and quickly got down to business. He proclaimed the innocence of Donté Drumm and said his execution was nothing more than a legal lynching. He blistered the police in a scathing condemnation, calling them "racist" and "determined to kill an innocent man." He ridiculed a judicial system that would allow an all-white jury to pass judgment on an innocent black man. Unable to resist, he asked the crowd: "How you supposed to get a fair trial when the prosecutor is sleeping with the judge?" "And the appeals courts said it was okay?" "Only in Texas!" He described the death penalty as a disgrace—an outdated tool of revenge that does not deter crime, is not used fairly, and has been abandoned by all civilized countries. Almost every sentence was followed with applause and shouting as the crowd grew louder. He called on the court system to stop the madness. He mocked the Texas Board of Pardons and Paroles. He called the governor a coward for not stopping the execution. He warned of unrest in Slone and East Texas and perhaps even the entire nation if the state went forward with the execution of an innocent black man.

Betts did a masterful job of raising emotions and tensions. When he finally wound down, he changed course and asked the crowd to behave, to stay off the streets tonight and tomorrow night. "We gain nothing by violence," he pleaded. When he finished, he introduced the Reverend Johnny Canty, pastor of the Bethel African Methodist Church, where the Drumm family had worshipped for over twenty years. Reverend Canty began with a message from the family. They were thankful for the support. They remained strong in their faith and were praying for a miracle. Roberta Drumm was doing as well as could be expected. Her plans were to travel to death row tomorrow and be there until the end. Reverend Canty then asked for quiet and began a long eloquent prayer that started with a plea for compassion for the family of Nicole Yarber, a family that had endured the nightmare of the death of an innocent child. Just like the Drumm family. He thanked the Almighty for the gift of life and the promise of eternity for all people. He thanked God for His laws, the most basic and most important being the Ten Commandments, which included the prohibition "Thou shalt not kill." He prayed for those "other Christians" out there who take the same Bible and twist it and use it as a weapon to kill others. "Forgive them, Father, for they know not what they do."

Canty had worked on his prayer for a long time, and he delivered it slowly, with perfect timing, and without notes. The crowd hummed and swayed and offered hearty "Amens" as he plodded along, no end in sight. It was far more a speech than a prayer, and Canty savored the moment. After praying for justice, he prayed for peace, not the peace that avoids violence, but the peace yet to be found in a society in which young black men are incarcerated in record numbers, in which they are executed far more often than those of other races, in which crimes committed by blacks are deemed more grievous than the same crimes committed by whites. He prayed for mercy, for forgiveness, for strength. Like most ministers, Canty went on too long and was losing his audience when he suddenly found it again. He began praying for Donté, "our persecuted brother," a young man snatched from his family nine years ago and thrown into a "hellhole" from which no man escaped alive. Nine years without his family and friends, nine years locked away like a caged animal. Nine years serving the time for a crime committed by someone else.

From the window of a small law library on the third floor, Judge Elias Henry watched and listened. The crowd was under control as the reverend prayed, yet it was the restlessness that frightened the judge.

Slone had known little racial discord over the decades, and the judge took most of the credit for

this, but only when talking to himself. Fifty years earlier, when he'd been a young lawyer struggling to pay
his bills, he'd taken a part-time job reporting and
writing editorials for the *Slone Daily News,* then a
prosperous weekly that was read by all. Now it was a
struggling daily with a lower readership. In the early
1960s, the newspaper was one of the few in East
Texas that recognized the fact that a sizable portion
of the population was black. Elias Henry wrote occasional stories about black sports teams and black history, and though this was not well received, it was not
openly condemned. His editorials, though, managed
to rile up the whites. He explained in layman's terms
the true meaning of *Brown v. Board of Education* and
criticized the segregated schools in Slone and Chester
County. The newspaper, through the growing influence of Elias and the declining health of its owner,
took bold stands in favor of voting rights for blacks,
as well as fair pay and fair housing. His arguments
were persuasive, his reasoning was sound, and most
of those who read his opinions realized he was far
smarter than they were. He bought the paper in 1966
and owned it for ten years. He also became a skilled
lawyer and politician and a leader in the community.
A lot of white folks disagreed with Elias, but few
challenged him publicly. When the schools were finally desegregated, at the end of a federal gun barrel,
white resistance in Slone had been softened after
years of crafty manipulation by Elias Henry.

After he was elected judge, he sold the paper and
assumed a loftier position. From there, he quietly but
firmly controlled a judicial system that was known to
be tough on those who were violent, strict on those
who needed guidance, and compassionate to those

who needed another chance. His defeat by Vivian Grale led to a nervous breakdown.

The conviction of Donté Drumm would not have happened on his watch. He would have known about the arrest not long after it occurred. He would have examined the confession and the circumstances surrounding it, and he would have called in Paul Koffee for an unofficial meeting, just the two of them with the door locked, to inform the DA that his case was rotten. The confession was hopelessly unconstitutional. It would not get to the jury. Keep looking, Koffee, because you have yet to find your killer.

Judge Henry looked at the throng packed tightly around the front of the courthouse. Not a white face anywhere, except for the reporters. It was an angry black crowd. The whites were hiding, and not sympathetic. His town was split, something he thought he would never see.

"God help us," he mumbled to himself.

The next speaker was Palomar Reed, a senior at the high school and vice president of the student body. He began with the obligatory condemnation of the death sentence and launched into a windy and technical diatribe against capital punishment, with heavy emphasis on the Texas version of it. The crowd stayed with him, though he lacked the drama of the more experienced speakers. Palomar, though, soon proved to have an incredible knack for the dramatic. Looking at a sheet of paper, he began calling the names of the black players on the Slone High School football team. One by one, they hurried to the podium and formed a line along the top step. Each wore the royal blue home jersey of the Slone Warriors. When all twenty-eight were packed shoulder to shoulder, Palomar made a shocking announcement: "These players stand here united with their brother Donté Drumm. A Slone Warrior. An African warrior. If the people of this city, county, and state succeed in their illegal and unconstitutional efforts to kill Donté Drumm tomorrow night, these warriors will not play in Friday's game against Longview."

The crowd exhaled in one massive cheer that rattled the windows of the courthouse. Palomar looked at the players, and on cue all twenty-eight reached for their shirttails and quickly yanked off the jerseys. They threw them at their feet. Under the jerseys, each player wore an identical white T-shirt with the unmistakable image of Donté's face. Under it, in bold lettering, was the word "INNOCENT." The players puffed their chests and pumped their fists, and the crowd drowned them in adoration.

"We will boycott classes tomorrow!" Palomar yelled into the microphone. "And Friday, too!

"And there will be no football game on Friday night!"

The rally was being broadcast live on the local channel, and most of the white folks in Slone were glued to their televisions. In banks and schools and homes and offices, the same muted utterances were heard:

"They can't do that, can they?"

"Of course they can. How do you stop them?"

"They've gone too far."

"No, we've gone too far."

"So, you think he's innocent?"

"I'm not sure. No one's sure. That's the problem. There's just too much doubt."

"He confessed."

"They never found the body."

"Why can't they just stop things for a few days, you know, a reprieve or something like that?"

"Why?"

"Wait till after football season."

"I'd prefer not to have a riot."

"If they riot, then they'll be prosecuted."

"Don't bet on it."

"This place is going to explode."

"Kick 'em off the team."

"Who do they think they are, calling the game off?"

"We got forty white boys who can play."

"Damn right we do."

"Coach oughtta kick 'em off the team."

"And they oughtta arrest 'em if they skip school."

"Brilliant. That'll throw gas on the fire."

At the high school, the football coach watched the protest in the principal's office. The coach was white, the principal black. They stared at the television and said nothing.

At the police department, three blocks down Main Street from the courthouse, Chief of Police Joe Radford watched the television with his assistant chief. The department had four dozen uniformed officers on the payroll, and at that moment thirty were watching nervously from the fringes of the rally.

"Will the execution take place?" the assistant chief asked.

"Far as I know," Radford answered. "I talked to Paul Koffee an hour ago, and he thinks it's a go."

"We might need some help."

"Naw. They'll throw a few rocks, but it'll blow over."

Paul Koffee watched the show alone at his desk with a sandwich and chips. His office was two blocks behind the courthouse, and he could hear the crowd when it roared. For him, such demonstrations were necessary evils in a country that valued the Bill of Rights. Folks could gather lawfully, with permission of course, and express their feelings. The same laws that protected this right also governed the orderly flow of justice. His job was to prosecute criminals and put the guilty ones away. And when a crime was grave enough, the laws of his state directed him to exact revenge and seek the death penalty. This he had done in the Drumm case. He had no regrets, no doubts, not the slightest uneasiness about his decisions, his tactics at trial, or the guilt of Drumm. His work had been ratified by seasoned appellate judges on numerous occasions. Dozens of these learned jurists had reviewed every word of the Drumm trial and affirmed his conviction. Koffee was at peace with himself. He regretted his involvement with Judge Vivian Grale, and the pain and embarrassment it had caused, but he had never doubted that her rulings were right.

He missed her. Their romance had cracked under the strain of all the negative attention it created. She ran away and refused any contact. His career as a prosecutor would soon be over, and he hated to admit that he would leave office under a cloud. The Drumm execution, though, would be his high-water mark, his vindication, a shining moment that the people of Slone, or at least the white ones, would appreciate.

Tomorrow would be his finest day.

*   *   *

The Flak Law Firm watched the rally on the wide-screen television in the main conference room, and when it was finally over, Robbie retreated to his office with half a sandwich and a diet cola. The receptionist had carefully arranged a dozen phone message slips on the center of his desk. The ones from Topeka caught his attention. Something rang a bell. Ignoring the food, he picked up the phone and punched in the number for a cell phone of the Reverend Keith Schroeder.

"Keith Schroeder please," he said when someone answered "Hello."

"Speaking."

"This is Robbie Flak, attorney in Slone, Texas. I have your message, and I think I saw an e-mail a few hours ago."

"Yes, thank you, Mr. Flak."

"It's Robbie."

"Okay, Robbie. It's Keith on this end."

"Fine, Keith. Where's the body?"

"In Missouri."

"I have no time to waste, Keith, and something tells me this call is a complete waste of time."

"Maybe it is, but give me five minutes."

"Talk fast."

Keith ran through the facts—his encounters with an unnamed parolee, his search into his background, the man's criminal record, his dire medical condition, everything he could cram into five uninterrupted minutes.

"Obviously, you're not worried about breaching confidentiality here," Robbie said.

"I'm troubled by it, but the stakes are too high. And I haven't told you his name."

"Where is he now?"

"He spent last night in a hospital, checked himself out this morning, and I haven't heard from him since. He'd due back at the halfway house at 6:00 p.m. sharp. I'll be there to see him."

"And he has four felony convictions for sex offenses?"

"At least."

"Pastor, this man has zero credibility. I can't do anything with this. There's nothing here. You gotta understand, Keith, that these executions always attract the nutcases. We had two fruitcakes show up last week. One claimed to know where Nicole is living now, she's a stripper by the way, and the other claimed to have killed her in a satanic ritual. Location of the body unknown. The first wanted some money, the second wanted out of prison in Arizona. The courts despise these last-minute fantasies."

"He says the body is buried in the hills south of Joplin, Missouri. That's where he grew up."

"How soon can he find the body?"

"I can't answer that."

"Come on, Keith. Give me something I can use."

"He has her class ring. I've seen it, held it, and examined it. SHS 1999, with her initials ANY. Blue stone, size about six."

"This is good, Keith. I like it. But where is the ring right now?"

"I assume it's around his neck."

"And you don't know where he is?"

"Uh, correct, at this moment, I don't know where he is."

"Who is Matthew Burns?"

"A friend of mine, a prosecutor."

"Look, Keith, I appreciate your concern. You've called twice, e-mailed once, got one of your friends to call. Thank you very much. I'm a very busy man right now, so please leave me alone." Robbie picked up his sandwich as he put down the phone.

14

Gill Newton had been the governor of Texas for five years, and though polls showed an enviable level of approval among the electorate, the polls were dwarfed by his own estimation of his popularity. He was from Laredo, far down in South Texas, where he'd been raised on a ranch that had been owned by his grandfather, who'd once been a sheriff. Gill had scratched his way through college and law school, and when no firm would hire him, he became an assistant prosecutor in El Paso. At the age of twenty-nine, he was elected district attorney in the first of many successful campaigns. He had never lost one. By the age of forty, he'd sent five men to death row. As governor, he'd watched two of them die, explaining that it was his duty since he'd prosecuted them. Though records were sketchy, it was widely believed that Newton was the only sitting governor of Texas to witness an execution. This was certainly true for the modern era. In interviews, he claimed that watching the men die had given him a sense of closure. "I remember the victims," he said. "I kept thinking about the victims. These were horrible crimes."

Newton seldom passed on a chance to be interviewed.

Brash, loud, vulgar (in private), he was wildly popular because of his antigovernment rhetoric, his unwavering beliefs, his outrageous comments that he never apologized for, and his love of Texas and its history of fierce independence. The vast majority of voters also shared his fondness for the death penalty.

With his second and final term secured, Newton was already gazing across the borders of Texas and contemplating a larger stage, something bigger. He was needed.

Late Wednesday afternoon he met with his two closest advisers, two old friends from law school who had helped with every major decision and most of the minor ones as well. Wayne Wallcott was the lawyer, or chief counsel, as his letterhead proclaimed, and Barry Ringfield was the mouthpiece, or director of communications. On a routine day in Austin, the three met in the governor's office at precisely 5:15 p.m. They took off their coats, dismissed the secretaries, locked the door, and at 5:30 p.m. poured the bourbon. Then they got down to business.

"This Drumm thing could get messy tomorrow," Barry was saying. "Blacks are pissed, and they got demonstrations scheduled all over the state tomorrow."

"Where?" the governor asked.

"Well, here, for starters. On the south lawn of the Capitol. Rumor has it that the Right Reverend Jeremiah Mays is flying in on his fancy jet to get the natives good and agitated."

"I love it," the governor said.

"The request for a reprieve has been filed and is on record," Wayne said, looking at some paperwork. He took a sip. The bourbon, Knob Creek, was poured each time into a heavy crystal Waterford glass with the state's seal on it.

"Definitely more interest in this one," Barry said. "Lots of calls, letters, e-mails."

"Who's calling?" Newton asked.

"The usual chorus. The Pope. President of France. Two members of the Dutch parliament. Prime minister of Kenya, Jimmy Carter, Amnesty International, that loudmouth from California who runs the Black Caucus in Washington. Lots of folks."

"Anybody important?"

"Not really. The circuit judge in Chester County, Elias Henry, has called twice and sent an e-mail. He's in favor of a reprieve, says he has grave doubts about the jury's verdict. Most of the noise from Slone, though, is gung ho in favor of the execution. They think the boy's guilty. The mayor called and expressed some concerns about trouble in Slone tomorrow night, says he might be calling for help."

"The National Guard?" Newton asked.

"I suppose so."

"I love it."

All three took a sip. The governor looked at Barry, who was not only his mouthpiece but also his most trusted, and most devious, adviser. "You got a plan?"

Barry always had a plan. "Sure, but it's a work in progress. I like the demonstration tomorrow, hopefully with Reverend Jeremiah stoking the fires. Big crowd. Tons of Africans. A real tense situation. And you take the podium, stare down the crowd, talk about the orderly flow of justice in this state, the usual spiel, then, right out there on the steps, with cameras rolling and the crowd booing and hissing and maybe throwing rocks at you, right then and there, you deny the request for a reprieve. The crowd erupts, you make your escape. It'll take some balls, but it's priceless."

"Wow," Newton said.

Wayne actually laughed.

Barry continued. "Three hours later they nuke him, but the front page will be taking on the mob of angry blacks. For the record, you got 4 percent of the black vote, Governor, 4 percent." A pause, a sip, but he wasn't finished. "I like the National Guard angle too. Later in the afternoon, but before the execution, hold a quick press conference and announce that you're sending in the Guard to quell the uprising in Slone."

"The numbers in Chester County?"

"You got 71 percent, Gill. They love you there. You protect them by sending in the Guard."

"But is the Guard necessary?" Wayne asked. "If we overreact, then it could backfire."

"It's fluid. Let's monitor the situation and decide later."

"Let's do that," the governor said, and the decision was made. "Any chance of some court issuing a last-minute stay?"

Wayne tossed some papers on the governor's desk and said, "I doubt it. Drumm's lawyers filed an appeal this morning claiming the boy's gone crazy and doesn't appreciate the gravity of what's coming. It's bullshit. I talked to Baker at the AG's office an hour ago, and they see nothing in the pipeline. It's all green lights."

"Should be fun," the governor said.

*   *   *

At Reeva's suggestion, or insistence, the Wednesday night prayer meeting at the First Baptist Church was canceled. This had happened only three times in the history of the church, once for an ice storm, once for a tornado, and once for a power outage. Brother Ronnie could not bring himself to use the word "canceled," so the prayer meeting was simply reclassified as a "prayer vigil" and was "moved" to another location. The weather cooperated. The sky was clear, and the temperature was almost seventy degrees.

They met at sunset, under a reserved pavilion at Rush Point State Park, on the edge of the Red River, as close to Nicole as they could possibly get. The pavilion was on a small bluff, with the river below, and about a hundred yards away was the sandbar that came and went with the level of water. Her gym card and student ID had been found there. In the minds of those who loved her, this had long been the spot of Nicole's final resting place.

During her many visits to Rush Point, Reeva had always alerted whatever media she could arouse in Slone. As the years passed, though, the local reporters lost interest. She often visited alone, sometimes with Wallis trailing along behind, always on her daughter's birthday and usually on December 4, the day she disappeared. But this vigil was far different. There was something to celebrate. *Fordyce—Hitting Hard!* was represented by a two-man crew with a small camera, the same one that had been following Reeva and a weary Wallis for two days now. There were two TV news crews and half a dozen print reporters. The presence of so much attention inspired the worshippers, and Brother Ronnie was pleased with such a large turnout. Forty miles from home!

They sang a few hymns as the sunlight faded, then

lit small candles and passed them around. Reeva sat in the front row and sobbed nonstop. Brother Ronnie could not resist the opportunity to preach, and his flock was in no hurry to leave. He dwelled on justice and relied on an avalanche of scripture to support God's commands for us to live as law-abiding citizens.

There were prayers by deacons and testimonials from friends of Nicole's, and even Wallis, after an elbow in the ribs, managed to stand and offer a few words. Brother Ronnie finished things up with a lengthy plea for compassion and mercy and strength. He asked God to walk the final mile with Reeva and Wallis and their family as they went through the ordeal of the execution.

They left the pavilion and moved in a solemn procession to the makeshift shrine closer to the river's edge. They laid flowers at the foot of a white cross. Some knelt and prayed again. Everybody had a good cry.

At 6:00 p.m. on Wednesday, Keith walked through the front door of Anchor House with every intention of corralling Travis Boyette and having a serious confrontation. The execution was exactly twenty-four hours away, and Keith was determined to do whatever he could to stop it. The task seemed utterly impossible, but at least he would try. An associate minister was handling the Wednesday night supper at St. Mark's.

Boyette was playing games, or maybe he was dead. During the day, he had not checked in with his parole officer, and had not been seen again at Anchor House. He was required to do none of these, but the fact that he seemed to have vanished was troubling. He was, however, required to check in for the night at 6:00 and could not leave until 8:00 the following morning, unless he had permission. He was not there at 6:00 p.m. Keith waited an hour, but there was no sign of Boyette. An ex-con named Rudy was manning the front desk. He mumbled to Keith, "You'd better go find his ass."

"I wouldn't know where to start," Keith said. He left his cell phone number with Rudy and started with the hospitals. He slowly drove from one to the other, killing time, waiting for a call from Rudy, watching the streets for any sign of a fortyish white weirdo limping along with a cane. None of the downtown hospitals had admitted a Travis Boyette. He was not loitering around the bus station, and he was not sharing a drink with the winos down by the river. At 9:00 p.m., Keith returned to Anchor House and sat in a chair at the front desk.

"He ain't here," Rudy said.

"What happens next?" Keith said.

"If he comes in later tonight, they'll cuss him but let it slide, unless he's drunk or drugged and then it hits the fan. They'll give you one screwup. But if he stays out all night, they'll probably revoke him and send him back to the pen. These guys are pretty serious. What's Boyette up to?"

"It's hard to say. He has trouble with the truth."

"I heard that. I got your number. If he shows, I'll give you a call."

"Thanks." Keith hung around for half an hour, then drove home. Dana heated up lasagna, and they ate on TV trays in the den. The boys were already asleep. The television was on mute. They said little.

Travis Boyette had consumed their lives for the better part of three days and they were tired of the man.

After dark, it became apparent that no one wanted to leave the train station. There was little legal work to be done, and nothing of any consequence could be thrown together at that hour to help Donté Drumm. The Texas Court of Criminal Appeals had not ruled on the insanity claim. Fred Pryor was still loitering on the outskirts of Houston, hoping for another drink or two with Joey Gamble, but that looked doubtful. This could well be the last night in the life of Donté Drumm. And his legal team needed the comfort of each other.

Carlos was sent to get pizza and beer, and when he returned, the long table in the conference room was used for dinner. When Ollie arrived later, a poker game materialized. Ollie Tufton was one of a handful of black lawyers in Slone and a close friend of Robbie's. He was shaped like a bowling ball and claimed to weigh four hundred pounds, though it was not clear why he wished to take credit for this. He was loud and hilarious and had huge appetites—food, whiskey, poker, and, sadly, cocaine. Robbie had rescued him from near disbarment on two occasions. He made an occasional buck with car wrecks, but the money always disappeared. When Ollie was in the room, most of the noise came from him. He assumed control of the poker game, appointed Carlos as dealer, established the rules, and told his latest dirty jokes, all while sipping a beer and finishing off the cold pizza. The players were Martha Handler, who usually won; Bonnie, the other paralegal; Kristi Hinze, who was still afraid of the game and even

more terrified of Ollie; and a part-time investigator/
runner named Ben Shoots.

Shoots had a pistol in his jacket hanging on the
wall. Robbie had two shotguns in his office, loaded.
Aaron Rey was always armed, and he moved quietly
around the train station, watching the windows and
the parking lot. The firm had received several threatening calls during the day, and they were on full alert.

Robbie took a beer to his office, left his door wide
open, and called DeDe, his live-in partner. She was at
yoga, blissfully unconcerned about the pending execution. They had been together for three years, and
Robbie was almost convinced they had a chance. She
showed almost no interest in whatever he did at the
office, and this was beneficial. His journey to find true
love was littered with women who could not accept
the fact that life with Robbie was heavily tilted in
Robbie's favor. The current girl went her own way,
and they met in bed. She was twenty years younger,
and Robbie was still smitten.

He called a reporter in Austin but said nothing
quotable. He called Judge Elias Henry and thanked
him for calling the governor. They wished each other
well, both knowing that the next twenty-four hours
would be remembered for a long time. The clock on
the wall seemed stuck at ten minutes after nine. Robbie would always remember that it was 9:10 p.m.
when Aaron Rey walked into his office and said,
"The First Baptist Church is burning."

The Battle of Slone had begun.

15

If Keith had fallen asleep, he wasn't aware of it. For the past three days, he had slept so little, and at such odd hours, that his routines and rhythms were out of sync. When the phone rang, he could have sworn he was wide-awake. Dana, though, heard it first and had to nudge her husband. He finally grabbed it after the fourth or fifth ring. "Hello," he said, in a daze, while Dana flipped on a lamp. It was 11:40. They had gone to bed less than an hour earlier.

"Hey, Pastor, it's me, Travis," the voice said.

"Hello, Travis," Keith said, and Dana scrambled for a bathrobe. "Where are you?"

"Here, Topeka, at a diner somewhere downtown, not far from Anchor House." His voice was slow, his tongue thick. Keith's second or third thought was that Boyette had been drinking.

"Why are you not at Anchor House?"

"It doesn't matter. Look, Pastor, I'm really hungry, nothing since this morning, and I'm sitting here with just a cup of coffee because I don't have any money. I'm starving, Pastor. Any ideas?"

"Have you been drinking, Travis?"

"Couple of beers. I'm okay."

"You spent money on beer but not on food?"

"I didn't call to fight with you, Pastor. Can you help me get something to eat?"

"Sure, Travis, but you need to get back to Anchor House. They're waiting for you. I talked to Rudy, and he says they'll write you up, but nothing serious. Let's get something to eat, then I'll take you where you belong."

"I ain't going back there, Pastor, forget it. I want to go to Texas, okay? I mean, now. I really want to go. I'll tell everybody the truth, tell them where the body is, everything. We gotta save that boy."

"We?"

"Who else, Pastor? We know the truth. If you and me get down there, we can stop this execution."

"You want me to take you to Texas right now?" Keith asked, staring into the eyes of his wife. She began shaking her head.

"There's no one else, Pastor. I got a brother in Illinois, but we don't talk. I suppose I could call my parole officer, but I doubt if he'd have any interest in hauling ass down to Texas. I know a few of the dudes around the halfway house, but they don't have cars. When you spend your life in prison, Pastor, you don't have a lot of friends on the outside."

"Where are you, Travis?"

"I told you. I'm in a diner. Hungry."

"Which one?"

"Blue Moon. You know it?"

"Yes. You order something to eat. I'll be there in fifteen minutes."

"Thank you, Pastor."

Keith hung up the phone and sat on the edge of the

bed next to his wife. Neither spoke for a few minutes. Neither wanted to fight.

"Is he drunk?" she finally asked.

"I don't think so. He's had a few, but seems sober. I don't know."

"What are you doing, Keith?"

"I'm buying dinner, or breakfast, or whatever it is. I'll wait for him to change his mind again. If he's serious, then I have no choice but to drive him to Texas."

"You do have a choice, Keith. You're not being forced to take this pervert to Texas."

"What about that young man on death row, Dana? Think about Donté Drumm's mother right now. This will be her last day to see her son."

"Boyette's pulling your leg, Keith. He's a liar."

"Maybe, and maybe not. But look at what's at stake here."

"At stake? Your job could be at stake. Your reputation, career, everything could be at stake. We have three little boys to think about."

"I'm not going to jeopardize my career, Dana, or my family. I might get a slap on the wrist, but that's all. I know what I'm doing."

"Are you sure?"

"No." He quickly shed his pajamas and put on a pair of jeans, sneakers, a shirt, and a red Cardinals baseball cap. She watched him dress without another word. He kissed her on the forehead and left the house.

Boyette was inspecting an impressive platter of food when Keith took the chair across from him. The diner was half-full, with several tables occupied by uniformed policemen, all eating pie, average weight at least 250. Keith ordered coffee and caught the irony of an unconvicted murderer and parole violator having a hearty meal thirty feet from a small squad of cops.

"Where have you been all day?" Keith asked.

The tic. A large bite of scrambled eggs. As he chewed, he said, "I really don't remember."

"We wasted an entire day, Travis. Our plan was to do the video, send it to the authorities and the press in Texas, and hope for a miracle. You ruined that plan by disappearing."

"The day's done, Pastor, leave it alone. You taking me to Texas or not?"

"So you're jumping parole?"

The tic, a sip of coffee, his hand shaking. Everything from his voice to his fingers to his eyes seemed to be engaged in a steady tremor. "Parole is the least of my worries right now, Pastor. Dying occupies most of my time. And that boy in Texas concerns me. I've tried to forget him, but I can't. And the girl. I need to see her before I die."

"Why?"

"I need to say I'm sorry. I hurt a lot of people, Pastor, but I only killed one." He glanced at the policemen, then kept going, his voice a bit lower. "And I don't know why. She was my favorite. I wanted to keep her forever, and when I realized I couldn't, well, I—"

"Got it, Travis. Let's talk logistics here. Slone, Texas, is 400 miles away, straight shot, as the crow flies, but it's more like 550 by car, with a lot of two-lane roads. It's midnight. If we left in the next hour or so and drove like maniacs, we might be there by noon. That's six hours before the execution. Any idea what we do when we get there?"

Boyette chewed on a piece of sausage and pondered the question, completely untouched by any sense of urgency. Keith noticed that he took very small bites, chewed them a long time, laid down his fork, and took a sip of either coffee or water. He did not seem to be overly hungry. Food was not important.

After more coffee, Boyette said, "I was thinking that we go to the local television station and I go on the air, tell my story, take responsibility, tell the idiots down there that they got the wrong guy for the murder, and they'll stop it."

"Just like that?"

"I don't know, Pastor. I've never done this before. You? What's your plan?"

"At this point, finding the body is more important than your confession. Frankly, Travis, given your lengthy record and the disgusting nature of your crimes, your credibility will be challenged. I've done some research since I met you on Monday morning, and I've run across some anecdotes about the nutcases who pop up around executions and make all sorts of claims."

"You calling me a nutcase?"

"No, I'm not. But I'm sure they'll call you a lot of names in Slone, Texas. They won't believe you."

"Do you believe me, Pastor?"

"I do."

"Would you like some eggs and bacon? You're paying for it."

"No, thanks."

The tic. Another glance at the cops. He pointed both index fingers at both temples and massaged them in tiny circles, grimacing as if he might scream. The pain finally passed. Keith looked at his watch.

Boyette began shaking his head slightly and said, "It'll take longer to find the body, Pastor. Can't be done today."

Since Keith had no experience in such matters, he simply shrugged and said nothing.

"Either we go to Texas, or I walk back to the halfway house and get yelled at. It's your choice, Pastor."

"I'm not sure why I'm supposed to make the decision."

"It's very simple. You have the car, the gas, the driver's license. I have nothing but the truth."

The car was a Subaru, four-wheel drive, 185,000 miles on the odometer, and at least 12,000 miles since the last oil change. Dana used it to haul the boys all over Topeka, and it showed the wear and tear of such a life on the streets. Their other car was a Honda Accord with a sticky oil light and a bad set of rear tires.

"Sorry for the dirty car," Keith said, almost embarrassed, as they crawled in and closed the doors. Boyette said nothing at first. He placed his cane between his legs.

"Seat belts are mandatory now," Keith said as he buckled up. Boyette did not move. There was a moment of silence in which Keith realized that the journey had begun. The man was in his car, along for a ride that would consume hours, maybe days, and neither knew where this little journey might take them.

Slowly, Boyette strapped himself in as the car began to move. Their elbows were inches apart. Keith got the first whiff of stale beer and said, "So, Travis, what's your history with booze?"

Boyette was breathing deeply, as if soothed by the

security of the car and its locked doors. Typically, he waited at least five seconds before responding. "Never thought of it as a history. I'm not a big drinker. I'm forty-four years old, Pastor, and I've spent just over twenty-three of those years locked away in various facilities, none of which had saloons, lounges, juke joints, strip clubs, all-night drive-thrus. Can't get a drink in prison."

"You've been drinking today."

"I had a few bucks, went to a bar in a hotel, and had some beers. They had a television in the bar. I saw a report on the Drumm execution in Texas. Had a picture of the boy. It hit me hard, Pastor, I gotta tell you. I was feeling pretty mellow, you know, kinda sentimental anyway, and when I saw that boy's face, I almost got choked up. I drank some more, watched the clock get closer and closer to 6:00 p.m. I made the decision to skip parole, go to Texas, do what's right."

Keith was holding his cell phone. "I need to call my wife."

"How is she?"

"Fine. Thanks for asking."

"She's so cute."

"You need to forget about her." Keith mumbled a few awkward phrases into the phone and then slapped it shut. He drove quickly through the deserted streets of central Topeka. "So, Travis, we're planning on this long drive down to Texas, where you face the authorities and tell the truth and try to stop this execution. And I'm assuming at some point very soon, you'll be expected to lead the authorities to Nicole's body. All this, of course, will lead to your arrest and being thrown in jail in Texas. They'll charge you with all sorts of crimes and you'll never get out. Is that the plan, Travis? Are we on the same page?"

The tic. The pause. "Yes, Pastor, we're on the same page. It doesn't matter. I'll be dead before they can get me properly indicted by the grand jury."

"I didn't want to say that."

"You don't have to. We know it, but I prefer that nobody in Texas knows about my tumor. It's only fitting that they get the satisfaction of prosecuting me. I deserve it. I'm at peace, Pastor."

"At peace with whom?"

"Myself. After I see Nicole again, and tell her I'm sorry, then I'll be ready for anything, including death."

Keith drove on in silence. He was facing a marathon trip with this guy, virtually shoulder to shoulder for the next ten, maybe twelve hours, and he hoped he wouldn't be as crazy as Boyette by the time they arrived in Slone.

He parked in the driveway, behind the Accord, and said, "Travis, I'm assuming you have no money, no clothes, nothing." This seemed painfully obvious.

Travis chuckled, raised his hands, and said, "Here I am, Pastor, with all my worldly assets."

"That's what I thought. Wait here. I'll be back in five minutes." Keith left the engine running and hurried into his house.

Dana was in the kitchen, throwing together sandwiches and chips and fruit and anything else she could find. "Where is he?" she demanded as soon as Keith walked through the door.

"In the car. He's not coming in."

"Keith, you can't be serious about this."

"What are the choices, Dana?" He'd made his decision, as unsettling as it was. He was prepared for a nasty fight with his wife, and he was willing to take the risks that his journey might entail. "We can't sit here and do nothing when we know the real killer. He's out there in the car."

She wrapped a sandwich and stuffed it into a small box. Keith took a folded grocery bag from the pantry and went into their bedroom. For his new pal Travis, he found an old pair of khakis, a couple of T-shirts, socks, underwear, and a Packers sweatshirt that no one had ever worn. He changed shirts, put on his clerical collar and a navy sport coat, and then packed a few things of his own in a gym bag. Minutes later, he was back in the kitchen, where Dana was leaning against the sink, arms locked defiantly across her chest.

"This is a huge mistake," she announced.

"Maybe so. I didn't volunteer for this. Boyette chose us."

"Us?"

"Okay, he chose me. He has no other means of getting to Texas, or so he says. I believe him."

She rolled her eyes. Keith glanced at the clock on the microwave. He was anxious to take off, but he also realized that his wife was entitled to a few parting shots.

"How can you believe anything he says?" she demanded.

"We've had this conversation, Dana."

"What if you get arrested down there?"

"For what? Trying to stop an execution. I doubt that's a crime, even in Texas."

"You're helping a man jump parole, right?"

"Right, in Kansas. They can't arrest me for it in Texas."

"But you're not sure."

"Look, Dana, I'm not going to get arrested in Texas. I promise. I might get shot, but not arrested."

"Are you trying to be funny?"

"No. No one's laughing. Come on, Dana, look at the big picture. I think Boyette killed this girl in 1998. I think he hid her body and knows where it is. And I think there's a chance for a miracle, if we can get down there."

"I think you're crazy."

"Maybe, but I'd rather take a chance."

"Look at the risk, Keith."

He had inched closer and now put his hands on her shoulders. She was rigid, her arms still crossed. "Look, Dana, I've never taken a chance in my life."

"I know. This is your big moment, isn't it?"

"No, this is not about me. Once we get there, I'm staying in the shadows, keeping a low profile—"

"Dodging bullets."

"Whatever. I'll be in the background. It's the Travis Boyette Show. I'm just his driver."

"Driver? You're a minister with a family."

"And I'll be back by Saturday. I'll preach on Sunday, and we'll have a picnic that afternoon. I promise."

Her shoulders sagged, and her arms fell to her sides. He squeezed her fiercely and then kissed her. "Please try to understand," he said.

She nodded gamely and said, "Okay."

"I love you."

"I love you. Please be careful."

Robbie's midnight wake-up call came at 12:30. He'd been in bed with DeDe for less than an hour when the phone erupted. DeDe, who'd gone to sleep without the aid of alcohol, jumped first and said, "Hello." Then she handed the phone to her mate, who was fogged in and trying to open his eyes.

"Who is it?" he growled.

"Wake up, Robbie, it's Fred. Got some interesting stuff here."

Robbie managed to rouse himself, at least to the next level. "What is it, Fred?" DeDe was already flipping to the other side. Robbie smiled at her fine rear end under the satin sheets.

Fred said, "Had another drink with Joey. Took him to a strip club. Second night in a row, you know. Not sure my liver can take much more of this project. I'm sure his cannot. Anyway, got the boy drunk as a pissant, and he finally admitted everything. Said he lied about seeing the green van, lied about the black person driving the damned thing, lied about everything. Admitted he was the one who called Kerber with the fake tip about Donté and the girl. It was beautiful. He was crying and carrying on, just a big blubbering fat boy knocking back beers and talking trash to the strippers. Said he and Donté were once good buddies, back in the ninth and tenth grades when they were football stars. Said he always thought the prosecutors and judges would figure things out. Can't believe it's come down to this. He's always thought the execution would never happen, thought Donté would one day get out of prison. Now he's finally convinced that they're gonna kill him, so he's all tore up about it. Thinks it's his fault. I assured him that it is. The blood will be on his hands. I really beat him up. It was wonderful."

Robbie was in the kitchen looking for water. "This is great, Fred," he said.

"It is, and it's not. He refuses to sign an affidavit."

"What!"

"Won't do it. We left the strip club and went to a coffeehouse. I begged him to sign an affidavit, but it's like talking to a tree."

"Why not?"

"His momma, Robbie, his momma and his family. He can't stomach the idea of admitting that he's a liar. He's got a lot of friends in Slone, and so on. I did everything I could possibly do, but the boy is not willing to sign on."

Robbie downed a glass of tap water and wiped his mouth with a sleeve. "Did you tape it?"

"Of course. I've listened to the tape once, about to go through it again. There's a lot of background noise—you ever been to a strip club?"

"Don't ask."

"Really loud music, a lotta rap shit and stuff like that. But his voice is there. You can understand what he's saying. We'll need to enhance it."

"There's no time for that."

"Okay. What's the plan?"

"How long is your drive?"

"Well, at this lovely time of the day, there's no traffic. I can be in Slone in five hours."

"Then get your ass on the road."

"You got it, Boss."

An hour later, Robbie was in bed, flat on his back, the dark ceiling doing strange things to his thought process. DeDe was purring like a kitten, dead to the world. He listened to her breathe heavily and wondered how she could be so untroubled by all of his troubles. He envied her. When she awoke hours later, her first priority would be an hour of hot yoga with a few of her dreadful friends. He would be at the office screaming at the telephone.

And so it had all come down to this: a drunk Joey Gamble confessing his sins and baring his soul in a strip club to a man with a concealed mike that produced a scratchy audio that no court in the civilized world would take heed of.

The fragile life of Donté Drumm would depend on the eleventh-hour recantation by a witness with no credibility.

PART TWO

THE PUNISHMENT

16

Lost in the frenzy of the departure was the issue of money. When he paid six bucks for Boyette's feast at the Blue Moon Diner, Keith realized he was low on cash. Then he forgot about it. He remembered it again after they were on the road and needed gas. They stopped at a truck stop on Interstate 335 at 1:15 a.m. It was Thursday, November 8.

As Keith pumped gas, he was aware of the fact that Donté Drumm would be strapped to the gurney in Huntsville in about seventeen hours. He was even more aware that the man who should be suffering through his final hours was, instead, sitting peacefully only a few feet away, snug inside the car, his pale slick head reflecting the overhead fluorescent lights. They were just south of Topeka. Texas was a million miles away. He paid with a credit card and counted $33 in cash in his left front pocket. He cursed himself for not raiding the slush fund he and Dana kept in a kitchen cabinet. The cigar box usually held around $200 in cash.

An hour south of Topeka, the speed limit increased to seventy miles per hour, and Keith and the old Subaru inched upward to seventy-five. Boyette so far had been quiet, seemingly content to sit crouched with his hands on his knees and stare at nothing through the right-side window. Keith preferred to ignore him. He preferred the silence. Sitting next to a stranger for twelve straight hours was a chore under normal circumstances. Rubbing shoulders with one as violent and weird as Boyette would make for a tense, tedious trip.

Just as Keith settled into a quiet, comfortable zone, he was suddenly hit with a wave of drowsiness. His eyelids snapped shut, only to be reopened when he jerked his head. His vision was blurred, foggy. The Subaru edged toward the right shoulder, then he moved back to the left. He pinched his cheeks. He blinked his eyes as wildly as possible. If he'd been alone, he would have slapped himself. Travis did not notice.

"How about some music?" Keith said. Anything to jolt his brain.

Travis just nodded his approval.

"Anything in particular?"

"It's your car."

Yes, it was. His favorite station was classic rock. He cranked up the volume and was soon thumping the steering wheel and tapping his left foot and mouthing the words. The noise cleared his brain, but he was still stunned by how quickly he had almost collapsed.

Only eleven hours to go. He thought of Charles Lindbergh and his solo flight to Paris. Thirty-three and a half straight hours, with no sleep the night before he took off from New York. Lindbergh later wrote that he was awake for sixty straight hours. Keith's brother was a pilot and loved to tell stories.

He thought about his brother, his sister, and his parents, and when he began to nod off, he said, "How many brothers and sisters do you have, Travis?"

Talk to me, Travis. Anything to keep me awake. You can't help with the driving, because you have no license. You have no insurance. You're not touching this wheel, so come on, Travis, help me out here before we crash.

"I don't know," Travis said, after the obligatory period of contemplation.

The answer did more to lift the fog than anything by Springsteen or Dylan. "What do you mean, you don't know?"

A slight tic. Travis had now shifted his gaze from the side window to the windshield. "Well," he said, then paused. "Not long after I was born, my father left my mother. Never saw him again. My mother took up with a man named Darrell, and since he was the first man I ever remembered, I just figured Darrell was my father. My mother told me he was my father. I called him Dad. I had an older brother and he called him Dad. Darrell was okay, never beat me or anything, but he had a brother who abused me. When they took me to court the first time—I think I was twelve—I realized that Darrell was not my real father. That really hurt. I was crushed. Then Darrell disappeared."

The response, like many of Boyette's, raised more mysteries than it solved. It also served to kick Keith's brain into high gear. He was suddenly wide-awake. And he was determined to unravel this psycho. What else was there to do for the next half day? They were in his car. He could ask anything he wanted.

"So you have one brother."

"There's more. My father, the real one, ran off to Florida and took up with another woman. They had a houseful of kids, so I guess I have outside brothers and sisters. And there was always this rumor that my mother had given birth to a child before she married my father. You ask how many. Pick a number, Pastor."

"How many are you in contact with?"

"I wouldn't call it contact, but I've written some letters to my brother. He's in Illinois. In prison."

What a surprise. "Why is he in prison?"

"Same reason everybody else is in prison. Drugs and booze. He needed cash for his habit, so he broke into a house, wrong one, ended up beating a man."

"Does he write back?"

"Sometimes. He'll never get out."

"Was he abused?"

"No, he was older, and my uncle left him alone, far as I know. We never talked about it."

"This was Darrell's brother?"

"Yes."

"So, he wasn't really your uncle?"

"I thought he was. Why are you asking so many questions, Pastor?"

"I'm trying to pass the time, Travis, and I'm trying to stay awake. Since I met you Monday morning, I have slept very little. I'm exhausted, and we have a long way to go."

"I don't like all these questions."

"Well, what exactly do you think you're about to hear in Texas? We show up, you claim to be the real murderer, and then you announce that you really don't like questions. Come on, Travis."

Several miles passed without a word. Travis stared to his right, at nothing but the darkness, and lightly tapped his cane with his fingertips. He had shown no signs of severe headaches for at least an hour. Keith glanced at the speedometer and realized he was doing eighty, ten over, enough for a ticket anywhere in Kansas. He slowed down and, to keep his mind going, played out the scene in which a state trooper pulled him over, checked his ID, checked Boyette's, then called for backup. A fleeing felon. A wayward Lutheran minister aiding the fleeing felon. Blue lights all over the road. Handcuffs. A night in jail, maybe in the same cell with his friend, a man who wouldn't be the least bit bothered by another night behind bars. What would Keith tell his boys?

He began to nod again. There was a phone call he had to make, and there was no good time to make it. The call was guaranteed to engage his mind at such a level that sleep would be forgotten momentarily. He removed his cell phone from his pocket and speed-dialed Matthew Burns. It was almost 2:00 a.m. Evidently, Matthew was a sound sleeper. It took eight rings to rouse him.

"This better be good," he growled.

"Good morning, Matthew. Sleep well?"

"Fine, Father. Why the hell are you calling me?"

"Watch your language, son. Look, I'm on the road headed for Texas, traveling with a man named Travis Boyette, a nice gentleman who visited our church last Sunday. You may have seen him. Walks with a cane. Anyway, Travis here has a confession to make to the authorities in Texas, a small town called Slone, and we're dashing off to stop an execution."

Matthew's voice cleared quickly. "Have you lost your mind, Keith? You've got that guy in the car?"

"Oh yes, left Topeka about an hour ago. The reason I'm calling, Matt, is to ask for your help."

"I'll give you some help, Keith. Free advice. Turn that damned car around and get back here."

"Thanks, Matt, but look, in a few hours I'll need you to make a couple of phone calls to Slone, Texas."

"What does Dana say about this?"

"Fine, fine. I'll need you to call the police, the prosecutor, and maybe a defense lawyer. I'll be calling them too, Matt, but since you're a prosecutor, they might listen to you."

"Are you still in Kansas?"

"Yes, I-35."

"Don't cross the state line, Keith. Please."

"Well, that might make it rather difficult to get to Texas, don't you think?"

"Don't cross the state line!"

"Get some sleep. I'll call you back around six, and we'll start working the phones, okay?"

Keith closed his phone, punched voice mail, and waited. Ten seconds later it buzzed. Matthew was calling back.

They were through Emporia and bearing down on Wichita.

Nothing prompted the narrative. Perhaps Boyette was getting sleepy himself, or maybe he was just bored. But the more he talked, the more Keith realized he was listening to the twisted autobiography of a dying man, one who knew no sense could be made of his life, but wanted to try anyway.

"Darrell's brother, we called him Uncle Chett, would take me fishing, that was what he told my parents. Never caught the first fish, never wet the first hook. We'd go to his little house out in the country, had a pond out back, and that's where all the fish were supposed to be. Never made it that far. He'd give me a cigarette, let me taste his beer. At first I didn't know what he was doing. Had no idea. I was just a kid, eight years old. I was too scared to move, to fight back. I remember how bad it hurt. He had all sorts of kiddie porn, magazines and movies, sick stuff he was generous enough to share with me. You cram all that garbage into the head of a little boy, and before long he sort of accepts it. I thought, well, maybe this is what kids do. Maybe this is what adults do to kids. It looked legitimate and normal. He wasn't mean to me; in fact, he bought me ice cream and pizza—anything I wanted. After each fishing trip, he would drive me home, and right before we'd get to my house, he would get real serious, sort of mean and threatening. He would tell me that it was important for me to keep our little secret. Some things are private. He kept a gun in his truck, a shiny pistol. Later, he would show me how to use it. But at first, he would take it out and place it on the seat, then explain that he loved his secrets, and if they were ever revealed, then he would be forced to hurt someone. Even me. If I told anyone, he would be forced to kill me, and then kill whomever I told, and that included Darrell and my mother. It was very effective. I never told anyone.

"We kept fishing. I think my mother knew, but she had her own problems, primarily with the bottle. She was drunk most of the time, didn't sober up until much later, until it was too late for me. When I was about ten or so, my uncle gave me some pot, and we started smoking together. Then some pills. It wasn't all bad. I thought I was pretty cool. A young punk smoking cigarettes and pot, drinking beer, watching porn. The other part was never pleasant, but it didn't last long. We were living in Springfield at the time, and one day my mother told me we had to move. My dad, her husband, whatever the hell he was, had found a job near Joplin, Missouri, where I was born. We packed in a hurry, loaded everything into a U-Haul, and fled in the middle of the night. I'm sure there was some unpaid rent involved. Probably a lot more than that—bills, lawsuits, arrest warrants, indictments—who knows. Anyway, I woke up the next morning in a double-wide trailer, a nice one. Uncle Chett got left behind. I'm sure it broke his heart. He finally found us and showed up a month or so later, asked me if I wanted to go fishing. I said no. He had no place to take me, so he just hung around the house, couldn't take his eyes off me. They were drinking, the adults, and before long they got into a fight over money. Uncle Chett left cussing. Never saw him again. But the damage was done. If I saw him now, I'd take a baseball bat and splatter his brains across forty acres. I was one screwed-up little boy. And I guess I've never gotten over it. Can I smoke?"

"No."

"Then can we pull over for a minute so I can smoke?"

"Sure." A few miles down the road, they pulled in to a rest stop and took a break. Keith's phone buzzed again. Another missed call from Matthew Burns. Boyette wandered away, last seen drifting into some woods behind the restrooms, a cloud of smoke trailing him. Keith was walking across the parking lot, back and forth, back and forth, trying to pump the blood, with one eye on his passenger. When Boyette was out of sight, gone in the darkness, Keith wondered if he was gone for good. He was already tired of the trip, and if there was an escape at this point, who would care? Keith would drive back home, wonderfully alone in the car, and face the music with his wife and get an earful from Matthew. With some luck, no one would ever know about the aborted mission. Boyette would do what he'd always done—drift here and there until he either died or got himself arrested again.

But what if he hurt someone? Would Keith share criminal responsibility?

Minutes passed with no movement from the woods. A dozen 18-wheelers were parked together at one end of the parking lot, their generators humming as their drivers slept.

Keith leaned on his car and waited. He'd lost his nerve, and he wanted to go home. He wanted Boyette to stay in the woods, to go deeper until there was no turning back, to simply disappear. Then he thought of Donté Drumm.

A puff of smoke wafted from the trees. His passenger had not escaped.

Miles passed without a word. Boyette seemed content to forget his past, though minutes earlier he'd been gushing details. At the first hint of numbness, Keith plowed ahead.

"You were in Joplin. Uncle Chett had come and gone."

The tic, five, ten seconds, then, "Yes, uh, we were living in a trailer out from town, a poor section. We were always in the poor section, but I remember being proud because we had a nice trailer. A rental, but I didn't know it then. Next to the trailer park, there was a little road, asphalt, that ran for miles into the hills south of Joplin, in Newton County. There were creeks and dells and dirt roads. It was a kid's paradise. We'd ride our bikes for hours along the trails and no one could ever find us. Sometimes we'd steal beer and booze out of the trailer, or even out of a store, and dash off into the hills for a little party. One time a kid named Damian had a bag of pot he'd stolen from his big brother, and we got so stoned we couldn't stay on our bikes."

"And this is where Nicole is buried?"

Keith counted to eleven before Boyette said, "I suppose. She's somewhere in there. Not sure I can remember, to tell you the truth. I was pretty drunk, Pastor. I've tried to remember, even tried to draw a map the other day, but it'll be difficult. If we get that far."

"Why did you bury her there?"

"Didn't want anybody to find her. It worked."

"How do you know it worked? How do you know her body hasn't been found? You buried her nine years ago. You've been in prison for the past six years, away from the news."

"Pastor, I assure you she has not been found."

Keith felt assured. He believed Boyette, and the fact that he believed so much from this hardened criminal was frustrating. He was wide-awake as they approached Wichita. Boyette had retreated into his sad little shell. He rubbed his temples occasionally.

"You went to court when you were twelve years old?" Keith asked.

The tic. "Something like that. Yes, I was twelve. I remember the judge making some comment about me being too young to launch a new career as a criminal. Little did he know."

"What was the crime?"

"We broke into a store and loaded up all the stuff we could carry. Beer, cigarettes, candy, lunch meat, chips. Had a regular feast in the woods, got drunk. No problem until somebody looked at the video. It was my first offense, so I got probation. My co-defendant was Eddie Stuart. He was fourteen, and it was not his first offense. They sent him to reform school, and I never saw him again. It was a rough neighborhood, and there was no shortage of bad boys. We were either making trouble or getting into trouble. Darrell yelled at me, but he came and went. My mother tried her best but couldn't stop drinking. My brother got sent away when he was fifteen. Me, I was thirteen. You ever been inside a reform school, Pastor?"

"No."

"Didn't think so. These are the kids nobody wants. Most are not bad kids, not when they first get there. They just didn't have a chance. My first stop was a place near St. Louis, and like all reform schools it was nothing but a penitentiary for kids. I got the top bunk in a long room crowded with kids from the streets of St. Louis. The violence was brutal. There were never enough guards or supervisors. We went to class, but the education was a joke. You had to join a gang to survive. Someone looked at my file and saw where I'd been sexually abused, so I was an easy target for the guards. After two years of hell, I was released. Now, Pastor, what's a fifteen-year-old kid supposed to do when he's back on the streets after two years of torture?" He actually looked at Keith as if he expected an answer.

Keith kept his eyes straight ahead and shrugged.

"The juvenile justice system does nothing but cultivate career criminals. Society wants to lock us up and throw away the key, but society is too stupid to realize that we'll eventually get out. And when we get out, it ain't pretty. Take me. I'd like to think I wasn't a hopeless case when I went in at thirteen. But give me two years of nothing but violence, hate, beatings, abuse, then society's got a problem when I walk out at fifteen. Prisons are hate factories, Pastor, and society wants more and more of them. It ain't working."

"Are you blaming someone else for what happened to Nicole?"

Boyette exhaled and looked away. It was a heavy question, and he sagged under its weight. Finally, he said, "You miss the whole point, Pastor. What I did was wrong, but I couldn't stop myself. Why couldn't I stop myself? Because of what I am. I wasn't born this way. I became a man with a lot of problems, not because of my DNA, but because of what society demanded. Lock 'em up. Punish the hell out of them. And if you make a few monsters along the way, too bad."

"What about the other 50 percent?"

"And who might those be?"

"Half of all inmates paroled from prison stay out of trouble and are never arrested again."

Boyette didn't appreciate this statistic. He reshifted his weight and fixated on the right-side mirror. He withdrew into his shell and stopped talking. When they were south of Wichita, he fell asleep.

The cell phone rang again at 3:40 a.m. It was Matthew Burns. "Where are you, Keith?" he demanded.

"Get some sleep, Matthew. Sorry I bothered you."

"I'm having trouble sleeping. Where are you?"

"About thirty miles from the Oklahoma state line."

"Still got your buddy?"

"Oh yes. He's sleeping now. Me, I just nap on and off."

"I've talked to Dana. She's upset, Keith. I'm worried too. We think you're losing your mind."

"Probably so. I'm touched. Relax, Matthew. I'm doing what's right, and I'll survive whatever happens. Right now, my thoughts are with Donté Drumm."

"Don't cross the state line."

"I heard you the first time."

"Good. I just wanted to be on record as warning you more than once."

"I'm writing it down."

"Okay, now, Keith, listen to me. We have no idea what might happen once you get to Slone and your buddy there starts running his mouth. I'm assuming he'll attract cameras like roadkill attracts buzzards. Stay out of the picture, Keith. Keep your head low. Don't talk to any reporters. One of two things will definitely happen. Number one, the execution will take place as scheduled. If so, then you've done your best, and it'll be time to scramble back home. Boyette has the option of staying there or catching a ride back. Doesn't really matter to you. Just get back home. There's a decent chance no one will know about your little adventure in Texas. The second scenario is that the execution will be stayed. If so, you've won, but don't celebrate. While the authorities grab Boyette, you sneak out of town and get back home. Either way, you gotta stay out of sight. Am I clear?"

"I think so. Here's the question: Where do we go when we get to Slone? The prosecutor, the police, the press, the defense attorney?"

"Robbie Flak. He's the only one who might listen. The police and the prosecutor have no reason to listen to Boyette. They have their man. They're just waiting for the execution. Flak is the only one who might believe you, and he certainly appears capable of making a lot of noise. If Boyette tells a good story, then Flak will take care of the press."

"That's what I thought. I'm planning on calling Flak at six. I doubt if he's sleeping much."

"Let's talk before we start making calls."

"You got it."

"And, Keith, I still think you're crazy."

"I don't doubt it, Matthew."

He put the phone in his pocket, and a few minutes later the Subaru left Kansas and entered Oklahoma. Keith was driving eighty miles an hour. He was also wearing his clerical collar, and he'd convinced himself that any decent trooper wouldn't ask too many questions of a man of God whose crime was nothing more than speeding.

17

The Drumm family spent the night in a budget motel on the outskirts of Livingston, less than four miles by car from the Allan B. Polunsky correctional facility, where Donté had been locked up for over seven years. The motel did a modest trade with the families of inmates, including the rather bizarre cult of death row wives from abroad. At any given time, around twenty condemned men were married to European women they could never actually touch. The weddings were not officially sanctioned by the state, but the couples nonetheless considered themselves married and carried on to the fullest extent possible. The wives corresponded with each other and often traveled together to Texas to see their men. They stayed at the same motel.

Four had eaten at a table near the Drumms late the night before. They were usually noticeable, with their thick accents and suggestive clothing. They liked to be noticed. Back home they were minor celebrities.

Donté had rebuffed all offers of matrimony. During his final days, he turned down book deals, requests for interviews, marriage proposals, and the chance to make an appearance on *Fordyce—Hitting Hard!* He had refused to meet with both the prison chaplain and his own minister, the Reverend Johnny Canty. Donté had given up on religion. He wanted no part of the same God so fervently worshipped by the devout Christians who were hell-bent on killing him.

Roberta Drumm awoke in the darkness of room 109. She had slept so little in the past month that her fatigue now kept her awake. The doctor had given her some pills, but they had backfired and made her edgy. The room was warm and she pulled back the sheets. Her daughter, Andrea, was in the other twin bed, only a few feet away, and seemed to be sleeping. Her sons Cedric and Marvin were next door. The rules of the prison allowed them to visit with Donté from 8:00 a.m. until noon on this, his final day. After their last farewell, he would be transported to the death chamber at the prison in Huntsville.

Eight in the morning was hours away.

The schedule was fixed, all movements dictated by a system famous for its efficiency. At 5:00 that afternoon, the family would report to a prison office in Huntsville and then take a short ride in a van to the death chamber, where they would be herded into a cramped witness room just seconds before the drugs were administered. They would see him on the gurney, tubes already in his arms, listen to his final words, wait ten minutes or so for the official declaration of death, then leave quickly. From there, they would drive to a local funeral home to retrieve the body and take it home.

Could it be a dream, a nightmare? Was she really there, awake in the darkness contemplating her son's final hours? Of course she was. She had lived the nightmare for nine years now, ever since the day she'd been told that Donté had not only been arrested but also confessed. The nightmare was a book as thick as her Bible, every chapter another tragedy, every page filled with sorrow and disbelief.

Andrea rolled from one side to another, the cheap bed squeaking and rattling. Then she was still and breathing heavily.

For Roberta, one horror had been replaced by the next: the numbing shock of seeing her boy in jail for the first time, in an orange jumpsuit, eyes wild and scared; the ache in her stomach as she thought about him in jail, locked away from his family and surrounded by criminals; the hope of a fair trial, only to suffer the shock of realizing it was anything but fair; her loud and unrestrained sobbing when the death sentence was announced; the last image of her son being led from the courtroom by thick deputies so smug in their work; the endless appeals and fading hopes; the countless visits to death row, where she watched a strong, healthy young man slowly deteriorate. She lost friends along the way and she really didn't care. Some were skeptical of the claims of innocence. Some grew weary of all the talk about her son. But she was consumed, and had little else to say. How could anyone else know what a mother was going through?

And the nightmare would never end. Not today, when Texas finally executed him. Not next week, when she buried him. Not at some point in the future, when the truth was finally known, if ever.

The horrors add up, and there were many days when Roberta Drumm doubted she had the strength to get out of bed. She was so tired of pretending to be strong.

"Are you awake, Momma?" Andrea asked softly.

"You know I am, honey."

"Did you sleep any?"

"No, I don't think so."

Andrea kicked off the sheets and stretched her legs. The room was very dark with no light filtering in from the outside. "It's four thirty, Momma."

"I can't see."

"My watch glows in the dark."

Andrea was the only one of the Drumm kids with a college degree. She taught kindergarten in a town near Slone. She had a husband and she wanted to be at home, in her bed, far away from Livingston, Texas. She closed her eyes in an effort to fall asleep, but only seconds passed before she was staring at the ceiling. "Momma, I gotta tell you something."

"What is it, honey?"

"I've never told anyone else this, and I never will. It's a burden I've carried a long, long time, and I want you to know it before they take Donté."

"I'm listening."

"There was a time, after the trial, after they'd sent him away that I began to doubt his story. I think I was looking for a reason to doubt him. What they said sort of made sense. I could see Donté fooling around with that girl, afraid of getting caught, and I could see her trying to break up and him not wanting to. Maybe he sneaked out of the house that night when I was asleep. And when I heard his confession in court, I have to admit it made me uneasy. They never found her body, and if he threw her in the river, then maybe that's why they'll never find her. I was trying to make sense out of everything that had happened. I wanted to believe that the system is not totally broken. And so I convinced myself that he was probably guilty, that they probably got the right man. I kept writing to him, kept coming over here to see him and all, but I was convinced he was guilty. For a while, it made me feel better, in some strange way. This went on for months, maybe a year."

"What changed your mind?"

"Robbie. You remember that time we went to Austin to hear the case on direct appeal?"

"Indeed I do."

"It was a year or so after the trial."

"I was there, honey."

"We were sitting in that big courtroom, looking at those nine judges, all white, all looking so important in their black robes and hard frowns, their airs, and across the room was Nicole's family and her big-mouthed mother, and Robbie got up to argue for us. He was so good. He went through the trial and pointed out how weak the evidence was. He mocked the prosecutor and the judge. He was afraid of nothing. He attacked the confession. And he brought up, for the first time, the fact that the police had not told him about the anonymous phone caller who said it was Donté. That shocked me. How could the police and the prosecutor withhold evidence? Didn't bother the court, though. I remember watching Robbie argue so passionately, and it dawned on me that he, the lawyer, the white guy from the rich part of town, had no doubt whatsoever that my brother was innocent. And I believed him right then and there. I felt so ashamed for doubting Donté."

"It's okay, honey."

"Please don't tell anyone."

"Never. You can trust your mother, you know."

They sat up and moved to the edges of their beds, holding hands, foreheads touching. Andrea said, "You wanna cry or you wanna pray?"

"We can pray later, but we can't cry later."

"Right. Let's have us a good cry."

The predawn traffic picked up as they approached Oklahoma City. Boyette's forehead was pressed against the passenger window, his mouth open in a pathetic drool. His nap was entering its second hour, and Keith was happy with the solitude. He'd stopped back near the state line for a cup of carryout coffee, a dreadful machine brew that he would normally pour into a ditch. But what it lacked in flavor it more than made up for in caffeine, and Keith was buzzing right along, his head spinning, his speedometer exactly eight miles per hour over the limit.

Boyette had requested a beer at the last stop. Keith declined and bought him a bottle of water. He found a bluegrass station out of Edmond and listened to it at low volume. At 5:30, he called Dana, but she had little to say. South of Oklahoma City, Boyette jerked from his slumber and said, "Guess I dozed off."

"You did indeed."

"Pastor, these pills I take really work on the bladder. Can we do a quick pit stop?"

"Sure," Keith said. What else could he say? He kept one eye on the clock. They would leave the expressway somewhere north of Denton, Texas, and head east on two-lane roads. Keith had no idea how long that would take. His best guess was arriving in Slone between noon and 1:00 p.m. The pit stops, of course, were not helping their progress.

They stopped in Norman and bought more coffee and water. Boyette managed to blaze through two cigarettes, sucking and blowing rapidly as if it might be his last smoke, while Keith quickly refueled. Fifteen minutes later, they were back on I-35, racing south through the flat country of Oklahoma.

As a man of God, Keith felt compelled to at least explore the subject of faith. He began, somewhat tentatively, "You've talked about your childhood, Travis, and we don't need to go back there. Just curious, though, if you were ever exposed to a church or to a preacher when you were a kid?"

The tic was back. So was the contemplation. "No," he said, and for a moment that seemed to be all. Then, "I never knew my mother to go to church. She didn't have much of a family. I think they were ashamed of her, so they kept away. Darrell certainly didn't do the church thing. Uncle Chett needed a good dose of religion, but I'm sure he's in hell right now."

Keith saw an opening. "So you believe in hell?"

"I suppose. I believe we all go somewhere after we die, and I can't imagine you and me going to the same place. Can you, Pastor? I mean, look, I've spent most of my life in prison, and, trust me, there's a species of mankind that's subhuman. These people were born mean. They're vicious, soulless, crazy men who cannot be helped. When they die, they gotta go to some bad place."

The irony was almost comical. A confessed murderer and serial rapist condemning violent men.

"Was there a Bible in the house?" Keith asked, trying to stay away from the subject of heinous crimes.

"Never saw one. Never saw much in the way of books. I was raised on porn, Pastor, fed to me by Uncle Chett and kept under Darrell's bed. That's the extent of my childhood reading."

"Do you believe in God?"

"Look, Pastor, I'm not talking about God and Jesus

and salvation and all that. I heard it all the time in prison. Lots of guys get really turned on when they're locked away and start thumping the Bible. I guess some are serious, but it also sounds good at the parole hearings. I just never bought into it."

"Are you prepared for death, Travis?"

A pause. "Look, Pastor, I'm forty-four years old, and my life has been one massive train wreck. I'm tired of living in prison. I'm tired of living with the guilt of what I've done. I'm tired of hearing the pitiful voices of the people I hurt. I'm tired of a lot of shit, Pastor, okay? Sorry for the language. I'm tired of being some degenerate who lives on the edges of society. I'm just so sick of it all. I'm proud of my tumor, okay? Hard to believe, but when it's not cracking my skull, I kinda like the damned thing. It tells me what's ahead. My days are numbered, and that doesn't bother me. I won't hurt anybody else. No one will miss me, Pastor. If I didn't have the tumor, I'd get a bottle of pills and a bottle of vodka and float away forever. Still might do that."

So much for a penetrating discussion on the subject of faith. Ten miles passed before Keith said, "What would you like to talk about, Travis?"

"Nothing. I just want to sit here and look at the road and think about nothing."

"Sounds good to me. You hungry?"

"No, thanks."

Robbie left the house at 5:00 a.m. and drove a circuitous route to the office. He kept his window down so he could smell the smoke. The fire had long since been extinguished, but the odor of freshly charred wood hung like a thick cloud over Slone. There was no wind. Downtown, anxious cops were blocking streets and diverting traffic away from the First Baptist Church. Robbie got just a glimpse of its smoking ruins, illuminated by the flashing lights of fire and rescue vehicles. He took the backstreets, and when he parked at the old train station and got out of his car, the smell was still pungent and fresh. All of Slone would be awakened and greeted with the ominous vapor of a suspicious fire. And the obvious question would be, will there be more?

His staff drifted in, all sleep deprived and anxious to see if the day would take a dramatic turn away from the direction it was headed. They gathered in the main conference room, around the long table still cluttered with the debris of the night before. Carlos gathered empty pizza boxes and beer bottles, while Samantha Thomas served coffee and bagels. Robbie, trying to appear upbeat, replayed for the gang his conversation with Fred Pryor about the surreptitious recording from the strip club. Pryor himself had not yet arrived.

The phone started ringing. No one wanted to answer it. The receptionist was not in yet. "Somebody punch 'Do Not Disturb,' " Robbie barked, and the phone stopped ringing.

Aaron Rey walked from room to room, looking out the windows. The television was on, but muted.

Bonnie entered the conference room and said, "Robbie, I just checked the phone messages for the past six hours. Nothing important. Just a couple of death threats, and a couple of rednecks happy the big day is finally here."

"No call from the governor?" Robbie asked.

"Not yet."

"What a surprise. I'm sure he lost sleep like the rest of us."

Keith would eventually frame the speeding ticket, and because of it he would always know exactly what he was doing at 5:50 a.m. on Thursday, November 8, 2007. The location wasn't clear, because there was no town in sight. Just a long, empty stretch of I-35, somewhere north of Ardmore, Oklahoma.

The trooper was hiding in some trees in the median, and as soon as Keith saw him and glanced at his speedometer, he knew he was in trouble. He hit his brakes, slowed considerably, and waited a few seconds. When the blue lights appeared, Boyette said, "Oh, shit."

"Watch your language." Keith was braking hard and hurrying to the shoulder.

"My language is the least of your problems. What're you gonna tell him?"

"That I'm sorry."

"What if he asks what we're doing?"

"We're driving down the highway, maybe a bit too fast, but we're okay."

"I think I'll tell him I'm jumping parole and you're my getaway driver."

"Knock it off, Travis."

The truth was that Travis looked exactly like the sort of character who would be jumping parole, right out of central casting. Keith stopped the car, turned off the ignition, straightened his clerical collar and made sure it was as visible as possible, and said, "Don't say a word, Travis. Let me do the talking."

As they waited for a very deliberate and purposeful state trooper, Keith managed to amuse himself by admitting that he was sitting beside the road, engaged in not one but two criminal activities, and that for some inconceivable reason he'd chosen as his partner in crime a serial rapist and murderer. He glanced at Travis and said, "Can you cover up that tattoo?" It was on the left side of his neck, a swirling creation that only a deviant might understand and wear with pride.

"What if he likes tattoos?" Travis said, without making a move for his shirt collar.

The trooper approached carefully, with a long flashlight, and when things appeared safe, he said gruffly, "Good morning."

"Morning," Keith said, glancing up. He handed over his license, registration, and insurance card.

"You a priest?" It was more of an accusation. Keith doubted there were many Catholics in southern Oklahoma.

"I'm a Lutheran minister," he said with a warm smile. The perfect picture of peace and civility.

"Lutheran?" the trooper grunted, as if that might be worse than a Catholic.

"Yes, sir."

He shined his light on the license. "Well, Reverend Schroeder, you were doing eighty-five miles an hour."

"Yes, sir. Sorry about that."

"Limit out here is seventy-five. What's the hurry?"

"No real hurry. Just wasn't paying attention."

"Where you headed?"

Keith wanted to fire back, "Why, sir, is that any of your business?" But he quickly said, "Dallas."

"Got a boy in Dallas," the trooper said, as if that fact were somehow relevant. He walked back to his car, got inside, slammed the door, and began his paperwork. His blue lights sparkled through the fading darkness.

When the adrenaline settled down and Keith got bored with the waiting, he decided to make use of the time. He called Matthew Burns, who appeared to be holding his cell phone. Keith explained where he was and what was happening to him at the moment and had trouble convincing Matthew that it was nothing but a routine speeding ticket. They managed to work through Matthew's overreaction and agreed to start calling Robbie Flak's office immediately.

The trooper eventually returned. Keith signed his ticket, retrieved his documents, apologized again, and after twenty-eight minutes they were back on the road. Boyette's presence was never acknowledged.

18

At one point in his blurred past, Donté knew the precise number of days he'd spent in cell number 22F, death row, at the Polunsky Unit. Most inmates kept such a tally. But he'd lost count, for the same reason he'd lost interest in reading, writing, exercising, eating, brushing his teeth, shaving, showering, trying to communicate with other inmates, and obeying the guards. He could sleep and dream and use the toilet when necessary; beyond that, he was unable or unwilling to try much else.

"This is the big day, Donté," the guard said when he slid the breakfast tray into the cell. Pancakes and applesauce again. "How you doin'?"

"Okay," Donté mumbled. They spoke through a narrow slit in the metal door.

The guard was Mouse, a tiny black guy, one of the nicer ones. Mouse moved on, leaving Donté to stare at the food. He did not touch it. An hour later, Mouse was back. "Come on, Donté, you gotta eat."

"Not hungry."

"How 'bout your last meal? You thought about that? You gotta place your order in a few hours."

"What's good?" Donté asked.

"I'm not sure anything's good as a last meal, but they tell me most of the guys eat like a horse. Steak, potatoes, catfish, shrimp, pizza, anything you want."

"How 'bout cold noodles and boiled leather, same as any other day?"

"Whatever you want, Donté." Mouse leaned a few inches closer, lowered his voice, and said, "Donté, I'll be thinking about you, you hear?"

"Thanks, Mouse."

"I'll miss you, Donté. You're a good guy."

Donté was amused at the thought that someone on death row would miss him. He did not respond and Mouse moved on.

Donté sat on the edge of his bunk for a long time and stared at a cardboard box they'd delivered yesterday. In it, he'd neatly packed his possessions—a dozen paperbacks, none of which he'd read in years, two writing tablets, envelopes, a dictionary, a Bible, a 2007 calendar, a zippered bag in which he kept his money, $18.40, two tins of sardines and a package of stale saltines from the canteen, and a radio that picked up only a Christian station from Livingston and a country one from Huntsville. He took a writing tablet and a pencil and began to calculate. It took some time, but he finally arrived at a total he believed to be fairly accurate.

Seven years, seven months, and three days, in cell number 22F—2,771 days. Before that, he'd spent about four months at the old death row at Ellis. He'd been arrested on December 22, 1998, and he'd been locked up since.

Almost nine years behind bars. It was an eternity, but not an impressive number. Four doors down, Oliver Tyree, age sixty-four, was in his thirty-first year on death row with no execution date on the calendar. There were several twenty-year veterans. It was changing, though. The newer arrivals faced a different set of rules. There were tougher deadlines for their appeals. For those convicted after 1990, the average wait before execution was ten years. Shortest in the nation.

During his early years in 22F, Donté waited and waited for news from the courts. They moved at a snail's pace, it seemed. Then it was all over, no more petitions to file, no more judges and justices for Robbie to attack. Looking back now, the appeals seemed to have flown by. He stretched out on his bed and tried to sleep.

You count the days and watch the years go by. You tell yourself, and you believe it, that you'd rather just die. You'd rather stare death boldly in the face and say you're ready because whatever is waiting on the other side has to be better than growing old in a six-by-ten cage with no one to talk to. You consider yourself half-dead at best. Please take the other half.

You've watched dozens leave and not return, and you accept the fact that one day they'll come for you. You're nothing but a rat in their lab, a disposable body to be used as proof that their experiment is working. An eye for an eye, each killing must be avenged. You kill enough and you're convinced that killing is good.

You count the days, and then there are none left. You ask yourself on your last morning if you are really ready. You search for courage, but the bravery is fading.

When it's over, no one really wants to die.

*   *   *

It was a big day for Reeva too, and to show the world she was suffering, she invited *Fordyce—Hitting Hard!* back into her home for breakfast. In her most stylish pantsuit, she cooked bacon and eggs and sat around the table with Wallis and their two children, Chad and Marie, both in their late teens. None of the four needed a heavy breakfast. They should've skipped the meal completely. But the cameras were rolling, and as the family ate, they prattled on about the fire that destroyed their beloved church, a fire that was still smoldering. They were stunned, angry. They were certain it was arson, but managed to restrain themselves and not make allegations against anyone—on camera. Off camera, they just knew the fire had been started by black thugs. Reeva had been a member of the church for over forty years. She had married both husbands there. Chad, Marie, and Nicole had been baptized there. Wallis was a deacon. It was a tragedy. Gradually, they got around to more important matters. They all agreed that it was a sad day, a sad occasion. Sad, but so necessary. For almost nine years they had waited for this day, for justice to finally arrive for their family, and yes, for all of Slone as well.

Sean Fordyce was still tied up with a complicated execution in Florida, but he had made his plans well-known. He would arrive, by private jet, at the Huntsville airport later in the afternoon for a quick interview with Reeva before she witnessed the execution. Of course, he would be there when it was over.

Without the host, the breakfast footage went on and on. Off camera, an assistant producer prompted the family with such gems as, "Do you think lethal injection is too humane?" Reeva certainly did. Wallis just grunted. Chad chewed his bacon. Marie, a chatterbox like her mother, said, between bites, that Drumm should suffer intense physical pain as he was dying, just like Nicole.

"Do you think executions should be made public?" Mixed reactions around the table.

"The condemned man is allowed a last statement. If you could speak to him, what would you say?" Reeva, chewing, burst into tears and covered her eyes. "Why, oh, why?" she wailed. "Why did you take my baby?"

"Sean will love this," the assistant producer whispered to the cameraman. Both were suppressing smiles.

Reeva pulled herself together, and the family plowed through breakfast. At one point, she barked at her husband, who'd said almost nothing, "Wallis! What are you thinking?" Wallis shrugged as if he hadn't been thinking at all.

Coincidentally, Brother Ronnie dropped by just as the meal was wrapping up. He'd been up all night watching his church burn, and he needed sleep. But Reeva and her family also needed him. They quizzed him about the fire. He appeared sufficiently burdened. They moved to the rear of the home, to Reeva's room, where they sat and huddled around a coffee table. They held hands, and Brother Ronnie led them in prayer. With an effort at drama, and with the camera two feet from his head, he pleaded for strength and courage for the family to endure what was ahead on this difficult day. He thanked the Lord for justice. He prayed for their church and its members.

He did not mention Donté Drumm or his family.

* * *

After a dozen trips to voice mail, a real person finally answered. "Flak Law Firm," she said quickly.

"Robbie Flak, please," Keith said as he perked up. Boyette turned and looked at him.

"Mr. Flak is in a meeting."

"I'm sure he is. Listen, this is very important. My name is Keith Schroeder. I'm a Lutheran minister from Topeka, Kansas. I spoke with Mr. Flak yesterday. I'm driving to Slone as we speak, and I have with me, here in my car, a man by the name of Travis Boyette. Mr. Boyette raped and killed Nicole Yarber, and he knows where her body is buried. I'm driving him to Slone so he can tell his story. It is imperative that I speak with Robbie Flak. Now."

"Uh, sure. Can I put you on hold?"

"I can't stop you from putting me on hold."

"Just a moment."

"Please hurry."

She put him on hold. She left her desk near the front door and hurried through the train station, rounding up the team. Robbie was in his office with Fred Pryor. "Robbie, you need to hear this," she said, and her face and voice left no room for discussion. They met in the conference room, where they gathered around a speakerphone. Robbie pushed a button and said, "This is Robbie Flak."

"Mr. Flak, this is Keith Schroeder. We spoke yesterday afternoon."

"Yes, it's Reverend Schroeder, right?"

"Yes, but now it's just Keith."

"You're on our speakerphone. Is that okay? My whole firm is here, plus some others. I'm counting ten people. Is that okay?"

"Sure, whatever."

"And the recorder is on, is that okay?"

"Yes, fine, anything else? Look, we've been driving all night, and we should be in Slone around noon. I have Travis Boyette with me, and he's ready to tell his story."

"Tell us about Travis," Robbie said. There was no movement, and little breathing, around the table.

"He's forty-four years old, born in Joplin, Missouri, a career criminal, registered sex offender in at least four states." Keith glanced at Boyette, who was looking through the passenger window, as if he were somewhere else. "His last stop was a prison in Lansing, Kansas, and he's now on parole. He was living in Slone at the time of Nicole Yarber's disappearance, staying at the Rebel Motor Inn. I'm sure you know where it is. He was arrested for drunk driving in Slone in January 1999. There is a copy of his arrest."

Carlos and Bonnie were hammering keys on their laptops, racing through the Internet, digging for anything on Keith Schroeder, Travis Boyette, the arrest in Slone.

Keith continued: "In fact, he was in jail in Slone while Donté Drumm was under arrest. Boyette posted bond, got out, then skipped town. He drifted to Kansas, tried to rape another woman, got caught, and is just finishing his sentence."

Tense looks were exchanged around the table. Everyone took a breath. "Why is he talking now?" Robbie asked, leaning down closer to the speakerphone.

"He's dying," Keith said bluntly, no need to soft-pedal things at this point. "He has a brain tumor, a glioblastoma, grade four, inoperable. He says that the doctors have told him he has less than a year to live. He says he wants to do the right thing. While he was in prison, he lost track of the Drumm case, said he figured the authorities in Texas would one day figure out that they had the wrong man."

"This guy's in the car with you?"

"Yes."

"Can he hear this conversation?"

Keith was driving with his left hand and holding his cell phone with his right. "No," he said.

"When did you meet this guy, Keith?"

"Monday."

"Do you believe him? If he is in fact a serial rapist and career criminal, then he'd rather lie than tell the truth. How do you know he has a brain tumor?"

"I checked that out. It's true." Keith glanced at Boyette, who was still staring at nothing through the passenger window. "I think it's all true."

"What does he want?"

"So far, nothing."

"Where are you right now?"

"Interstate 35, not far from the Texas line. How does this work, Robbie? Is there a chance of stopping the execution?"

"There's a chance," Robbie said as he looked into the eyes of Samantha Thomas. She shrugged, nodded, a weak "Maybe."

Robbie rubbed both hands and said, "Okay, Keith, here's what we have to do. We have to meet Boyette and ask him a lot of questions, and if that goes well, then we'll prepare an affidavit for him to sign and file it with a petition. We have time, but not much."

Carlos handed Samantha a photo of Boyette he'd just printed out from a Web site for the Kansas Department of Corrections. She pointed at his face and whispered, "Get him on the phone."

Robbie nodded and said, "Keith, I'd like to talk to Boyette. Can you put him on?"

Keith lowered his cell phone and said, "Travis, this is the lawyer. He wants to talk to you."

"I don't think so," Boyette said.

"Why not? We're driving to Texas to talk to the man, here he is."

"Nope. I'll talk when we get there."

Boyette's voice was clear on the speakerphone. Robbie and the rest were relieved to know that Keith actually had someone else in the car with him. Maybe he wasn't some nut playing games at the eleventh hour.

Robbie pressed on. "If we can talk to him now, we can start to work on his affidavit. That'll save some time, and we don't have much of it."

Keith relayed this to Boyette, whose reaction was startling. His upper body pitched forward violently as he grabbed his head with both hands. He tried to suppress a scream, but a very loud "Aghhhhh!" escaped, followed by deep guttural lurches that made the man sound as if he were dying in horrendous pain.

"What was that?" Robbie asked.

Keith was driving, talking on the phone, and suddenly distracted by another seizure. "I'll call you back," he said and put the phone down.

"I'm throwing up," Boyette said, reaching for the door handle. Keith hit the brakes and steered the Subaru onto the shoulder. An 18-wheeler behind him swerved and sounded the horn. They finally came to a stop, and Boyette clutched his seat belt. When he was free, he leaned through the cracked door and began vomiting. Keith got out, walked to the rear bumper, and decided not to watch. Boyette puked for a long time, and when he finally finished, Keith handed him a bottle of water. "I need to lie down," Boyette said, and crawled into the backseat. "Don't move the car," he directed. "I'm still sick."

Keith walked a few feet away and called his wife.

After another noisy bout of gagging and throwing up, Boyette seemed to settle down. He returned to the rear seat, with the right-side door open, his feet hanging out.

"We need to move along, Travis. Slone is not getting any closer."

"Just a minute, okay? I'm not ready to move." He was rubbing his temples, and his slick skull seemed ready to crack. Keith watched him for a minute, but felt uncomfortable gawking at such agony. He stepped around the vomit and leaned on the hood of the car.

His phone buzzed. It was Robbie. "What happened?" he asked.

Robbie was seated now, still at the conference table, with most of the crew still there. Carlos was already working on an affidavit. Bonnie had found Boyette's arrest record in Slone and was trying to determine which lawyer had represented him. Kristi Hinze arrived around 7:30 and soon realized she was missing the excitement. Martha Handler typed furiously, another episode in her evolving story about the execution. Aaron Rey and Fred Pryor roamed around the train station, sipping cup after cup of coffee and nervously watching all doors and windows. Thankfully, the sun was now up and they didn't really expect trouble. Not at the office, anyway.

"He has these seizures," Keith said, as an 18-wheeler roared by, its wind blowing his hair. "I guess it's the tumor, but when they hit, they're pretty frightening. He's been throwing up for the past twenty minutes."

"Is the car moving, Keith?"

"No. We'll take off in a minute."

"The minutes are getting by us, Keith. You understand this, right? Donté will be executed at six o'clock tonight."

"I got that. If you'll recall, I tried to talk to you yesterday, and you told me to get lost."

Robbie took a deep breath as he collected the stares from around the table. "Can he hear you right now?"

"No. He's lying in the backseat, rubbing his head, afraid to move. Me, I'm sitting on the hood, dodging 18-wheelers."

"Tell us why you believe this guy."

"Well, let's see, where do I start? He knows a lot about the crime. He was in Slone when it happened. He's obviously capable of such violence. He's dying. There's no proof against Donté Drumm other than the confession. And Boyette has her senior class ring on a chain around his neck. That's the best I can do, Robbie. And, I'll admit, there's a slight chance this is all a big lie."

"But you're helping him jump parole. You're committing a crime."

"Don't remind me, okay? I just talked to my wife and she happened to mention that."

"How soon can you get here?"

"I don't know. Three hours, maybe. We've stopped twice for coffee because I haven't slept in three nights.

I bought myself a speeding ticket, one written by the slowest trooper in Oklahoma. Now Boyette is puking his guts out, and I'd rather him do that in a ditch and not in my car. I don't know, Robbie. We're trying."

"Hurry up."

19

With the sun up and the town anxiously coming to life, the Slone police were on high alert, with holsters unfastened, radios squawking, patrol cars darting up and down the streets, and every officer looking for the next hint of trouble. It was expected at the high school, and for good measure the chief sent half a dozen men there early on Thursday morning. When the students arrived for class, they saw police cars parked near the main entrance, an ominous sign.

All of Slone knew that the black players had boycotted practice on Wednesday and had vowed not to play Friday. There could be no greater insult to a community that loved its football. The fans, so ardent and loyal only a week earlier, now felt betrayed. Feelings were strong; emotions were raw all over Slone. On the white side of town, the bitterness was caused by football, and now the burning of a church. On the black side, it was all about the execution.

As with most violent and sudden conflicts, the precise manner in which the riot began would never be known. In the endless retelling of it, two things became obvious: the black students blamed the white students, and the whites blamed the blacks. The question of time was a bit clearer. Just seconds after the first bell at 8:15, several things happened at once. Smoke bombs were lit in the boys' restrooms on the first and second floors. Cherry bombs were rolled down the main hallway, exploding like howitzers under the metal lockers. A string of firecrackers went off near the central stairwell, and panic swept the school. Most of the black students walked out of class and mingled in the halls. A brawl erupted in a junior homeroom class when a black hothead and a white hothead exchanged insults and started swinging. Others were quick to take sides and join in. The teacher ran from the room screaming for help. One fight sparked a dozen more. Before long, students were rushing out of the building, running for safety. Some were yelling, "Fire! Fire!" though no flames had been seen. The police called for backups and fire trucks. Firecrackers were popping all over the first and second floors. The smoke grew thicker and thicker as the chaos spread. Near the entryway to the gymnasium, some black kids were ransacking the trophy cases when they were seen by a gang of whites. Another fight broke out, one that spilled into a parking lot next to the gym. The principal stayed in his office and barked nonstop into the PA system. His warnings were ignored and only added to the confusion. At 8:30, he announced that school had been canceled for that day and the next. The police, with reinforcements, eventually settled things down and evacuated Slone High School. There were no fires, only smoke and the acrid smell of cheap explosives. There was some broken glass, clogged toilets, upended lockers, and stolen backpacks, and a soft drink machine was vandalized. Three students—two whites and one black—were taken to the hospital and treated for cuts. There were a lot of cuts and bruises that went unreported. Typical of such a melee, with so many taking part, it was not possible to determine who was causing trouble and who was trying to flee, so no arrests were made at the time.

Many of the older boys, black and white, went home to get their guns.

Roberta, Andrea, Cedric, and Marvin were cleared through the security desk at Polunsky's front building and led by a supervisor to the Visitors' Room, a process and a walk they had endured many times in the past seven years. And though they had always hated the prison and everything about it, they realized that it would soon be a part of their past. If it meant nothing else, Polunsky was where Donté lived. That would change in a matter of hours.

There are two private rooms used by attorneys in the visiting area. They are slightly wider than the other booths used by visitors, and they are fully enclosed so no guard or prison official, or other inmate or lawyer, can eavesdrop. On his final day, a condemned man is allowed to see his family and friends in one of the attorney's rooms. The Plexiglas is still there, and all conversations are through black phones on each side of it. No touching.

The Visitors' Room is a loud and busy place on weekends, but on weekdays there is little traffic. Wednesdays are set aside as "Media Days," and a man "with a date" is typically interviewed by a couple of reporters from the town where the murder took place. Donté had declined all requests for interviews.

When the family entered the visiting area at 8:00

a.m., the only other person there was a female guard named Ruth. They knew her well. She was a thoughtful soul who liked Donté. Ruth welcomed them and said how sorry she was.

Donté was already in the attorney's booth when Roberta and Cedric entered. A guard could be seen through the window of a door behind him. As always, he placed the palm of his left hand flat on the Plexiglas, and Roberta did the same from the other side. Though the touch was never completed, it was a long, warm embrace in their minds. Donté had not touched his mother since the last day of his trial, in October 1999, when a guard allowed them a quick hug as he was being led from the courtroom.

He held the phone with his right hand and said with a smile, "Hi, Momma. Thanks for coming. I love you." Their hands were still together, pressed against the glass. Roberta said, "And I love you right back, Donté. How are you today?"

"The same. I've already had my shower and a shave. Everybody's real nice to me. Got fresh clothes on, a new pair of boxers. This is a lovely place. They get real nice around here right before they kill you."

"You look great, Donté."

"And so do you, Momma. You're as beautiful as always."

During one of her first visits, Roberta had wept and had been unable to stop herself. Afterward, Donté wrote to her and explained how upsetting it was to see her so distraught. In the solitude of his cell, he wept for hours, but he couldn't bear to watch his mother do the same. He wanted her to visit him whenever possible, but the tears did more harm than good. There had been no more tears, not from Roberta, Andrea, Cedric, Marvin, or any other relative or friend. Roberta made this very clear with each visit. If you can't control yourself, get out of the room.

"I talked to Robbie this morning," she said. "He has one or two more plans for the final appeals, plus the governor has not ruled on your request for a reprieve. So there's still hope, Donté."

"There's no hope, Momma, so don't kid yourself."

"We can't give up, Donté."

"Why not? There's nothing we can do. When Texas wants to kill somebody, they're gonna do it. Killed one last week. Got another planned later this month. It's an assembly line around here, can't nobody stop it. You might get lucky and get a stay every now and then, happened to me two years ago, but sooner or later your time is up. They don't care about guilt or innocence, Momma, all they care about is showing the world how tough they are. Texas don't fool around. Don't mess with Texas. Ever heard that?"

Softly she said, "I don't want you to be angry, Donté."

"I'm sorry, Momma, I'm gonna die angry. I can't help it. Some of these guys go peacefully, singing hymns, quoting scripture, begging for forgiveness. Dude last week said, 'Father, unto you I commend my spirit.' Some don't say a word, just close their eyes and wait for the poison. A few go out kicking. Todd Willingham died three years ago, always claimed to be innocent. They said he started a house fire that burned up his three little girls. Yet he was in the house and got burned too. He was a fighter. He cussed 'em in his final statement."

"Don't do that, Donté."

"I don't know what I'll do, Momma. Maybe nothing. Maybe I'll just lie there with my eyes closed and start counting, and when I get to a hundred, I'll just float away. But, Momma, you're not gonna be there."

"We've had this conversation, Donté."

"Well, now we're having it again. I don't want you to witness this."

"I don't want to either, believe me. But I'll be there."

"I'm gonna talk to Robbie."

"I've already talked to him, Donté. He knows how I feel."

Donté slowly withdrew his left hand from the glass, and Roberta did the same. She placed the phone on the counter and removed a sheet of paper from her pocket. No purses were allowed past the front desk. She unfolded the paper, picked up the phone, and said, "Donté, this is a list of the folks who've called or stopped by to ask about you. I promised them I would pass along their thoughts."

He nodded and tried to smile. Roberta went through the names—neighbors, old friends from down the street, classmates, beloved church members, and a few distant relatives. Donté listened without a word, but seemed to drift away. Roberta went on and on, and with each name she added a brief commentary about the person or an anecdote.

Andrea was next. The touching ritual was followed. She described the burning of the Baptist church, the tension in Slone, the fears that things would get worse. Donté seemed to like that—the thought of his people fighting back.

The family had learned years earlier that it was important to arrive at the Visitors' Room with a pocketful of coins. Vending machines lined the walls, and the guards delivered the food and drinks to the inmates during the visits. Donté had lost serious weight in prison, but he craved a certain cinnamon bun coated with thick frosting. While Roberta and Andrea handled the first round of the visit, Marvin bought two of the buns, with a soft drink, and Ruth took them to Donté. The junk food helped his mood.

Cedric was reading a newspaper, not far from the attorney's room, when the warden popped in for a friendly hello. He wanted to make sure all was well, everything in his prison running smooth.

"Anything I can do to help?" he asked as if he were running for office. He was trying hard to appear compassionate.

Cedric stood up, thought for a second, and then got angry. "Are you kidding me? You're about to put my brother to death for something he didn't do, and you pop in here with some happy horseshit about wanting to help."

"We're just doing our jobs, sir." Ruth was walking over.

"No, you're not, unless your job allows you to kill innocent people. You wanna help, stop the damned execution."

Marvin stepped between them and said, "Let's be cool here." The warden backed away and said something to Ruth. They had a serious conversation as the warden walked to the door. He soon left.

The Texas Court of Criminal Appeals (TCCA) has sole jurisdiction over capital murder cases and is the court of last resort in Texas before an inmate hits the federal circuit. It has nine members, all elected, all required to run statewide. In 2007, it still clung to the archaic rule that all pleadings, petitions, appeals, documents, and such had to be filed as hard copies.

Nothing online. Black ink on white paper, and tons of it. Each filing had to include twelve copies, one for each justice, and one for the clerk, one for the secretary, and one for the official file.

It was a bizarre and cumbersome procedure. The federal court for the Western District of Texas, housed a few blocks from the TCCA, adopted electronic filing in the mid-1990s. By the turn of the century, paper filings were rapidly becoming obsolete as technology marched on. In law, both in courts and in offices, the electronic file became far more popular than the paper file.

At 9:00 a.m. on Thursday, the Flak firm and the Defender Group lawyers were notified that the insanity claim was denied by the TCCA. The court did not believe Donté was mentally ill. This was expected. Minutes after this denial was received, the identical petition was filed electronically in the federal court for the Eastern District of Texas in Tyler.

At 9:30 a.m., a Defender Group lawyer named Cicely Avis walked into the clerk's office at the TCCA with the latest filing by the lawyers for Donté Drumm. It was a claim of actual innocence based on the secretly recorded statements by Joey Gamble. Cicely routinely showed up with similar filings, and she and the clerk knew each other well.

"What else is coming?" the clerk asked as he processed the petition.

"I'm sure there will be something," Cicely said.

"Usually is."

The clerk finished his paperwork, handed a marked copy back to Cicely, and wished her a good day. Because of the obvious urgency of the matter, the clerk hand delivered a copy of the petition to the offices of all nine justices. Three happened to be in Austin.

The other six were scattered around the state. The chief justice was a man by the name of Milton Prudlowe, a longtime member of the court who lived in Lubbock most of the year but kept a small apartment in Austin.

Prudlowe and his law clerk read the petition and paid particular attention to the eight-page transcript of the recording of Joey Gamble spilling his guts in a Houston strip club the night before. While it was entertaining, it was far from sworn testimony, and there was little doubt he would deny making the statements if confronted with them. No consent had been given to the recording. Everything about it was tinged with sleaze. The young man was obviously drinking heavily. And, if his statements could be delivered, and if he had indeed lied at trial, what would it prove? Almost nothing, in Prudlowe's opinion. Donté Drumm had confessed, plain and simple. The Drumm case had never bothered Milton Prudlowe.

Seven years earlier, he and his colleagues had first considered the direct appeal of Donté Drumm. They remembered it well, not because of the confession, but because of the absence of a dead body. His conviction was affirmed, though, and in a unanimous opinion. Texas law had long been settled on the issue of a murder trial without clear evidence of murder. Some of the usual elements were just not necessary.

Prudlowe and his law clerk agreed that this latest claim had no merit. The clerk then polled the clerks of the other justices, and within an hour a preliminary denial was being circulated.

Boyette was in the backseat, where he'd been for almost two hours. He'd taken a pill, and evidently it was working splendidly. He didn't move, didn't make a sound, but did appear to be breathing the last time Keith checked.

To stay awake, and to get his blood boiling, Keith had called Dana twice. They had words, neither retreated, neither apologized for saying too much. After each conversation, Keith found himself wide-awake, fuming. He called Matthew Burns, who was at the office in downtown Topeka and anxious to help. There was little he could do.

When the Subaru drifted onto the right shoulder of a two-lane road, somewhere close to Sherman, Texas, Keith was suddenly awakened. And mad. He stopped at the nearest convenience store and bought a tall cup of strong coffee. He stirred in three packs of sugar and walked around the store five times. Back in the car, Boyette had not moved. Keith gulped the hot coffee and sped away. His cell phone rang, and he snatched it from the passenger seat.

It was Robbie Flak. "Where are you?" he asked.

"I don't know. Highway 82, headed west, outside of Sherman."

"What's taking so long?"

"I'm doing the best I can."

"What are the chances of me talking to Boyette, now, by phone?"

"Slim. Right now he's passed out in the backseat, still very sick. And he said he was not talking until he got there."

"I can't do anything, Keith, until I talk to this guy, okay? I have to know how much he is willing to say. Is he going to admit that he killed Nicole Yarber? Can you answer this?"

"Well, Robbie, it's like this. We left Topeka in the middle of the night. We're driving like crazy to get to

your office, and the sole purpose, according to Boyette when we left Topeka, was for him to come clean,
admit to the rape and murder, and try to save Donté
Drumm. That's what he said. But with this guy nothing is predictable. He may be in a coma right now, for
all I know."

"Should you check his pulse?"

"No. He doesn't like to be touched."

"Just hurry, damn it."

"Watch your language, please. I'm a minister and I
don't appreciate that language."

"Sorry. Please hurry."

20

____

The march had been whispered about since Monday, but its details had not been finalized. When the week began, the execution was days away, and there was a fervent hope in the black community that a judge somewhere would wake up and stop it. But the days had passed and the higher powers were still asleep. Now the hour was near, and the blacks in Slone, especially the younger ones, were not about to sit idly by. The closing of the high school had energized them and left them free to look for a way to make noise. Around 10:00 a.m., a crowd began to gather at Washington Park, at the corner of Tenth Street and Martin Luther King Boulevard. Aided by cell phones and the Internet, the crowd multiplied, and before long a thousand blacks were milling about, restless, certain that something was about to happen but not sure exactly what. Two police cars arrived and parked down the street, safely away from the crowd.

Trey Glover was Slone High School's starting tailback, and he drove an SUV with tinted windows, oversize tires, glistening chrome wheel covers, and an audio system that could break glass. He parked it on the street, opened all four doors, and began playing "White Man's Justice," an angry rap song by T. P. Slik. The song electrified the crowd. Others streamed in, most of them high school students, but the gathering was also attracting the unemployed, some housewives, and a few retirees. A drum ensemble materialized when four members of the Marching Warriors arrived with two bass drums and two snares. A chant began, "Free Donté Drumm," and it echoed through the neighborhood. In the distance, away from the park, someone lit a round of firecrackers, and for a split second everyone thought it could've been gunfire. Smoke bombs were set off, and as the minutes passed, the tension grew.

The brick was not thrown from Washington Park. It came from behind the police cars, from behind a wooden fence next to a house owned by Mr. Ernie Shylock, who was sitting on the porch watching the excitement. He claimed no knowledge of who threw it. It crashed into the rear window of a police car, jolted the two cops into a near panic, and caused a roaring wave of approval from the crowd. The police ran around for a few seconds, guns drawn, ready to shoot anything that moved, with Mr. Shylock being the first possible target. He raised his hands and yelled, "Don't shoot. I didn't do it." One cop sprinted behind the house as if he might chase down the assailant, but after forty yards he was winded and gave up. Within minutes, reinforcements arrived, and the sight of more police cars fired up the crowd.

The march finally began when the drummers stepped onto Martin Luther King Boulevard and headed north, in the general direction of downtown. They were followed by Trey Glover in his SUV, windows down, rap at full volume. Behind him were the others, a long line of protesters, many holding posters that demanded justice, a stop to the killing, and freedom for Donté. Children on bikes joined the fun. Blacks sitting idly on porches got up and began walking with the crowd. The parade grew in size as it inched along, seemingly without a destination.

No one had bothered with a permit, as required by Slone ordinance. The rally the day before in front of the courthouse had been legally conducted, but not this march. The police, though, played it cool. Let 'em protest. Let 'em yell. It'll be over tonight, hopefully. Blocking the parade route, or trying to disperse the crowd, or even arresting a few, would incite them and only make matters worse. So the police held back, some following at a distance while others circled ahead, clearing the way, diverting traffic.

A black officer on a motorcycle pulled alongside the SUV and yelled, "Where you going, Trey?"

Trey, apparently the unofficial leader of the event, replied, "We're going back to the courthouse."

"Keep it peaceful and there won't be trouble."

"I'll try," Trey said with a shrug. He and the officer both knew that trouble could erupt at any moment.

The parade turned onto Phillips Street and inched along, a loosely organized assemblage of concerned citizens enthralled by their freedom of expression, and who were also enjoying the attention. The drummers repeated their precise, impressive routines. The rap shook the ground with its deadening lyrics. The students shook and gyrated with the beat while chanting a variety of battle cries. The mood was at once festive and angry. The kids were quite proud of their ballooning numbers, yet they wanted to do more. Ahead of them, the police blocked off Main Street and spread the word among the downtown merchants that a march was headed their way.

The 911 call was recorded at 11:27 a.m. The Mount Sinai Church of God in Christ was burning, not far from Washington Park. A white van with a logo and phone numbers had been parked behind the church, according to the caller, and two white men in uniforms, like plumbers or electricians, had hurried from the church into the van and left. Minutes later, there was smoke. Sirens erupted as the first responders answered the call. Fire trucks rumbled from two of the three stations in Slone.

At the corner of Phillips and Main, the march came to a halt. The drummers were still. The rap was turned down. They watched the fire trucks go racing by, headed into their part of town. The same black officer on the motorcycle stopped at the SUV and informed Trey that one of their churches was now burning.

"Let's disband this little march, Trey," the officer said.

"I don't think so."

"Then there's gonna be trouble."

"There's already trouble," Trey said.

"Ya'll need to break up before this thing gets outta hand."

"No, you need to get outta the way."

Ten miles west of Slone there was a country store and deli called the Trading Post. It was owned by a large, loud, garrulous man named Jesse Hicks, a second cousin of Reeva's. Jesse's father had opened the Trading Post fifty years earlier, and Jesse had never worked anywhere else. The Post, as it was known, was a gathering place for gossip and lunch, and it had even hosted a few campaign barbecues for politicians. On Thursday, there was more traffic than usual, more folks stopping by to hear the latest on the execution. Jesse kept a photo of his favorite niece, Nicole Yarber, on the wall behind the counter next to the cigarettes, and he would discuss her case with anyone who would listen. Technically, she was a third cousin, but he called her a niece since she'd become something of a celebrity. For Jesse, 6:00 p.m. on Thursday, November 8, could not arrive soon enough.

The store was in the front part of the building, the small eating area in the rear, and around an ancient potbellied stove there were half a dozen rocking chairs, all occupied as lunch drew near. Jesse was working the cash register, selling gas and beer, and talking nonstop to his small crowd. With the riot at the high school only a few hours old, and the First Baptist Church still smoldering, and, of course, the looming execution, the gossip was hot and the men chatted away excitedly. A man called Shorty walked in and announced, "The Africans are marchin' downtown again. One of 'em threw a brick through the window of a police car."

This, on top of all the other stories, led to a near overload of news that had to be discussed and analyzed and put in perspective, and quickly. Shorty had the floor for a few minutes, but was soon overshadowed by Jesse, who always dominated the conversations. Various opinions were put forth on what the police should be doing, and no one argued that the police were handling things properly.

For years, Jesse had boasted that he would witness the execution of Donté Drumm, couldn't wait to watch it, would, in fact, pull the switch himself if given the chance. He had said many times that his dear Reeva was insistent that he be there, on account of his fondness for and closeness to Nicole, his beloved niece. Every man rocking away had seen Jesse get choked up and wipe his eyes when talking about Nicole. But now a last-minute bureaucratic snafu was keeping Jesse away from Huntsville. There were so many journalists and prison officials and other big shots wanting to watch that Jesse got bumped. It was the hottest ticket in town, and Jesse, though on the approved list, had somehow been left out.

A man named Rusty walked in and announced, "Another church is on fire! One of those black Pentecostal ones."

"Where?"

"In Slone, near Washington Park."

The thought of a retaliatory church burning was at first inconceivable. Even Jesse was stunned. But the more they talked about it and analyzed it, the more they liked it. Why not? Tit for tat. An eye for an eye. If they want war, we'll give 'em a war. There was a general agreement that Slone was a powder keg and they were in for a long night. This was disturbing, but also stimulating. Every man sitting around the stove had at least two guns in his truck and more in the house.

Two strangers entered the Trading Post: one, a man of the cloth with a collar and navy jacket, the other man a slick-headed cripple who shuffled along with a cane. The minister walked to a display case and took out two bottles of water. The other man went to the restroom.

Keith set the two bottles on the counter and said "Good morning" to Jesse. Behind him, the experts in the rockers were all talking at once and Keith understood none of it.

"You from around here?" Jesse asked as he rung up the water.

"No, just passing through," Keith said. His speech was crisp, precise, no accent at all. Yankee.

"You a preacher?"

"Yes. I'm a Lutheran minister," Keith said as he caught a nose full of onion rings being removed from hot grease. A hunger pain hit and buckled his knees. He was starving, and exhausted, but there was no time for food. Boyette was shuffling over. Keith handed him a bottle, said "Thanks" to Jesse, and turned for the door. Boyette nodded at Jesse, who said, "You boys have a good day."

And with that, Jesse spoke to the man who murdered his niece.

In the parking lot, an Audi stopped abruptly next to the Subaru, and two men—Aaron Rey and Fred Pryor—crawled out. Quick introductions were made. Aaron and Fred looked closely at Boyette, sizing him up, asking themselves if the guy was real. Robbie would want to know as soon as they got back in the car and called him.

Aaron said, "We're about fifteen minutes from the office, and we'll have to detour around downtown. There's a lot going on. Just stick close, okay?"

"Let's go," Keith said, anxious to finish this interminable drive. They drove away, the Subaru tailgating the Audi. Boyette seemed calm, even detached. The cane was resting between his legs. He thumped its handle with his fingers, in much the same way he'd been doing for the past ten hours. When they passed the sign indicating the municipal boundaries of Slone,

Boyette said, "I never thought I'd see this place again."

"Recognize it?"

The tic, the pause. "Not really. I've seen a lot of these places, Pastor, small hick towns everywhere. After a while, they tend to blur together."

"Anything special about Slone?"

"Nicole. I killed her."

"And she was the only one you killed?"

"I didn't say that, Pastor."

"So there are others?"

"Didn't say that either. Let's talk about something else."

"And what would you like to talk about, Travis?"

"How'd you meet your wife?"

"I've told you before, Travis, leave her out of it. You're much too concerned with my wife."

"She's so cute."

On the conference table, Robbie pushed a button for the speakerphone and said, "Talk to me, Fred."

"We met them; they're behind us now, and they appear to be a genuine minister and one seriously weird sidekick."

"Describe Boyette."

"White male, you wouldn't call him handsome. Five ten, 150, shaved scalp with a bad tattoo on the left side of his neck, several more covering his arms. Has the look of a sick puppy who's spent his life locked away. Green shifty eyes that don't blink. I wanted to wash my hand after shaking his. Weak handshake, a dishrag."

Robbie took a deep breath and then said, "So they're here."

"They are indeed. We'll be there in a matter of minutes."

"Hurry up." He turned off the speakerphone and looked at his team scattered around the table, all watching him. "It might be somewhat intimidating for Boyette to walk in here and have ten people staring at him," Robbie said. "Let's pretend like it's business as usual. I'll take him to my office and ask the first questions."

Their file on Boyette was getting thicker. They had found records of his convictions in four states and a few details of his incarcerations, and they had located the lawyer in Slone who'd represented him briefly after his arrest there. The lawyer vaguely remembered him and had sent over his file. They had an affidavit from the owner of the Rebel Motor Inn, one Inez Gaffney, who had no recollection of Boyette, but did find his name in an old ledger from 1998. They had the building records from the Monsanto warehouse where Boyette allegedly worked in the late fall of that year.

Carlos tidied up the conference table and they waited.

When Keith parked at the train station and opened his door, he heard sirens in the distance. He smelled smoke. He sensed trouble.

"The First Baptist Church burned last night," Aaron said as they walked up the steps to the old loading platform. "Now there's a fire at a black church over there." He nodded to his left, as if Keith was supposed to know his way around town.

"They're burning churches?" he asked.

"Yep."

Boyette struggled up the steps, leaning on his cane, and then they stepped into the lobby. Fanta pretended to be busy with a word processor, barely looking up.

"Where's Robbie?" Fred Pryor asked, and she nodded toward the back.

Robbie met them in the conference room. Awkward introductions were made. Boyette was reluctant to speak or to shake hands. Abruptly, he said to Robbie, "I remember you. I saw you on television after the boy was arrested. You were upset, almost yelling at the camera."

"That's me. Where were you?"

"I was here, Mr. Flak, watching it all, couldn't believe they had arrested the wrong guy."

"That's right, the wrong guy." For someone as high-strung and quick-tempered as Robbie Flak, it was difficult to remain calm. He wanted to slap Boyette, and grab his cane and beat him senseless, and curse him for a long list of transgressions. He wanted to kill him with his bare hands. Instead, he pretended to be cool, detached. Harsh words would not help Donté.

They left the conference room and walked into Robbie's office. Aaron and Fred Pryor stayed outside, ready for whatever came next. Robbie directed Keith and Boyette to a small table in the corner, and all three sat down. "Would you like some coffee or something to drink?" he asked, almost pleasantly. He stared at Boyette, who stared back without flinching or blinking.

Keith cleared his throat and said, "Look, Robbie, I hate to ask for favors, but we haven't eaten in a long time. We're starving."

Robbie picked up the phone, rang Carlos, and ordered a tray of deli sandwiches and water.

"No sense beating around the bush, Mr. Boyette. Let's hear what you have to say."

The tic, the pause. Boyette shifted and squirmed, suddenly unable to make eye contact. "Well, the first thing I want to know is if there's any reward money on the table."

Keith dropped his head and said, "Oh my God."

"You're not serious, are you?" Robbie asked.

"I suppose everything is serious right now, Mr. Flak," Boyette said. "Wouldn't you agree?"

"This is the first mention of reward money," Keith said, completely exasperated.

"I have needs," Boyette said. "I don't have a dime and no prospects of finding one. Just curious, that's all."

"That's all?" Robbie repeated. "The execution is less than six hours away, and our chances of stopping it are very slim. Texas is about to execute an innocent man, and I'm sitting here with the real killer, who suddenly wants to get paid for what he's done."

"Who says I'm the real killer?"

"You," Keith blurted. "You told me you killed her and you know where the body is buried because you buried it. Stop playing games, Travis."

"If I recall correctly, her father put up a bunch of dough when they were trying to find her. Something like $200,000. That right, Mr. Flak?"

"That was nine years ago. If you think you're in line for the reward money, you're badly mistaken." Robbie's words were measured, but an explosion was imminent.

"Why do you want money?" Keith asked. "According to your own words, you'll be dead in a few months. The tumor, remember?"

"Thanks for reminding me, Pastor."

Robbie glared at Boyette with unrestrained hatred. The truth was that Robbie, at that moment, would sign over every asset he could find in exchange for a nice thick affidavit that told the truth and might save his client. There was a long stretch of silence as the three contemplated what to do next. Boyette grimaced and then began rubbing his slick head. He placed both palms on both temples and pressed as hard as possible, as if pressure from the outside world would relieve the pressure from within.

"Are you having a seizure?" Keith asked, but there was no response.

"He has these seizures," Keith said to Robbie, as if an explanation would help matters. "Caffeine helps."

Robbie jumped to his feet and left the room. Outside his office, he told Aaron and Pryor, "The son of a bitch wants money." He walked to the kitchen, grabbed a pot of stale coffee, found two paper cups, and returned to his office. He poured a cup for Boyette, who was bent double at the waist, elbows on knees, cradling his head, and moaning. "Here's some coffee."

Silence.

Finally, Boyette said, "I'm going to be sick. I need to lie down."

"Take the sofa," Robbie said, pointing to it across the room. Boyette struggled to his feet and with Keith's help made it to the sofa, where he wrapped his arms around his head and pulled his knees to his chest. "Can you turn off the lights?" Boyette said. "I'll be okay in a minute."

"We don't have time for this!" Robbie said, ready to scream.

"Please, just a minute," Boyette said pathetically

as his body vibrated and he gasped for air. Keith and Robbie left the office and stepped into the conference room. A crowd soon gathered, and Robbie introduced Keith to the rest of the gang. The food arrived and they ate quickly.

21

They came for Donté at noon. Not a minute before, not a minute after. Everything precise and well rehearsed. There was a knock on the metal door behind him. Three loud raps. He was talking to Cedric, but when he knew it was time, he asked for his mother. Roberta was standing behind Cedric, with Andrea and Marvin at her sides, all four squeezed into the small room, all four crying now with no effort to hold back the tears. They had watched the clock for four hours, and there was nothing left to say. Cedric exchanged places with Roberta, who took the phone and placed her palm on the Plexiglas. Donté did the same from the other side. His three siblings embraced behind his mother, all four huddled together, touching, with Andrea in the middle and on the verge of collapse.

"I love you, Momma," Donté said. "And I'm so sorry this is happening."

"I love you too, baby, and you don't have to say you're sorry. You did nothing wrong."

Donté wiped his cheeks with a sleeve. "I always wished I could've gotten outta here before Daddy died. I wanted him to see me as a free man. I wanted him to know that I did nothing wrong."

"He knew that, Donté. Your daddy never doubted you. When he died, he knew you were innocent." She wiped her face with a tissue. "I've never doubted you either, baby."

"I know. I guess I'll be seeing Daddy pretty soon."

Roberta nodded, but could not respond. The door behind him opened, and a large male guard appeared. Donté hung up the phone, stood, and placed both palms flat on the Plexiglas. His family did the same. One final embrace, and then he was gone.

With his hands cuffed again, Donté was led from the visitors' wing, through a series of clicking metal doors, out of the building, over a lawn crisscrossed with sidewalks, and into a wing where he was taken back to his cell for the last time. Everything, now, was for the last time, and as Donté sat on his bunk and stared at his box of assets, he almost convinced himself that it would be a relief to get away.

His family was given a few minutes to collect themselves. As Ruth was leading them out of the room, she gave them a hug. She said she was sorry, and they thanked her for her kindness. Just as they were walking through a metal door, she said, "You folks headed to Huntsville?"

Yes, of course, they were.

"Might want to get on over there. Rumor is there might be trouble on the roads."

They nodded but were not sure how to respond. They walked through security at the front building, got their driver's licenses and purses, and walked out of Polunsky for the last time.

*   *   *

The "trouble on the roads" mentioned by Ruth was a clandestine Facebook conspiracy inspired by two black students at Sam Houston State University in Huntsville. The code name was Detour, and the plan was so simple and so brilliant that it attracted dozens of volunteers.

In 2000, soon after Donté arrived on death row, the inmates were moved from Huntsville to Polunsky. The inmates were moved; the death chamber was not. For seven years and two hundred executions, it had been necessary to haul the condemned men from Polunsky to Huntsville. Elaborate movements were planned and used, but after a few dozen transfers, with no ambushes, no heroic efforts to rescue the condemned, without a hitch of any kind, the authorities realized that no one was watching. No one really cared. The elaborate plans were discarded, and the same route was used with every transfer. They left the prison at 1:00 p.m., turned left on 350, turned left again on 190, a four-lane road with plenty of traffic, and an hour later the trip was over.

Inmates were placed in the rear of an unmarked passenger van, surrounded by enough muscle and weaponry to protect the president, and escorted, for good measure, by an identical van filled with another squad of bored guards hoping for a little excitement.

The last execution had been on September 25, when Michael Richard was injected. Ten students, all members of Operation Detour, used five vehicles and plenty of cell phones to track the movements of the two white vans from Polunsky to Huntsville. The students were not detected. No one suspected them. No one was looking for them. By early November, their plan was complete, and their operatives were itching for trouble.

At 12:50 p.m., a guard, a black one sympathetic to Donté, tipped off a member of Detour. The two white vans were being loaded; the transfer had begun. At 1:00 p.m., the vans left the prison for a service road near the maximum security unit. They turned onto Route 350 and headed for Livingston. There was little traffic. Two miles from the prison, the traffic increased, became heavy, then stopped completely. Ahead of the vans, a car had stalled in the right lane. Oddly, one had stalled in the left lane, and another on the shoulder. The three cars blocked any passage. Their drivers were out checking under their hoods. Then, behind the three cars, there were three more, all stalled in a neat line across the road. The vans did not move, and seemed to be in no hurry. Behind them, in the right lane, another car came to a stop. Its driver, a young black woman, popped the hood, got out, feigned exasperation because her Nissan had quit on her. A Volkswagen Beetle pulled beside her in the left lane, suffered a mechanical failure on cue, and the hood went up. More vehicles materialized from nowhere and bunched together behind the first wave, thoroughly blocking the road, its shoulders, and all exits and entrances to it. Within five minutes, a traffic jam of at least twenty vehicles had occurred. The white vans were surrounded by disabled cars and SUVs, all with their hoods up, the drivers loitering about, talking, laughing, chatting on cell phones. Several of the male students went from car to car, disabling each by pulling the wires to the distributor caps.

The state and local police arrived in minutes, dozens of marked cars with sirens screaming. They were followed by a brigade of tow trucks, all of which had been rounded up in Livingston on short notice. Operation Detour had briefed its volunteers well. Each driver was adamant that his or her car had quit, and under Texas law this was not a crime. Citations would certainly be written for blocking traffic, but Detour had found a lawyer who would fight those in court. Officers did not have the right to take keys and check the engines for themselves. And if they tried, the engines were dead. The students had been told to resist searches of their vehicles; to peacefully resist any attempts at being arrested; to threaten legal action in the face of an arrest; and, if arrested, consider it an honor, a badge of courage in the fight against injustice. Detour had other lawyers who would handle their cases. The students relished the thought of being locked up, an act of defiance in their minds. Something they could talk about for years.

As the police cars and wreckers parked haphazardly near the traffic jam, and as the first troopers were approaching the students, the second phase of the plan fell beautifully into place. Another wave of students in cars turned onto Route 350 from Livingston and were soon approaching the melee. They parked three abreast and three deep behind the tow trucks. All hoods popped open, more roadside breakdowns. Since the tow truck drivers were expected to react with anger and maybe violence to being penned in, the second wave of drivers remained in their cars with the windows up and doors locked. Most cars were full of students, and many were healthy young men who could take care of themselves. They wouldn't mind a fight. They were angry to begin with.

A tow truck driver approached the first car parked

behind him, realized it was full of blacks, and began swearing and making threats. A state trooper yelled at him and told him to shut up. The trooper was Sergeant Inman, and he took charge of a truly unique situation, one that included, so far, eight police cars, seven tow trucks, at least thirty "disabled" vehicles, and two prison vans, one of which was transporting a man to his death. To make matters worse, the locals who routinely used Route 350 were backing up, unaware they had chosen the wrong time to get from one place to another. The road was hopelessly clogged.

Inman was a cool professional, and he knew something the students didn't. As he walked through the jam, headed for the vans, he nodded politely at the students, smiled, asked if they were having a nice day. At the vans, security details for Donté unloaded, thick men in blue SWAT-style uniforms with automatic weapons. Most of the students made their way close to the vans. One seemed to lead the pack. Inman approached him, extended a hand, and politely said, "I'm Sergeant Inman. May I ask your name?"

"Quincy Mooney." He reluctantly shook Inman's hand.

"Mr. Mooney, I'm sorry about your car breaking down."

"Don't mention it."

Inman looked around, smiled at the other students. "All these folks friends of yours?"

"I've never seen 'em before."

Inman smiled. "Look, Mr. Mooney, we need to get these cars off the road. Traffic is backing up. Everything is blocked."

"Guess we need to call some mechanics."

"No, we're just gonna tow 'em, Quincy. Unless, of course, ya'll would like to save a hundred bucks and drive away. If you chose to do so, then we wouldn't be forced to write a bunch of tickets. That's another hundred bucks a car."

"So, it's against the law for your car to break down?"

"No, sir, it's not. But you and I both know why you're here. The judge will know too."

"I know why I'm here. Why are you here?"

"I'm doing my job, Quincy. Traffic control and keeping the peace." Inman nodded his head and said, "Come with me." Quincy followed him to the first van. Its double side doors were open. Inman looked inside, then invited Quincy to do the same. The van was empty. They walked to the second van. Both looked inside. It, too, was empty. The security guards were snickering. The whirling thump-thump of a helicopter could be heard.

"Where's Donté Drumm?" Quincy asked, stunned.

"He ain't here, is he?" Inman asked with a smirk. Quincy stared at the darkened windows of the empty van. They walked back to the front of the first one. Inman looked to the sky, in the direction of Polunsky. Everyone waited and waited, and seconds later a helicopter roared directly over them.

Inman pointed at it and said, "There goes Donté."

Quincy's jaw dropped, his shoulders slumped. Word spread through the students, and there were looks of shock and disbelief. A perfect operation had been compromised. Donté Drumm would arrive at the death chamber ahead of schedule.

"Too much Internet chatter," Inman said. "Here's the deal, Quincy. You guys have fifteen minutes to clear this road and get outta here. In fifteen minutes, we start writing tickets and towing. And, just so you know, there won't be any arrests, so don't provoke us. Got it?"

Quincy walked away, thoroughly defeated.

Boyette, after a sandwich and three cups of coffee, was feeling better. He was at the table, lights on, shades opened. Robbie and Keith were staring at him, and no one was smiling. Evidently, the issue of money had been put aside by Boyette, at least for the moment.

"So if I tell you what happened with Nicole, what happens to me?" he asked, looking at Robbie.

"Nothing, at least nothing for a long time. The cops and prosecutors have their man. If he's killed tonight, then they'll never consider pursuing someone else. If Donté gets a stay, I'm not sure what they'll do, but it'll be a long time before they admit that anybody but Donté killed Nicole. They have far too much invested in their wrongful conviction."

"So I won't be arrested today or tomorrow or the next day?"

"I can't speak for these clowns, Mr. Boyette. I don't know what they'll do. As a general rule, the cops here are stupid, and Detective Kerber is a moron. But to arrest you is to admit they were wrong about Donté, and that's not going to happen. If you walked into the police station right now, swore on a Bible, and gave them every detail of the abduction, rape, and murder, they would dismiss you outright as a lunatic. They'll have no desire to believe you, Mr. Boyette. Your admission destroys them."

The tic, the pause. Robbie leaned forward and glared at him. "Time's up, Mr. Boyette. I want to hear it. Tell me the truth. Did you kill the girl?"

"Yes, just like I've told Keith here. I grabbed her, raped her for two days, then choked her and hid the body."

"Where is the body? Finding the body will stop the execution, I guarantee it. Where is it?"

"In the hills south of Joplin, Missouri. Deep in the hills."

"Joplin, Missouri, is at least five hours from here."

"More than that. Nicole and I drove there."

"So she was alive when you left Texas."

The tic, the pause, finally, "Yes. I killed her in Missouri. Raped her from here to there."

"Is it possible to call the authorities in Joplin and tell them how to find the body?"

Boyette managed to laugh at such foolishness. "You think I'm stupid? Why would I bury her where someone could find her? I'm not even sure I can find her after all these years."

Robbie anticipated this and didn't miss a beat. "Then we need to take your statement, by video, and quickly."

"Okay. I'm ready."

They walked to the conference room, where Carlos was waiting with a camera and a court reporter. Boyette was directed to a chair facing the camera. The court reporter sat to his right, Robbie to his left. Carlos worked the camera. The other members of the firm suddenly materialized—Robbie wanted them as witnesses—and they stood with Keith ten feet away. Boyette looked at them and was suddenly nervous. He felt like a man facing his own, well-attended execution. The court reporter asked him to raise his right hand and swear to tell the truth. He did, and then Robbie began the questioning. Name, place of birth, address, employment, current status as a parolee, and criminal record. He asked if Boyette was giving his statement voluntarily. Nothing had been promised. Was he living in Slone in December 1998? Why? How long?

Robbie's questions were gentle but efficient. Boyette looked squarely at the camera, no flinching or blinking, and seemed to warm to the task. Oddly, the tic went away.

Tell us about Nicole.

Boyette thought for a second and then launched into his narrative. The football games, the fascination with Nicole, the obsession, the stalking, and finally the abduction outside the mall, not a single witness anywhere. On the floor of his truck, he put a gun to her head and threatened to kill her if she made a sound, then he bound her wrists and ankles with duct tape. He taped her mouth. He drove somewhere into the country, he was not sure where, and after he raped her the first time, he almost dumped her in a ditch, injured but not dead, but wanted to rape her again. They left Slone. The cell phone in her handbag kept ringing and ringing so he finally stopped at a bridge over the Red River. He took her cash, credit card, and driver's license, then threw the handbag off the bridge. They drifted through southeastern Oklahoma. Just before sunrise, near Fort Smith, he saw a cheap motel he'd stayed in before, alone. He paid cash for a room and, with a gun to her head, got her inside without being seen. He taped her wrists, ankles, and mouth again and told her to go to sleep. He slept a few hours, not sure if she did. They spent a long day at the motel. He convinced her that if she would cooperate, give him what he wanted, then he would release her. But he already knew the truth. After dark, they moved on, headed north. At daybreak on Sunday, they were south of Joplin, in a heavily wooded, remote area. She begged him, but he killed her anyway. It wasn't easy, she fought hard, scratched him, drew blood. He stuffed her body in a large toolbox and buried it. No one would ever find her. He drove back to Slone and got drunk.

Robbie was taking notes. The court reporter pressed the keys of her stenotype machine. No one else moved. No one seemed to breathe.

Boyette went silent, his story complete. His detached narration and his command of details were chilling. Martha Handler would later write: "Watching Boyette's eyes and face as he talked about his crimes left no doubt that we were in the presence of a ruthless killer. The story that we will never know, and perhaps prefer not to know, is the suffering this poor girl endured throughout the ordeal."

Robbie, calm but also anxious to finish the testimony, pressed on: "Approximately what time on Sunday did you kill her?"

"The sun was barely up. I waited until I could see things, see where I was, and find the best place to hide her."

"And this was Sunday, December 6, 1998?"

"If you say so. Yes."

"So sunrise would be around 6:30 a.m.?"

"That sounds about right."

"And you returned to Slone and went where?"

"I went to my room at the Rebel Motor Inn, after I'd bought a case of beer with the cash I took from Nicole."

"You got drunk at the Rebel Motor Inn?"

"Yes."

"How long did you live in Slone after the murder?"

"I don't know, maybe a month and a half. I was arrested here in January, you got the records. After I got outta jail, I took off."

"After you killed her, when did you hear that Donté Drumm had been arrested?"

"Don't know exactly. I saw it on television. I saw you yelling at the cameras."

"What did you think when he was arrested?"

Boyette shook his head and said, "I thought, what a bunch of idiots. That kid had nothing to do with it. They got the wrong guy."

It was a perfect place to end. Robbie said, "That's all." Carlos reached for the camera.

Robbie asked the court reporter, "How long before we have a transcript?"

"Ten minutes."

"Good. Hurry." Robbie huddled with the rest of his firm at the conference table and everyone talked at once. Boyette was forgotten for a moment, though Fred Pryor kept an eye on him. Boyette asked for water, and Pryor handed him a bottle. Keith stepped outside to call Dana and Matthew Burns and to get some fresh air. But the air wasn't refreshing; it was heavy with smoke and tension.

There was a loud thud, followed by a shriek, as Boyette fell out of his chair and hit the floor. He grabbed his head, pulled his knees to his chest, and began shaking as the seizure consumed him. Fred Pryor and Aaron Rey knelt over him, uncertain what to do. Robbie and the others crowded around, staring in horror at a fit so violent that the ancient wooden floor seemed to shake. They actually felt sorry for the man. Keith heard the commotion and joined the crowd.

"He needs a doctor," Sammie Thomas said.

"He has meds, doesn't he, Keith?" Robbie asked in a hushed tone.

"Yes."

"Have you seen this before?"

Boyette was still thrashing about, groaning pitifully. Surely the man was dying. Fred Pryor was patting him softly on the arm.

"Yes," Keith said. "About four hours ago, somewhere in Oklahoma. He vomited forever and then passed out."

"Should we take him to the hospital? I mean, look, Keith, could he be dying right now?"

"I don't know, I'm not a doctor. What else do you need from him?"

"We must have his signature on his affidavit, signed under oath." Robbie stepped back and motioned for Keith to join him. They spoke softly. Robbie continued, "And then there's the matter of finding the body. Even with his affidavit, there's no guarantee the court will stop the execution. The governor will not. Either way, we have to find the body, and soon."

Keith said, "Let's put him on the sofa in your office, turn off the lights. I'll give him a pill. Maybe he's not dying."

"Good idea."

It was 1:20 p.m.

22

Donté's first helicopter ride was intended to be his last. Courtesy of the Texas Department of Public Safety, he was moving through the air at ninety miles per hour, three thousand feet above the rolling hills, and he could see nothing below. He was wedged between two guards, thick young men scowling out the windows as if Operation Detour might have a surface-to-air missile or two in its arsenal. Up front were the two pilots, grim-faced boys thrilled with the excitement of their mission. The rocky, noisy ride made Donté nauseous, so he closed his eyes, leaned his head back against hard plastic, and tried to think of something pleasant. He could not.

He practiced his last statement, mouthing the words, though with the racket in the helicopter he could have barked them out and no one would have noticed. He thought of other inmates—some friends, some enemies, almost all guilty, but a few who claimed innocence—and how they faced their deaths.

The ride lasted twenty minutes, and when the helicopter landed at the old rodeo grounds inside Huntsville prison, a small army awaited the prisoner.

Donté, laden with chains and shackles, was practically carried by his guards to a van. Minutes later, the van pulled into an alley lined with chain-link fencing covered by a thick windscreen and topped with glistening razor wire. Donté was escorted from the van, through a gate, along a short sidewalk to a small, flat, redbrick building where Texas does its killing.

Inside, he squinted and tried to focus on his new surroundings. There were eight cells to his right, each emptying onto a short hallway. On a table, there were several Bibles, including one in Spanish. A dozen guards milled about, some chatting about the weather as if the weather were important at that moment. Donté was positioned in front of a camera and photographed. The handcuffs were removed, and a technician informed him they would now fingerprint him.

"Why?" Donté asked.

"Routine," came the response. He took a finger and rolled it on the ink pad.

"I don't understand why you need to fingerprint a man before you kill him."

The technician did not respond.

"I get it," Donté said. "You wanna make sure you got the right man, right?"

The technician rolled another finger.

"Well, you got the wrong man this time; I can assure you of that."

When the fingerprinting was over, he was led to the holding cell, one of the eight. The other seven were not used. Donté sat on the edge of the bunk. He noticed how shiny the floors were, how clean the sheets were, how pleasant the temperature. On the other side of the bars, in the hallway, were several prison officials. One stepped to the bars and said,

"Donté, I'm Ben Jeter, the warden here at Huntsville."

Donté nodded but did not stand. He stared at the floor.

"Our chaplain is Tommy Powell. He's here and he'll stay here all afternoon."

Without looking up, Donté said, "Don't need a chaplain."

"It's your call. Now listen to me because I want to tell you how things happen around here."

"I think I know what happens."

"Well, I'll tell you anyway."

After a round of speeches, each more strident than the one before, the rally lost some steam. A large mob of blacks packed around the front of the courthouse, and even spilled onto Main Street, which had been closed. When no one else took up the bullhorn, the drum corps came to life, and the crowd followed the music down Main Street, heading west, chanting, waving banners, singing "We Shall Overcome." Trey Glover assumed his role as parade master and maneuvered his SUV in front of the drummers. The rap blasted the downtown shops and cafés where the owners, clerks, and customers stood in the windows and doors. Why were the blacks so upset? The boy confessed. He killed Nicole; he said he did it. An eye for an eye.

There was no trouble, but the town seemed ready to erupt.

When Trey and the drummers came to Sisk Avenue, they turned right, not left. A left turn would have routed the march to the south, the general direction of where it started. A turn to the right meant they were headed into the white section. Still, no one had thrown anything. No threats had been made. A few police cars followed well behind, while others shadowed the march from parallel streets. Two blocks north of Main and they were in the older residential section. The noise brought people to their porches, and what they saw sent them back inside, to their gun cabinets. They also went to their phones to call the mayor and the police chief. Surely, this was disturbing the peace. What are these folks so upset about? The boy confessed. Do something.

Civitan Park was a complex of youth baseball and softball fields on Sisk, five blocks north of Main, and Trey Glover decided they had walked far enough. The drums were put aside, and the march came to an end. It was now a gathering, a volatile mix of youth, anger, and a sense of having nothing better to do for the afternoon and evening. A police captain estimated the crowd at twelve hundred, almost all under the age of thirty. Most of the older blacks had fallen aside and returned home. Cell phones confirmed details, and cars full of more young blacks headed for Civitan Park.

Across town, another crowd of angry blacks watched as the fire crews saved what was left of the Mount Sinai Church of God in Christ. Because of the quick 911 call, and the quick response, the damage was not as extensive as that inflicted on the First Baptist Church, but the sanctuary was fairly gutted. The flames had been extinguished, but the smoke still poured from the windows. With no wind, it too lingered over the town and added another layer of tension.

*   *   *

Reeva's departure for Huntsville was properly recorded. She invited some family and friends over for another gut-wrenching performance, and everybody had a good cry for the cameras. Sean Fordyce was on a jet at that moment, zipping in from Florida, and they would hook up in Huntsville for the pre-execution interview.

With Wallis, her other two children, and Brother Ronnie, there were five in her party, and for a three-hour drive that might be uncomfortable. So Reeva had prevailed upon her pastor to borrow one of the church vans, and even suggested that he do the driving. Brother Ronnie was exhausted, and emotionally spent as well, but he was in no position to argue with Reeva, not at that moment, not on "the most important day of her life." They loaded up and pulled away, Brother Ronnie behind the wheel of a ten-passenger van with "First Baptist Church of Slone, Texas" painted boldly on both sides. Everyone waved at the friends and well-wishers. Everyone waved at the camera.

Reeva was crying before they reached the outskirts of town.

After fifteen minutes in the quiet darkness of Robbie's office, Boyette rallied. He stayed on the sofa, his mind numb from pain, his feet and hands still wobbly. When Keith peeked through the door, Boyette said, "I'm here, Pastor. Still alive."

Keith walked closer and asked, "How you doing, Travis?"

"Much better, Pastor."

"Can I get something for you?"

"Some coffee. It seems to help ease the pain."

Keith left and closed the door. He found Robbie and reported that Boyette was still alive. At the moment, the court reporter was transcribing Boyette's statement. Sammie Thomas and both paralegals, Carlos and Bonnie, were frantically putting together a filing that was already known as "the Boyette petition."

Judge Elias Henry walked into the office, past the receptionist, and into the conference room. "Over here," Robbie said, and led the judge into a small library. He closed the door, picked up a remote, and said, "You gotta see this."

"What is it?" Judge Henry asked as he fell into a chair.

"Just wait." He pointed the remote at a screen on a wall, and Boyette appeared. "This is the man who killed Nicole Yarber. We just taped this."

The video ran for fourteen minutes. They watched it without a word.

"Where is he?" Judge Henry asked when the screen went dark.

"In my office, on the sofa. He has a malignant brain tumor, or so he says, and he's dying. He walked into the office of a Lutheran minister in Topeka, Kansas, Monday morning and spilled his guts. He played some games, but the minister finally got him in a car. They arrived in Slone a couple of hours ago."

"The minister drove him here?"

"Yep. Hang on." Robbie opened the door and called Keith over. He introduced him to Judge Henry. "This is the man," Robbie said, patting Keith on the back. "Have a seat. Judge Henry is our circuit court judge. If he had presided over the trial of Donté Drumm, we wouldn't be here right now."

"A pleasure to meet you," Keith said.

"Sounds like you're having quite an adventure."

Keith laughed and said, "I don't know where I am or what I'm doing."

"Then you've come to the right law firm," Judge Henry said. They shared a laugh, a quick one, and then all humor vanished.

"What do you think?" Robbie asked Judge Henry.

The judge scratched his cheek, thought hard for a moment, and then said, "The question is, what will the court of appeals think? You can never tell. They hate these last-minute surprise witnesses who pop up and begin changing facts that are ten years old. Plus, a man who's made a career out of aggravated rape is not likely to be taken seriously. I'd give you a slight chance of getting a stay."

"That's a lot more than we had two hours ago," Robbie said.

"When do you file? It's almost two o'clock."

"Within the hour. Here's my question. Do we tell the press about Mr. Boyette? I'm sending the video to the court and to the governor. I can also give it to the local TV station, or I can send it to every station in Texas. Or, better yet, I can arrange a press conference here or at the courthouse and let the world listen as Boyette tells his story."

"To what benefit?"

"Maybe I want the world to know that Texas is about to execute the wrong man. Here's the killer, listen to him."

"But the world cannot stop the execution. Only the courts or the governor can do that. I'd be careful here, Robbie. There's smoke in the air now, and if people see Boyette on television, claiming responsibility, this place could blow up."

"It's blowing up anyway."

"You want a race war?"

"If they kill Donté, yes. I wouldn't mind a race war. A small one."

"Come on, Robbie. You're playing with dynamite here. Think strategically, not emotionally. And keep in mind that this guy could be lying. This would not be the first execution where a fraud claimed responsibility. The press can't resist it. The nut gets on television. Everybody looks stupid."

Robbie was pacing, four steps one way, four steps the other. He was fidgety, frantic, but still thinking clearly. He had great admiration for Judge Henry, and Robbie was smart enough to know he needed advice at that moment.

The room was quiet. On the other side of the door, the voices were tense, the phones were ringing.

Judge Henry said, "I assume it's not possible to search for the body."

Robbie shook his head and deferred to Keith, who said, "Not now. Two days ago, Tuesday I think it was, I'm not sure—I feel as though I've lived with this guy for a year—but anyway, Tuesday I suggested the best way to stop the execution was to find the body. He said that it would be difficult. He buried her nine years ago in a secluded area that is heavily wooded. He also said that he's gone back to visit her several times—I'm not sure what that meant, and I really didn't want to pursue it. Then I lost contact with him. I searched and searched and I was determined to somehow corral him and insist that we notify the authorities, here and in Missouri, if that is in fact where Nicole is buried, but he would not agree. Then we lost contact again. He's a strange guy, very strange. He called me around midnight last night; I was already in bed, sound asleep, and he said he wanted to come here, to tell his story, to stop the execution. I felt as though I had no choice. I've never done anything like this before, I can promise you that. I know it's wrong to help a convict violate his parole, but so be it. Anyway, we left Topeka around 1:00 this morning, and again I suggested that we notify the authorities and at least begin the search for the body. He wanted no part of that."

"It would not have worked, Keith," Robbie said. "The authorities here are useless. They would laugh at you. They have their man, the case is solved. Almost closed, I guess. Nobody in Missouri would lift a finger because there is no active investigation. You can't just call a sheriff and suggest that he and his boys go out in the woods and start digging somewhere down by the creek. It doesn't work that way."

"Then who looks for the body?" Keith asked.

"I guess we do."

"I'm going home, Robbie. My wife is barking at me. My lawyer friend thinks I'm crazy. I think I'm crazy. I've done my best. Boyette's all yours. I'm sick of the guy."

"Relax, Keith. I need you right now."

"For what?"

"Just hang around, okay? Boyette trusts you. Besides, when was the last time you had front-row seats at a race riot?"

"Not funny."

"Sit on the video, Robbie," Judge Henry said. "Show it to the court and to the governor, but don't make it public."

"I can control the video, but I cannot control Mr. Boyette. If he wants to talk to the press, I can't stop him. God knows he's not my client."

*   *   *

By 2:30 Thursday afternoon, every church in Slone, black and white, was being guarded by preachers, deacons, and Sunday school teachers, all men, all heavily armed and visible. They sat on the front steps and chatted anxiously, shotguns across their knees. They sat under shade trees near the streets, waving at the passing cars, many of which honked in solidarity. They patrolled the rear doors and back property, smoking, chewing, watching for any movement. There would be no more church burnings in Slone.

The cotton gin had been abandoned two decades earlier when a newer one replaced it east of town. It was an eyesore, a badly decaying old building, and under normal circumstances a good fire would have been welcomed. The 911 call was recorded at 2:44. A teenager driving by saw heavy smoke and called on her cell phone. The beleaguered firemen rushed to the old gin, and by the time they arrived, the flames were roaring through the roof. Since it was an empty, abandoned building, and not a great loss anyway, they took their time.

The black smoke boiled into the sky. The mayor could see it from his second-story office, near the courthouse, and after consulting with the chief of police, he called the governor's office. The situation in Slone was not likely to improve. The citizens were in danger. They needed the National Guard.

23

The petition was finished just before 3:00 p.m., and with Boyette's affidavit included, it ran for thirty pages. Boyette swore in writing that he was telling the truth, and Sammie Thomas e-mailed the petition to the Defender Group's office in Austin. The staff there was waiting. It was printed, copied twelve times, and handed off to Cicely Avis, who sprinted from the office, hopped in her car, and raced across town to the offices of the Texas Court of Criminal Appeals. The petition was filed at 3:35.

"What's this?" the clerk asked, holding a disc.

"It's a video of a confession by the real murderer," Cicely replied.

"Interesting. I assume you want the judges to see this fairly soon."

"Right now, please."

"I'll get it done."

They chatted for a second, and Cicely left the office. The clerk immediately delivered the petition to the offices of the nine judges. In the chief justice's office, he spoke to the law clerk and said, "You might want to watch the video first. Some guy just confessed to the murder."

"And where is this guy?" asked the clerk.

"He's in Donté Drumm's lawyer's office in Slone, according to the Defender Group lawyer."

"So Robbie Flak's found him a new witness?"

"Looks like it."

As Cicely Avis left the TCCA offices, she detoured two blocks and drove past the State Capitol. The "Rally for Donté" was drawing a nice crowd on the south lawn. Police were everywhere. A permit had been issued, and the First Amendment appeared to be working.

The crowd, almost all black, was streaming in. The permit was valid for three hours, from 3:00 p.m. to 6:00 p.m., the moment of execution, but it was obvious things were behind schedule—in Austin, but certainly not in Huntsville.

The governor was in a meeting, an important one, one that had nothing to do with Donté Drumm. At 3:11, the video was received by an assistant who handled the requests for reprieves, and she watched all fourteen minutes of it before she could decide what to do next. While she found Boyette somewhat believable and chilling, she was skeptical because of his background and the timing of his sudden desire to come clean. She went to find Wayne Wallcott, the governor's lawyer and close friend, and described the video.

Wallcott listened closely, then shut the door of his office and told her to sit down. "Who has seen this video?" he asked.

"Only me," the assistant answered. "It was

e-mailed from Mr. Flak's office, with a pass code. I watched it immediately and here I am."

"And it's a full confession?"

"Oh yes, with lots of details."

"And you believe this guy?"

"I didn't say that. I said he seems to know what he's talking about. He's a serial rapist, and he was in Slone when the girl disappeared. It's a full confession."

"Does he mention Drumm?"

"Why don't you just watch the video?"

"I didn't ask for any suggestions, did I?" Wallcott snapped. "Just answer my questions."

"Sorry." The assistant took a breath. She was suddenly nervous and uneasy. Wallcott was listening, but he was also scheming. "He mentioned Drumm only to say that he's never met him and he had nothing to do with the crime."

"He's obviously lying. I'm not bothering the governor with this, and I want you to keep the video to yourself. I don't have the time to look at it. Neither does the governor. You understand?"

She did not, but she nodded anyway.

Wallcott narrowed his eyes and frowned. "You do understand, don't you?" he asked gravely. "This video stays in your computer."

"Yes, sir."

As soon as she left, Wallcott practically jogged to the office of Barry Ringfield, the governor's chief spokesman and closest friend. The office suite was crawling with staff and interns, so they took a stroll down the hall.

After a few minutes of discussing their options, they agreed that the governor would not see the video. If Boyette was lying, then the video would be irrelevant and the right man was executed. But if Boyette was telling the truth, which they strongly doubted, and the wrong man was executed, the fallout could be messy. The only way to protect Governor Gill Newton was for one of them, or perhaps the assistant, to take the fall by admitting they sat on, or maybe even lost, the video. Gill Newton had never granted a reprieve in a death case, and with the thrilling attention being stirred up by the Drumm case, he was not about to back down now. Even if he watched the video, and even if he believed Boyette, he would not retreat.

Wayne and Barry walked to the governor's office. They were expected there promptly at 4:00 p.m., two hours before the execution, and they would not tell the governor about the video.

At 3:30 p.m., the Flak Law Firm gathered once again around the main conference table. All were present and accounted for, including Keith, who, though fighting the worst fatigue of his life, was finding it hard to believe he had somehow acquired a ticket to this circus. He and Judge Henry sat away from the table, against a wall. Aaron Rey and Fred Pryor read newspapers on the other side of the room. Travis Boyette was still alive, still resting in the dark on Robbie's sofa.

It was past time for Robbie to leave for Huntsville, and the strain was showing. But he couldn't leave yet. The Boyette petition had energized the team and given them hope.

Robbie worked from a checklist. Yellow legal pad, as always. Sammie Thomas and Bonnie would track the Boyette petition before the court of appeals, and also continue to press the governor's office on the reprieve. Gill Newton had yet to grant or deny, and he usually waited until the last moment. He loved the drama and attention. Carlos would track the insanity petition, which was still with the Fifth Circuit in New Orleans. If denied there, they would appeal to the U.S. Supreme Court. Fred Pryor would remain at the office and tend to Boyette. No one knew what to do with Boyette, but he didn't appear to be leaving. As always, Aaron Rey would accompany Robbie to Huntsville. Martha Handler would also go, to observe and record. Robbie barked orders, answered questions, refereed conflicts, and then suddenly looked at the reverend and asked, "Keith, can you go with us to Huntsville?"

For a few seconds, the reverend couldn't speak. "Why, Robbie?" he managed to ask.

"Donté might need you."

Keith's mouth fell open and no words came out. The room was quiet, all eyes on Keith. Robbie pressed on: "He was raised in a church, Keith, but he now takes a dim view of religion. His jury had five Baptists, two Pentecostals, one Church of Christ, and I guess the others were lost. Over the past few years, he's come to believe that white Christians are the reason he's on death row. He wants no part of their God, and I don't expect him to change his views anytime soon. Still, at the very end, he might appreciate someone to pray with."

What Keith wanted was a nice bed in a clean motel and twelve hours of sleep. But, as a man of God, he couldn't say no. He nodded slowly and said, "Sure."

"Good. We'll leave in five minutes."

Keith closed his eyes and rubbed his temples and

said to himself, "Lord, what am I doing here? Help me."

Fred Pryor suddenly jumped from his chair. He held his cell phone at arm's length, as if it were white-hot, and said loudly, "Oh, boy! It's Joey Gamble. He wants to sign the affidavit and recant his testimony."

"Is he on the phone?" Robbie said.

"No. It's a text message. Should I call him?"

"Of course!" Robbie snapped. Pryor stepped to the center of the table and pressed the keys on the speakerphone. No one moved as the phone rang and rang. Finally, a timid "Hello."

"Joey, Fred Pryor here, in Slone, just got your message, what the hell's going on?"

"Uh, I wanna help, Mr. Pryor. I'm really upset by all this."

"You think you're upset, what about Donté? He's got two and a half hours to live, and now you finally wake up and want to help."

"I'm so confused," Joey said.

Robbie leaned forward and took charge. "Joey, this is Robbie Flak. Remember?"

"Of course."

"Where are you?"

"Mission Bend, in my apartment."

"Are you willing to sign an affidavit admitting that you lied at Donté's trial?"

With no hesitation, Joey said, "Yes."

Robbie closed his eyes and dropped his head. Around the table, there were silent fist pumps, quick prayers of thanks, and a lot of tired smiles.

"All right, here's the plan. There's a lawyer in Houston by the name of Agnes Tanner. Her office is downtown on Clay Street. Do you know the city?"

"I guess."

"Can you find an office downtown?"

"I don't know. I'm not sure I should drive."

"Are you drunk?"

"Not drunk, but I've been drinking." Robbie instinctively glanced at his watch. Not yet 4:00 p.m. and the boy was already thick tongued.

"Joey, call a cab. I'll reimburse you later. It's crucial that you get to Tanner's office as quickly as possible. We'll e-mail an affidavit, you sign it, and we'll get it filed in Austin. Can you do this, Joey?"

"I'll try."

"It's the least you can do, Joey. Right now Donté is in the holding cell in Huntsville, thirty feet from the little room where they kill people, and your lies helped put him there."

"I'm so sorry." His voice cracked.

"The office is at 118 Clay Street, you got that, Joey?"

"I think so."

"Get there, Joey. The paperwork will be waiting for you. Every minute is crucial, Joey, do you understand?"

"Okay, okay."

"Call us back in ten minutes."

"You got it."

After the call ended, Robbie barked orders and everyone scrambled. As he headed for the door, he said, "Let's go, Keith." They jumped in the van, with Martha Handler racing to keep up with them, and Aaron Rey sped away. Robbie called Agnes Tanner in Houston and urgently confirmed the details.

Keith leaned forward and looked at Aaron in the rearview mirror. "Someone said it's a three-hour drive to Huntsville."

"It is," Aaron replied. "But we're not driving."

The Slone Municipal Airport was two miles east of town. It had one runway, west to east, four small hangars, the usual collection of old Cessnas in a row on the deck, and a square metal building for the terminal. They parked, ran through the tiny lobby area, nodded at a deckhand behind the desk, and stepped onto the tarmac, where a shiny twin-engine King Air was waiting. It was owned by a wealthy lawyer friend of Robbie's who was an avid pilot. He got them on board, locked the door, made them fasten their seat belts, then strapped himself in and began flipping switches.

Keith had not talked to his wife in several hours, and things were happening so fast he wasn't sure where to begin. Dana answered during the first beep, as if she'd been staring at her cell phone. The engines started, and the cabin was suddenly loud and shaking. "Where are you?" she asked.

"In an airplane, leaving Slone, flying to Huntsville to meet Donté Drumm."

"I can barely hear you. Whose airplane?"

"A friend of Robbie Flak's. Look, Dana, I can't hear you either. I'll call you when we land in Huntsville."

"Please be careful, Keith."

"Love you."

Keith was facing the front of the plane, his knees almost touching Martha Handler's. He watched the pilot run through the checklist as they taxied away to the runway. Robbie, Martha, and Aaron were all on the phone, and Keith wondered how they could carry on a conversation amid the racket. At the end of the runway, the King Air did a 180 and pointed west. The pilot revved the engines, the plane shook harder and harder as if it might explode, then the pilot yelled,

"Hold on," and released the brakes. They jerked forward, and all four passengers closed their eyes. Within seconds, they were in the air. The landing gear folded with a thud, but Keith had no idea what he was hearing. In the blur of the moment, he realized that he had never before flown in a small airplane.

Nor had he ever been to Texas, chauffeured a serial rapist and murderer, listened to his chilling confession, witnessed the chaos of a law firm trying to save an innocent man, gone four days with virtually no sleep, picked up a speeding ticket in Oklahoma, or said yes to an invitation to pray with a man minutes before his death.

They flew over Slone at two thousand feet and climbing. The old cotton gin was still burning, thick smoke boiling into a cloud.

Keith closed his eyes again and tried to convince himself that he was where he was and doing what he was doing. He was not convinced. He prayed and asked God to take his hand and guide him now, because he had no idea what to do. He thanked God for this rather unusual situation and acknowledged that only divine intervention could be responsible for it. At five thousand feet, his chin hit his chest, the fatigue finally taking its toll.

The bourbon was usually Knob Creek, but on special occasions the really fine stuff was pulled out of the drawer. A shot each of Pappy Van Winkle's, and all three smacked their lips. They were starting a bit early, but the governor said he needed a stiff one. Barry and Wayne had never said no. They had their coats off, sleeves rolled up, ties loosened, busy men with a lot on their minds. They stood near a credenza in a corner, sipping, watching the rally on a small television. If they had opened a window, they could have heard the noise. One long-winded speaker after another delivered scathing attacks on the death penalty, racism, and the Texas judicial system. The term "judicial lynching" was used freely. So far, every speaker had demanded that the governor stop the execution. Capitol security estimated the crowd at ten thousand.

Behind the governor's back, Barry and Wayne exchanged nervous glances. If the crowd could see the video, a riot would break out. Should they tell him? No, maybe later.

"Gill, we need to make a decision about the National Guard," Barry said.

"What's happening in Slone?"

"As of thirty minutes ago, they've burned two churches, one white and one black. Now an abandoned building is on fire. They canceled classes this morning at the high school after fights broke out. The blacks are marching and roaming the streets, looking for trouble. One brick was thrown through the rear window of a police car, but so far there's been no other violence. The mayor is scared and thinks the town could blow up after the execution."

"Who's available?"

"The unit in Tyler is getting ready and can be deployed within an hour. Six hundred guardsmen. That should be enough."

"Do it and issue a press release."

Barry darted from the office. Wayne took another sip and with hesitation said, "Gill, should we at least have the conversation about a thirty-day stay? Let things cool off a bit."

"Hell no. We can't back down just because the

blacks are upset. If we show weakness now, then they'll get louder next time. If we wait thirty days, then they'll just start this crap again. I'm not blinking. You know me better than that."

"Okay, okay. Just wanted to mention it."

"Don't mention it again."

"You got it."

"Here he is," the governor said and took a step closer to the television.

The crowd roared as the Reverend Jeremiah Mays took the podium. Mays was currently the loudest black radical roaming the country and was quite adept at somehow wedging himself into every conflict or episode where race was an issue. He raised his hands, called for quiet, and launched into a flowery prayer in which he beseeched the Almighty to look down upon the poor misguided souls running the State of Texas, to open their eyes, to grant them wisdom, to touch their hearts so that this grave injustice could be stopped. He asked for the hand of God, for a miracle, for the rescue of their brother Donté Drumm.

When Barry returned, he refilled the shot glasses, his hands visibly shaking. The governor said, "Enough of this nonsense," and hit the mute button. "Gentlemen," he said, "I want to watch it one more time." They had watched "it" together several times, and with each viewing all lingering doubts were erased. They walked to the other side of the office, to another television, and Barry picked up the remote.

Donté Drumm, December 23, 1998. He was facing the camera, a can of Coke and an uneaten doughnut on the table in front of him. No one else could be seen. He was subdued, tired, and frightened. He spoke slowly, in a monotone, his eyes never looking directly into the camera.

Off camera, Detective Drew Kerber said,

"You've been read your Miranda rights, correct?"

"Yes."

"And you're giving this statement of your own free will, no threats, no promises of any kind, right?"

"That's right."

"Okay, tell us what happened on Friday night, December 4, nineteen days ago."

Donté leaned forward on his elbows and looked as though he might pass out. He picked a spot on the table, stared at it, spoke to it. "Well, me and Nicole had been sneaking around, having sex, having a good time."

"How long had this been going on?"

"Three or four months. I liked her, she liked me, things were getting serious, and she got scared because she was afraid people would find out. We started to fight some, she wanted to break it off, I didn't want to. I think I was in love with her. Then she wouldn't see me anymore, and this drove me crazy. All I could think about was her, she was so fine. I wanted her more than anything in the world. I was obsessed. I was crazy, couldn't stand to think that somebody else might have her. So that Friday night, I went looking for her. I knew where she liked to hang out. I saw her car at the mall, over on the east side of the mall."

"Excuse me, Donté, but I believe you said earlier that her car was parked on the west side of the mall."

"That's right, the west side. So I waited and waited."

"And you were driving a green Ford van, owned by your parents?"

"That's right. And I guess it was around ten o'clock Friday night, and—"

Kerber said, "Excuse me, Donté, but you said earlier that it was closer to eleven."

"That's right, eleven."

"Go ahead, you were in the green van, looking for Nicole, and you saw her car."

"That's right, I was really wanting to see her, and so we were driving around, looking for her car, and—"

"Excuse me, Donté, but you said 'we' were driving around, you said earlier—"

"Yeah, me and Torrey Pickett were—"

"But you said earlier that you were alone, that you had dropped Torrey off at his mother's house."

"That's right, sorry about that. At his mother's house, right. And so I was by myself at the mall and I saw her car and I parked and waited. When she came out, she was alone. We talked for a minute, and she agreed to get in the van. We used the van a few times on dates, when we were sneaking around. And so I drove and we talked. We both got upset. She was determined to break up, and I was determined to stay together. We talked about running away together, to get out of Texas, go to California, where nobody would bother us, you know. But she wouldn't listen to me. She started crying, and that made me start crying. We parked behind Shiloh Church, out on Travis Road, one of our places, and I said I *wanted to have sex one last time. At first, she seemed okay with it, and we started making out. Then she pulled away, said stop it, said no, said she wanted to get back because her friends would be looking for her, but I couldn't stop. She started pushing me away, and I got mad, real mad, just all of a sudden I hated her because she was pushing me away, because I couldn't have her. If I was white, then I could have her, but because I'm not, then I'm not good enough, you know. We started fighting, and at some point she realized that I was not going to stop. She didn't resist, but she didn't give in either. When it was over, she got mad, real mad. She slapped me and said I'd raped her. And then, something just happened, I snapped or something, I don't know, but I just went crazy. She was still under me, and I, uh, well ... I hit her, and I hit her again, and I couldn't believe I was hitting that beautiful face, but if I couldn't have her, then nobody else could either. I just went into a rage, like some kinda wild man, and before I realized what I was doing, my hands were around her neck. I just shook her and shook her, and then she was still. Everything was very still. When I came to my senses, I just looked at her, and at some point I realized she wasn't breathing.* [Donté took the first sip and only sip from the Coke can.] *I started driving around; I had no idea where to go. I kept waiting for her to wake up, but she didn't. I'd call back there, but she wouldn't answer. I guess I panicked. I didn't know what time it was. I drove north, and when I realized the sun was coming up, I panicked again. I saw a sign for the Red River. I was on Route 344, and—"*

"Excuse me, Donté, but you said earlier it was Route 244."

"That's right: 244. I drove onto the bridge, it was still dark, no other car lights anywhere, not a sound, and I got her out of the back of the van and tossed her into the river. When I heard her splash, it made me sick. I remember crying all the way back home."

The governor stepped forward and punched the off button. "Boys, that's all I need to see. Let's go." All three straightened their ties, buttoned their cuffs, put on their jackets, and walked out of the office. In the hallway, they were met with a security detail, one beefed up for the occasion. They took the stairs down to the street level and walked quickly to the Capitol. They waited, unseen by the crowd, until the Reverend Jeremiah Mays finished his incendiary remarks. The crowd roared when he signed off, vowing revenge. When their governor suddenly appeared at the podium, the mood changed remarkably. For a moment, those present were confused, but when they heard the words "I'm Gill Newton, governor of the great State of Texas," they drowned him out in an avalanche of boos.

He yelled back, "Thank you for coming here and expressing your First Amendment right to assemble. God bless America." Even louder boos. "Our country is great because we love democracy, the greatest system in the world." Loud boos for democracy. "You've assembled here today because you believe Donté Drumm is innocent. Well, I'm here to tell you he is not. He was convicted in a fair trial. He had a good lawyer. He confessed to the crime." The boos and whistles and angry shouts were now continuous, and Newton was forced to yell into the microphone. "His case has been reviewed by dozens of judges, sitting on five different courts, state and federal, and every ruling against him has been unanimous."

When the roar became too loud to continue, Newton stood and smirked at the crowd, a man with power facing those with none. He nodded, acknowledging their hatred of him. When the noise subsided slightly, he leaned closer to the microphone and, with as much drama as he could muster and knowing full well that what he was about to say would play on every evening and late newscast in Texas, said, "I refuse to grant a reprieve to Donté Drumm. He is a monster. He is a guilty man!"

The crowd roared again and pressed forward. The governor waved and saluted for the cameras and stepped away. He was swarmed by his security team and whisked away to safety. Barry and Wayne followed, neither able to suppress a smile. Their man had just pulled off another beautiful stunt, one that would no doubt win every election from then on.

24

The last meal, the last walk, the last statement. Donté had never understood the significance of these final details. Why the fascination with what a man consumed just before he died? It wasn't as though the food gave comfort, or strengthened the body, or postponed the inevitable. The food, along with the organs, would soon be flushed out and incinerated. What good did it do? After feeding a man gruel for decades, why pamper him with something he might enjoy just before you kill him?

He could vaguely recall the early days on death row and his horror of what he was supposed to eat. He'd been raised by a woman who appreciated and enjoyed the kitchen, and though Roberta relied too heavily on grease and flour, she also grew her own vegetables and was careful with processed ingredients. She loved to use herbs, spices, and peppers, and her chickens and meats were highly seasoned. The first meat Donté was served on death row was allegedly a slice of pork, and completely devoid of taste. He lost his appetite the first week and never regained it.

Now, at the end, he was expected to order a feast and be thankful for this one last favor. As silly as it was, virtually all condemned men gave thought to the final meal. They had so little else to think about. Donté had decided days earlier that he wanted to be served nothing that even remotely resembled dishes his mother once prepared. So he ordered a pepperoni pizza and a glass of root beer. It arrived at 4:00 p.m., rolled into the holding cell on a small tray by two guards. Donté said nothing as they left. He'd been napping off and on throughout the afternoon, waiting on his pizza, waiting on his lawyer. Waiting on a miracle, though by 4:00 p.m. he'd given up.

In the hallway, just beyond the bars, his audience watched without a word. A guard, a prison official, and the chaplain who'd tried twice to talk to him. Twice Donté had rejected the offers of spiritual counseling. He wasn't sure why they watched him so closely, but presumed it was to prevent a suicide. How he might go about killing himself wasn't clear, not in this holding cell. If Donté could have committed suicide, he would have done so months earlier. And now he wished he had. He would already be gone, and his mother could not watch him die.

For a palate neutralized by tasteless white bread, bland applesauce, and an endless stream of "mystery meats," the pizza was surprisingly delicious. He ate it slowly.

Ben Jeter stepped to the bars and asked, "How's the pizza, Donté?"

Donté did not look at the warden. "It's fine," he said softly.

"Need anything?"

He shook his head no. I need a lot of things, pal,

not a damned one of which you can provide. And if you could, you wouldn't. Just leave me alone.

"I think your lawyer's on the way."

Donté nodded and picked up another slice.

At 4:21, the Fifth Circuit Court of Appeals in New Orleans denied relief under Donté's claim of mental illness. The Flak Law Firm immediately filed in the U.S. Supreme Court a petition for a writ of certiorari, or cert, as it's known; a request that the Court hear the appeal and consider the merits of the petition. If cert was granted, the execution would be stopped, and time would pass while the dust settled and briefs were filed. If cert was denied, the claim would be dead, and so would the claimant, in all likelihood. There was no other place to appeal.

At the Supreme Court Building in Washington, the "death clerk" received the cert petition electronically and distributed it to the offices of the nine justices.

There was no word on the Boyette petition pending before the Texas Court of Criminal Appeals.

When the King Air landed in Huntsville, Robbie called the office and was informed of the adverse ruling in the Fifth Circuit. Joey Gamble had not yet found his way to the law office of Agnes Tanner in Houston. The governor had denied a reprieve, in spectacular fashion. There were currently no new fires in Slone, but the National Guard was on the way. A depressing phone call, but then Robbie had expected little else.

He, Aaron, Martha, and Keith jumped into a minivan driven by an investigator Robbie had used before, and they raced off. The prison was fifteen minutes away. Keith called Dana and tried to explain what was happening in his life, but the explanation got complicated, and others were listening. She was beyond bewildered and certain that he was doing something stupid. He promised to call back in a few moments. Aaron called the office and talked to Fred Pryor. Boyette was up and moving about, but slowly. He was complaining because he had not talked to any reporters. He expected to tell his side of the story to everyone, and it seemed as if no one wanted to hear him. Robbie was frantically trying to reach Joey Gamble, with no luck. Martha Handler took her usual pages of notes.

At 4:30, Chief Justice Milton Prudlowe convened the Texas Court of Criminal Appeals, by teleconference, to consider the Boyette petition in the case of Donté Drumm. The court had not been impressed with Boyette. The general feeling was that he was a publicity seeker with serious credibility issues. After a brief discussion, he called the roll. The vote was unanimous; not a single judge voted to grant relief to Donté Drumm. The clerk of the court e-mailed the decision to the attorney general's office, the lawyers fighting Donté's appeals; to Wayne Wallcott, the governor's lawyer; and to the law office of Robbie Flak.

The van was almost at the prison when Robbie got the call from Carlos. Though he'd been reminding himself throughout the afternoon that relief was unlikely, he still took it hard. "Sons of bitches!" he snapped. "Didn't believe Boyette. Denied, denied, denied, all nine of them. Sons of bitches."

"What happens next?" Keith asked.

"We run to the U.S. Supreme Court. Let 'em see

Boyette. Pray for a miracle. We're running out of options."

"Did they give a reason?" Martha asked.

"Nope, they don't have to. The problem is that we want desperately to believe Boyette, and they, the chosen nine, have no interest in believing him. Believing Boyette would upset the system. Excuse me. I gotta call Agnes Tanner. Gamble's probably in a strip club getting plastered while a lap dancer works him over."

There were no strippers, no stops or detours, just a couple of wrong turns. Joey walked into the law office of Agnes Tanner at 4:40, and she was waiting at the door. Ms. Tanner was a hard-nosed divorce lawyer who, when bored, occasionally volunteered for a capital murder defense. She knew Robbie well, though they had not spoken in over a year.

She was holding the affidavit and, after a tense "Nice to meet you," led Joey to a small meeting room. She wanted to ask him where he had been, why it took so long, whether he was drunk, if he realized they were out of time, and why he lied nine years ago and had sat on his fat ass ever since. She wanted to grill him for an hour, but there was no time; plus, he was moody and unpredictable, according to Robbie.

"You can read this, or I'll tell you what it says," she said, waving the affidavit.

Joey sat in a chair, buried his face in his hands, and said, "Just tell me."

"It gives your name, address, all that crap. It says you testified at the trial of Donté Drumm on such and such date in October 1999; that you gave crucial testimony on behalf of the prosecution, and in your testimony you told the jury that on the night of Nicole's disappearance, at about the same time, you saw a green Ford van driving suspiciously through the parking lot where her car was parked, and that the driver appeared to be a black male, and that the van was very similar to the one owned by Donté Drumm. There are a lot more details, but we don't have time for details. Are you with me, Joey?"

"Yes." His eyes were covered, and he appeared to be crying.

"You now recant that testimony and swear that it was not true. You're saying that you lied at trial. Got that, Joey?"

He nodded his head in the affirmative.

"And it goes on to say that you made the anonymous phone call to Detective Drew Kerber in which you informed him that Donté Drumm was the killer. Again, lots of details, but I'll spare you. I think you understand all this, Joey, don't you?"

He uncovered his face, wiped tears, and said, "I've lived with this for a long time."

"Then fix it, Joey." She slapped the affidavit on the table and thrust a pen at him. "Page five, bottom right. Quickly."

He signed the affidavit, and after it was notarized, it was scanned and e-mailed to the Defender Group office in Austin. Agnes Tanner waited for a confirmation, but it bounced back. She called a lawyer at the Defender Group—it had not been received. There had been some problems with their Internet server. Agnes sent it again, and again it was not received. She barked at a clerk who began faxing the five pages.

Joey, suddenly neglected, left the office without being noticed. He at least expected someone to say thanks.

*   *   *

The prison in Huntsville is called the Walls Unit. It's the oldest prison in Texas, built the old way with tall, thick brick walls, thus the name. Its storied history includes the incarcerations of once-famous outlaws and gunslingers. Its death chamber has been used to execute more men and women than any other state. The Walls Unit is proud of its history. A block of the oldest cells has been preserved and presents a step back in time. Tours can be arranged.

Robbie had been there twice before, always hurried and burdened and disinterested in the history of the Walls Unit. When he and Keith walked in the front door, they were met by Ben Jeter, who managed a smile. "Hello, Mr. Flak," he said.

"Hello, Warden," Robbie said grimly, grabbing his wallet. "This is Donté's spiritual adviser, the Reverend Keith Schroeder." The warden shook hands cautiously. "Wasn't aware that Drumm had a spiritual adviser."

"Well, he does now."

"Okay. Give me some ID."

They handed Jeter their driver's licenses, and he gave them to a guard behind a counter. "Follow me," he said.

Jeter had been the warden at the Walls Unit for eleven years, and every execution belonged to him. It was a duty he assumed but didn't ask for; it was just part of the job. He was noted for his detachment and professionalism. All movements were precise, all details followed without variation. Texas was so efficient in its death work that other states sent over prison officials for consultation. Ben Jeter could show them precisely how it should be done.

He had asked 298 men and 3 women if they had any last words. Fifteen minutes later, he declared them all dead.

"What about the appeals?" he asked, one step ahead of Robbie, two ahead of Keith, who was still in a daze. They were zipping down a hallway, its walls lined with fading black and whites of former wardens and dead governors.

"Doesn't look good," Robbie said. "Couple of balls in the air, but nothing much."

"So you think we'll go at six?"

"I don't know," Robbie said, unwilling to offer much.

"Go at six," Keith said to himself. As if they were catching a flight or waiting for a kickoff.

They stopped at a door and Jeter waved a card. It opened and they stepped outside, walked twenty feet, then entered the death house. Keith's heart was pounding, and he was so dizzy he needed to sit down. Inside, he saw bars, rows of bars in a dimly lit block of cells. There were guards in the way, two men in bad suits, the warden, all looking at the holding cell.

"Donté, your lawyer is here," Jeter announced, as if he were delivering a gift. Donté rose to his feet and smiled. Metal clanged, the door slid open, and Donté took a step. Robbie grabbed him, clutched him, whispered something in his ear. Donté squeezed his lawyer, the first real human contact in almost a decade. Both were crying when they separated.

Next to the holding cell was the visiting cell, a space identical except for a wall of glass behind the bars that allowed privacy as the lawyer met with his client for the last time. The rules allowed one hour of visitation. Most condemned men saved a few minutes for the last prayer with the prison chaplain. The rules

stated that the hour of visitation ran from 4:00 p.m.
to 5:00 p.m., leaving the inmate all alone at the end.
Warden Jeter, though a stickler for the rules, knew
when to bend them. He also knew that Donté
Drumm had been a model prisoner, unlike many, and
that meant a lot in his business.

Jeter tapped his watch and said, "It's 4:45, Mr.
Flak, you have sixty minutes."

"Thank you."

Donté entered the visiting cell and sat on the edge
of the bed. Robbie followed him and sat on a stool. A
guard closed the glass door, then rolled the bars in
place.

They were alone, knees touching; Robbie put a
hand on Donté's shoulder and worked to keep his
composure. He had agonized over whether he should
bring up Boyette. On the one hand, Donté had probably accepted the inevitable and, with an hour to go,
was ready for whatever stood beyond. He certainly
seemed to be at peace. Why upset him with a wild
new story? On the other hand, Donté might appreciate knowing that the truth would finally be known.
His name would be cleared, even though posthumously. The truth, though, was far from certain, and
Robbie decided not to mention Boyette.

"Thanks for coming, Robbie," Donté said in a
whisper.

"I promised I'd be here until the end. I'm sorry I
couldn't stop this, Donté, I'm truly sorry."

"Come on, Robbie, you did the best you could.
You're still fighting, aren't you?"

"Oh yes. We have some last-minute appeals still
out there, so there's a chance."

"How much of a chance, Robbie?"

"A chance. Joey Gamble has admitted he lied at

trial. He got drunk last night in a strip club and admitted everything. We secretly recorded it, and filed a petition this morning. The court turned us down. Then around 3:30 this afternoon, Joey contacted us and said he wants to admit everything."

Donté's only reaction was to slowly shake his head in disbelief.

"We're trying to file another petition, one that includes his sworn affidavit, and it gives us a chance."

They were hunched over, their heads almost touching, speaking in whispers. There was so much to say, and so little. Robbie was bitter at the system, angry to the point of violence, burdened by his lack of success in defending Donté, but most of all he was, at that moment, just sad.

For Donté, the brief stay in the holding cell was confusing. Ahead, not thirty feet away, was a door that led to death, a door he preferred not to open. Behind him was death row and the maddening existence of isolation in a cell he preferred to never see again. He thought he was ready for the door, but he was not. Nor did he wish to ever see Polunsky again.

"Don't beat yourself up, Robbie. I'll be all right."

Keith, with permission, stepped outside and tried to breathe. It had snowed Monday morning in Topeka; now it felt like eighty degrees in Texas. He leaned against a fence and stared at the razor wire above him.

He called Dana and told her where he was, what he was doing, what he was thinking. She seemed as astonished as he was.

With the Drumm matter out of the way, Chief Justice Milton Prudlowe left his office and hurried to the

Rolling Creek Country Club in west-central Austin. He had a 5:00 p.m. tennis match with a major contributor to his last, and next, campaigns. In traffic, his cell phone rang. The clerk of the court informed him that they had received a call from the Defender Group, and that another petition was in the works.

"What time do you have?" Prudlowe demanded.

"Four forty-nine."

"I get so tired of this crap," Prudlowe said. "We close at five, and everybody knows it."

"Yes, sir," the clerk said. The clerk knew quite well that Justice Prudlowe despised the last-minute Hail Marys thrown by desperate defense lawyers. The cases drag on for years with little activity, then with hours to go, the lawyers suddenly shift into high gear.

"Any idea what they're filing?" Prudlowe asked.

"I think it's the same thing they filed this morning—an eyewitness is recanting. They're having trouble with their computers."

"Gee, that's original. We close at five, and at five I want the door locked, and not a minute after. Understand?"

"Yes, sir."

At 4:45, Cicely Avis and two paralegals left the Defender Group offices with the petition and Gamble's affidavit. All twelve copies. As they sped through traffic, Cicely called the clerk's office with the heads-up that they were on the way. The clerk informed her that the office would close at five, the usual time, five days a week.

"But we have a petition that includes a sworn affidavit from the only eyewitness at trial," she insisted.

"I think we've already seen that one," the clerk said.

"You have not! This has a sworn statement."

"I just talked to the chief justice. We close at five."

"But we'll be a few minutes late!"

"We close at five."

Travis Boyette was sitting by a window in the conference room, cane across his knees, watching the chaos of frantic people yelling at each other. Fred Pryor was close by, also watching.

Unable to make sense of what was happening, Boyette stood and approached the table. "Can anybody tell me what's going on?" he asked.

"Yep, we're losing," Carlos snapped at him.

"What about my statement? Is anybody listening to me?"

"The answer is no. The court was not impressed."

"They think I'm lying?"

"Yes, Travis, they think you're lying. I'm sorry. We believe you, but we don't have a vote."

"I want to talk to the reporters."

"I think they're busy chasing fires."

Sammie Thomas looked at her laptop, scribbled down something, and handed it to Boyette. "This is the cell phone number of one of our local TV idiots." She pointed to a table near the television. "That is a telephone. Feel free to do whatever you want, Mr. Boyette." Travis shuffled over to the phone, punched the numbers, and waited. He was being watched by Sammie, Carlos, Bonnie, and Fred Pryor.

He held the receiver and stared at the floor. Then he flinched, and said, "Uh, yes, is this Garrett? Okay, look, my name is Travis Boyette, and I'm down at the law office of Robbie Flak. I was involved in the murder of Nicole Yarber, and I'd like to go on the air and make a confession." Pause. The tic. "I want to confess to the murder of the girl. Donté Drumm had nothing to do with it." Pause. The tic. "Yes, I want to say that on the air, and I have a lot more to say as well." The others could almost hear the frantic thrill in Garrett's voice. What a story!

Boyette said, "Okay," and hung up. He looked around the conference room and said, "They'll be here in ten minutes."

Sammie said, "Fred, why don't you take him out front, somewhere near the landing, and find a good spot."

Boyette said, "I can leave if I want to, right? I don't have to stay here?"

"You're a free man as far as I'm concerned," Sammie said. "Do whatever you want. I really don't care."

Boyette and Pryor left the conference room and waited outside the train station.

Carlos took the call from Cicely Avis. She explained that they arrived at the court at 5:07, the doors were locked, the offices closed. She called the clerk's cell phone. The clerk said he was not there, he was in fact driving home.

Donté's final petition would not be filed.

According to club records, Chief Justice Milton Prudlowe and his guest played tennis on court 8 for an hour, beginning at 5:00 p.m.

25

Paul Koffee's cabin was on a small lake ten miles south of Slone. He'd owned it for years and used it as an escape, a hiding place, a fishing hole. He'd also used it as a love nest during his romp with Judge Vivian Grale, an unfortunate episode that led to an ugly divorce that almost led to the loss of the cabin. His ex-wife got their home instead.

After lunch on Thursday, he left his office and drove to the cabin. The town was in a meltdown, it was beginning to feel dangerous, the phone was ringing nonstop, and no one in his office was even attempting to appear productive. He escaped the frenzy and was soon in the peaceful countryside, where he prepared for a party he'd thrown together a week earlier. He iced down the beer, stocked the bar, puttered around the cabin, and waited for his guests. They began arriving before 5:00 p.m.—most had left work early—and everyone needed a drink. They gathered on a deck near the edge of the water—retired lawyers, active lawyers, two assistant prosecutors in Koffee's office, an investigator, and other assorted friends, almost all of whom had some connection to the law.

Drew Kerber and another detective were there. Everyone wanted to talk to Kerber, the cop who broke the case. Without his skillful interrogation of Donté Drumm, there would have been no conviction. He'd found the bloodhounds that picked up Nicole's scent in the green Ford van. He'd deftly manipulated a jailhouse snitch into obtaining yet another confession from their suspect. Good, solid police work. The Drumm case was Kerber's crowning moment, and he intended to savor its final moments.

Not to be outdone, Paul Koffee commanded his share of attention. He would retire in a few years, and in his old age he would have something to brag about. Against a ferocious defense mounted by Robbie Flak and his team, Koffee and his boys had fought on, fought for justice, fought for Nicole. The fact that he had gotten his prized death verdict without a body was even more reason to gloat.

The booze loosened the tension. They howled with laughter at the story of their beloved governor shouting down a black mob and calling Drumm a monster. Things were a bit quieter when Koffee described the petition, filed hardly two hours ago, in which some nut claimed to be the killer. But have no fear, he assured them, the court of appeals had already denied relief. Only one other appeal was in play, a bogus one—"hell, they're all bogus"—but it was as good as dead in the Supreme Court. Koffee happily assured his guests that justice was on the verge of prevailing.

They swapped stories about the church burnings, the cotton gin fire, the growing mob in Civitan Park, and the coming of the cavalry. The National Guard was expected by 6:00 p.m., and there was no shortage of opinions about whether it was actually needed.

Koffee was barbecuing chicken on a grill, breasts and thighs coated with a thick sauce. But the treat of the night, he announced, would be "Drumm sticks." A chorus of laughter echoed across the lake.

Huntsville is also the home of Sam Houston State University. The school has an enrollment of sixteen thousand—81 percent white, 12 percent black, 6 percent Hispanic, and 1 percent other.

Late Thursday afternoon, many of the black students were drifting toward the prison, some eight blocks away in central Huntsville. Operation Detour may have failed in its attempt to block roads, but it would not fail in its efforts to raise a little hell. The streets closer to the prison were sealed off by Texas state troopers and Huntsville police. The authorities were expecting trouble, and security around the Walls Unit was tight.

The black students gathered three blocks from the prison and began making noise. When Robbie stepped out of the death house to work the phone, he heard in the distance the organized chanting of a thousand voices. "Donté! Donté!" He could see nothing but the exterior walls of the death house and chain-link fencing, but he could tell the crowd was close.

What difference did it make? It was too late for protests and marches. He listened for a second, then called the office. Sammie Thomas answered by blurting, "They wouldn't let us file the Gamble petition. They locked the doors at 5:00 p.m., Robbie, and we got there seven minutes late. They knew we were coming too."

His first impulse was to launch the phone against the nearest brick wall and watch it shatter into a thousand pieces, but he was too stunned to move. She went on, "The Defender Group called the clerk a few minutes before five. They were actually in a car racing to file. Clerk said too bad, said he'd talked to Prudlowe and the office closed at five. Are you there, Robbie?"

"Yes, no. Go on."

"Nothing left but the cert petitions before the Supremes. No word yet."

Robbie was leaning on a chain-link fence, trying to steady himself. A tantrum would not help matters now. He could throw things and curse and maybe file lawsuits tomorrow, but he needed to think. "I don't expect any help from the Supreme Court, do you?" he asked.

"No, not really."

"Well, then, it's almost over."

"Yes, Robbie, that's the feeling around here."

"You know, Sammie, all we needed was twenty-four hours. If Travis Boyette and Joey Gamble had given us twenty-four hours, we could've stopped this damned thing, and there's a very good chance Donté would one day walk out of here. Twenty-four hours."

"Agreed, and speaking of Boyette, he's outside waiting for a TV crew. He called them, not us, though I did give him the number. He wants to talk."

"Let him talk, damn it. As of now, let him tell the world. I don't care. Is Carlos ready with the video blast?"

"I think so."

"Then turn him loose. I want every big newspaper and television station in the state to get the video right now. Let's make as much noise as possible. If we're going down, then let's go down in flames."

"You got it, Boss."

Robbie listened to the distant chants for a moment while staring at his phone. Who could he call? Was there anyone in the world who could help?

Keith flinched when the metal bars closed behind him. This was not his first prison visit, but it was the first time he'd been locked in a cell. His breathing was labored and his colon was in knots, but he had prayed for strength. It was a very short prayer: God, please give me courage and wisdom. Then please get me out of here.

Donté did not rise when Keith entered the visitors' cell, but he did smile and offer a hand. Keith shook it, a soft, passive handshake. "I'm Keith Schroeder," he said as he sat on the stool, his back to the wall, his shoes inches from Donté's.

"Robbie said you were a good guy," Donté said. He seemed to concentrate on Keith's collar, as if to confirm that he was in fact a minister.

Keith's voice froze as he thought about what to say. A grave "How are you doing?" seemed ludicrous. What do you say to a young man who will die in less than an hour, whose death is certain, and could be avoided?

You talk about death. "Robbie tells me you didn't want to talk to the prison chaplain," Keith said.

"He works for the system. The system has persecuted me for nine years, and it will soon get what it wants. So I concede nothing to the system."

Makes perfect sense, Keith thought. Donté was sitting straighter, his arms folded across his chest, as though he would welcome a good debate about religion, faith, God, heaven, hell, or anything else Keith wanted to discuss.

"You're not from Texas, are you?" Donté asked.

"Kansas."

"The accent. Do you believe the state has the right to kill people?"

"No."

"Do you think Jesus would approve of the killing of inmates for retribution?"

"Of course not."

"Does 'Thou shalt not kill' apply to everybody, or did Moses forget the exemption for state governments?"

"The government is owned by the people. The commandment applies to everyone."

Donté smiled and relaxed a little. "Okay, you pass. We can talk. What's on your mind?"

Keith breathed a little easier, pleased to have survived the entrance exam. He half expected to meet a young man without all of his mental assets, and he was wrong. Robbie's noisy claim that Donté had been driven insane by death row seemed misguided.

Keith plunged ahead. "Robbie tells me you were raised in a church, baptized at an early age, had a strong faith, raised by parents who were devout Christians."

"All true. I was close to God, Mr. Schroeder, until God abandoned me."

"Please call me Keith. I read a story about a man who once sat right here, in this cell, his name was Darrell Clark, young man from West Texas, Midland, I think. He'd killed some people in a drug war, got convicted and sent to death row, at the old unit at

Ellis. While he was on death row, someone gave him a Bible, and someone else shared a Christian testimony. Clark became a Christian and grew very close to the Lord. His appeals ran out, and his execution date was set. He embraced the end. He looked forward to death because he knew the exact moment when he would enter the kingdom of heaven. I can't think of another story quite like Darrell Clark's."

"What's your point?"

"My point is you're about to die, and you know when it will happen. Very few people know this. Soldiers in battle may feel like dead men, but there's always a chance they'll survive. I suppose some victims of horrible crimes know they're at the end, but they have such short notice. You, though, have had this date for months. Now the hour is at hand, and it's not a bad time to make amends with God."

"I know the legend of Darrell Clark. His final words were 'Father, into your hands I commit my spirit.' Luke 23, verse 46, the last words of Jesus before he died on the cross, according to Luke anyway. But you're missing something here, Keith. Clark killed three people, execution style, and after they convicted him, he never made a serious claim of innocence. He was guilty. I am not. Clark deserved to be punished, not to be killed, but imprisoned for life. Me, I am innocent."

"True, but death is death, and in the end nothing else matters except your relationship with God."

"So you're trying to convince me that I should go running back to God here at the last minute, and just sort of forget the past nine years."

"You blame God for the past nine years?"

"Yes, I do. This is what happened to me, Keith. I

was eighteen years old, a longtime Christian, still active in church, but also doing some things that most kids do, nothing bad, but, hell, when you grow up in a house as strict as mine, you're gonna rebel a little. I was a good student, the football thing was on hold, but I wasn't running drugs and beating people. I stayed off the streets. I was looking forward to college. Then, for some reason I guess I'll never understand, a bolt of lightning hits me square in the forehead. I'm wearing handcuffs. I'm in jail. My picture is on the front page. I'm declared guilty long before the trial. My fate is determined by twelve white people, half of them good, solid Baptists. The prosecutor was a Methodist, the judge was Presbyterian, or at least their names were on church rolls somewhere. They were also screwing each other, but I guess we all have a weakness for flesh. Most of us anyway. Screwing each other, yet pretending to give me a fair trial. The jury was a bunch of rednecks. I remember sitting in the courtroom, looking at their faces as they condemned me to death—hard, unforgiving, Christian faces—and thinking to myself, 'We don't worship the same God.' And we don't. How can God allow His people to kill so often? Answer that, please."

"God's people are often wrong, Donté, but God is never wrong. You can't blame Him."

The fight left him. The weight of the moment returned. Donté leaned forward with his elbows on his knees and hung his head. "I was a faithful servant, Keith, and look what I get."

Robbie walked in from the outside and stood by the visitors' cell. Keith's time was up. "Would you pray with me, Donté?"

"Why? I prayed the first three years I was in prison, and things just got worse. I could've prayed ten times a day, and I would still be sitting right here, talking to you."

"All right, mind if I pray?"

"Go right ahead."

Keith closed his eyes. He found it hard to pray under the circumstances—Donté staring at him, Robbie anxiously waiting, the clock ticking louder and louder. He asked God to give Donté strength and courage, and have mercy on his soul. Amen.

When he finished, he stood and patted Donté on the shoulder, still not believing that he would be dead in less than an hour. Donté said, "Thanks for coming."

"I'm honored to meet you, Donté."

They shook hands again. Then the metal clanged and the doors opened. Keith stepped out, Robbie stepped in. The clock on the wall, indeed the only clock that mattered, gave the time as 5:34.

The looming execution of a man claiming innocence did nothing to arouse the national media. The stories had become so commonplace. However, the tit-for-tat angle of the church burnings on the eve of the execution woke up a few producers. The melee at the high school added some fuel. But the possibility of a race riot—now, that was too good to be ignored. Toss in the drama of the National Guard, and by late afternoon Slone was buzzing with brightly painted television vans from Dallas and Houston and other cities, most providing direct feeds to network and cable stations. When word spread that a man claiming to be the real killer wanted to confess on camera, the train station became an instant magnet for the media. With Fred Pryor directing things, or at least attempting to keep some order, Travis Boyette stood on the bottom step of the platform and looked at the reporters and the cameras. Microphones were thrust at him like bayonets. Fred stood at his right side, actually shoving some of the reporters back.

"Quiet!" Fred barked at them. Then he nodded at Travis and said, "Go ahead."

Travis was as stiff as a deer in headlights, but he swallowed hard and plunged in. "My name is Travis Boyette, and I killed Nicole Yarber. Donté Drumm had nothing to do with her murder. I acted alone. I abducted her, raped her repeatedly, then strangled her to death. I disposed of her body, and it's not in the Red River."

"Where is it!"

"It's in Missouri, where I left it."

"Why'd you do it!"

"Because I can't stop myself. I've raped other women, lots of them, sometimes I got caught, sometimes I didn't."

This startled the reporters, and a few seconds elapsed before the next question. "So you are a convicted rapist?"

"Oh yes. I have four or five convictions."

"Are you from Slone?"

"No, but I was living here when I killed Nicole."

"Did you know her?"

Dana Schroeder had been parked in front of the television in the den for the past two hours, glued to CNN, waiting for more news from Slone. There had been two reports, brief little snippets about the unrest and the National Guard. She had watched the governor make a fool of himself. The story, though, was gathering momentum. When she saw the face of Travis Boyette, she said out loud, "There he is."

Her husband was at death row consoling the man convicted of the killing, and she was watching the one who had actually committed the crime.

Joey Gamble was in a bar, the first one he'd seen when he left the office of Agnes Tanner. He was drunk but still aware of what was happening. There were two televisions hanging from the ceiling at opposite ends of the bar, one was on SportsCenter, the other on CNN. When Joey saw the story from Slone, he walked closer to the television. He listened to Boyette as he talked about killing Nicole. "You son of a bitch," Joey mumbled, and the bartender gave him a quizzical look.

But then he felt good about himself. He had finally told the truth, and now the real killer had come forward. Donté would be spared. He ordered another beer.

Judge Elias Henry was sitting with his wife in the den of their home, not far from Civitan Park. The doors were locked; his hunting rifles were loaded and ready. A police car drove by every ten minutes. A helicopter watched from above. The air was thick with the smell of smoke—smoke from the fireworks party at the park, and smoke from the destroyed buildings. The mob could be heard. Its nonstop drumming and booming rap and screeching chants had only intensified throughout the afternoon. Judge and Mrs. Henry had discussed leaving for the night. They had a son in Tyler, an hour away, and he had encouraged them to flee, if only for a few hours. But they decided to stay, primarily because the neighbors were staying and there was strength in numbers. The judge had chatted with the chief of police, who somewhat nervously assured him that things were under control.

The television was on, another breaking story from Slone. The judge grabbed the remote and turned up the volume, then there was the man he'd seen in the video, not three hours earlier. Travis Boyette was talking, giving details, staring at a bunch of microphones.

"Did you know the girl?" a reporter asked.

"I'd never met her, but I had followed her. I knew who she was, knew she was a cheerleader. I picked her out."

"How did you abduct her?"

"I found her car, parked next to it, waited until she came out of the mall. I used a gun, she didn't argue. I've done this before."

"Have you been convicted in Texas before?"

"No. Missouri, Kansas, Oklahoma, Arkansas. You can check the records. I'm telling the truth here, and the truth is that I did the crime. Not Donté Drumm."

"Why are you coming forward now, and not a year ago?"

"I should have, but I figured the courts down here would finally realize they had the wrong guy. I just got out of prison in Kansas, and a few days ago I saw in the paper where they were getting ready to execute Drumm. Surprised me. So here I am."

"Right now, only the governor can stop the execution. What would you say to him?"

"I'd say you're about to kill an innocent man. You give me twenty-four hours, and I'll show you the body of Nicole Yarber. Just twenty-four hours, Mr. Governor."

Judge Henry scratched his chin with his knuckles and said, "A bad night just got worse."

Barry and Wayne were in the governor's office watching Boyette on CNN. Their governor was down the hall being interviewed for the fifth or sixth time since his courageous handling of the angry mob. "We'd better go get him," Wayne said.

"Yep. I'll go; you keep an eye on this."

Five minutes later, the governor was watching a rerun of Boyette. "He's obviously a crackpot," Newton said after a few seconds. "Where's the bourbon?"

Three glasses were filled, and the bourbon was sipped as they listened to Boyette talk about the body.

"How did you kill Nicole?" Strangled her with her belt, black leather with a round silver buckle, still around her neck. Boyette reached under his shirt and pulled out a ring. He thrust it at the cameras. "This is Nicole's. I've worn it since the night I took her, has her initials and everything."

"How did you dispose of the body?"

"Let's just say it's underground."

"How far from here?"

"I don't know, five or six hours. Again, if the governor would give us twenty-four hours, we can find it. That'll prove I'm right."

"Who is this guy?" the governor asked.

"A serial rapist, rap sheet a mile long."

"It's amazing how they always manage to pop up right before the execution," Newton said. "Probably getting money from Flak."

All three managed a nervous laugh.

*   *   *

The laughter at the lake was interrupted when a guest walked past a TV inside and saw what was happening. The party quickly moved indoors, and thirty people huddled around the small screen. No one spoke; no one seemed to breathe as Boyette went on and on, perfectly willing to answer any question with a blunt response.

"Ya'll ever hear of this guy, Paul?" asked one of the retired lawyers.

Paul shook his head no.

"He's at Flak's office, the train station."

"Robbie's up to his old tricks."

Not a smile, not a grin, not a forced chuckle. When Boyette produced her ring, and freely displayed it for the cameras, fear swept through the cabin, and Paul Koffee found his way to a chair.

The breaking news was not heard by everyone. At the prison, Reeva and her gang were gathered in a small office where they waited for the van ride to the death chamber. Not far away, the family of Donté waited too. For the next hour, the two groups of witnesses would be in close proximity to each other, but carefully separated. At 5:40, the family of the victim was loaded in a white unmarked prison van and driven to the death house, a ride that lasted less than ten minutes. Once there, they were led through an unmarked door into a small square room twelve feet long and twelve feet wide. There were no chairs, no benches. The walls were blank, unmarked. Before them was a closed curtain, and they had been told that on the other side of the curtain was the actual death chamber. At 5:45, the Drumm family made the same trip and entered their witness room through another door. The witness rooms were side by side. A loud cough in one could be heard in the other.

They waited.

26

At 5:40, the U.S. Supreme Court, by a vote of 5–4, refused to hear Donté's insanity petition. Ten minutes later, the Court, again 5–4, denied cert on the Boyette petition. Robbie took the calls outside the holding cell. He closed his phone, walked inside to Warden Jeter, and whispered, "It's over. No more appeals."

Jeter nodded grimly and said, "You got two minutes."

"Thanks." Robbie reentered the holding cell and broke the news to Donté. There was nothing else to do, the fight was over. Donté closed his eyes and breathed deeply as the reality set in. Until that moment there had always been hope, however distant, however remote and unlikely.

Then he swallowed hard, managed a smile, and inched closer to Robbie. Their knees were touching, their heads just inches apart. "Say, Robbie, you think they'll ever catch the dude who killed Nicole?"

Again, Robbie wanted to tell him about Boyette, but that story was far from over. The truth was anything but certain. "I don't know, Donté, I can't predict. Why?"

"Here's what you gotta do, Robbie. If they never find the guy, then folks will always believe it was me. But if they find him, then you gotta promise me you'll clear my name. Will you promise me, Robbie? I don't care how long it takes, but you gotta clear my name."

"I'll do that, Donté."

"I got this vision that one day my momma and my brothers and sister will stand beside my grave and celebrate because I'm an innocent man. Won't that be great, Robbie?"

"I'll be there too, Donté."

"Throw a big party, right there in the cemetery. Invite all my friends, raise all sorts of hell, let the world know that Donté is innocent. Will you do that, Robbie?"

"You have my word."

"That'll be great."

Robbie slowly took both of Donté's hands and squeezed them in his. "I gotta go, big man. I don't know what to say, except that it's been an honor being your lawyer. I have believed you from the very beginning, and I believe you even more today. I've always known you are innocent, and I hate the sons of bitches who are making this happen. I'll keep fighting, Donté. I promise."

Their foreheads touched. Donté said, "Thank you, Robbie, for everything. I'll be all right."

"I'll never forget you."

"Take care of my momma, okay, Robbie?"

"You know I will."

They stood and embraced, a long painful hug that neither wanted to end. Ben Jeter was by the door, waiting. Robbie finally left the holding cell and walked to the end of the short hallway where Keith sat in a folding chair, praying fervently. Robbie sat down beside him and began weeping.

Ben Jeter asked Donté for the last time if he wanted to see the chaplain. He did not. The hallway began to fill with uniformed guards, large healthy boys with stern faces and thick arms. The beef had arrived, just in case the inmate had second thoughts about going peacefully to the death chamber. There was a flurry of activity, and the place was filled with people.

Jeter approached Robbie and said, "Let's go." Robbie slowly got to his feet and took a step before he stopped and looked down at Keith. "Come on, Keith," he said.

Keith looked up blankly, not sure where he was, certain that his little nightmare would end soon and he'd wake up in bed with Dana. "What?"

Robbie grabbed an arm and yanked hard. "Come on. It's time to witness the execution."

"But—"

"The warden gave his approval." Another hard pull. "You're the spiritual adviser to the condemned man, thus, you qualify as a witness."

"I don't think so, Robbie. No, look, I'll just wait—"

Several of the guards were amused by the altercation. Keith was aware of their smirks, but didn't care.

"Come on," Robbie said, now dragging the minister. "Do it for Donté. Hell, do it for me. You live in Kansas, a death-penalty state. Come watch a little democracy in action."

Keith was moving, and everything was a blur. They walked by the columns of guards, past the holding cell where Donté, eyes down, was being handcuffed again, to a narrow unmarked door Keith had not noticed before. It opened and closed behind them. They were in a small boxlike room with dim lights. Robbie finally let loose of him, then walked over and hugged the Drumm family. "No more appeals," he said softly. "There's nothing left to do."

It would be the longest ten minutes in Gill Newton's lengthy career in public service. From 5:50 until 6:00 p.m., he vacillated as never before. On one side, literally on one side of his office, Wayne pushed harder and harder for a thirty-day reprieve. He argued that the execution could be delayed for thirty days, and thirty days only, while the dust settled and the claims of this Boyette clown could be investigated. If he was telling the truth, and the body could be found, then the governor would be a hero. If he turned out to be a flake, as they strongly suspected, then Drumm would live another thirty days and then get the needle. There was no long-term harm, politically. The only permanent damage would occur if they ignored Boyette, executed Drumm, then found the body exactly where Boyette took them. That would be fatal, and not just for Drumm.

The mood was so tense that they were ignoring the bourbon.

On the other side, Barry argued that any form of retreat would be nothing but a show of weakness, especially in light of the governor's performance before the mob less than three hours earlier. Executions, especially high-profile ones, attract all sorts of attention seekers, and this guy Boyette was a perfect example. He was obviously looking for the spotlight, his fifteen minutes onstage, and to allow him to derail a proper execution was wrong from a judicial point of view, and even more so from a political one. Drumm confessed to the murder, Barry said over and over. Don't let some serial pervert cloud the truth. It was a fair trial! The appeals courts, all of them, had affirmed the conviction!

Play it safe, Wayne countered. Just thirty days, maybe we'll learn something new about the case.

But it's been nine years, Barry retorted. Enough is enough.

"Are there any reporters outside?" Newton asked.

"Sure," Barry said. "They have been hanging around all day."

"Line 'em up."

The final walk was a short one, some thirty feet from the holding cell to the death chamber, the entire pathway lined with guards, some of whom watched from the corners of their eyes to see the dead man's face, others stared at the floor as if they were sentries guarding a lonely gate. One of three faces could be expected from the condemned man. The most common was a hard frown with wide eyes, a look of fear and disbelief. The second most common was a passive surrender, eyes half-open, as if the chemicals were already at work. The third and least common was the angry look of a man who'd kill every guard in sight if he had a gun. Donté Drumm did not resist; that rarely happens. With a guard holding each elbow, he marched on, his face calm, his eyes on the floor. He refused to allow his captors to see the fear he felt, nor did he wish to acknowledge them in any way.

For such a notorious room, the Texas death chamber is remarkably small, a near-square box twelve feet long and wide, with a low ceiling and a permanent metal bed in the center, adorned in clean white sheets for each occasion. The bed fills the room.

Donté could not believe how cramped it was. He sat on the edge of the bed, and four guards quickly took over. They swung his legs around, stretched them out, then methodically secured his body with five thick leather straps, one around his chest, midsection, groin, thighs, and calves. His arms were placed on extensions 45 degrees from his body and secured with more leather straps. As they prepped him, he closed his eyes, listened to and felt the urgent business about him. There were grunts and a few words, but these men knew their tasks. This was the last stop on the system's assembly line, and the workers were well experienced.

When all the straps were tightened, the guards retreated. A medical technician who smelled of antiseptic hovered and said, "I'm going to poke and find a vein, left arm first, then the right. You understand?"

"Be my guest," Donté said and opened his eyes. The technician was rubbing his arm with alcohol. To prevent infection? How thoughtful. Behind him was a darkened window, and below it was an opening from which two ominous tubes ran toward the bed. The warden was to his right, watching it all carefully, very much in charge. Behind the warden were two identical windows—the witness rooms—sealed off by curtains. If he'd been so inclined, and were it not for all the damned leather straps, Donté could've reached out and touched the nearest window.

The tubes were in place, one in each arm, though

only one would be used. The second one was a backup, just in case.

At 5:59, Governor Gill Newton hurriedly stepped in front of three cameras outside of his office and, without notes, said, "My denial of a reprieve still stands. Donté Drumm confessed to this atrocious crime and must pay the ultimate price. He received a fair trial eight years ago, by a jury of his peers, and his case has been reviewed by five different courts, dozens of judges, and all have confirmed his conviction. His claim of innocence is not believable, nor is this last-minute sensational effort by his attorneys to produce a new killer. The judicial system of Texas cannot be hijacked by some criminal looking for attention and a desperate lawyer who will say anything. God bless Texas."

He refused to answer questions and returned to his office.

When the curtains were suddenly opened, Roberta Drumm nearly collapsed at the sight of her youngest son strapped tightly to the bed with tubes running from both arms. She gasped, covered her mouth with both hands, and had Cedric and Marvin not braced her, she would have been on the floor. The shock hit all of them. They squeezed tighter together, and Robbie joined the huddle, adding support.

Keith was too stricken to move. He stood a few feet away. Some strangers were behind him, witnesses who had entered at some point, Keith wasn't sure when. They inched forward straining for a view. It was Thursday, the second one in November, and at that moment the Ladies' Bible Class was meeting in the vestry of St. Mark's Lutheran for the continuation of their study of the Gospel of Luke, to be followed by a pasta dinner in the kitchen. Keith, Dana, and the boys were always invited to the dinner and usually attended. He really missed his church, and his family, and he wasn't sure why he was having such thoughts as he stared at the very dark head of Donté Drumm. It contrasted sharply with the white shirt he was wearing and the snow-white sheets around him. The leather straps were light brown. Roberta sobbed loudly and Robbie was mumbling and the unknown witnesses behind him were pressing for a better view, and Keith wanted to scream. He was tired of praying, and his prayers weren't working anyway.

Keith asked himself if he would feel differently if Donté was guilty. He didn't think so. Guilt would certainly take away some of the sympathy for the kid, but as he watched the preliminaries unfold, he was struck by the coldness, the ruthless efficiency, the sanitized neatness of it. It was similar to killing an old dog, a lame horse, or a laboratory rat. Who, exactly, gives us the right to kill? If killing is wrong, then why are we allowed to kill? As Keith stared at Donté, he knew the image would never go away. And he knew that he would never be the same.

Robbie stared at Donté too, at the right side of his face, and thought of all the things he would have changed. In every trial, the lawyer makes a dozen snap decisions, and Robbie had relived them all. He would have hired a different expert, called different witnesses, toned down his attitude toward the judge, been nicer to the jury. He would always blame himself, though no one else did. He had failed to save an innocent man, and that burden was too heavy. A big piece of his life was about to perish also, and he doubted he would ever be the same.

Next door, Reeva wept at the sight of her daughter's killer flat on his back, helpless, hopeless, waiting to take his last breath and go on to hell. His death—quick and rather pleasant—was nothing compared to Nicole's, and Reeva wanted more suffering and pain than she was about to witness. Wallis boosted her with an arm around her shoulder. She was held by her two children. Nicole's biological father was not there, and Reeva would never let him forget it.

Donté turned hard to his right, and his mother finally came into focus. He smiled, gave a thumbs-up, then turned back and closed his eyes.

At 6:01, Warden Jeter stepped to a table and picked up a phone, a direct line to the attorney general's office in Austin. He was informed that all appeals were final; there was no reason to stop the execution. He replaced the receiver, then picked up another one, identical to the first. It was a direct line to the governor's office. The message was the same, green lights all around. At 6:06, he stepped to the bed and said, "Mr. Drumm, would you like to make a final statement?"

Donté said, "Yes."

The warden reached toward the ceiling, grabbed a small microphone, and pulled it to within twelve inches of Donté's face. "Go ahead," he said. Wires ran to a small speaker in each witness room.

Donté cleared his throat, stared at the microphone, and said, "I love my mother and my father and I'm so sad my dad died before I could say good-bye. The State of Texas would not allow me to attend his funeral. To Cedric, Marvin, and Andrea, I love ya'll and I'll see you down the road. I'm sorry I've put you through all this, but it wasn't my fault. To Robbie, I love you, man. You're the greatest. To the family of Nicole Yarber, I'm sorry about what happened to her. She was a sweet girl, and I hope someday they find the man who killed her. Then I guess you all will have to be here and do this again."

He paused, closed his eyes, then yelled, "I am an innocent man! I've been persecuted for nine years by the State of Texas for a crime I didn't do! I never touched Nicole Yarber and I don't know who killed her." He took a breath, opened his eyes, and went on. "To Detective Drew Kerber, Paul Koffee, Judge Grale, all those bigots on the jury, all those blind mice on the appeals courts, and to Governor Newton, your day of judgment is coming. When they find the real killer, I'll be there to haunt you."

He turned and looked at his mother. "Good-bye, Momma. Love you."

After a few seconds of silence, Ben Jeter pushed the microphone toward the ceiling. He took a step backward and nodded at the faceless chemist who hid behind the black window to the left of the bed. The injection began—three different doses given in quick succession. Each of the three was lethal enough if used alone. The first was sodium thiopental, a powerful sedative. Donté closed his eyes, never to reopen them. Two minutes later, a dose of pancuronium bromide, a muscle relaxer, stopped his breathing. Third was a shot of potassium chloride that stopped his heart.

With all the leather strapping, it was difficult to tell

when Donté's breathing stopped. But stop it did. At 6:19, the medical technician appeared and prodded the corpse with a stethoscope. He nodded at the warden, who announced at 6:21 that Donté Drumm was dead.

27

The curtains closed; the death chamber vanished.

Reeva hugged Wallis and Wallis hugged Reeva, and they hugged their children. The door to their witness room opened, and a prison official hurried them through it. Two minutes after the announcement of death, Reeva and her family were back in the van, whisked away with an amazing efficiency. After they left, the Drumm family was escorted through a different door, but along the same route.

Robbie and Keith were alone for a few seconds in the witness room. Robbie's eyes were wet, his face pale. He was thoroughly defeated, drained, but at the same time looking for someone to fight. "Are you glad you watched it?" he asked.

"No, I am not."

"Neither am I."

At the train station, news of Donté's death was received without a word. They were too stunned to speak. In the conference room, they stared at the television, heard the words, but still couldn't believe that the miracle had somehow slipped away. Only three hours earlier, they had been frantically working on the Boyette petition and the Gamble petition, two eleventh-hour gifts from above that seemed so hopeful. But the TCCA rejected Boyette and literally slammed the door on Gamble.

Now Donté was dead.

Sammie Thomas cried softly in one corner. Carlos and Bonnie stared at the television, as if the story might change to a happier ending. Travis Boyette sat hunched over, rubbing his head, while Fred Pryor watched him. They worried about Robbie.

Boyette suddenly stood and said, "I don't understand. What happened? Those people didn't listen to me. I'm telling the truth."

"You're too late, Boyette," Carlos snapped.

"Nine years too late," Sammie said. "You sit on your ass for nine years, perfectly willing to let someone else serve your time, and then you pop in here with five hours to go and expect everyone to listen to you."

Carlos was walking toward Boyette, pointing a finger. "All we needed was twenty-four hours, Boyette. If you had shown up yesterday, we could've searched for the body. We find the body, there's no execution. There's no execution because they got the wrong guy. They got the wrong guy because they're stupid, but also because you're too much of a coward to come forward. Donté is dead, Boyette, because of you."

Boyette's face turned crimson and he reached for his cane. Fred Pryor, though, was quicker. He grabbed Boyette's hand, looked at Carlos, and said, "Let's cool it. Everybody calm down."

Sammie's cell phone buzzed. She glanced at it and said, "It's Robbie." Carlos turned away and Boyette sat down, with Pryor close by. Sammie listened for a few minutes, then laid down the phone. She wiped a tear and said, "The press got it right for a change. He's dead. He said Donté was strong to the bitter end, proclaimed his innocence, did so very convincingly. Robbie's leaving the prison now. They'll fly back and be here around 8:00. He would like for us to wait." She paused and wiped her face again.

The National Guardsmen had just fanned out through the streets around Civitan Park in the white section and Washington Park in the black section when the news hit that Donté had been executed. The crowd in Civitan Park had grown steadily throughout the afternoon, in both size and volume, and it immediately pressed outward toward the guardsmen. The soldiers were taunted, cursed, insulted, a few rocks were thrown, but the violence, seething just under the surface, was suppressed. It was near dark, and there was little doubt that nighttime would see the situation deteriorate. In Washington Park, the crowd was older and made up primarily of neighbors. The younger, rowdier ones headed across town, where trouble was more likely.

Homes were locked, vigils commenced on front porches, and weapons were at the ready. The sentries stepped up their patrols at every church in Slone.

Ten miles to the south, the mood was much merrier at the cabin. Huddled around the television, fresh drinks in hand, they grinned smugly when death was confirmed. Paul Koffee toasted Drew Kerber, then

Drew Kerber toasted Paul Koffee. Glasses clinked together. The discomforting hesitation they had felt with that Boyette thing was quickly forgotten. At least for the moment.

Justice had finally prevailed.

Warden Jeter walked Robbie and Keith back to the front of the prison, shook their hands, said goodbye. Robbie thanked him for his thoughtfulness. Keith wasn't sure if he wanted to thank him or insult him—his last-second approval of Keith as a witness had led to a horrific experience—but he was gracious anyway, as was his nature. When they stepped through the front door, they saw where the noise was coming from. To the right, three blocks away, and on the other side of a wall of police and state troopers, students were yelling and waving homemade banners and placards. They were packed together in the middle of a street that had been cordoned off. Beyond them, traffic was backed up. A wave of cars had tried to reach the prison, and when they were blocked, their drivers simply got out and joined the crowd. Operation Detour had planned to choke the prison with people and vehicles, and the plan was working. The goal of preventing the execution had not been reached, but Donté's supporters had at least been mobilized, and they had been heard.

Aaron Rey was waiting on the sidewalk, waving Keith and Robbie over. "We've found an escape route," he said. "This place is ready to blow up." They hurried to the minivan and took off. The driver began darting through side streets, dodging parked cars and angry students. Martha Handler studied Robbie's face, but he did not make eye contact.

"Can we talk?" she asked.

He shook his head no. Keith did the same. Both closed their eyes.

A Huntsville funeral home had the contract. One of its black hearses was inside the Walls Unit, out of sight, and when the last of the witnesses and officials left the death house, it backed to the same gate where the vans had come and gone. A collapsible gurney was pulled out, extended, and rolled inside to the death chamber, where it was wedged tightly next to the bed where Donté lay motionless and unrestrained. The tubes had been removed and recoiled into the dark room where the chemist, still unseen, was filling out his paperwork. On the count of three, four guards lifted the corpse gently and placed it on the gurney, where it was once again strapped, but not as tightly this time. A blanket, owned by the funeral home, was tucked over him, and when all was in place, the gurney was rolled back to the hearse. Twenty minutes after the pronouncement of death, the body was leaving the Walls Unit, through a different route, to avoid the protesters and cameras.

At the funeral home, the body was taken to a prep room. Mr. Hubert Lamb and his son, Alvin, owners of Lamb & Son Funeral Home, Slone, Texas, were waiting. They would embalm the body at their place in Slone, on the same table where they had prepared Riley Drumm five years earlier. But Riley had been an old man of fifty-five when he passed, his body shrunken and decayed, and his death had been anticipated. It could be explained. His son's could not. As men who dealt in death, constantly handling corpses, the Lambs figured they had seen it all. But they were taken aback by the sight of Donté lying peacefully on the gurney, his face content, his body undisturbed, a young man of twenty-seven. They had known him since he was a boy. They had cheered for him on the football field and, like all of Slone, expected a long, glorious career. They had whispered and gossiped with the rest of the town when he was arrested. They were stunned by the confession, and quick to believe Donté when he immediately recanted. The Slone police, and Detective Kerber in particular, were not trusted on their side of town. The boy was tricked; they beat a confession out of him, just like in the old days. They watched with frustration as he was tried and convicted by a white jury, and after he was sent away, they, like the rest of the town, half expected the girl's body to show up, or maybe even the girl herself.

With the help of two others, they lifted Donté from the gurney and gently placed him in a handsome oak casket selected by his mother on Monday. Roberta had paid a small deposit—she had burial insurance—and the Lambs were quick to agree to a full refund if the casket became unnecessary. They would have happily forgone the use of it. They had prayed they would not be where they were at that moment—collecting the body, then driving it home, then preparing for a painful wake, memorial, and funeral.

The four men wrestled the casket into the Lamb & Son hearse, and at 7:02 Donté left Huntsville and headed home.

*　*　*

The *Fordyce—Hitting Hard!* set was in a small "ballroom" in a cheap chain motel on the fringe of Huntsville. Reeva and Wallis were perched on director's chairs and made up for the cameras while Sean Fordyce stomped around in his usual manic mode. He'd just "jetted" in from an execution in Florida, barely made it to Huntsville, but so glad he did because the Nicole Yarber case had become one of his best ever. In preliminary chitchat, as the technicians worked frantically on the sound, the lighting, the makeup, the script, Fordyce realized that Reeva had not yet heard about the appearance of Travis Boyette. She had been inside the prison, preparing for the big event, when the story broke. Instinctively, he decided not to tell her. He would save it for later.

The post-execution interview was the most dramatic segment of his show. Catch 'em just minutes after they've watched the bastard die and they might say anything. He snapped at a technician, cursed a cameraman, yelled that he was ready to go. A final dusting of powder on his forehead, then an instant change of demeanor as he looked at the camera, smiled, and became a man of great compassion. With tape running, he explained where he was, gave the time, the hour, the gravity of the moment, then he walked to Reeva and said, "Reeva, it's over. Tell us what you saw."

Reeva, a Kleenex in each hand—she'd gone through a box since lunch—dabbed her eyes and said, "I saw him, for the first time in eight years, I saw the man who killed my baby. I looked him in the eyes, but he would not look at me." Her voice was strong, no breakdown yet.

"What did he say?"

"He said he was sorry, and I appreciate that."

Fordyce leaned in closer, frowning. "Did he say he was sorry for killing Nicole?"

"Something like that," she said, but Wallis shook his head and glanced at his wife.

"You disagree, Mr. Pike?"

"He said he was sorry for what happened, not sorry for anything he did," Wallis grunted.

"Are you sure?" Reeva fired back at her husband.

"I'm sure."

"That's not what I heard."

"Tell us about the execution, the dying," Fordyce pleaded.

Reeva, still pissed at Wallis, shook her head and wiped her nose with a Kleenex. "It was much too easy. He just went to sleep. When they opened the curtains, he was already on the little bed in there, all strapped down, looking very much at peace. He made his last statement, then he closed his eyes. We couldn't tell anything, nothing, no sign that the drugs had been administered, nothing. He just went to sleep."

"And you were thinking about Nicole and how horrible her death must have been?"

"Oh, God, yes, exactly, my poor baby. She suffered greatly. Just terrible..." Her voice choked and the camera zoomed even closer.

"Did you want him to suffer?" Fordyce asked, prodding, prompting.

She nodded vigorously, her eyes closed. Fordyce asked Wallis, "What changes now, Mr. Pike? What does this mean for your family?"

Wallis thought for a second, and while he was

thinking, Reeva blurted, "It means a lot, knowing he's dead, knowing he's been punished. I think I'll sleep better at night."

"Did he claim to be innocent?"

"Oh yes," Reeva said, the tears gone for the moment. "Same old stuff we've been hearing for years. 'I'm an innocent man!' Well, now he's a dead man, that's all I can say."

"Have you ever thought that he might be innocent, that someone else might have killed Nicole?"

"No, not for a minute. The monster confessed."

Fordyce pulled back a little. "Have you heard of a man named Travis Boyette?"

A blank face. "Who?"

"Travis Boyette. At 5:30 this afternoon, he went on television in Slone and claimed to be the killer."

"Nonsense."

"Here's the tape," Fordyce said, pointing to a twenty-inch screen off to the right. On cue, the video of Travis Boyette appeared. The volume was high; the rest of the set was perfectly still. As he talked, Reeva watched closely, frowning, almost smirking, then shaking her head no. An idiot, a fraud. She knew who the killer was. But when Boyette pulled out the class ring, shoved it at the cameras, and said he had kept it for nine years, Reeva's face turned pale, her jaw dropped, her shoulders slumped.

Sean Fordyce may have been a noisy proponent of the death penalty, but like most cable screamers he never let ideology get in the way of a sensational story. The possibility that the wrong man had just been executed would undoubtedly strike a blow against capital punishment, but Fordyce couldn't have cared less. He was smack in the middle of the hour's hottest story—number two on CNN's home page—and he planned to make the most of it.

And he saw nothing wrong with ambushing his own guest. He'd done it before, and he would do it again if it produced great drama.

Boyette vanished from the screen.

"Did you see the ring, Reeva?" Fordyce boomed.

Reeva looked as though she'd seen a ghost. Then she collected herself and remembered that everything was being filmed. "Yes," she managed to say.

"And is it Nicole's?"

"Oh, there's no way to tell. Who is this guy and where did he come from?"

"He's a serial rapist with a rap sheet a mile long, that's who he is."

"Well, there. Who can believe him?"

"So you don't, Reeva?"

"Of course not." But the tears were gone, as was the spunk. Reeva appeared confused, disoriented, and very tired. As Fordyce moved in for another question, she said, "Sean, it's been a long day. We're going home."

"Yes, sure, Reeva, just one more question. Now that you've seen an execution, do you think they should be televised?"

Reeva yanked the mike off her jacket and bounced to her feet. "Come on, Wallis. I'm tired."

The interview was over. Reeva, Wallis, and their two children walked out of the motel with Brother Ronnie behind them. They piled into the church van and headed for Slone.

At the airport, Keith called Dana with the latest update on his little road trip. He was free-falling now, with no idea where he was going and not sure where he'd been. When he explained, gently, that he had just witnessed the execution, she was speechless. So was he. The conversation was brief. She asked if he was okay, and he replied that he definitely was not.

The King Air lifted off at 7:05 and was soon in heavy clouds. The plane dipped and lurched, much like an old truck on a bumpy road. "Moderate turbulence" the pilot had called it as they boarded. With the noise of the engines, the sense of being tossed about, and the mind-bending blur of images from the past two hours, Keith found it easy to close his eyes and withdraw into his own little cocoon.

Robbie was withdrawn too. He sat forward, elbows on knees, chin in hand, eyes closed, deep in thought and painful memories. Martha Handler wanted to talk, to take notes, to capture the moment fully, but there was no one to interview. Aaron Rey stared nervously out the window, as if waiting for a wing to break off.

At five thousand feet, the ride smoothed somewhat and the cabin noise died down. Robbie reclined in his seat and smiled at Martha. "What were his last words?" she asked.

"He loves his momma and he's an innocent man."

"Is that all?"

"That's enough. There's a Web site for the Texas death row, an official one, and they post all of the last statements. Donté's will be up by noon tomorrow. It was beautiful. He called 'em by name, the bad guys—Kerber, Koffee, Judge Grale, the governor. Beautiful, just beautiful."

"So he went down fighting?"

"He was not able to fight, but he did not give an inch."

* * *

The car was an old Buick owned by an old widow, Ms. Nadine Snyderwine, and it was parked beside her modest home on a concrete pad, under a willow oak. She drove it three times a week, max, and with her failing eyesight she knew her driving days were numbered. Ms. Snyderwine had never worked outside the home, never met a lot of people, and certainly never provoked anyone. Her car was chosen because it was accessible and, more important, because it was parked on a quiet, dark street in a very white part of town. The Buick was unlocked, not that a lock would have mattered. The driver's door was opened, a Molotov cocktail was lit and tossed inside, and the arsonists disappeared into the night without a trace. A neighbor saw flames, and the 911 call was recorded at 7:28.

If there was a chance that the old Buick's wiring shorted, that the car somehow ignited on its own, such thoughts were dashed when the second 911 call came at 7:36. Another car was on fire, a Volvo wagon parked on a street halfway between the courthouse and Civitan Park. Fire trucks screamed back and forth across town, with police escorts clearing the way. The sirens were applauded by the mob at the park, a mob that was growing larger as the night grew later. But aside from underage drinking and possession of pot, no crimes were being committed. Yet. Perhaps disturbing the peace, but given the tension of the moment, the police were not inclined to enter the park and break up the fun. The crowd was in a belligerent mood, fueled by the news of Donté's death, the statements of Travis Boyette, the angry rap blasting from car stereos, and some drugs and alcohol.

The police watched and pondered their options. They huddled with the National Guardsmen and plotted strategy. The wrong move could provoke a response that was unpredictable, primarily because the crowd had no real leader at that point and had no idea where the night would lead it. Every half hour or so, some clown lit a string of firecrackers, and for a split second the policemen and guardsmen froze and strained to tell if the noise was gunfire. So far, only firecrackers.

The third call was recorded at 7:40, and it was the most ominous so far. In fact, when the police chief got the details, he thought about leaving town himself. At Big Louie's honky-tonk west of town, the gravel parking lot was packed as usual for a Thursday night, the unofficial beginning of the weekend. To kick things off, Louie offered a variety of drink specials, all involving reduced prices, and the Bubbas responded with enthusiasm. Of the vehicles parked outside the cheap metal building, virtually all were pickup trucks, an even split between Ford and Chevrolet. The arsonists picked one of each, broke the windows, tossed the cocktails, and disappeared into the darkness. A latecomer, in a pickup, thought he saw a "coupla black boys" running away, crouching low, very suspicious. But he wasn't close and didn't see their faces. In fact, he wasn't even sure they were black.

When the Bubbas stampeded outside and saw flames roaring out of both trucks, they scrambled for their own. A melee ensued, a near demolition derby, as they frantically tried to get away from the fires. Many of them left, evidently no longer thirsty and anxious to get home, lock the doors, get the guns loaded. Every pickup at Big Louie's had at least one gun under the seat or in the glove box. Many had hunting rifles in the window racks.

It was the wrong crowd to start a fight with. You burn a man's pickup, and he's ready for war.

28

By eight o'clock, the drumsticks were gone, too much booze had been consumed, and most of Koffee's guests were anxious to get home and see how bad things were in town. The television crews were darting around, trying to keep up with the arsonists, and the fires effectively ended the celebration by the lake. Drew Kerber hung around, stalling, waiting for everyone to leave. He opened another beer and said to Paul Koffee, "We need to talk."

They walked to the edge of the narrow dock, as far away from the cabin as possible, though no one else was there. Koffee also had a bottle of beer. They leaned on the railing and looked at the water below them.

Kerber spat, sipped his beer, and said, "This guy Boyette, does he worry you?"

Koffee appeared to look surprised, or at least attempted to. "No, but he obviously worries you."

A long, slow pull on the beer, and Kerber said, "I grew up in Denton, and there were some Boyettes in the neighborhood. Ted Boyette was a good friend, finished high school together, then he joined the Army and disappeared. I heard he got into some trouble, but I moved away, ended up here, and sort of forgot about him. You know how it is with childhood friends, you don't ever forget them, but you don't ever see them either. Anyway, in January 1999, and I remember the month because we had Drumm locked up, I was at the station and some of the other guys were laughing about a thug they'd caught in a stolen pickup. They ran his record; guy's got three convictions for sexual assault. A registered sex offender in three states, and he was only in his mid-thirties. The cops were wondering, what's the record? Which pervert is registered in the most states? Someone asked his name. Someone else said, 'T. Boyette.' I didn't say a word, but I was curious as to whether it might be the kid from our neighborhood. I checked his file, saw his name was Travis, but I was still curious. A couple of days later, he was led into the courtroom for a quick appearance before the judge. I didn't want him to see me, because if it had been my old pal, I didn't want to embarrass him. The courtroom was busy, it was easy to not be noticed. But it wasn't him. It was Travis Boyette, the same guy who is in town right now. I recognized him the second I saw him on television—same slick head, same tattoo on the left side of his neck. He was here, Paul, in Slone, in jail, at approximately the same time the girl disappeared."

Koffee thought hard for a few seconds, then said, "Okay, assume he was here. That doesn't mean he's telling the truth about killing her."

"What if he is telling the truth?"

"You can't be serious."

"Humor me, Paul. What if? What if Boyette is telling the truth? What if Boyette really has the girl's ring? What if Boyette takes them to the body? What if, Paul? Help me here. You're the lawyer."

"I'm not believing this."

"Can we face charges?"

"For what?"

"How about murder?"

"Are you drunk, Kerber?"

"I've had too much."

"Then sleep here, don't drive. Why aren't you in town with every other cop?"

"I'm a detective, not a street cop. And I'd like to keep my job, Paul. Hypothetically, what happens if this Boyette is telling the truth?"

Koffee drained his bottle, then tossed it into the lake. He lit a cigarette, and blew a long trail of smoke. "Nothing happens. We're immune. I control the grand jury, thus I control who gets prosecuted for what. There's never been a case of a detective or a prosecutor facing charges for a bad conviction. We are the system, Kerber. We might get sued in a civil court, but that's a long shot too. Plus, we're insured by the city. So there, stop worrying. We're Teflon."

"Would I get fired?"

"No, because that would harm you and the city in the civil suit. But they'll probably offer you early retirement. The city will take care of you."

"So we'll be okay?"

. "Yes, and please stop this, will you?"

Kerber smiled, breathed deeply, and took another long drink. "Just curious," he said. "That's all. I'm really not worried."

"Could've fooled me."

They stared at the water for a while, both lost in their thoughts, but both thinking the same thing.

Finally, Koffee said, "Boyette was in jail here, and out on parole from another state, right?"

"Right. I think it was Oklahoma, maybe Arkansas."

"Then how did he get away?"

"I don't remember everything, but I'll check the file in the morning. Seems as though he posted bond, then disappeared. I had nothing to do with the case, and as soon as I realized it was a different Boyette, I forgot about him. Until today."

Another gap in the conversation, then Koffee said, "Just relax, Kerber. You built a good case, he got a fair trial, and his guilt was affirmed by all the courts. What else can we expect? The system worked. Hell, Drew, the boy confessed."

"Of course he did. I've often wondered, though, what would've happened without the confession."

"You're not worried about the confession, are you?"

"Oh, no. I played it by the book."

"Forget about it, Drew. Look, it's over, really over. It's too late to second-guess anything we did. The boy is on the way home in a box."

The Slone airport was closed. The pilot activated the landing lights by radio signal from his controls, and the approach and touchdown were smooth. They taxied to the small terminal, and as soon as the props came to rest, they hurried off the plane. Robbie thanked the pilot and promised to call him later. The pilot passed along his condolences. By the time they were in the van, Aaron had spoken with Carlos and had a full report. "Fires all over town," he said. "They're burning cars. Carlos says there are three television crews in the parking lot at the office. They want to talk to you, Robbie, and they want to see more of Boyette."

"Why don't they burn the TV vans?" Robbie asked.

"Are you gonna talk to them?"

"I don't know. Make 'em wait. What's Boyette doing?"

"Watching television. Carlos says he's pissed off because no one listened to him, and he's refusing to say anything else to the reporters."

"If I attack him with a baseball bat, will you please keep me from killing him?"

"No," Aaron said.

As they entered the city limits, all four strained to see signs of the unrest. Aaron kept to the backstreets, away from downtown, and minutes later they arrived at the train station. All the lights were on. The parking lot was full, and there were indeed three TV vans waiting. By the time Robbie got out, the reporters were waiting for him. He politely asked them where they were from and what they wanted. One crew was from Slone, one from a station in Dallas, and one from Tyler. There were several newspaper reporters, including one from Houston. Robbie offered them a deal—if he organized a small press conference, outside, on the platform, and answered their questions, would they then leave and not come back? He reminded them that they were on his property and they could be asked to leave at any time. They accepted his deal; everything was pleasant.

"What about Travis Boyette?" a reporter asked.

Robbie said, "I'm not in charge of Mr. Boyette. I understand he's still inside and doesn't wish to say anything else. I'll speak with him, see what he wants to do."

"Thank you, Mr. Flak."

"I'll be back in thirty minutes," he said, and climbed the steps. Keith, Aaron, and Martha followed. Emotions hit hard when they walked into the conference room and saw Carlos, Bonnie, Sammie Thomas, Kristi Hinze, Fanta, and Fred Pryor. There were hugs and condolences and tears.

"Where's Boyette?" Robbie asked.

Fred Pryor pointed to the closed door of a small office.

"Good, keep him there. Let's gather around the conference table. I'd like to describe what it was like, while it's fresh. Reverend Schroeder might want to help, because he was there. He spent time with Donté and watched him die."

Keith was already in a chair against the wall, drained, fatigued, and wiped out. They looked at him in disbelief. He nodded without a smile.

Robbie took off his jacket and loosened his tie. Bonnie brought a tray of sandwiches and placed it in front of him. Aaron grabbed one, as did Martha. Keith waved them off; he'd lost his appetite. When they were settled in, Robbie began by saying, "He was very brave, but he expected a last-minute miracle. I guess they all do."

Like a third-grade teacher at story time, Robbie led them through the last hour of Donté's life, and when he finished, they were all crying again.

Rocks began flying, some thrown by teenagers hiding behind groups of other teenagers, and some thrown by persons unseen. They landed on Walter Street, where the police and the guardsmen maintained a casual line of defense. The first injury was to a Slone officer who took a rock in the teeth and went down hard, much to the delight of the crowd. The sight of a cop down inspired more rock throwing, and Civitan Park was finally exploding. A police sergeant made the decision to break up the crowd and with a bullhorn ordered everyone to disperse immediately or face arrest. This provoked an angry response, and the launching of more rocks and debris. The crowd jeered at the police and soldiers, spewing profanities and threats and showing no signs of obeying the order. The police and soldiers, with helmets and shields, formed a wedge, crossed the street, and entered the park. Several students, including Trey Glover, the tailback and initial leader of the protest, walked forward with their hands thrust out, volunteering for arrest. As Trey was being handcuffed, a rock bounced off the helmet of the officer arresting him. The officer yelled and cursed, then forgot about Trey and began chasing the kid who threw the rock. A few of the protesters scattered and ran through the streets, but most fought on, throwing whatever they could find. The dugouts on one of the baseball fields were made of cinder block, perfect for breaking into pieces and hurling at the men and women in uniform. One student wrapped a string of firecrackers around a stick, lit the fuse, and tossed it into the wedge. The explosions caused the cops and soldiers to break ranks and run for cover. The mob roared. From somewhere behind the wedge, a Molotov cocktail dropped from the sky and landed on the roof of an unmarked and unoccupied police car parked at the edge of Walter Street. The flames spread quickly as the gasoline splashed over the vehicle. This created another wave

of delirious cheering and yelling from the crowd. A
TV van arrived as the action picked up. The reporter,
a serious blonde who should've stuck to the weather,
scrambled out with a microphone and was met by an
angry policeman who demanded that she get back in
the van and get the hell out of there. The van, painted
white with bold red and yellow lettering, made an
easy target, and seconds after it slid to a stop, it was
being pelted with rocks and debris. Then a jagged
piece of cinder block struck the reporter in the back
of the head, opening a wide gash and knocking her
unconscious. More cheers, more obscenities. Lots of
blood. Her cameraman dragged her to safety as the
police called for an ambulance. To add to the fun and
frenzy, smoke bombs were tossed at the police and
soldiers, and at that point the decision was made to
respond with tear gas. The first canisters were fired,
and panic swept through the crowd. It began to break
up, with people running away, fanning through the
neighborhood. On the streets around Civitan Park,
men were on their front porches, listening to the
chaos not far away, watching for any sign of movement or trouble. With the women and children safe
inside, they stood guard with their shotguns and rifles, just waiting for a black face to appear. When
Herman Grist of 1485 Benton Street saw three young
blacks walking down the middle of the street, he fired
two shotgun blasts into the air from his porch and
yelled at the kids to get back to their part of town.
The kids began running away. The blasts cut through
the night, a grave signal that vigilantes had entered
the fray. Fortunately, though, Grist did not fire again.

The crowd continued to disperse, a few throwing
rocks in retreat. By 9:00 p.m., the park had been secured, and the police and soldiers walked through the

debris—empty cans and bottles, fast-food containers, cigarette butts, fireworks wrappers, enough litter for a landfill. The two dugouts were gone, nothing left but metal benches. The concession stand had been broken into, but there was nothing to take. In the wake of the tear gas, several vehicles had been abandoned, including Trey Glover's SUV. Trey and a dozen others were already at the jail. Four had volunteered, the rest had been caught. Several had been taken to the hospital because of the tear gas. Three policemen had been injured, along with the reporter.

The acrid smell of the gas permeated the park. A gray cloud from the smoke bombs hung not far above the ball fields. The place resembled a battlefield without the casualties.

The breakup of the party meant that a thousand or so angry blacks were now moving around Slone with no intention of going home and with no plans to do anything constructive. The use of tear gas infuriated them. They had been raised with the black-and-white videos of the dogs in Selma, the fire hoses in Birmingham, and the tear gas in Watts. That epic struggle was a part of their heritage, their DNA, a glorified chapter in their history, and suddenly here they were, on the streets protesting and fighting and being gassed, just like their ancestors. They had no intention of stopping the fight. If the cops wanted to play dirty, so be it.

The mayor, Harris Rooney, was monitoring the deteriorating condition of his little city from the police department, which had become the command center. He and the police chief, Joe Radford, had made the decision to scatter the crowd at Civitan Park and break things up, and they both had agreed that tear gas should be used. Reports were now flooding in, by radio and cell phone, that the protesters were roaming in packs, breaking windows, yelling threats at passing motorists, throwing rocks and debris, all manner of hooligan behavior.

At 9:15, he called the Reverend Johnny Canty, pastor of Bethel African Methodist Church. The two had met on Tuesday, when Reverend Canty had pleaded with the mayor to intervene with the governor and support a stay. The mayor had declined. He did not know the governor, had no clout with him whatsoever, and besides, anyone begging for a reprieve was wasting his time with Gill Newton. Canty had warned Mayor Rooney of the potential for unrest if the execution of Donté took place. The mayor had been skeptical.

All skepticism had now been replaced by fear.

Mrs. Canty answered the phone and explained that her husband was not home. He was at the funeral home waiting for the Drumm family to return. She gave the mayor a cell phone number, and Reverend Canty finally answered. "Well, good evening, Mayor," he said softly in his rich preacher's voice. "How are things tonight?"

"Things are pretty exciting right now, Reverend. How are you?"

"I've had better days. We're here at the funeral home, waiting for the family to return with the body, so I'm not doing too well right now. What can I do for you?"

"You were right about the unrest, Reverend. I didn't believe you, and I'm sorry. I should have listened, and I didn't. But things seem to be going from bad to worse. We've had eight fires, I think, a dozen arrests, half a dozen injuries, and there's no reason to believe those numbers will not go up. The crowd at Civitan Park has been dispersed, but the crowd at Washington Park is growing by the minute. I wouldn't be surprised if someone doesn't get killed very soon."

"There's already been a killing, Mayor. I'm waiting on the body."

"I'm sorry."

"What's the purpose of this call, Mayor?"

"You are a well-regarded leader in your community. You are the Drumms' pastor. I ask you to go to Washington Park and appeal for calm. They will listen to you. This violence and unrest serves no purpose."

"I have one question for you, Mayor. Did your police use tear gas on those kids in Civitan Park? I heard that rumor only minutes ago."

"Well, yes. It was considered necessary."

"No, it wasn't necessary, and it was a monumental mistake. By gassing our children, the police made a bad situation worse. Don't expect me to go rushing in to repair your damage. Good night."

The line was dead.

Robbie, with Aaron Rey on one side and Fred Pryor on the other, stood before the mikes and cameras and answered questions. He explained that Travis Boyette was still in the building and did not wish to speak to anyone. One reporter asked if he could go inside and interview Boyette. Only if you want to get arrested and perhaps shot was Robbie's sharp reply. Stay away from the building. They asked about Donté's last meal, visit, statement, and so on. Who were the witnesses? Any contact with the victim's family? Useless questions, in Robbie's opinion, but then the whole world seemed worthless at that point.

After twenty minutes, he thanked them. They thanked him. He asked them to leave and not come back. In the event Boyette changed his mind and wanted to talk, Robbie would give him a phone and a number.

Keith watched the press conference from a dark spot on the platform, outside the office but under its veranda. He was on the phone with Dana, recounting the events of the day, trying to stay awake, when she suddenly said that Robbie Flak was on the screen. She was watching the cable news and there he was, live from Slone, Texas.

"I'm about fifty feet behind him, in the shadows," Keith said, voice lower.

"He looks tired," she said. "Tired and maybe a bit crazy."

"Both. The fatigue comes and goes, but I suspect he's always a little crazy."

"He looks like a wild man."

"Certified, but there's a sweet man under the surface."

"Where's Boyette?"

"He's in a room, inside the building, with a television and some food. He prefers not to come out, and that's a good thing. These people knew Donté and loved him. Boyette has no friends around here."

"A few minutes ago they showed the fires and talked to the mayor. He seemed a bit jumpy. Are you safe, Keith?"

"Sure. I can hear sirens in the distance, but nothing close."

"Please be careful."

"Don't worry. I'm fine."

"You're not fine. You're a wreck, I can tell. Get some sleep. When are you coming home?"

"I plan to leave here in the morning."

"What about Boyette? Is he coming back?"

"We have not had that conversation."

29

Slone had three funeral homes, two for the whites (upper and lower) and one for the blacks. Integration had been achieved in some important areas of life—schools, politics, employment, and commercial activity. But in other areas, integration would never occur because neither race really wanted it. Sunday worship was segregated, by choice. A few blacks attended the larger white churches in town, and they were welcome. Even fewer whites could be found in black churches, where they were treated like everyone else. But the vast majority stuck with their own kind, and bigotry had little to do with it. It was more a matter of tradition and preference. The whites preferred an orderly, more subdued ritual on Sunday morning. Opening prayer at 11:00 a.m., followed by some beautiful music, then a nice crisp sermon, out by noon and certainly no later than 12:10 because by then they were starving. In the black churches, time was not as important. The spirit flowed more freely and made for a more spontaneous style of worship. The crack of noon was never heard. Lunch was often on the grounds, whenever, with no one in a hurry to leave.

And dying was so different. There was never a hurry to bury a black person, while the whites usually wanted it done within three days max. The black funeral home was busier, with more visitors, longer wakes, longer good-byes. Lamb & Son had been providing dignified service in its part of town for decades. When its hearse arrived a few minutes after 10:00 p.m., there was a solemn crowd waiting on the lawn in front of the small chapel. The mourners were silent, with heads down, faces somber. They watched as Hubert and Alvin opened the rear door of the hearse, then gave directions to the pallbearers—eight friends of Donté's, most of whom had once played football for the Slone Warriors. They carried the casket a few feet, following Hubert Lamb, then disappeared through a side door. The funeral home was closed and would not open until the following morning when Donté was properly prepared and ready to be viewed.

Sirens wailed in the distance. The air was thick, tense, heavy with smoke and fear. Those who were not making trouble were certainly expecting it.

A car pulled into the parking lot and parked next to the hearse. Roberta Drumm, with Marvin, Cedric, and Andrea, got out and moved slowly to the front entrance, where they greeted their friends. There were hugs and whispers and tears. The family eventually went inside, but the friends did not leave. Another car turned in and parked near the hearse. It was Robbie, with Aaron Rey, and they slipped past the crowd and entered through the side door. In the front parlor, Robbie met the family. They sat together and embraced and cried as if they had not seen each other in months. Only a few hours earlier they had watched Donté die, but that time and place were so distant now.

During the drive back from Huntsville, the Drumm family had listened to the radio and talked on cell phones. They quizzed Robbie about this Boyette character, and Robbie gave all the details he had. They knew things were grim in Slone, and expected to get worse, and Roberta repeatedly said she wanted the violence to stop. It's not within your power, Robbie assured her. It's out of control.

Hubert Lamb entered the parlor and said, "Roberta, Donté is ready."

She entered the prep room alone, closed the door behind her, and locked it. Her beautiful boy was lying on a narrow table, one covered in white sheets for the moment. He was dressed in the same clothes they had killed him in—cheap white shirt, worn khakis, bargain shoes—courtesy of the State of Texas. She gently placed her hands on his cheeks and kissed him on the face—the forehead, the lips, the nose, the chin—she kissed him and kissed him as her tears dropped like rain. She had not touched him in eight years, the last embrace a quick, stolen hug as they led him out of the courtroom the day they sentenced him to die, and as she wept now, she remembered the unspeakable agony of watching him hauled away, the leg chains rattling, the fat deputies crowding around him as if he just might kill someone else, the hard, smug faces of the prosecutors, the jurors, and the judge, proud of their work.

"I love you, Momma," he called over his shoulder,

then they shoved him through a door and he was gone.

His skin wasn't cold, nor was it warm. She touched the small scar under his chin, a small consolation prize from a neighborhood rock fight he'd lost when he was eight years old. Other rock fights followed. He had been a tough kid, made tougher by his older brother Cedric, who teased him constantly. A tough kid, but a sweet boy. She touched the lobe of his right ear, the tiny hole barely visible. He bought an earring when he was fifteen, a small fake diamond, and wore it when he was out with his friends. He hid it from his father, though. Riley would have chastised him.

Her beautiful boy, lying there so peaceful, and so healthy. Dead but not diseased. Dead but not injured. Dead but not maimed. She examined his arms and could find no trace of the needle pricks used for the injections. There was no evidence of the killing, nothing external. He seemed to be resting and waiting for the next drug to be administered, one that would gently wake him and allow him to go home with his mother.

His legs were straight; his arms were by his sides. Hubert Lamb said the stiffening would begin soon, so she had to get busy. From her purse, she removed a tissue to wipe her cheeks and a pair of scissors to cut away the prison garb. She could have unbuttoned the shirt, but instead she cut it down the front, then along the sleeves, removing it piece by piece and dropping the scraps on the floor. Tears still ran down her cheeks, but she was humming now, an old gospel song, "Take My Hand, Precious Lord." She paused to rub his flat stomach and his soft chest and shoulders, and she marveled at how much he'd shrunk in prison.

The fierce athlete was gone, replaced by the broken prisoner. He had died slowly in prison.

She unbuckled the cheap canvas belt, and for good measure cut it in half and dropped it on the pile. Tomorrow, when she was alone, she planned to burn the prison scraps in her backyard, in a private ceremony that only she would attend. She unlaced the dreadful shoes, removed them, and pulled off the white cotton socks. She touched the scars along his left ankle, permanent reminders of the injury that ended his football career. She cut the khakis, carefully up the inseams and delicately through the crotch. Of her three boys, Cedric had been the dresser, the clotheshorse who would work two part-time jobs so he could buy better labels. Donté preferred jeans and pullovers and looked good in anything. Anything but the jumpsuits they wore in prison. She clipped away, dropping the pieces of khaki onto the pile. She paused occasionally to wipe her cheeks with the back of a hand, but she had to hurry. The body was stiffening. She stepped to a sink and turned on the faucet.

The boxer shorts were white and oversized. She snipped away like a seamstress and removed them. The pile was complete. He was naked, leaving the world the same way he had entered it. She poured liquid soap into the sink, splashed the water, adjusted the temperature, then turned off the faucet. She dipped a cloth and began bathing her son. She rubbed his legs, then dried them quickly with a small towel. She washed his genitals, and wondered how many grandchildren he would have fathered. He loved the girls, and they loved him. She gently washed his chest and arms, neck and face, drying him as she went.

When the bath was finished, she moved to the last and most difficult part of her preparation. Before the family left for Huntsville, Cedric stopped by the funeral home with a new suit Roberta had purchased and altered. It was hanging on a wall, along with a new white shirt and a handsome gold tie. She assumed the shirt and coat would be the most difficult, the pants and shoes the easiest to finesse. And she was right. His arms would not bend now, and she carefully threaded the shirt over his right arm, then gently maneuvered Donté onto his left side. She brought the shirt around, laid him back down, wiggled it over his left arm, and quickly buttoned it. She did the same with the coat, a dark gray wool blend, and when she wrapped it around him, she paused for a second to kiss the side of his face. His legs were stiff. She methodically inched upward a pair of black cotton boxers, size large and too big. She should have bought mediums. The pants took a while. She tugged gently from side to side, straining to lift Donté at his midsection for a moment to complete the task. When the pants were in place at the waist, she tucked in the shirttail, zipped the pants, then fished a belt through the loops and buckled it. His feet were stiff, his ankles wouldn't bend, and the socks were more of a challenge than she had expected. The shoes were the black leather lace-ups Donté had worn to church as a teenager.

The shoes had been taken from his closet, one he'd shared with Marvin when they were boys. Donté had assumed full ownership when his brother got married, and for nine years now it had remained virtually untouched. Roberta cleaned it, dusted the clothing, killed the insects, arranged things just so. Hours earlier when she had removed the shoes, she had stood in the closet door for a long time, wondering, what now?

For years after he was sent away, she lived with the fervent belief that Donté would one day be freed. One glorious day their nightmare would end and he would come home. He would sleep in his bed, eat his mother's cooking, nap on the sofa, and need the things in his closet. One day a judge or a lawyer or someone toiling in the impenetrable maze of the judicial system would discover the truth. The phone call from heaven would arrive and they would celebrate. But the appeals ran their course, no miracles occurred, the years dragged on, and her hope and the hopes of many others slowly faded. The shirts and jeans and sweaters and shoes in his closet would never be used again, and she wondered what to do with them.

Roberta told herself to worry about it later.

She laced his shoes, adjusted his socks, pulled down the cuffs of his pants. Now that he was dressed, she could relax. Cedric had tied the necktie into a perfect knot, and she looped it over Donté's head and managed to fit it under his collar. She tightened the knot and fiddled with the tie until it was perfect. She adjusted here and there, flattened a few wrinkles in the pants, then she took a step back and admired her work. What a handsome young man. Gray suit, white shirt, gold tie; she had chosen well.

She leaned over and kissed him again. Get up Donté and let's go to church. You'll find a wife there and have ten children. Hurry now, there's so much you've missed. Please. Let's go show you off in your fine new outfit. Hurry now.

She was aware of the grislier aspects of death, the embalming and fluids and such, and she knew that in a few hours Mr. Lamb and his son would be warming the body, removing the clothes, and going about their unspeakable tasks. That's why she wanted these few precious moments with her son, while he was still whole and intact.

Tomorrow she would plan the funeral and tend to the other details. She would be strong and brave. Now, though, she wanted to be alone with her child, to grieve and ache and cry without restraint, as any mother would.

PART THREE

THE EXONERATION

30

Before sunrise Friday, a short caravan of vehicles departed the town and traveled east. The lead vehicle was Robbie's customized van, with Aaron Rey at the wheel and Carlos riding shotgun. Robbie sat in his favorite chair, sipped coffee, glanced through the newspapers, and generally ignored Martha Handler, who was gulping coffee and scribbling notes and trying to wake up. Behind them was the Subaru, with Keith driving and Boyette gripping his cane and staring into the darkness. Behind the Subaru was a three-quarter-ton pickup truck with Fred Pryor at the wheel. His passengers were two private security guards who had worked off and on during the past few days to protect Robbie's law office and his home. The truck was Fred's, and it carried shovels, flashlights, and other equipment. Behind the truck was another van, white and unmarked, owned by the TV station in Slone and driven by a news director named Bryan Day, nicknamed Hairspray Day for obvious reasons. With Day was a cameraman called Buck.

The four vehicles had gathered in the long driveway of Robbie's home at 5:00 a.m. and managed to weave through side streets and back roads for a stealthy and successful getaway. The office had received enough phone calls and e-mails to convince Robbie that certain people were curious about where he might be headed on Friday.

He'd slept five hours, and it took a pill to achieve that. He was beyond the point of exhaustion, but there was so much left to do. After leaving Lamb & Son, and briefly seeing the body, he took his entourage home, where DeDe managed to produce enough food to feed everyone. Keith and Boyette slept on sofas in the basement while a maid washed and ironed their clothes.

Everyone was exhausted, but no one had trouble jumping out of bed.

Carlos was on his cell phone, listening more than talking, and when the conversation was over, he announced, "That was my man at the radio station. Forty or so arrests, two dozen injuries, but no fatalities, which is a miracle. They have sealed off most of downtown, and things have settled down for the moment. Lots of fires, too many to count. Fire trucks here from Paris, Tyler, other places. At least three police cars have been hit with Molotov cocktails, which has become the weapon of choice. They torched the press box at the football field and it's still burning. Most of the fires are in empty buildings. No homes, yet. Rumor is that the governor is sending in more guardsmen. Nothing confirmed, though."

"And what happens if we find the body?" Martha asked.

Robbie shook his head and thought for a second. "Then last night was child's play."

They had debated the various combinations and arrangements for the trip. To make sure Boyette didn't vanish, Robbie wanted him secured in his van under the watchful eye of Aaron Rey and Fred Pryor. But he just couldn't stomach the thought of being confined in a small place for several hours with the creep. Keith was adamant that he was driving his Subaru, primarily because he was determined to be in Topeka by late Friday afternoon, with or without Boyette. Like Robbie, he had no desire to sit near Boyette, but since he had done it once, he assured Robbie that he could do it again.

Fred Pryor had suggested they toss Boyette in the rear seat of the club cab of his truck and keep guns on him. Among Robbie's team, there was a yearning for retribution, and if Boyette did indeed lead them to the body, Fred Pryor and Aaron Rey could easily be convinced to take him somewhere behind the trees and put him out of his misery. Keith sensed this, and they respected his presence. There would be no violence.

The inclusion of Bryan Day had been complicated. Robbie trusted no reporter, period. However, if they found what they were looking for, it would need to be properly recorded, and by someone outside his circle. Of course Day had been eager to tag along, but he had been forced to agree to a list of firm conditions that basically prevented him from reporting anything until so directed by Robbie Flak. If he tried, he and Buck the cameraman would in all likelihood be either beaten or shot, or both. Day and Buck understood that the stakes were high and the rules would be followed. Because Day was the station's news director, he was able to slip away without leaving clues at the office.

"Can we talk?" Martha asked. They had been on the road for half an hour, and there were hints of orange in the sky ahead of them.

"No," Robbie said.

"It's been almost twelve hours since he died. What are you thinking?"

"I'm fried, Martha. My brain is not working. There are no thoughts."

"What did you think when you saw his body?"

"It's a sick world when we kill people because we assume we have the right to kill them. I thought he looked great, this handsome young man lying there asleep, no visible injuries, no signs of a struggle. Put down like an old dog by bigots and idiots too lazy and too stupid to realize what they're doing. You know what I'm really thinking about, Martha?"

"Tell me."

"I'll tell you. I'm thinking about Vermont, cool summers, no humidity, no executions. A civilized place. A cabin on a lake. I can learn to shovel snow. If I sell everything and close my firm, maybe I can net a million. I'll retire to Vermont and write a book."

"About what?"

"I have no idea."

"No one believes that, Robbie. You'll never leave. You might take some time off, catch your breath, but before long you'll find another case and get mad and file a lawsuit, or ten. You'll be doing that until you're eighty, and they'll carry you out of the station on a stretcher."

"I'll never see eighty. I'm fifty-two now and I feel like a geezer."

"You'll be suing people when you're eighty."

"I don't know."

"I do. I know where your heart is."

"Right now my heart is broken, and I'm ready to quit. A half-ass lawyer could've saved Donté."

"And what could this half-ass lawyer have done differently?"

Robbie showed her both palms and said, "Not now, Martha. Please."

In the car behind them, the first words were spoken when Boyette said, "Did you really watch the execution?"

Keith took a sip of coffee and waited awhile. "Yes, I did. It wasn't planned; it just happened at the last second. I didn't want to watch it."

"Do you wish you hadn't?"

"That's a very good question, Travis."

"Thank you."

"On the one hand, I wish I had not watched a man die, especially a man who claimed to be innocent."

"He is innocent, or was."

"I tried to pray with him, but he refused. He said he doesn't believe in God, though he once did. As a minister, it's very difficult to be with someone who is facing death and does not believe in God or Christ or heaven. I've stood at hospital beds and watched my members die, and it's always comforting to know that their souls are bound for a glorious hereafter. Not so with Donté."

"Nor with me."

"On the other hand, I saw something in the death chamber that should be seen by everyone. Why hide what we are doing?"

"So you would watch another one?"

"I didn't say that, Travis." It was a question Keith could not answer. He was struggling with his first execution; he couldn't imagine the next one. Just hours earlier, seconds before he'd finally fallen asleep, the image of Donté strapped to the deathbed came into focus, and Keith ran through it again in slow motion.

He remembered staring at Donté's chest as it lifted slightly, then fell. Lifted, then fell. Up and down, barely noticeable. And then it stopped. He had just watched a man exhale for the final time. Keith knew the image would never go away.

The sky was lighter to the east. They crossed into Oklahoma.

Boyette said, "I guess that's my last trip to Texas."

Keith could not think of a response.

The governor's helicopter touched down at 9:00 a.m. Since the media had received plenty of advance notice and were waiting anxiously, there was considerable debate among the governor and Barry and Wayne about the details of the landing. En route, they finally settled on the parking lot next to the football field. The media were informed and scrambled to Slone High School for this late-breaking development. The press box was badly damaged, charred, and smoldering. Firemen were still on the scene, cleaning up. When Gill Newton emerged from his chopper, he was met by state police, colonels from the Guard, and a few carefully selected and weary firefighters. He shook their hands warmly as if they were Marines returning from combat. Barry and Wayne were quick to survey the surroundings, and they organized the press conference so that the backdrop would be the football field and, most important, the burned-out press box. The governor was wearing jeans, cowboy boots, no tie, and a Windbreaker—a real working man.

With a troubled face but an enthusiastic spirit, he faced the cameras and reporters. He condemned the violence and unrest. He promised to protect the citizens of Slone. He announced he was calling in more guardsmen and would mobilize the entire Texas National Guard, if need be. He talked about justice, Texas style. He engaged in a bit of race-baiting by calling on black leaders to rein in the hooligans. He said nothing of the sort about white troublemakers. He ranted and raved, and when he was finished, he ducked away from the microphones without taking questions. Neither he nor Barry and Wayne wanted to deal with the Boyette matter.

For an hour he buzzed around Slone in a patrol car, stopping to drink coffee with soldiers and policemen, and to chat with citizens, and to survey, with a grim and pained face, the ruins of the First Baptist Church, and all the while the cameras were rolling, recording it all for the glory of the moment, but also for future campaigns.

After five hours, the caravan finally stopped at a country store north of Neosho, Missouri, twenty miles south of Joplin. After a restroom break and more coffee, they headed north, now with the Subaru in the lead and the other vehicles close behind.

Boyette was visibly nervous, the tic more active, his fingers thumping the cane. "We're getting close to the turnoff," he said. "It's to the left." They were on Highway 59, a busy two-lane road in Newton County. They turned left at the bottom of a hill, next to a gas station. "This looks right," Travis kept saying, obviously anxious about where he was taking them. They were on a county road with bridges over small creeks, sharp curves, steep hills. Most of the homes were trailers with an occasional square red-brick from the 1950s.

"This looks right," Boyette said.

"And you lived around here, Travis?"

"Yep, right up here." He nodded, and when he did so, he began rubbing his temples. Please, Keith thought, not another seizure. Not at this moment. They stopped at an intersection in the middle of a small settlement. "Keep going straight," Boyette said. Past a shopping center with a grocery, hair salon, video rental. The parking lot was gravel. "This looks right," he said again.

Keith had questions, but he said little. Was Nicole still alive, Travis, when you drove through here? Or had you already taken her life? What were you thinking, Travis, when you drove through here nine years ago with that poor girl bound and gagged and bruised, traumatized after a long weekend of sexual assault?

They turned to the left, onto another road that was paved but narrower, and drove a mile before they passed a dwelling. "Old man Deweese had a store up here," Travis said. "I'll bet it's gone now. He was ninety years old when I was a kid." They stopped at a stop sign in front of Deweese's Country Market.

"I robbed that place once," Travis said. "Couldn't have been more than ten. Crawled through a window. Hated the old bastard. Keep going straight."

Keith did as he was told and said nothing.

"This was gravel last time I was here," Boyette said, as if recalling a pleasant boyhood memory.

"And when was that?" Keith asked.

"I don't know, Pastor. My last visit to see Nicole."

You sick puppy, Keith thought. The road had sharp turns, so sharp that at times Keith thought they would loop back and meet themselves. The two vans and the pickup stayed close behind. "Look for a little creek with a wooden bridge," Boyette said. "This looks right." A hundred yards past the bridge, Boyette said, "Slow down now."

"We're going ten miles an hour, Travis."

Travis was looking to their left, where thick underbrush and weeds lined the road. "There's a gravel road here, somewhere," he said. "Slower." The caravan was almost bumper-to-bumper.

In the van, Robbie said, "Come on, Travis, you sick little weasel. Don't make liars out of us."

Keith turned left onto a shaded gravel road with oaks and elms entangled above it. The trail was narrow and dark like a tunnel. "This is it," Boyette said, relieved, for the moment. "This road sort of follows the creek for a while. There's a camping area down here on the right, or at least there was." Keith checked his odometer. They went 1.2 miles into the near darkness with the creek showing up occasionally. There was no traffic, no room for traffic, and no sign of human life anywhere in the vicinity. The camping area was just an open space with room for a few tents and cars, and it appeared to have been forgotten. The weeds were knee-high. Two wooden picnic tables were broken and turned on their sides. "We camped here when I was a kid," Boyette said.

Keith almost felt sorry for him. He was trying to remember something pleasant and normal from his wretched childhood.

"I think we should stop here," Boyette said. "I'll explain."

The four vehicles stopped and everyone gathered in front of the Subaru. Boyette used his cane as a pointer and said, "There's a dirt trail that goes up that hill. You can't see the trail from here, but it's here, or it used to be. Only the truck can get up there. The other vehicles should stay here."

"How far up there?" Robbie asked.

"I didn't check the odometer, but I'd say a quarter of a mile."

"And what will we find when we get there, Boyette?" Robbie asked.

Boyette leaned on his cane and studied the weeds at his feet. "That's where the grave is, Mr. Flak. That's where you'll find Nicole."

"Tell us about the grave," Robbie pressed on.

"She's buried in a metal box, a large toolbox I took from the construction site where I worked. The top of the box is two feet under the ground. It's been nine years, so the ground is thick with vegetation. It will be difficult to locate. But I think I can get close. This is all coming back to me now, now that I'm here."

They discussed the logistics and decided that Carlos, Martha Handler, Day and Buck, and one of the security guards (armed) would stay at the campsite. The rest would pile into Fred's pickup and assault the hill with a video camera.

"One last thing," Boyette said. "Years ago this property was known as Roop's Mountain, owned by the Roop family, pretty tough folks. They took a dim view of trespassers and hunters, and they were notorious for running off campers. That's one reason I picked this place. I knew there wouldn't be much traffic." A pause as Boyette grimaced and rubbed his temples. "Anyway, there were a lot of Roops, so I figure it's still in the family. If we bump into someone, we better be prepared for trouble."

"Where do they live?" Robbie asked, somewhat nervously.

Boyette waved his cane in another direction. "A good ways off. I don't think they will hear or see us."

"Let's go," Robbie said.

* * *

What had begun on Monday morning with a seemingly routine pastoral conference now came down to this—Keith was riding in the rear of a pickup truck, bouncing up the side of Roop's Mountain, which was nothing more than a medium-size hill dense with kudzu and poison ivy and thick woods, facing a real chance of armed conflict with surly landowners no doubt high on meth, in the final push to determine whether Travis Boyette was, in fact, telling the truth. If they did not find Nicole's remains, Boyette was a fraud, Keith was a fool, and Texas had just executed the right person, in all likelihood.

If, however, they found the body, then, well, Keith could not comprehend what would happen next. Certainty had become a fuzzy concept, but he was reasonably certain that he would be home sometime that night. He couldn't begin to imagine what would happen in Texas, but he was sure he wouldn't be there. He would watch it all on television, from a safe distance. He was fairly certain events down there would be sensational and probably historic.

Boyette was in the front seat, rubbing his head and straining to see something familiar. He pointed to his right—he was sure the grave was to the right of the trail—and said, "This might be familiar." The area was a dense patch of weeds and saplings. They stopped, got out, and grabbed two metal detectors. For fifteen minutes, they scoured the thick undergrowth looking for clues and waiting for the detectors to make their noise. Boyette limped along, whacking weeds with his cane, followed by Keith and watched by everyone. "Look for an old tire, a tractor tire," Boyette said more than once.

But there was no tire, and no noise from the detectors. They retook their positions in the truck and moved slowly onward, inching up the incline on a logging trail that gave no indication of having been used in decades. Strike one.

The trail disappeared, and for twenty yards Fred Pryor inched the truck forward through vegetation, flinching as it was scraped by branches and vines. Those in the rear of the truck ducked for cover as limbs whipped about. Just as Fred was about to stop, the trail appeared again, vaguely, and Boyette said, "Keep going." Then the trail split. Fred stopped as Boyette studied the fork and shook his head. He doesn't have a clue, Fred said to himself. In the rear, Robbie looked at Keith and shook his head.

"Over there," Boyette said, motioning to his right, and Fred followed his direction.

The woods became thicker, the trees younger and closer together. Like a bloodhound, Boyette raised his hand and pointed, and Fred Pryor turned off the ignition. The search party fanned out, looking for an old tractor tire, looking for anything. A beer can aroused one of the metal detectors, and for a few seconds the tension spiked. A small airplane flew low overhead, and everyone froze, as if someone were watching. Robbie said, "Boyette, do you remember if the grave is under the trees or in an open area?" The question seemed reasonable. Boyette replied, "I think it was more out in the open, but the trees have grown in nine years."

"Great," Robbie mumbled, then continued stomping around, crushing weeds, gawking at the ground as if the perfect clue were just one step away. After half an hour, Boyette said, "This is not it. Let's move on."

Strike two.

Keith crouched in the back of the truck and exchanged glances with Robbie. Both seemed to say, "We should've known better." But neither spoke. No one spoke because there was absolutely nothing to say. There were a thousand thoughts.

The road turned, and when it straightened, Boyette pointed again. "This is it," he said as he yanked open the door before the engine was turned off. He launched himself into a clearing of weeds waist-high as the others scrambled to follow. Keith took a few steps and tripped over something, falling hard. As he scrambled to his feet, brushing off bugs and brush, he realized what had tripped him. The remains of a tractor tire, virtually buried in vegetation.

"Here's a tire," he announced, and the others stopped moving. Boyette was only a few feet away. "Get the metal detectors," he said. Fred Pryor had one, and within seconds it was clicking and buzzing, giving all indications of being highly agitated. Aaron Rey produced two shovels.

The terrain was strewn with rocks, but the soil was soft and moist. After ten minutes of furious digging, Fred Pryor's shovel struck what clearly sounded like metal.

"Let's stop for a second," Robbie said. Both Fred and Aaron needed a break.

"All right, Boyette," Robbie said. "Tell us what we are about to find."

The tic, the pause, then, "It's a metal box used for hydraulic tools, heavy as hell, almost ruined my back dragging the damned thing over here. It's orange in color with the name of the company, R. S. McGuire and Sons, Fort Smith, Arkansas, painted on the front. It opens from the top."

"And inside?"

"Nothing but bones by now. It's been nine years." He spoke with an air of authority, as if this wasn't his first hidden grave site. "Her clothing was wadded together and placed next to her head. There's a belt around her neck, should be intact." His voice trailed off, as if this were somehow painful for him. There was a pause while the others glanced at each other, then Travis cleared his throat and continued. "In her clothing, we should find her driver's license and a credit card. I didn't want to get caught with them."

"Describe the belt," Robbie said. The security guard handed Robbie a video camera.

"Black, two inches wide, with a round silver buckle. It is the murder weapon."

The digging continued as Robbie captured it on video. "It's about five feet long," Boyette said, pointing, indicating an outline for the box. With its shape clear, each shovelful of dirt revealed more. It was indeed orange. Deeper, the name "R. S. McGuire and Sons, Fort Smith, Arkansas," became visible.

"That's enough," Robbie said, and the digging stopped. Aaron Rey and Fred Pryor were sweating and breathing heavily. "We won't be removing it."

The toolbox presented an obvious challenge, one that had gradually become more and more evident. The top lid was secured by a latch, and the latch was secured by a combination lock, the inexpensive kind found in every hardware store. Fred did not have the proper tools to cut the lock, but there was little doubt that they would somehow snap it free. After coming this far, they would not be denied a look inside. The six men huddled close together and gawked at the orange toolbox and the combination lock. Robbie said, "So, Travis, what's the combination?"

Travis actually smiled, as though, finally, he was

about to be vindicated. He lowered himself to the edge of the grave, touched the box as if it were an altar, then gently took the lock and shook dirt from it. He turned the dial a few times to clear the code, then slowly turned to the right, to 17, then back to the left, to 50, then to the right, to 4, and finally back to the left, to 55. He hesitated and lowered his head as if to hear something, then he pulled sharply. There was a soft click, and the lock was open.

Robbie was filming from five feet away. Keith couldn't suppress a grin, in spite of where he was and what he was doing.

"Don't open it," Robbie said. Pryor hustled to the truck and returned with a package. He passed out sanitary gloves and masks, and when everyone had put them on, Robbie handed him the camera and told him to start filming. He instructed Aaron to step down and slowly open the lid. He did so. There was no corpse, only bones, the skeletal remains of someone, Nicole they assumed. Her hands and fingers were laced together below her ribs, but her feet were near her knees, as if Boyette had been forced to fold her to fit her in the toolbox. Her skull was intact but a molar was missing. She'd had perfect teeth; they knew that from the photographs. Around the skull there were strands of long blond hair. Between the skull and the shoulder, there was a length of black leather, the belt, they assumed. Next to the skull, in the corner of the box, there appeared to be clothing.

Keith closed his eyes and said a prayer.

Robbie closed his eyes and cursed the world.

Boyette stepped back and sat on the edge of the tractor tire, in the weeds, and began rubbing his head.

With Fred filming, Robbie directed Aaron to gently remove the roll of clothing. The articles were intact, though frayed along some of the edges and stained in places. A blouse, blue and yellow with some type of fringe, and a large ugly hole made by either insects or decaying flesh. A short white skirt, badly stained. Brown sandals. Matching bra and panties, dark blue. And two plastic cards, one her driver's license and one a MasterCard. Nicole's things were placed neatly on the side of her grave.

Boyette returned to the truck, where he sat in the front seat and massaged his head. For ten minutes, Robbie gave orders and made plans. Dozens of photographs were taken, but nothing else was touched. It was a crime scene now, and the local authorities would take charge.

Aaron and the security guard stayed behind while the others retreated down Roop's Mountain.

31

By 10:00 a.m., the parking lot at Lamb & Son Funeral Home was full, and cars lined both sides of the street. The mourners, dressed in their Sunday best, formed a line that began at the front door and ran three and four abreast through the small lawn, down the street, and around the corner. They were sad and angry, tired and anxious, and uncertain about what was happening to them and their quiet town. The sirens, fireworks, gunshots, and urgent voices from the street had finally subsided not long before sunrise, allowing a few hours of rest. But no one expected the streets to return to normal on Friday or over the weekend.

They had seen the eerie face of Travis Boyette on television, and they had heard his poisonous confession. They believed him because they had always believed Donté. So much more of the story had yet to be told, and if Boyette really had killed the girl, then someone would pay a heavy price.

The Slone Police Department had eight black officers, and all eight volunteered for the assignment. Though most had not slept in hours, they were determined to pay tribute. They secured the street in front of the funeral home, directed traffic, and, most important, kept the reporters at bay. There was a pack of them, all neatly cordoned off and barricaded a block away.

When Hubert Lamb unlocked the front door, he greeted the first wave of mourners and asked them to sign the register. The crowd began to move slowly, in no hurry. It would take a week to bury Donté, and there would be plenty of time to pay proper respects.

He was on display in the main parlor, his casket open and draped with flowers. His senior class photo had been enlarged and sat on a tripod at the foot of his casket—an eighteen-year-old in a coat and tie, a handsome face. The portrait had been taken a month before he was arrested. He was smiling, still dreaming of playing football. His eyes were full of expectation and ambition.

His family stood near the casket, where they had been for the past hour, touching him, weeping, trying to be strong for their guests.

At the campsite, Robbie described the scene to Carlos and the others. Bryan Day wanted to get to the grave immediately and record everything before the police arrived, but Robbie wasn't so sure. They argued, though both knew Robbie would make the decision. Fred Pryor was on his cell phone trying to locate the sheriff of Newton County. Martha Handler was talking to Aaron on her cell phone and taking notes. Suddenly there was a shriek, an anguished cry, as Boyette fell to the ground and began trembling violently. Keith knelt over him, and the others gathered to watch helplessly. Quizzical looks were exchanged.

After a minute or so, the seizure seemed to pass, and the shaking and jerking subsided. Boyette clutched his head and whimpered in pain. Then he seemed to die. His body went limp and was perfectly still. Keith waited, then touched his shoulder and said, "Hey, Travis, can you hear me?" Evidently, Travis could not; there was no response.

Keith stood and said, "He usually blacks out for a few minutes."

"Let's put him out of his misery," Robbie said. "One quick pop to the head. There's a grave not far from here that's about to be empty."

"Come on, Robbie," Keith said.

The others seemed to like Robbie's idea. They backed away and were soon occupied with other matters. Five minutes passed. Boyette had not moved. Keith knelt down and checked his pulse. It was steady but faint. A few minutes later, Keith said, "Robbie, I think this is serious. He's unconscious."

"I'm not a brain surgeon, Keith. What do you want me to do?"

"He needs attention."

"He needs a funeral, Keith. Why don't you take him back to Kansas and bury him?"

Keith stood and walked a few steps to where Robbie was standing. He said, "That's a little harsh, don't you think?"

"I'm sorry, Keith. There's a lot happening right now, in case you haven't noticed. Boyette's health is not one of my priorities."

"We can't just let him die out here."

"Why not? He's practically dead anyway, right?"

Boyette grunted, then shook from head to toe, as if an aftershock were rumbling through. Then he was still again.

Keith swallowed hard and said, "He needs a doctor."

"Great. Go find one."

Minutes dragged by, and Boyette was not responsive. The others didn't care, and Keith almost persuaded himself to get in his car and leave, alone. But he could not bring himself to ignore a dying man. The security guard helped Keith load Boyette into the rear seat of the Subaru. Fred Pryor walked from the direction of the creek and said, "That was the sheriff. I finally got him, finally convinced him that we're for real, and that we've found a dead body in his jurisdiction. He's on his way."

As Keith was opening his car door, Robbie approached him and said, "Call me when you get to a hospital, and keep an eye on Boyette. I'm sure the authorities here will want to talk to him. There's no open investigation at this point, but that could change quickly, especially if Boyette admits he killed the girl in this state."

"His pulse is almost gone," the security guard reported from the rear seat.

"I'm not planning on standing guard, Robbie," Keith said. "I'm done. I'm outta here. I'll drop him off at a hospital, God knows where, and then hustle back to Kansas."

"You have our cell numbers. Just keep us posted. As soon as the sheriff sees the grave, I'm sure he'll send someone to see Boyette."

The two shook hands, not sure if they would see each other again. Death binds people in odd ways, and they felt as though they had known each other for years.

As the Subaru disappeared into the woods, Robbie checked his watch. It had taken about six hours to drive from Slone and find the body. If Travis Boyette had not delayed, Donté Drumm would be alive and on his way to a quick exoneration. He spat on the ground and quietly wished Boyette a slow and painful death.

During the forty-five-minute drive from the campsite, complete with at least four stops to ask for directions, Boyette had not moved and had not uttered a sound. He still appeared to be dead. At the emergency room entrance, Keith told a doctor about Boyette's tumor, but little else. The doctor was curious as to why a minister from Kansas was traveling through Joplin with a gravely ill man who was neither a relative nor a member of his congregation. Keith assured him it was a very long story, one he would happily tell when they had the time. Both knew they would never have the time and the story would never be told. They placed Boyette on a stretcher, with his cane, and rolled him down the hall for examination. Keith watched him disappear behind swinging doors and found a seat in the waiting area. He called Dana to check in. His wife had received his updates with a growing sense of disbelief, one shocker after another, and she seemed to be numb to anything new. Fine, Keith. Yes, Keith. Sure, Keith. Please come home, Keith.

He called Robbie and told him where they were at that moment. Boyette was alive and being examined. Robbie was still waiting for the sheriff to arrive at the site. He was anxious to hand over the crime scene to the professionals, though he knew that would take time.

Keith called Matthew Burns, and when Matthew

answered, Keith began with a happy "Well, good morning, Matt. I'm now in Missouri, where an hour ago we opened the grave and saw the remains of Nicole Yarber. Top that for a Friday morning."

"So what else is new? What did she look like?"

"All bones. Positive ID, though. Boyette is telling the truth. They executed the wrong man. It's unbelievable, Matt."

"When are you coming home?"

"I'll be there for dinner. Dana's freaking out, so I won't be long."

"We need to meet first thing in the morning. I've watched the coverage nonstop, and there hasn't been a word about you. Maybe you've slid under the radar. We gotta talk. Where's Boyette?"

"In a hospital in Joplin, dying, I think. I'm with him."

"Leave him, Keith. Maybe he'll die. Let someone else worry about him. Just get in your car and haul ass."

"That's my plan. I'll hang around here until I hear something, then I'm on the road. Kansas is just minutes away."

An hour passed. Robbie called Keith with the news that the sheriff had arrived and Roop's Mountain was now crawling with police. Two state policemen were on their way to the hospital to secure Mr. Boyette. Keith agreed to wait for them, then he was leaving.

"Thanks, Keith, for everything," Robbie said.

"It wasn't enough."

"No, but what you did took courage. You tried. That's all you could do."

"Let's keep in touch."

The state troopers, Weshler and Giles, were both sergeants, and after terse introductions they asked

Keith if he would fill in some gaps. Sure, why not, what else was there to do in an ER waiting room? It was almost 1:00 p.m., and they bought sandwiches from a machine and found a table. Giles took notes, and Weshler handled most of the questions. Keith began with Monday morning and hit the high points of this rather unusual week. As he told his story, they seemed to doubt him at times. They had not been following the Drumm case, but when Boyette went public with his claim of guilt, and mentioned the body being buried near Joplin, phones started ringing. They tuned in, and they had seen Boyette's face and performance several times. Now that a body had been found, they were smack in the middle of a growing story.

A doctor interrupted them. He explained that Boyette was stable and resting. His vital signs were near normal. They had X-rayed his head and confirmed the presence of an egg-size tumor. The hospital needed to contact a family member, and Keith tried to describe what little he knew about Boyette's relatives. "There's a brother in prison in Illinois, that's all I know," Keith said.

"Well," the doctor said, scratching his jaw, "how long do you want us to keep him?"

"How long should he be kept?"

"Overnight, but beyond that I'm not sure what we can do for him."

"He doesn't belong to me, Doc," Keith said. "I'm just driving him around."

"And this is part of the very long story?"

Both Giles and Weshler nodded. Keith suggested the doctor contact the doctors at St. Francis Hospital in Topeka, and perhaps the little group could devise a plan for dealing with Travis Boyette.

"Where is he now?" Weshler asked.

"He's in a small ward on the third floor," the doctor said.

"Could we see him?"

"Not now, he needs to rest."

"Then could we station ourselves outside the ward," Giles said. "We anticipate this man being charged with murder, and we have orders to secure him."

"He's not going anywhere."

Weshler bristled at this, and the doctor sensed the futility of arguing. "Follow me," he said. As they began to walk away, Keith said, "Hey, fellas, I'm free to go, right?"

Weshler looked at Giles, and Giles studied Weshler, then both looked at the doctor. Weshler said, "Sure, why not?"

"He's all yours," Keith said, already backing away. He left through the ER entrance and jogged to his car in a nearby parking garage. He found $6 in his dwindling cash reserves, paid the attendant, and gunned the Subaru onto the street. Free at last, he said to himself. It was exhilarating to glance over at the empty seat and know that he, with luck, would never again be near Travis Boyette.

Weshler and Giles were given folding chairs and took their positions in the hallway by the door to Ward 8. They called their supervisor and reported on Boyette's status. They found some magazines and began killing time. Through the door, there were six beds, each separated by flimsy curtains, all occupied by people suffering from serious afflictions. At the far end, there was a large window that overlooked a vacant lot, and next to the window was a door the janitors used on occasion.

The doctor returned, spoke to the troopers, then stepped inside for a quick check on Boyette. When he pulled the curtain by bed 4, he froze in disbelief.

The IVs were dangling. The bed was neatly made with a black walking cane across it. Boyette was gone.

32

Robbie Flak and his little team stood by and watched the circus for two hours. Not long after the sheriff arrived and saw that there was indeed a grave site, Roop's Mountain attracted every cop within fifty miles. Local deputies, state troopers, the county coroner, investigators from the Missouri State Highway Patrol, and, finally, a crime scene expert. Radios squawked, men yelled, a helicopter hovered overhead. When the news arrived that Boyette had vanished, cops cursed his name as if they had known him forever. Robbie called Keith's cell phone and passed along the news. Keith explained what had happened at the hospital. He could not imagine Boyette being physically able to go far. They agreed that he would be caught, and soon.

By 2:00 p.m., Robbie was tired of the scene. He had told his story and answered a thousand questions from the investigators, there was nothing left to do. They had found Nicole Yarber, and they were ready to return to Slone and face a multitude of issues. Bryan Day had enough footage for a miniseries, but would be forced to sit on it for a few hours. Robbie informed the sheriff that they were leaving. The caravan, minus the Subaru, worked its way through the traffic until it was back on the highway and headed south. Carlos e-mailed dozens of photographs to the office, as well as the video. A presentation was being put together.

"Can we talk?" Martha Handler asked after a few minutes on the road.

"No," Robbie answered.

"You talked to the police, what's next?"

"They will keep the remains in the toolbox and move it all to a satellite crime lab in Joplin. They will do what they do, and we'll see."

"What will they look for?"

"Well, first they will attempt to identify the body using dental records. That should be easy, probably take a few hours. We may hear something tonight."

"They have her dental records?"

"I gave them a set. Before Donté's trial, the prosecution dumped several boxes of discovery on us a week before we picked the jury. Not surprisingly, the prosecution screwed up, and in one file there was a set of X-rays of Nicole's teeth. Several sets were floating around during the initial days of the search, and Koffee had one. He inadvertently gave it to us. It was no big deal because her dental records were not an issue at trial. As we know, there was no dead body. A year later, I sent the file back to Koffee, but I made a copy for myself. Who knows what you'll need one day?"

"Did he know you kept a copy?"

"I don't remember, but I doubt it. It's no big deal."

"There's no violation of privacy here?"

"Of course not. Whose privacy? Nicole's?"

Martha scribbled notes as her tape recorder ran on. Robbie closed his eyes and tried not to frown.

"What else will they look for?" she asked.

Robbie frowned but did not open his eyes. "Cause of death in a strangulation case is impossible after nine years. They'll look for DNA evidence, maybe in dried blood or hair. Nothing else—semen, skin, saliva, earwax, sweat—none of it holds up after this long in a decomposing corpse."

"Does DNA matter? I mean, we know who killed her."

"We do, but I would love to have the DNA proof. If we get it, then this will be the first case in U.S. history in which we know by DNA evidence that the wrong man has been executed. There are a dozen or so cases where we strongly suspect the state killed the wrong guy, but none with clear biological proof. Would you like a drink? I need a drink."

"No."

"A drink, Carlos?"

"Sure. I'll take a beer."

"Aaron?"

"Driving, Boss."

"Just joking."

Robbie pulled two beers out of the fridge and handed one to Carlos. After a long drink from the bottle, he closed his eyes again.

"What are you thinking?" Martha asked.

"Boyette, Travis Boyette. We came so close, and if he had just given us twenty-four hours, we could have saved Donté. Now we just deal with the aftermath."

"What happens to Boyette?"

"They'll indict him for murder here in Missouri. If he lives long enough, they'll prosecute him."

"Will he be prosecuted in Texas?"

"Of course not. They will never, ever admit they killed the wrong guy. Koffee, Kerber, Judge Vivian Grale, the jurors, the appellate judges, the governor—none of those responsible for this travesty will ever admit fault. Watch 'em run. Watch 'em point fingers. Maybe they won't deny their mistakes, but they damned sure won't admit them. I suspect they will just keep quiet, hunker down, ride out the storm."

"Can they?"

Another pull on the bottle. Robbie smiled at the beer and licked his lips. "No cop has ever been indicted for a wrongful conviction. Kerber should go to jail. Koffee should too. They are directly responsible for Donté's conviction, but Koffee controls the grand jury. He's in charge of the system. So, criminal prosecutions are unlikely, unless, of course, I can convince the Justice Department to investigate. I will certainly try. And we still have the civil courts."

"Lawsuits?"

"Oh yes, lots of them. I'll sue everybody. Can't wait."

"Thought you were moving to Vermont."

"I may have to put that on hold. I'm not quite finished here."

The Slone Municipal School Board met in an emergency session at 2:00 Friday afternoon. The only item on the agenda was the game. Longview was scheduled to arrive at 5:00 p.m. for a 7:30 p.m. kickoff. The school officials and coaches in Longview were worried about the safety of their players and fans, and with good reason. The unrest in Slone was now routinely being referred to as a "race riot," a sensational description that was as inaccurate as it was catchy.

There had been a constant flow of threatening phone calls to the Slone Police Department and the school. If they tried to play the game, there would be trouble, and lots of it. The chief of police, Joe Radford, pleaded with the board to cancel the game, or somehow postpone it. A crowd of five thousand people, almost all of whom would be white, would provide too enticing a target for those wanting trouble. And just as troubling was the prospect of all the empty and unprotected homes of the fans during the game. The football coach admitted he really didn't want to play either. The kids were too distracted, not to mention the fact that his best players, the twenty-eight black ones, were boycotting. His star tailback, Trey Glover, was still in jail. Both teams had six wins and two losses and were eligible for the state play-offs. The coach knew he had no chance with an all-white team. But a forfeit was a loss, and this perplexed him and everybody else in the room.

The principal described the burned-out press box, the tension of the past two days, the canceled classes, and the phone threats his office had received throughout the day. He was exhausted and jumpy and practically begged the board to cancel.

A honcho from the National Guard reluctantly attended the meeting. He thought it was possible to secure the stadium area and play the game without incident. But he shared the chief's concerns about what might happen in the rest of the town for the three hours. When pressed, he admitted that the safest route was to cancel.

The board members squirmed and fretted and passed notes. While they routinely grappled with budgets and curriculum and discipline and dozens of important issues, they had never been faced with something as momentous as canceling a high school football game. They stood for election every four years, and the prospect of alienating the voters weighed heavily. If they voted to cancel and Slone was forced to forfeit, they would be seen as caving in to the boycotters and troublemakers. If they voted to play and people got hurt in an ugly incident, their opponents would lay blame on them.

A compromise was suggested, seized upon, and quickly gained momentum. A flurry of phone calls were made, and the compromise became a reality. The game would not be played that night in Slone; rather, it would be played the following day at an undisclosed site in a nearby town. Longview agreed. Their coach knew of the boycott and smelled blood. The location of the neutral site would be kept secret until two hours before kickoff. Both teams would drive about an hour, play the game without spectators, and the show would go on. The compromise pleased everyone but the head coach. He gamely gritted his teeth and predicted a win. What else could he do?

Throughout the morning and into the afternoon, the train station had been a magnet for reporters. It was the last place Boyette had been seen, and he was in demand. His chilling confession had been on the nonstop cable loop for almost a full day now, but his past had caught up with him. His colorful criminal record was in play, his credibility in serious question. Experts of all stripes were on the air, proffering opinions about his background, his profile, his motives. One windbag flat-out called him a liar and went on and on about how "these creeps" want their fifteen minutes of fame and enjoy tormenting the families of victims. A former Texas prosecutor opined as to the fairness of the Drumm trial and appeals and assured those listening that all was well with the system. Boyette was obviously a nut job.

As the saga wore on, it lost some of its shock value. Boyette wasn't around anymore to add details, or to defend himself. And neither was Robbie Flak. The reporters knew that Flak's car was not at the office. Where was he?

Inside the station, Sammie Thomas, Bonnie, and Fanta adopted a siege mentality and tried to work. It was impossible. The phones rang and rang, and every hour or so one of the ruder reporters would almost make it to the front door before being accosted by one of the security guards. With time, the mob began to understand that Boyette wasn't there, and neither was Robbie.

Out of boredom, the reporters left and drove around Slone looking for a fire or a fight. To get to the bottom of things, they interviewed guardsmen as they walked the streets, and they filmed and re-filmed the burned-out churches and buildings. They talked to angry young blacks outside of pool halls and honky-tonks, and they stuck microphones into pickup trucks for priceless comments from white vigilantes. Bored again, they returned to the train station and waited on some word from Boyette. Where the hell was he?

By late afternoon, a crowd was beginning to assemble in Washington Park. News of this development spread through the media, and off they went. Their presence attracted more young blacks, and soon the rap was booming and fireworks were popping. It was Friday night—payday, beer day, the start of the weekend, time to blow off some steam.

The tension was rising.

Some forty hours after leaving the parsonage with an unwanted passenger, Keith returned to it, alone. When he turned off the ignition, he sat in the car for a moment to get his bearings. Dana was waiting at the kitchen door with a hug and a kiss and a very pleasant "You look tired."

"I'm fine," he said. "Just need a good night's sleep. Where are the boys?"

The boys were at the table eating ravioli. They jumped at their father as if he'd been gone for a month. Clay, the oldest, was dressed in his soccer uniform, ready for a game. After a long hug, the family sat down and finished dinner.

In the bedroom, Keith dressed after a quick shower as Dana sat on the bed and watched him. She was saying, "Not a word from anyone around here. I've talked to Matthew a few times. We're watching the news and spending hours online. Your name has not been mentioned anywhere. A thousand photos, but no sign of you. The church thinks you were called away on some emergency, so no suspicions there. We might get lucky."

"What's the latest from Slone?"

"Not much. They postponed the football game tonight, and that was reported as urgently as a major plane crash."

"No news from Missouri?"

"Not a word."

"It'll blow up soon enough. I can't imagine the

shock waves when they announce they have found the body of Nicole Yarber. The town will explode."

"When will it happen?"

"I don't know. I'm not sure what Robbie's plans are."

"Robbie? You sound like you're old friends."

"We are. I met him yesterday, but we have traveled a long way together."

"I'm proud of you, Keith. What you did was crazy, but it was also courageous."

"I don't feel brave. I'm not sure what I feel right now. More shock than anything else. I think I'm still numb. It was a rather unique adventure, but we failed."

"You tried."

Keith pulled on a sweater, tucked in his shirttail, and said, "I just hope they catch Boyette. What if he finds another victim?"

"Come on, Keith, he's a dying man."

"But he left his cane behind, Dana. Can you explain that? I've been around the guy for five days—seems like a year—and he had trouble walking without the cane. Why would he leave it behind?"

"Maybe he thought he would be easier to spot with a cane."

Keith pulled his belt tight and buckled it. "He was fixated on you, Dana. He mentioned you several times, something like, 'That cute little wife of yours.'"

"I'm not worried about Travis Boyette. He'd be a fool to come back to Topeka."

"He's done dumber things. Look at all the arrests."

"We need to go. The game is at 6:30."

"I can't wait. I need something to distract me.

Do we have a bottle of Communion wine around here?"

"I think so."

"Good. I need a drink. Let's go watch a little soccer, then we'll spend the rest of the night debriefing."

"I want to hear everything."

33

The meeting was arranged by Judge Elias Henry, and while he did not have the authority to order people around on a Friday night, his powers of persuasion were more than enough. Paul Koffee and Drew Kerber arrived in the judge's chambers promptly at 8:00 p.m. Joe Radford followed them in, and the three sat together on one side of the judge's worktable. Robbie had been there for thirty minutes, along with Carlos, and the atmosphere was already toxic. There were no greetings, no handshakes, no pleasantries. A moment later Mayor Rooney arrived and sat by himself, away from the table.

Judge Henry, as always in a dark suit, white shirt, and orange tie, began solemnly. "Everyone is here. Mr. Flak has some information."

Robbie was seated directly across from Kerber, Koffee, and Radford, all three still and subdued as if waiting for a death sentence. Robbie started by saying, "We left Slone this morning around five and drove to Newton County, Missouri. Travis Boyette was with us. The trip took just under six hours. With Boyette giving directions, we worked our way through a remote section of the county, along back roads, then dirt trails, then to a place known locally as Roop's Mountain. Secluded, remote, overgrown. Boyette struggled to remember it at times, but eventually led us to the place where he claims he buried Nicole Yarber." Robbie nodded at Carlos, who punched a key on his laptop. At the far end of the room, on a whiteboard, a photo of the overgrown clearing appeared. Robbie continued, "We found the site and began to dig." The next photo was of Aaron Rey and Fred Pryor with shovels. "When Boyette was here in Slone in the fall of 1998, he worked for a company called R. S. McGuire and Sons out of Fort Smith. He kept a large metal box, one that was once used for hydraulic tools, in the back of his truck, and he used it to bury her." Next photo: the top of the orange toolbox. "The soil was not hard, and within ten, maybe fifteen minutes we found this." Next photo: the top half of the toolbox with "R. S. McGuire and Sons" stenciled on it. "As you can see, the toolbox opened from the top with a latch to the side. The latch was secured by a combination lock, which Boyette claimed he bought at a hardware store in Springdale, Arkansas. Boyette remembered the combination and unlocked it." Next photo: Boyette kneeling at the grave, handling the lock. The color drained from Koffee's face, and Kerber had perspiration on his forehead. "When we opened the box, this is what we found." Next photo: the skeleton. "Before we opened it, Boyette told us there would be a wad of clothing next to her head." Next photo: the clothing next to the skull. "He also told us that rolled up in the clothing we would find Nicole's driver's license and a credit card. He was right." Next photo: a close-up of the MasterCard, also stained but with her name easily readable. "Boyette told us he killed her by choking her with her black leather belt with a silver buckle." Next photo: a length of black leather, partially decomposed, but with the silver buckle. "I have a complete set of these photos for you boys to take home and look at all night. At this point, we called the sheriff of Newton County and surrendered the site." Next photo: the sheriff and three of his deputies gawking at the skeletal remains. "The site was soon crawling with police and investigators, and the decision was made to leave her remains in the box and take it to the satellite crime lab there in Joplin. That's where it is now. I gave the authorities a copy of Nicole's dental X-rays, a copy of the same set you boys inadvertently handed over when you were playing games with discovery before the trial. I have talked to the crime lab, and the case has priority. They expect to finish the preliminary identification tonight. We are expecting a phone call any moment. They will examine everything in the toolbox and hopefully find evidence for DNA testing. This is a long shot, but DNA is not crucial. It's pretty clear who was buried in the box, and there's no doubt who did the killing. Boyette has a lethal brain tumor—that's one reason he came forward—and he's subject to violent seizures. He collapsed at the site and was taken to a hospital in Joplin. Somehow, he managed to leave the hospital without being detected, and as of now no one knows where he is. He's considered a suspect, but he was not under arrest when he disappeared."

Robbie stared at Koffee and Kerber as he delivered his narrative, but they were unable to maintain eye contact. Koffee was pinching the bridge of his nose, while Kerber picked his cuticles. There were three identical black binders in the center of the table, and

Robbie gently slid them over, one each for Koffee, Kerber, and Radford. Robbie continued, "In these, you each have a complete set of the photos, along with a few other goodies—Boyette's arrest record here in Slone, which proves he was here at the time of the murder. In fact, you boys actually had him in jail at the same time Donté Drumm was locked up. There is also a copy of his extensive criminal record and history of incarcerations. His affidavit is included, but you don't really need to read it. It's a detailed account of the abduction, sexual assaults, murder, and burial; the same story you have no doubt seen a dozen times now on television. There's also an affidavit signed yesterday by Joey Gamble in which he says he lied at the trial. Any questions?"

Silence.

He continued, "I have chosen to proceed in this manner out of respect for Nicole's family. I doubt if any of you have the backbone to meet with Reeva tonight and tell her the truth, but at least you have that option. It would be a shame for her to hear it secondhand. Someone needs to tell her tonight. Comments? Anything?"

Silence.

The mayor cleared his throat and asked softly, "When will this go public?"

"I have asked the authorities in Missouri to sit on it until tomorrow. At nine in the morning, I'm holding a press conference."

"God, Robbie, is that really necessary?" the mayor blurted.

"It's Mr. Flak to you, Mr. Mayor, and, yes, it is quite necessary. The truth must be told. It's been buried for nine years by the police and the prosecutor, so, yes, it is time to tell the truth. The lies will finally be exposed. After nine years and the execution of an innocent man, the world will finally know that Donté's confession was bogus, and I'll explain the brutal methods used by Detective Kerber to obtain it. I plan to go into great detail describing the lies used at trial—Joey Gamble's and the jailhouse snitch Kerber and Koffee rounded up and cut a deal with—and I'll describe all the dirty tactics used at trial. I'll probably have the opportunity to remind everyone that Mr. Koffee was sleeping with the judge during the trial, just in case anyone has forgotten. I wish the blood-hound were still alive—what was his name?"

"Yogi," Carlos said.

"How could I forget? I wish ol' Yogi were still alive so I could show him to the world and call him a stupid son of a bitch again. I figure it might be a long press conference. You boys are invited. Questions? Comments?"

Paul Koffee's mouth opened slightly as if words were being formed, but words failed him. Robbie was far from finished. "And just so you boys will know what's coming in the next few days, I'll file at least two lawsuits Monday morning, one here in state court, naming you as defendants, along with the city, county, and half the state. Another one will be filed in federal court, a civil-rights action with a long list of allegations. You will be named in that one also. I might file another one or two, if I can find a cause of action. I plan to contact the Justice Department and request an investigation. For you, Koffee, I plan to file a complaint with the state bar association for ethics violations, not that I expect the state bar to show much of an interest, but you will get chewed up in the process. You might want to start thinking about a res-ignation. For you, Kerber, early retirement is now a real option. You should be fired, but I doubt the mayor and the city council have the balls to do that. Chief, you were the assistant chief when this investigation got off track. You will be named as a defendant, too. But don't take it personally. I'm suing everybody."

The chief slowly stood up and walked toward the door. "You're leaving, Mr. Radford?" the judge asked, in a tone that left no doubt such an abrupt exit would be frowned upon.

"My job does not require me to sit and listen to pompous assholes like Robbie Flak," the chief replied.

"The meeting is not over," Judge Henry said sternly.

"I'd stay if I were you," the mayor said, and the chief decided to stay. He assumed a position by the door.

Robbie stared at Kerber and Koffee, then said, "So last night you had a little party by the lake to celebrate; now I guess the party is over."

"We always thought Drumm had an accomplice," Koffee managed to blurt out, though his words trailed off under the weight of their own absurdity. Kerber nodded quickly, ready to pounce on any new theory that might save them.

"Good God, Paul," Judge Henry roared in disbelief. Robbie was laughing. The mayor's jaw had dropped in shock.

"Great!" Robbie yelled. "Wonderful, brilliant. Suddenly a new theory, one that has never been mentioned before. One with absolutely no relation to the truth. Let the lying begin! We have a Web site, Koffee, and my sidekick Carlos here is going to keep a tally of the lies. Lies from the two of you, from the governor, the courts, maybe even dear Judge Vivian Grale, if we can find her. You have lied for nine years in order to kill an innocent man, and now that we know the truth, now that your lies will be exposed, you insist on doing precisely what you have always done. Lie! You make me want to puke, Koffee."

"Judge, can we leave now?" Koffee asked.

"Just a moment."

A cell phone rang and Carlos grabbed it. "It's the crime lab, Robbie." Robbie reached over, took the phone. The conversation was brief, and there were no surprises. When it ended, Robbie said, "Positive ID, it's Nicole."

The room was quiet as they thought about the girl. Judge Henry eventually said, "I am concerned about her family, gentlemen. How do we break the news?"

Drew Kerber was perspiring and appeared to be on the brink of an attack of some variety. He was not thinking about Nicole's family. He had a wife, a houseful of kids, lots of debts, and a reputation. Paul Koffee could not even begin to imagine a conversation with Reeva about this little twist to their story. No, he would not do it. He would rather run like a coward than deal with that woman. Admitting they had prosecuted and executed the wrong man was, at that moment, far beyond the limits of his imagination.

There were no volunteers. Robbie said, "Obviously, Judge, I'm not the guy. I have my own little trip to make, over to the Drumm home to deliver the news."

"Mr. Kerber?" the judge asked.

He shook his head no.

"Mr. Koffee?"

He shook his head no.

"Very well. I will call her mother myself and break the news."

"How late can you wait, Judge?" the mayor asked. "If this hits the streets tonight, then God help us."

"Who is in the loop, Robbie?" the judge asked.

"My office, the seven of us in this room, the authorities in Missouri. We also took a TV crew with us, but they won't air anything until I say so. It's a small world right now."

"I'll wait two hours," Judge Henry said. "This meeting is adjourned."

Roberta Drumm was at home with Andrea and a few friends. The kitchen table and counters were covered with food—casseroles, platters of fried chicken, cakes, and pies, enough food to feed a hundred. Robbie had forgotten to eat dinner, so he snacked as he and Martha waited for the friends to leave. Roberta was thoroughly drained. After a day receiving guests at the funeral home, and crying with most of them, she was emotionally and physically spent.

And so Robbie made things much worse by delivering the news. He had no choice. He began with the journey to Missouri and finished with the meeting in Judge Henry's office. He and Martha helped Andrea put Roberta in bed. She was conscious, but barely. Knowing that Donté was about to be exonerated, and before he was buried, was simply too much.

The sirens were quiet until ten minutes after 11:00 p.m. Three quick 911 calls got them started. The first reported a fire in a shopping center north of town. Evidently, someone tossed a Molotov cocktail through the front window of a clothing store, and a passing motorist saw flames. The second call, anonymous, reported a burning school bus parked behind the junior high. And the third, and most ominous, was from a fire alarm system at a feed store. Its owner was Wallis Pike, Reeva's husband. The police and guardsmen, already on high alert, stepped up their patrols and surveillance, and for the third straight night Slone endured the sirens and the smoke.

Long after the boys were asleep, Keith and Dana sat in the dark den and sipped wine from coffee cups. As Keith told his story, the details poured out, and he remembered facts and sounds and smells for the first time. The little things surprised him—the sound of Boyette heaving in the grass beside the interstate, the lethargy of the state trooper as he went about the task of writing the speeding ticket, the stacks of paperwork on the long table in Robbie's conference room, the looks of fear on the faces of his staff, the antiseptic smell of the holding room in the death house, the ringing in Keith's ears as he watched Donté die, the lurching of the airplane as they flew over Texas, and on and on. Dana peppered him with questions, random and insightful. She was as intrigued by the adventure as Keith, and at times incredulous.

When the bottle was empty, Keith stretched out on the sofa and fell into a deep sleep.

34

With Judge Henry's approval, the press conference was held in the main courtroom of the Chester County Courthouse, on Main Street in downtown Slone. Robbie had planned to hold it in his office, but when it became apparent that a mob would attend, he changed his mind. He wanted to make sure every possible reporter could be accommodated, but he didn't want a bunch of curious strangers poking around his train station.

At 9:15 a.m., Robbie stepped to the podium in front of Judge Henry's bench and surveyed the throng. Cameras clicked and tape recorders were turned on to catch every word. He wore a dark three-piece suit, his finest, and though exhausted, he was also wired. He wasted little time getting to the point. "Good morning and thanks for coming," he said. "The skeletal remains of Nicole Yarber were found yesterday morning in a remote section of Newton County, Missouri, just south of the city of Joplin. I was there, along with members of my staff, accompanying a man named Travis Boyette. Boyette led us to the site where he buried Nicole almost nine years ago,

two days after he abducted her here in Slone. Using
dental records, the crime lab in Joplin made a positive identification last night. The crime lab is working
around the clock to examine her remains, and their
work should be completed in a couple of days." He
paused, took a sip of water, and scanned the crowd.
Not a sound. "I'm in no hurry, folks. I plan to go into
considerable detail, then I will answer all the questions you have." He nodded at Carlos, who was
seated nearby with his laptop. On a large screen next
to the podium, a photo of the grave site appeared.
Robbie began a methodical description of what they
had found, illustrated by one photo after another.
Pursuant to an agreement with the authorities in Missouri, he did not show the skeletal remains. The site
was being treated as a crime scene. He did use the
photos of Nicole's driver's license, credit card, and the
belt Boyette used to strangle her. He talked about
Boyette and gave a brief explanation of his disappearance. There was not yet a warrant for his arrest,
so Boyette wasn't a wanted man.

It was obvious that Robbie was relishing the moment. His performance was being broadcast live. His
audience was captive, spellbound, and hungry for
every detail. He could not be interrupted or challenged on any point. It was his press conference, and
he was finally getting the last word. The moment was
a lawyer's dream.

There would be several points during the morning
when Robbie belabored a topic, beginning with his
heartfelt ramblings about Donté Drumm. The audience, though, refused to be bored. He eventually got

around to the crime, and this prompted a photo of Nicole, a very pretty, wholesome high school girl.

Reeva was watching. Phone calls had roused her. They had been up all night dealing with the fire at the feed store, a fire that was contained quickly and could've been much worse. It was certainly arson, a criminal act obviously carried out by black thugs seeking revenge against the family of Nicole Yarber. Wallis was still there, and Reeva was alone.

She cried when she saw her daughter's face, displayed by a man she loathed. She cried and she seethed and she ached. Reeva was confused, tormented, thoroughly bewildered. The phone call last night from Judge Henry had spiked her blood pressure and sent her to the emergency room. Add the fire, and Reeva was practically delirious.

She had asked Judge Henry many questions—Nicole's grave? Skeletal remains? Her clothing and driver's license, belt and credit card, and all the way up in Missouri? She had not been dumped in the Red River near Rush Point? And worst of all—Drumm was not the killer?

"It's true, Mrs. Pike," the judge said patiently. "It's all true. I'm sorry. I know that it is a shock."

A shock? Reeva couldn't believe it and for hours refused to believe it. She'd slept little, ate nothing, and was still grasping for answers when she turned on the television and there was Flak, the peacock, live on CNN talking about her daughter.

There were reporters outside, in the driveway, but the house was locked, the curtains drawn, the blinds down, and one of Wallis's cousins was on the front porch with a 12-gauge shotgun. Reeva was fed up with the media. She had no comment. Sean Fordyce was holed up in a motel south of town fuming because she would not chat with him on camera. He had made a fool of her already. He reminded her of their agreement, of the signed contract, to which she responded, "Just sue me, Fordyce."

Watching Robbie Flak, Reeva, for the first time, allowed herself to think the unthinkable. Was Drumm innocent? Had she spent the last nine years hating the wrong person? Had she watched the wrong man die?

And what about the funeral? Now that her baby had been found, she would need to be properly buried. But the church was gone. Where would they have the funeral? Reeva wiped her face with a wet cloth and mumbled to herself.

Eventually, Robbie moved on to the confession. Here he picked up steam and was consumed by a controlled rage. It was very effective. The courtroom was silent. Carlos projected a photo of Detective Drew Kerber, and Robbie announced with great drama, "And here is the principal architect of the wrongful conviction."

Drew Kerber was watching, at the office. He had spent a horrible night at home. After leaving Judge Henry's, he had gone for a long drive and tried to imagine a happier ending to this nightmare. None appeared. Around midnight, he sat down with his wife at the kitchen table and bared his soul: the grave, the bones, the ID, the unmentionable idea that "evidently" they had nailed the wrong guy; Flak and his lawsuits and his threats of vigilante-style suing that would follow Kerber to his grave and the high probability of future unemployment, legal bills, and judgments. Kerber unloaded a mountain of grief upon his poor wife, but he did not tell the whole truth. Detective Kerber had never admitted, and he never would, that he had bullied Donté into confessing.

As a chief detective with sixteen years of experience, he earned $56,000 a year. He had three teenagers and a nine-year-old, a mortgage, two car payments, an IRA with around ten grand, and a savings account with $800. If fired, or retired, he might be entitled to a small pension, but he could not survive financially. And his days as a police officer would be over.

"Drew Kerber is a rogue cop with a history of obtaining fake confessions," Robbie said loudly, and Kerber flinched. He was at his desk, in a small locked office, all alone. He had instructed his wife to keep the TVs off in the house, as if they could somehow hide this story from his kids. He cursed Flak, then watched with horror as the slimeball explained to the world exactly how he, Kerber, had obtained the confession.

Kerber's life was over. He might handle the ending by himself.

Robbie moved on to the trial. He introduced more characters—Paul Koffee and Judge Vivian Grale. Photos, please. On the large screen, Carlos projected them side by side, as if still attached, and Robbie assailed them for their relationship. He mocked the "brilliant decision to move the trial all the way to Paris, Texas, forty-nine miles from here." He drove home the point that he tried valiantly to keep the confession away from the jury, while Koffee fought just as hard to keep it in evidence. Judge Grale sided with the prosecution and "her lover, the Honorable Paul Koffee."

Paul Koffee was watching, and seething. He was at the cabin by the lake, very much alone, watching the local station's "exclusive live coverage" of the Robbie Flak show, when he saw his face next to Vivian's. Flak was railing against the jury, as white as a Klan rally because Paul Koffee had systematically used his jury strikes to eliminate blacks, and, of course, his girl-friend up on the bench went along with it. "Texas-style justice," Robbie lamented, over and over.

He eventually moved away from the more tawdry aspects of the judge-prosecutor relationship and found his rhythm railing against the lack of evidence. Grale's face disappeared from the screen, and Koffee's was enlarged. No physical evidence, no dead body, only a trumped-up confession, a jailhouse snitch, a bloodhound, and a lying witness named Joey Gamble. Meanwhile, Travis Boyette was free, certainly not worried about getting caught, not by these clowns.

Koffee had tried all night to conjure up a revised theory that would somehow link Donté Drumm and Travis Boyette, but fiction failed him. He felt lousy. His head ached from too much vodka, and his heart pounded as he tried to breathe under the crushing weight of a ruined career. He was finished, and that troubled him much more than the notion that he had helped kill an innocent young man.

When he finished with the jailhouse snitch and the bloodhound, Robbie attacked Joey Gamble and his fraudulent testimony. With perfect timing, Carlos flashed up Gamble's affidavit, the one signed in Hous-ton on Thursday, an hour before the execution. High-lighted were Joey's statements admitting he lied at

trial and admitting he was the first to suggest that
Donté Drumm was the killer.

Joey Gamble was watching. He was at his
mother's house in Slone. His father was away; his
mother needed him. He had told her the truth, and
the truth had not been well received. Now he was
shocked to see and hear his transgressions broadcast
in such a startling way. He had assumed that when he
came clean, he would be subjected to some level of
embarrassment, but nothing like this.

"Joey Gamble lied repeatedly," Flak announced at
full throttle, and Joey almost reached for the remote.
"And now he admits it!" Joey's mother was upstairs
in her bedroom, too upset to be around him. "You
helped kill that boy," she had said more than once,
not that Joey needed reminding.

Robbie continued, "Moving on from the incompetent
investigation, the travesty of a trial, and the wrongful
conviction, I would like to now discuss the Texas
Court of Criminal Appeals. This court heard Donté's
first appeal in February 2001. The body of Nicole
Yarber was still missing. The court noted that there
was no physical evidence in the trial. The court
seemed slightly bothered by the lies of the jailhouse
snitch. It nibbled at the edges of Donté's confession
but refused to criticize Judge Grale for allowing the
jury to hear it. It commented on the use of the bloodhound testimony, saying perhaps it wasn't the 'best
evidence' to use in such a serious trial. But all in all,
the court saw nothing wrong. The vote was nine to
affirm the conviction, zero to overturn it."

Chief Justice Milton Prudlowe was watching. A
frantic call from his law clerk had alerted him to the

press conference, and he was with his wife in their small apartment in Austin, glued to CNN. If Texas had indeed executed an innocent man, he knew his court was in for an avalanche of scorching criticism. Mr. Flak seemed prepared to lead the attack.

"Last Thursday," Robbie was saying, "at exactly 3:35 p.m., lawyers for Donté Drumm filed a petition for relief, and we included a video that we had just taken of Travis Boyette confessing to the rape and murder. This was two and a half hours before the execution. I assume the court considered this matter and was not impressed with the video, or the affidavit, because an hour later the court denied relief and refused to stop the execution. Again, the vote was nine to zero." On cue, Carlos flashed up the times and actions by the court. Robbie plowed ahead. "The court closes for business each day at 5:00 p.m., even when an execution is pending. Our final filing was the last-minute affidavit and recantation by Joey Gamble. In Austin, attorneys for Donté called the court clerk, a Mr. Emerson Pugh, and informed him that they were on their way with the petition. He said the court would close at 5:00. And he was right. When the attorneys arrived at the court at 5:07, the door was locked. The petition could not be filed."

Prudlowe's wife glared at him and said, "I hope he's lying."

Prudlowe wanted to assure her that of course this loudmouthed lawyer was lying, but he hesitated. Flak was too shrewd to make such damning statements in public without having the facts to back them up.

"Milton, tell me this guy is lying."

"Well, honey, I'm not sure right now."

"You're not sure? Why would the court close if the lawyers were trying to file something?"

"Well, uh, we—"

"You're stuttering here, Milton, and that means you're struggling to tell me something that may or may not be entirely accurate. Did you see Boyette's video two hours before the execution?"

"Yes, it was passed—"

"Oh my God, Milton! Then why didn't you stop things for a few days? You're the chief justice, Milton; you can do anything you want. Executions are delayed all the time. Why not give it another thirty days, or a year for that matter?"

"We thought it was bogus. The guy is a serial rapist with no credibility."

"Well, right now he's got a helluva lot more credibility than the Texas Court of Criminal Appeals. The murderer confesses, no one believes him, so he shows them exactly where he buried the body. Sounds pretty credible to me."

Robbie paused and took a sip of water. "As for the governor, his office received a copy of the Boyette video at 3:11 Thursday afternoon. I don't know for sure whether the governor saw the video. We do know that at 4:30 he addressed a crowd of protesters and publicly denied a reprieve for Donté."

The governor was watching. He was standing in his office in the Governor's Mansion, dressed for a golf game that would not be played, with Wayne on one side and Barry on the other. When Robbie paused, he demanded, "Is that true? Did we have the video at 3:11 p.m.?"

Wayne lied first. "Don't know. So much stuff was happening. They were filing junk by the truckload."

Barry told the second lie. "This is the first I've heard of it."

"Did anyone see the video when it came in?" he asked, his irritation growing by the second.

"Don't know, Boss, but we'll find out," Barry said.

The governor stared at the television, his mind spinning, trying to grasp the severity of what he was hearing. Robbie was saying, "Even after denying clemency, the governor had the right to reconsider and stop the execution. He refused to do so."

The governor hissed the word "Asshole," then yelled, "Get to the bottom of this, and now!"

Carlos closed his laptop, and the screen went blank. Robbie flipped through his legal pad to make sure he'd said enough. He lowered his voice and in a grave tone said, "In closing, it is now obvious that we have finally done it. Those who study the death penalty, and those of us who fight it, have long feared the day when this would happen, when we would wake up to the horrible fact that we have executed an innocent man, and that it can be proven by clear and convincing evidence. Innocent men have been executed before, but the proof was not clear. With Donté, there is no doubt." A pause. The courtroom was still and silent. "What you will see in the days to come will be a pathetic game of finger-pointing, lying, and dodging blame. I have just given you the names and some of the faces of those responsible. Go after them, listen to their lies. This did not have to happen. This was not an unavoidable mistake. This was a willful disregard for the rights of Donté Drumm. May he rest in peace. Thank you."

Before the onslaught of questions, Robbie stepped

to the bar and took the hand of Roberta Drumm. She rose and walked stiffly to the podium, Robbie by her side. She pulled the microphone down a bit closer and said, "My name is Roberta Drumm. Donté was my son. I have little to say at this moment. My family is grieving. We are in shock. But I beg of you, I plead with the people of this town, to stop the violence. Stop the fires and the rock throwing, the fighting, the threats. Please stop it. It does no good. Yes, we are angry. Yes, we are wounded. But the violence serves no purpose. I call on my people to lay down your arms, to respect everyone, and to get off the streets. The violence does nothing but harm the honor of my son."

Robbie led her back to her seat, then smiled at the crowd and said, "Now, does anyone have a question?"

35

Matthew Burns joined the Schroeder family for a late breakfast of pancakes and sausage. The boys ate quickly and returned to their video games. Dana made more coffee and began clearing the table. They discussed the press conference, Robbie's brilliant presentation of the case, and Roberta's poignant remarks. Matthew was curious about Slone, the fires and violence, but Keith had seen little of it. He had felt the tension, smelled the smoke, heard the police helicopter hovering overhead, but he had not seen much of the town.

With fresh coffee, the three sat at the table and talked about Keith's improbable journey and the whereabouts of Travis Boyette. Keith, though, was growing weary of the details. He had other issues, and Matthew was prepared for the conversation.

"So, Counselor, how much trouble could I be in?" Keith asked.

"The law is not real clear. There is no specific prohibition against aiding a convicted felon in his efforts to violate the terms of his parole. But it's still against the law. The applicable code section deals with ob-

struction of justice, which is a huge net for a lot of behavior that would otherwise be difficult to classify. By
driving Boyette out of this jurisdiction, and with the
knowledge that it was a violation of his parole, you
violated the law."

"How serious?"

Matthew shrugged, grimaced, stirred his coffee
with a spoon. "It's a felony, but not a serious one.
And it's not the type of violation that we get excited
about."

"We?" Dana asked.

"As in prosecutors. The district attorney would
have jurisdiction, a different office. I'm with the city."

"A felony?" Keith asked.

"Probably. It appears that your trip to Texas has
gone unnoticed here in Topeka. You managed to
avoid the cameras, and I have yet to see your name in
print."

"But you know about it, Matthew," Dana said.

"I do, and I suppose that, technically, I'm expected
to inform the police, to turn you in. But it doesn't
work that way. We can process only so much crime.
We're forced to pick and choose. This is not a violation that any prosecutor would want to deal with."

"But Boyette is a famous guy right now," Dana
said. "It's just a matter of time before a reporter here
picks up on the story. He jumped parole, took off to
Texas, and we've seen his face for three days now."

"Yes, but who can link Keith to Boyette?"

"Several folks in Texas," Keith said.

"True, but I doubt if they care what happens here.
And these folks are on our side, right?"

"I guess."

"So, who can make the link? Did anyone see you
with Boyette?"

"What about the guy at the halfway house?" Dana asked.

"It's possible," Keith said. "I went there several times looking for Boyette. I signed the register, and there was a guy at the desk, Rudy, I think, who knew my name."

"But he didn't see you drive away with Boyette late Wednesday night?"

"No one saw us. It was after midnight."

Matthew shrugged, satisfied. All three worked on their coffee for a moment, then Keith said, "I can make the link, Matthew. I knew I was violating the law when I left with Boyette because you made things very clear. I made a choice. At the time, I knew I was doing the right thing. I have no regrets now, so long as Boyette is found before he hurts anyone else. But if he's not found, and if someone gets hurt, then I'll have a ton of regrets. I am not going to live with a possible criminal violation hanging over my head. We plan to deal with it now."

Dana and Keith were both looking at Matthew, who said, "That's sort of what I figured."

"I'm not running from this," Keith said. "And we can't live with the threat of an officer knocking on the door. Let's get it over with."

Matthew shook his head and said, "Okay, but you'll need a lawyer."

"What about you?" Dana asked.

"A defense lawyer, as in criminal defense. Me? I'm now on the other side of the street, and, frankly, I can help more over there."

"Could Keith possibly go to jail?" she asked.

"Get right to the point, don't you?" Keith said with a smile. Dana was not smiling. Her eyes were moist.

Matthew stretched his arms above his head, then leaned forward on his elbows. "Here's my worst-case scenario. I'm not predicting this; it's just the worst case. If you admit your role in taking him to Texas, get ready for some coverage. Then, if Boyette rapes another woman, all hell breaks loose. I can see the DA playing hardball with you, but I cannot, under any scenario, see you going to jail. You may have to plead guilty, get probation, pay a small fine, but I doubt it."

"I'd stand in court, in front of a judge, and plead guilty?"

"That's what usually happens."

Keith took Dana's hand on the table. There was a long moment of reflection, then she said, "What would you do, Matthew?"

"Hire a lawyer, and pray Boyette is either dead or too ill to attack someone."

At noon, the forty-one white members of the Slone High football team met in the parking lot of a small elementary school on the edge of town. There, they quickly boarded a chartered bus and left town. Their equipment was in a rental van behind the bus. An hour later, they arrived at Mount Pleasant, population fifteen thousand. From there, the bus followed a police car to the high school football field. The players dressed quickly and hustled to the field for their pregame routines. It was odd, warming up with no lights and no fans. Security was tight; police cars blocked every possible route to the field. The Lobos of Longview High took the field minutes later. There were no cheerleaders, no band, national anthem, pregame prayer, or public address announcer. As the coin was tossed, the Slone coach looked across the field at the Lobos and wondered how bad the slaughter might be. They had eighty players on a roster that was at least 70 percent black. Slone had not beaten Longview since the days of Donté Drumm, and the Warriors had no chance today.

What was happening in Slone was being felt throughout East Texas, if not far beyond.

Slone won the toss and elected to receive. It really didn't matter, but the Slone coach wanted to avoid a long kickoff return and a quick seven points. His receiving team took the field, and the Lobos lined up to kick. Ten black kids and a white kicker. At the whistle, the player closest to the ball suddenly stepped forward and grabbed it. It was a move that had never been seen before, and for a second everyone was startled. The ten black members of the kickoff team then yanked off their helmets and laid them on the turf. The referees blew their whistles, the coaches yelled, and for a few seconds there was total confusion. On cue, the other black Longview players walked onto the field, dropping their helmets and jerseys as they went. The Slone players on the field backed away in disbelief. The game was over before it began.

The black players formed a tight circle and sat together at midfield, the modern-day version of a sit-in. The officials, four white and two black, huddled briefly and kept their cool. None of the six volunteered to attempt to get the football. The Longview coach walked to midfield and said, "What the hell is going on here?"

"Game's over, Coach," said Number 71, a 330-pound tackle and co-captain.

"We ain't playing," said Number 2, the other co-captain.

"Why not?"

"It's a protest," said Number 71. "We're solid with our brothers in Slone."

The coach kicked the turf and weighed his options. It was clear that this situation was not about to change, not anytime soon. "Well, just so you understand what you are doing here, this means we'll have to forfeit, which knocks us out of the play-offs, and they'll probably find some kind of probation for us. That what you guys want?"

All sixty or so said "Yes!" in unison.

The coach threw up his hands, walked off the field, and sat on the bench. The Slone coach called his players off the field. From both sidelines, the white players stared at the black players. Green Lobo jerseys and helmets littered the field. The officials retreated to an end zone and watched; their day was done.

Minutes passed as reality set in. Then from the Longview sideline, Number 35, a white backup fullback, stepped onto the field, removed his helmet and jersey, and took a seat on the forty-yard line, near his black teammates. One by one the other players followed, until only the coaches were left on the sideline.

The Slone coach wasn't sure what to do. He was thinking that perhaps he had just been handed a victory, snatched by a miracle from certain defeat. He was about to tell his players to leave the field when Number 88, Denny Weeks, the starting tight end and the son of a Slone police officer, stepped onto the field, dropped his helmet, and pulled off his jersey. He sat on the field with the Longview players, one of whom reached over and shook his hand. One by one the Warriors followed, until all forty-one had left the sideline.

At 3:00 p.m., the governor's office issued a statement for the press. Drafted by Barry Ringfield and rewritten by Wayne Wallcott and the governor himself, its final version read:

> *Governor Gill Newton is deeply concerned about recent events in the matter of Donté Drumm. The allegations that this office received a videotape of a confession by the alleged killer, just before the execution, are simply false. The governor first saw the video yesterday, Friday, approximately sixteen hours after the execution. The governor will be available on Monday for additional comments.*

The train station finally closed Saturday afternoon. Aaron Rey placed two armed guards on the landing, with orders to threaten anyone who came near. The Flak firm gathered at Robbie's house for an impromptu party. Everyone was there, along with spouses. DeDe hired a caterer who specialized in barbecue, and the rich smell of ribs on the grill wafted over the patio. Fred Pryor manned the bar and the drinks flowed. Everyone lounged in the pool house and tried to relax. The Longhorns were playing football and the television drew some interest. Robbie tried to prohibit any discussion of the Drumm case, but the conversation drifted there anyway. They couldn't help themselves. They were exhausted, drained, and defeated, but managed to unwind. The booze helped a lot.

The Longview game was making the rounds, and they tipped a glass in honor of the sit-in.

Fred Pryor, while bartending, monitored the police chatter on his radio. The streets of Slone were remarkably calm, which they attributed to Roberta Drumm's emotional plea. They had also heard that Roberta, Marvin, Cedric, and Andrea had gone to Washington Park and pleaded with the people to go home, to stop the violence.

Though Robbie had ordered all cell phones turned off, the call came through anyway. Carlos received it and relayed the news to a hushed audience. The authorities in Joplin had expedited their examination and had some interesting news. On Nicole's underwear, they had found a significant semen sample. DNA testing matched it to Travis Boyette. His DNA sample was in the Missouri data bank due to a previous conviction there.

There was reason to celebrate, and reason to weep. With emotions torn both ways, they decided to have another drink.

36

Sunday. What had been probable on Thursday, even likelier on Friday, and virtually certain on Saturday became the numbing truth during the night, so that on Sunday morning the country awoke to the sensational reality that an innocent man had been executed. Led by *The New York Times* and *The Washington Post*, the big dailies railed and ranted, and all reached the same conclusion—it's time to stop the killing. The story was page one in both papers, and in dozens of others from Boston to San Francisco. Lengthy articles gave the history of the case, and the characters were well advertised, with Robbie Flak getting as much attention as Donté. Screeching editorials called for a moratorium on executions. There were countless guest columns by legal experts, defense lawyers, death-penalty abolitionists, professors, activists, ministers, even a couple of men on death row, and the same conclusion was reached: now that we have unassailable evidence of a wrongful execution, the only fair and sensible course is to stop them forever, or, if that can't be done, at least stop them until the death penalty system can be studied and over-hauled.

In Texas, the *Houston Chronicle*, a paper that had gradually grown weary of the death penalty but had stopped short of calling for its abolition, covered its front page with an unrestrained summary of the case. It was a condensed version of Robbie's press conference, with large photographs of Donté, Nicole, and Robbie on page one, and a dozen more on page five. The stories, all six of them, hit hard at the mistakes and peeled skin off Drew Kerber, Paul Koffee, and Judge Vivian Grale. The identities of the villains were clear; blame was inescapable. One reporter was on the trail of the Texas Court of Criminal Appeals, and it was obvious that there would be no place for the court to hide. Chief Justice Milton Prudlowe was unavailable for comment, as were the other eight justices. The clerk of the court, Mr. Emerson Pugh, refused comment. However, Cicely Avis, the Defender Group lawyer who tried to enter Pugh's office at 5:07 Thursday afternoon, had plenty to say. The details were emerging, with more stories sure to come. Another *Chronicle* reporter was stalking the governor and his staff, all evidently in full retreat.

Reactions varied around the state. Newspapers known to be generally moderate in their politics—those in Austin and San Antonio—called for outright abolition of the death penalty. The Dallas paper was on record calling for a moratorium. Newspapers that were firmly on the right went light on the editorials but could not resist full-blown coverage of the events in Slone.

On television, the Sunday morning talk shows all found room for the story, though the presidential campaign was still the main topic. On cable, Donté

Drumm had been the lead story since Robbie's press conference twenty-four hours earlier, and it showed no signs of slipping to number two. At least one of the subplots had been deemed important enough to have its own title: "The Hunt for Travis Boyette" could be seen every thirty minutes. On the Internet, the story was all the rage, showing five times more hits than anything else. Anti-death-penalty bloggers railed with uncontrolled fury.

As tragic as it was, the story was a huge gift for those on the left. On the right, things were predictably quiet. Those who supported the death penalty were not likely to change, not overnight anyway, but there seemed to be a general feeling that it was a good time to say nothing. The hard-right cable shows and AM radio commentators simply ignored the story.

In Slone, Sunday was still a day of worship. At the Bethel African Methodist Church, a crowd much larger than normal gathered for the 8:00 a.m. call to worship, to be followed by Sunday school, a men's prayer breakfast, choir practice, Bible lessons, coffee and doughnuts, and eventually the worship hour, which would go on far longer than sixty minutes. Some were there in hopes of seeing one of the Drumms, preferably Roberta, and maybe offering a quiet word of condolence. But the Drumm family needed rest and stayed at home. Some were there because they needed to talk, to hear the gossip, to lend support or to receive it.

Whatever the motive, the sanctuary was overflowing when the Reverend Johnny Canty stepped to the pulpit and warmly welcomed the crowd. It didn't take long to get to the issue of Donté Drumm. It would've been easy to stir up his people, to throw gas on the fire, to hit all the open targets, but Reverend Canty was not inclined to do so. He talked about Roberta and her grace under pressure, her agony in watching her son die, her strength, her love for her children. He talked about the urge for revenge, and how Jesus turned the other cheek. He prayed for patience and tolerance and the wisdom of good men to deal with what had happened. He talked about Martin Luther King and his courage in bringing about change by eschewing violence. It's man's nature to strike back, but the second blow leads to the third, and the fourth. He thanked his flock for laying down their arms and getting off the streets.

Remarkably, it had been a quiet night in Slone. Canty reminded his people that Donté Drumm's name was now famous; it was a symbol that would bring about change. "Let us not smear it with more blood, more violence."

After a thirty-minute warm-up, the worshippers fanned out through the church to pursue the usual Sunday morning activities.

A mile away, members of the First Baptist Church began arriving for a unique worship experience. The rubble of their sanctuary was still lined with yellow police tape, still a crime scene under active investigation. In a parking lot, a large white tent had been erected. Beneath it were rows of folding chairs and tables covered with food. The dress was casual, the mood generally upbeat. After a quick breakfast they sang hymns, old-time gospel tunes with a beat and lyrics they knew by heart. The chairman of the deacons spoke about the fire and, more important, about the new church they would build. They had insurance, they had faith, they would borrow, if necessary, but a beautiful new sanctuary would rise from the ashes, all to the glory of the Lord.

Reeva was not in attendance. She had not come out of the house. Frankly, she was hardly missed. Her friends felt her pain, now that her daughter had been found, but with Reeva the pain had been relentless for nine years. Her friends could not help but remember the vigils by the Red River, the marathon prayer sessions, the endless tirades in the press, the enthusiastic embrace of victimhood, all in an effort to extract revenge on that "monster" Donté Drumm. Now that they had executed the wrong monster, and with Reeva happily watching him die, few of her fellow church members wanted to face her. Fortunately, she did not want to face them.

Brother Ronnie was a troubled soul. He had watched his church burn, which was no fault of his, but he had also watched Donté die, and with no small measure of satisfaction. There was a sin in there somewhere. He was a Baptist, a breed noted for its creative ways of finding new versions of sin, and he needed forgiveness. He shared this with his congregation. He bared his soul, admitted he was wrong, and asked them to pray for him. He seemed genuinely humbled and distressed.

Arrangements for Nicole's funeral were incomplete. Brother Ronnie explained that he had talked with Reeva by phone—she was not taking visitors—and the church Web site would post the details when the family made decisions. Nicole was still in Missouri, and the authorities there had not said when they would release her.

The tent was being watched closely. Across the street, on property that did not belong to the church, two dozen or so reporters loitered about, most with cameras. If not for the presence of several quite edgy police officers, the reporters would have been under the tent, recording every word, making a nuisance of themselves.

Slone had never been more divided than on that Sunday morning, but even at that dark hour there was some circling of the wagons. The number of reporters and cameras had steadily increased since Thursday, and everyone in town felt an element of the siege. The man on the street had stopped talking to reporters. City officials had nothing but "No comment." Not a single word could be pried out of the courthouse. And in certain places, the police increased their presence and sharpened their attitude. Any reporter trying to get near the Drumm home was likely to be handled roughly. The funeral home where Donté was resting was strictly off-limits. Reeva's house was being guarded by cousins and friends, but the police were nearby, just waiting for some clown with a camera to intrude. Robbie Flak could take care of himself, and was doing a fine job of it, but his home and office were patrolled every hour. And on Sunday morning, the devoted Christians who worshipped at the Bethel African Methodist Church, and at the First Baptist Church, were able to do so without intrusion. The Slone Police Department made sure of it.

At St. Mark's Lutheran, the Reverend Keith Schroeder assumed the pulpit and startled his congregation with the most gripping opening of any sermon yet. "Last Thursday, the State of Texas executed an innocent man. If you've missed the story, then I don't know where you've been. Most of you know the facts of the case, but what you don't know is that the real killer was here last Sunday, sitting right over there. His name is Travis Boyette, a convicted felon, released a few weeks ago from the prison in Lansing and assigned to a halfway house on Seventeenth Street here in Topeka."

No one in the crowd of two hundred seemed to be breathing. Those who had been planning naps were suddenly wide-awake. Keith was amused at the odd looks he was getting. He went on: "No, I'm not kidding. And while I would like to say that Mr. Boyette was attracted to our little church because of its reputation for great preaching, the truth is that he came because he was troubled. First thing Monday morning, he was in my study to talk about his problems. He then made his way down to Texas and tried to stop the execution of Donté Drumm. He was unsuccessful. Somehow, he got away."

Keith's initial plan was to describe his adventures in Texas, in what would undoubtedly be his most fascinating sermon ever. He was not afraid of the truth; he wanted it told. He assumed his church would find out sooner or later, and he was determined to confront the issue head-on. However, Dana had maintained that the wiser course was to wait until he met with a lawyer. Admitting to a crime, especially in such a public manner, without the advice of counsel, seemed risky. She prevailed, and Keith decided on a different message.

As a minister, he steadfastly refused to mix politics and religion. In the pulpit, he had stayed away from issues such as gay rights, abortion, and war, preferring instead to teach what Jesus taught—love your neighbor, help the less fortunate, forgive others because you have been forgiven, and follow God's laws.

However, after witnessing the execution, Keith was a different person, or at least a different preacher. Suddenly, confronting social injustice was far more important than making his flock feel good each Sunday. He would begin hitting the issues, always from the Christian perspective and never from the politician's, and if it rankled folks, too bad. He was tired of playing it safe.

"Would Jesus witness an execution without trying to stop it?" he asked. "Would Jesus approve of laws that allow us to kill those who have killed?" The answer to both was no, and for a full hour, in the longest sermon of his career, Keith explained why not.

Before dark on Sunday afternoon, Roberta Drumm, with her three children, their spouses, and her five grandchildren, walked a few blocks to Washington Park. They had made the same walk the day before, and for the same purpose. They met with the young people congregated there and in one-on-one conversations talked about Donté's death and what it was doing to all of them. The rap was turned off. The crowd became quiet and respectful. At one point, several dozen gathered around Roberta and listened as she pleaded for civility. In a strong, eloquent voice, and sometimes pointing for emphasis, she said, "Please don't desecrate the memory of my son with more bloodshed. I don't want the name of Donté Drumm to be remembered as the reason for a race riot here in Slone. Nothing you do out here on the streets will help our people. Violence creates more violence, and in the end we lose. Please, go home and hug your mother."

To his people, Donté Drumm was already a legend. The courage of his mother inspired them to go home.

37

Slone High School did not open Monday morning. Though the tension appeared to be easing, the school authorities and the police were still nervous. Another round of fights and smoke bombs could spill over into the streets and disrupt the fragile truce. The white students were ready to return to class, to their normal routines and activities. As a rule, they were shocked, even appalled by what had happened over the weekend. They were as stunned by the Drumm execution as their black friends, and they were anxious to confront it, discuss it, and try to move on. The joining of the sit-in by the white football players at the Longview game was the topic of nonstop chatter around town, and that simple act of solidarity was viewed as one huge offer of an apology. A momentous mistake had been made, but others were to blame. Let's meet and shake hands and deal with it. For most of the black students, the thought of continued violence was not appealing. They had the same routines and activities as their white friends, and they, too, wanted a return to normalcy.

The school board met again with the mayor and

the police. The term "powder keg" was used often to describe the atmosphere in Slone. There were enough hotheads on both sides to make trouble. Anonymous phone calls were still being recorded. There were threats of violence as soon as the school reopened. In the end, it was decided that the safest route was to wait until after the funeral of Donté Drumm.

At 9:00 a.m., the football team met with their coaches in the locker room at the field. The meeting was closed. The twenty-eight black players were there, as were their white teammates, all forty-one of them. The meeting had been suggested by Cedric and Marvin Drumm, both of whom had played as Warriors, though at a level far below their brother's. Standing side by side, they addressed the team. They thanked the white players for their courage in joining the Longview players in protest. They spoke fondly, even emotionally, of their brother and said that Donté would not approve of the divisiveness. The football team was the pride of the town, and if it managed to heal itself, then there was hope for everyone. They appealed for unity. Cedric said, "When we bury Donté, I ask that all of you be there. It will mean so much to our family, and to the rest of our community."

Denny Weeks, the son of a Slone policeman and the first player to remove his helmet and jersey and sit with the Longview players, asked if he could speak. He faced the team and began by describing how sickened he was by the execution and its aftermath. He, along with most of the whites he knew, had felt all along that Donté was guilty and getting what he deserved. He was wrong, so incredibly wrong, and he would always carry the guilt. He apologized for what he'd believed, that he'd favored the execution. Denny became emotional and, trying to keep his composure, finished by saying that he hoped Cedric and Marvin, the rest of the family, and his black teammates could find it in their hearts to forgive him. Other confessionals followed, and the meeting became a prolonged and fruitful effort at reconciliation. It was a team, complete with petty grudges and fierce rivalries, but most of the boys had played football together since middle school and knew each other well. They had nothing to gain by allowing the bitterness to fester.

The state officials were still trying to resolve the baffling issues presented by the Longview standoff. It was generally believed that both teams would be given a forfeit, but the regular season would go on. There was one game left on the schedule. The coach said that it was all or nothing—if they could not come together as a team, then the last game would be forfeited. With Cedric and Marvin standing before them, the players had no choice. They could not say no to the brothers of Donté Drumm. After two hours, they shook hands and decided to meet that afternoon for a long practice.

The spirit of reconciliation had not reached the Flak Law Firm, and it probably would not. Energized by a quiet Sunday, and facing a mountain of work, Robbie pushed the troops to prepare for an assault on various fronts. Top priority was the civil litigation. Robbie was determined to file suit that day, both in state and in federal court. The state action, for wrongful death, would be a shotgun blast aimed at the City of Slone, its police department, the county and its district attorney, the state and its judges, prison officials, and appeals court justices. The members of the judi-

ciary were immune from liability, but Robbie planned
to sue them anyway. He would sue the governor, who
was absolutely immune. Much of the lawsuit would
be dismantled and eventually dismissed, but Robbie
didn't care. He wanted revenge, and embarrassing
those responsible and forcing them to hire lawyers
were things he relished. He loved bare-knuckle litigation, especially when he was throwing the punches
and the press was watching. His clients, the Drumms,
were sincerely opposed to more violence in the streets,
as was Robbie, but he knew how to create violence
in the courts. The litigation would drag on for years
and consume him, but he was confident of prevailing
eventually.

The lawsuit in federal court would be a civil-rights
action, with many of the same defendants. There, he
would not waste time suing the judges, justices, and
the governor, but would hit hard at the City of Slone,
its police, and Paul Koffee. In light of what had become obvious, he foresaw a lucrative settlement, but
far down the road. The city and county, and, more
important, their insurance companies, would never
run the risk of having their dirty laundry aired before
a jury in such a notorious case. When they were fully
exposed, the actions of Drew Kerber and Paul Koffee
would terrify the well-paid lawyers for the insurers.
Robbie was obsessed with revenge, but he also
smelled money.

Other strategies on the table included an ethics
complaint against Paul Koffee. A win there could
mean disbarment and further humiliation, though
Robbie was not overly optimistic. He also made plans
to file a complaint against Chief Justice Milton Prudlowe with the State Commission on Judicial Conduct,
but this would take more time. So few of the facts sur-

rounding the aborted filing were known. It appeared, though, as if the facts would be forthcoming. Something akin to a hornet's nest of reporters was already attacking the Texas Court of Criminal Appeals. Robbie was content to sit back and watch the press flush out the truth.

He contacted the Justice Department in Washington. He took calls from death-penalty opponents around the country. He chatted with reporters. His office was chaos, and he thrived on it.

The law office Keith and Dana walked into Monday morning was far different from the last one Keith had seen. The Flak Law Firm had been filled with people, tension, and activity. The office of Elmo Laird was small and quiet. Matthew's scouting report described Elmo as a sole practitioner, a sixty-year-old veteran of the criminal courts who dispensed solid advice but rarely went to trial. He and Matthew were friends, and, more important, Elmo played golf with the district attorney.

"I've never had a case like this," Elmo admitted after listening to Keith for a few minutes. He had done his homework and, like everyone who enjoys the morning paper, knew the basics of the Drumm mess down in Texas.

"Well, it's something new for me too," Keith said.

"There's no clear statute on point. You provided assistance to a man who was determined to violate his parole anyway by leaving this jurisdiction. It's not exactly a major crime, but you could be prosecuted for obstruction of justice."

"We've read the statutes," Dana said. "Matthew

sent them over, along with a few cases from other states. Nothing is clear."

"I haven't been able to find a similar case in Kansas," Elmo said. "Not that that means anything. If the district attorney chooses to prosecute, then I'd say he has a pretty good case. You're admitting everything, aren't you?"

"Sure," Keith said.

"Then I suggest we explore the possibility of a plea agreement, and the sooner, the better. Boyette is on the loose. He may strike again, maybe not. Perhaps this week, maybe never. It's to your advantage to cut a deal, a good deal, before he makes any more trouble. If he hurts someone, you become more culpable, and a simple case could get complicated."

"What's a good deal?" Keith asked.

"No jail and a slap on the wrist," Elmo said with a shrug.

"And what does that mean?"

"Not much. A quick court appearance, a small fine of some sort, certainly no time in jail."

"I was hoping you would say that," Dana said.

"And after some time, I could probably get your record expunged," Elmo added.

"But the conviction would be a public record, right?" Keith asked.

"Yes, and that is worrisome. Boyette was front-page news this morning here in Topeka, and I suspect there will be more about him in the coming days. It's our own little connection to this sensational episode. If a reporter sniffs around, he might stumble across your conviction. It's a pretty good story, if you think about it. Local minister gives assistance to the real killer, and so on. I can see a big splash in the paper, but no permanent damage. The bigger story will be written if and when he commits another crime. Then the prosecutor will take some heat and might be harder to deal with."

Keith and Dana exchanged uncertain looks. It was their first visit to a law office together, and hopefully their last. Keith said, "Look, Mr. Laird, I really don't want this hanging over my head. I'm guilty of doing what I did. If I committed a crime, I'll take my punishment. Our question is simple: What now?"

"Give me a few hours to talk to the district attorney. If he agrees, then we cut a quick deal and get it over with. With some luck, you'll slide under the radar."

"How soon could this happen?"

Another shrug. "This week."

"And you promise he's not going to jail?" Dana asked, almost pleading.

"No promises, but it's very unlikely. Let's talk first thing in the morning."

Keith and Dana sat in the car outside Laird's office and stared at the side of his building. "I can't believe we're here, doing this, talking about pleading guilty, worrying about going to jail," she said.

"Isn't it great? I love it."

"You what?"

"I gotta tell you, Dana, other than our honeymoon, this past week has been the greatest week of my life."

"You're sick. You've spent too much time with Boyette."

"I sorta miss Travis."

"Drive, Keith. You're cracking up."

*　*　*

The governor was officially hard at work grappling with the state's budget. He was too busy to comment on the Drumm matter; the case was closed as far as he was concerned.

Unofficially, he was locked in his office with Wayne and Barry, all three dazed and hungover, eating ibuprofen, and bitching about what to do next. Reporters were camped outside the building—they'd actually filmed him as he left the Governor's Mansion that morning at 7:30 with his security detail, something he did five days a week, as if such a movement were now breaking news. The office was being flooded with calls, faxes, e-mails, letters, people, even packages.

Barry said, "It's a shit storm, growing worse by the minute. Thirty-one editorials yesterday, coast-to-coast, another seventeen today. At this rate, every newspaper in the country will take a shot. Nonstop yakking on cable, experts popping up by the dozens with advice on what to do next."

"And what should we do next?" the governor asked.

"Moratoriums, moratoriums. Give up capital punishment, or at least study it to death."

"Polls?"

"The polls say we screwed up, but it's too early for something like this. Give it a few days, let the aftershocks die down, then we'll ease back into the market. I suspect we'll lose a few points, but my guess is at least 65 percent are still in favor of the needle. Wayne?"

Wayne was buried in his laptop, but not missing a word. "Sixty-nine, still my favorite number."

"I'll split it," the governor said. "Sixty-seven. All in?"

Barry and Wayne gave a quick thumbs-up. The standard polling bet was now in play—each of the three with $100 on the line.

The governor walked to his favorite window for the hundredth time, but saw nothing outside. "I gotta talk to someone. Staying in here and ignoring the press makes me look like I'm hiding."

"You are so hiding," Barry said.

"Find me an interview with someone we can trust."

"There's always Fox. I talked to Chuck Monahand two hours ago, and he would love to have a chat. He's harmless and his numbers are way up."

"Will he give us the questions ahead of time?"

"Of course he will. He'll do anything."

"I like it. Wayne?"

Wayne cracked his knuckles with enough force to break them, then said, "Not so fast. What's the urgency? Sure you're hunkered down, but give it some time. Let's think of where we'll be a week from now."

"My guess is that we'll be right here," Barry said. "With the door locked, pulling our hair out and trying to decide what to do next."

"But it's such a big moment," the governor said. "I hate to let it pass."

"Let it pass," Wayne said. "You look bad right now, Gov, and there's no way to fix that. What we need is time, and lots of it. I say we lie low, dodge the bullets, let the press chew on Koffee and the cops and the court of appeals. Let a month go by. It won't be pleasant, but the clock will not stop."

"I say we go to Fox," Barry said.

"And I say we don't," Wayne shot back. "I say we cook up a trade mission to China and leave for ten days. Explore foreign markets, more outlets for Texas products, more jobs for our people."

"I did that three months ago," Newton said. "I hate Chinese food."

"You'll look weak," Barry said. "Running away smack in the middle of the biggest story since that last hurricane. Bad idea."

"I agree. I'm not leaving."

"Then can I go to China?" Wayne asked.

"No. What time is it?" The governor wore a watch, and there were at least three clocks in his office. When that question was asked late in the afternoon, it meant only one thing. Barry stepped to the cabinet and pulled out a bottle of Knob Creek bourbon.

The governor sat behind his massive desk and took a sip. "When is the next execution?" he asked Wayne. His lawyer punched keys, stared at his laptop, and said, "Sixteen days."

Barry said, "Oh, boy."

"Who is it?" Newton asked.

Wayne said, "Drifty Tucker. Male, white, fifty-one years old, Panola County, killed his wife when he caught her in bed with the next-door neighbor. Shot the neighbor too, eight times. Had to reload."

"Is that a crime?" Barry asked.

"Not in my book," Newton said. "No claim of innocence?"

"Nope. He claimed insanity, but it looks as if the reloading bit nailed him."

"Can we get a court somewhere to issue a stay?" Newton asked. "I'd rather not deal with it."

"I'll work on it."

The governor took another sip, shook his head,

and mumbled, "Just what we need right now, another execution."

Wayne suddenly reacted as if he'd been slapped. "Get a load of this. Robbie Flak just filed a lawsuit in state court in Chester County, naming a bunch of defendants; one of them is the Honorable Gill Newton, Governor. Fifty million dollars in damages for the wrongful death of Donté Drumm."

"He can't do that," the governor said.

"He just did. Looks like he e-mailed a copy of it to all defendants, as well as to every newspaper in the state."

"I'm immune."

"Of course you are, but you've been sued anyway."

Barry sat down and began scratching his hair. The governor closed his eyes and mumbled to himself. Wayne gawked at his laptop, mouth wide open. A bad day just took a turn for the worse.

38

Keith sat in his office at the church, hands locked behind his head, shoeless feet on the desk, eyes gazing at the ceiling, his thoughts still scrambled after all of it. Once or twice in the past few days, his mind had returned to family and church matters, but those pleasant diversions were always ruined when he thought of Travis Boyette loose on the streets. Keith had reminded himself countless times that he did not help Boyette escape—the man was already roaming the streets of Topeka, a convict who'd served his time and was lawfully reentering society. He, Boyette, had made the decision to leave Anchor House and violate his parole before he convinced Keith to become his chauffeur. But Keith was living with a knot in his stomach, a constant nag that assured him he had done something wrong.

To take a break from Boyette, he yanked his feet off the desk and turned to face his computer. The monitor was showing a Web site for the Kansas chapter of AADP, Americans Against the Death Penalty, and Keith decided to join. Using his credit card, he paid the $25 annual fee, now one of three thousand members and as such entitled to the online newsletter, a monthly magazine with all the latest, and other periodic updates from the staff. The group met once a year in Wichita, details to follow. Outside of the church, it was the first organization he'd ever joined.

Out of curiosity, he looked at the sites of anti-death-penalty groups in Texas, and found plenty. He noticed the names of several groups he'd seen in the news coverage the past two days; the abolitionists down there were making the most of the Drumm execution, and there was no shortage of activity. Execution Watch, Students Against the Death Penalty, Texas Network Moratorium, TALK (Texans Against Legalized Killing), Texans for Alternatives to the Death Penalty. One familiar name was Death Penalty Focus. Keith went to its Web site and was impressed. Membership was only $10. Keith pulled out his credit card and signed up. He was enjoying himself and not thinking about Boyette.

The largest and oldest group in Texas was ATeXX, an acronym for Abolish Texas Executions. It not only published extensively on the subject of capital punishment but also pushed its policies on the legislature, built support groups for the men and women on death row, raised money to defend those charged with capital crimes, networked with dozens of other groups around the country, and, most impressively, at least in Keith's opinion, reached out to both families—those of the victims and those of the condemned. ATeXX had fifteen thousand members and an annual budget of $2 million and offered membership to anyone willing to pay $25. Keith was in the mood, and moments later he joined his third group.

Sixty dollars later, he felt like a certified abolitionist.

His intercom beeped and broke the silence. Charlotte Junger announced, "There's a reporter on the phone. I think you should talk to her."

"Where's she from?"

"Houston, and she's not going away."

"Thanks." He answered the phone. "This is the Reverend Keith Schroeder."

"Reverend Schroeder, my name is Eliza Keene. I'm with the *Houston Chronicle*." Her voice was soft, her words unhurried, her accent similar to the twang Keith had heard in Slone. "I have some questions about Travis Boyette."

His life flashed before his eyes. Headlines, controversy, handcuffs, jail.

Keith froze long enough to convince Ms. Keene that she was on the right trail. "Sure," he said. What was he supposed to say? He would not lie and deny knowing Boyette. For a split second, he thought about refusing to talk to her, but that would set off alarms.

"Do you mind if I record our conversation?" she asked pleasantly.

Yes. No. He had no idea. "Well, no," he said.

"Good. It helps me keep things accurate. Just a second." A pause. "Now the recorder is on."

"Okay," Keith said, but only because it seemed as though something was needed on his end. He decided to stall as he tried to gather his thoughts. "Say, uh, Ms. Keene, I don't spend a lot of time talking to reporters. Is there some way I can verify that you are indeed a reporter for the *Houston Chronicle*?"

"Is your computer on?"

"It is."

"Then I'm sending you my bio right now. I'm also sending a photo taken outside the law office of Robbie Flak. It was last Thursday as Mr. Flak and his team were leaving. There are four people in the photo, one wearing a dark jacket and a white collar. I'll bet that's you."

Keith opened the e-mail, checked the attachment. It was him. He scanned her bio but knew it wasn't necessary.

"Nice-looking guy," Keith said.

"We thought so. That you?"

"Yep."

"Did you witness the execution of Donté Drumm?" she asked, and Keith's mouth went dry. He grunted, cleared his throat, and said, "Why do you think I witnessed the execution?"

"We have obtained the records from the prison. You're listed as a witness for the inmate. Plus, one of the men standing behind you during the execution was a reporter, not for us, but for another paper. He did not get your name. I found it."

What would Elmo Laird advise him to do at this point? Stop talking, perhaps. He wasn't sure, but he was impressed. If she had the prison records and a photo, then what else had she found? His curiosity took over. "Then I guess I witnessed the execution," he said.

"Why would a Lutheran minister from Topeka witness an execution in Texas?" she asked. It was the same question Keith had posed to himself at least a thousand times.

Keith forced a chuckle and said, "It's a long story."

"A friend of Donté Drumm's?"

"No."

"Travis Boyette was staying at a halfway house in Topeka, then he pops up in Slone, Texas. Any idea how he got there?"

"Perhaps."

"Do you drive a maroon Subaru, Kansas plates, registration LLZ787?"

"I'm assuming you have a copy of my registration."

"I do, and one of our reporters noticed the car in Slone. Not many Kansans stop over in Slone. Any chance Boyette hitched a ride with you?"

Another chuckle, this one for real. "All right, Ms. Keene, what do you want from me?"

"I want the story, Reverend Schroeder, all of it."

"That would take hours, and I'm not willing to spend the time, not right now."

"When did you first meet Travis Boyette?"

"One week ago today, last Monday."

"And at that time, did he admit to the murder of Nicole Yarber?"

Surely, all confidentiality was gone. Boyette had broadcast his admissions to the world; there weren't too many secrets left. Some things, though, should be kept private. Keith wasn't obliged to answer the question, or any others for that matter. He was not afraid of the truth; in fact, he was determined not to hide it. If his tracks were this easy to follow, other reporters would be calling soon. Let's get it over with.

"This is what I'm willing to say, Ms. Keene. Travis Boyette visited our church Sunday of last week. He wanted to talk, so he came back the following day.

He confided in me, and we eventually made our way down to Slone, Texas, arriving last Thursday around midday. He was determined to stop the execution because Donté Drumm was innocent. Boyette went on the air, admitted that he was the killer, and gave the statement that we've all seen. Mr. Flak asked me to travel with him to Huntsville. I reluctantly said yes, and one thing led to another. I met Donté and, quite unexpectedly, witnessed the execution. The following morning, Boyette led Mr. Flak and others, including me, to the place in Missouri where he'd buried the girl. After that, Boyette fell ill. I took him to a hospital in Joplin, and from there he managed to walk away. I drove home. I've had no contact with Boyette since."

There was a pause on the other end as she digested this. "Reverend Schroeder, I have about a thousand questions."

"And I'm late for soccer practice. Good day, ma'am." Keith hung up and hurriedly left the office.

Fordyce—Hitting Hard! ran a one-hour segment during prime time Monday night. The event had been shamelessly advertised throughout the weekend, and Sean Fordyce spoke to the world live from Slone, Texas, where he was still darting around in search of another fire or, hopefully, a dead body or a bomb blast. The first half hour was the Reeva show, with lots of tears and anticipation of the execution. There was footage of Nicole as a little girl dancing in a recital, and more of her bounding on the sideline as she cheered on the Warriors. There was a clip of Donté mauling a running back. And lots of Reeva, with the highlight being the post-execution interview. In light of the obvious, she looked foolish, almost pathetic, and it was obvious Fordyce set her up for the kill. There were close shots of Reeva bawling without restraint, then going mute as she watched the tape of Boyette for the first time. She was visibly shaken when Boyette displayed Nicole's class ring. After that, no more Reeva. In the second half, Fordyce ran a collage of videos and interviews and produced nothing that wasn't already known. The piece was a mess. It was ironic that a mouthpiece so enamored of the death penalty was airing an exclusive about a wrongful execution, but irony was lost on Sean Fordyce. He cared for nothing but ratings.

Keith and Dana watched it. During his chaotic hours in Slone, and the frenzy to actually get there, he had seen nothing of Nicole's family. He'd read about Reeva online but had not heard her speak. At least the Fordyce piece was good for something. Not having dealt with Reeva, he could easily feel sorry for her.

There was a phone call he had been delaying for several hours. As Dana prepped the boys for bed, Keith retreated to the bedroom and called Elmo Laird. He apologized for disturbing him at home, but things were changing rapidly and Keith deemed the call important. Elmo said not to worry. After Keith explained in detail the conversation with Eliza Keene, Elmo suggested that perhaps they should worry. "Probably not a good idea" was his first response.

"But she had the story, Mr. Laird, the facts, the paperwork, the photo. She knew everything. I would've sounded stupid trying to deny things."

"You're not required to speak to reporters, you know?"

"I know, but I'm not running from anyone. I did what I did. The truth is on the table."

"I appreciate that, Pastor, but you hired me to give advice. There would've been a better time and place to tell your story, a setting of our choosing."

"I'm sorry. I don't understand legalities. Right now, I'm overwhelmed with the law and its endless procedures."

"Of course, my clients usually are. That's why they hire me."

"So I screwed up?"

"Not necessarily. But get ready for all hell to break loose, pardon my language, Pastor. I expect coverage of this. I'm not sure the Drumm story can take any more ink, but your story will certainly be a new wrinkle."

"I'm confused, Mr. Laird. Help me here. How will the coverage affect my case?"

"Keith, come on, you really don't have a case. There are no charges pending, and there may never be. I spoke with the district attorney this afternoon, he and I are friends, and while he was captivated with your story, he wasn't gung ho to crank up a prosecution. He didn't rule it out, and again I'm afraid Boyette is the key. He's probably the most famous convict on the loose right now. He was indicted for murder in Missouri today, did you see—"

"I saw it a couple of hours ago," Keith said.

"His face is everywhere, so maybe he'll be caught. I doubt if he comes back to Kansas. Let Missouri have him. If he's locked up before he hurts someone, I think the DA here might close the book."

"And the publicity about my involvement?"

"We'll see. A lot of people around here will admire

you for what you did. I can't see much room to criticize you for trying to save Donté Drumm, especially in light of what we know now. We'll ride it out, but, please, no more interviews."

"You got it, Mr. Laird."

39

Keith slept, off and on, for four hours, then finally got out of bed and went to the kitchen. He checked CNN, saw nothing new, then opened his laptop and checked in with Houston. On Chron.com there were several stories, with Robbie and his lawsuits getting the lead. There was a photo of him waving some papers on the steps of the Chester County Courthouse. He was quoted at length, with predictable statements about hounding those responsible for the wrongful death of Donté Drumm to their graves. None of the defendants, including the governor, commented.

The next story was about the reactions of the various anti-death-penalty groups in the state, and Keith was proud to see ATeXX taking the lead. There were demands for a number of drastic responses—the usual moratorium on executions, investigations of the Slone Police Department, the Texas Court of Criminal Appeals, the governor's handling of clemency, the trial itself, Paul Koffee and his office, and on and on. Demonstrations were planned for noon Tuesday at the State Capitol in Austin, Sam Houston State

University in Huntsville, Texas Southern University, and a dozen other schools.

The longest-serving member of the Texas Senate was a feisty black attorney from Houston, Rodger Ebbs, and he had a lot to say. He was demanding that the governor call an emergency session of the legislature so that a special inquiry could be initiated to investigate all aspects of the Drumm fiasco. Ebbs was vice chairman of the Senate Finance Committee, and thus had considerable influence over every aspect of the state's budget. He promised to shut down the state government if a special session did not take place. No comment from the governor.

Drifty Tucker, the next man scheduled to be executed, was suddenly in the news. His date was November 28, a little over two weeks away, and his case, dormant for a decade, was attracting a lot of attention.

Eliza Keene's article was number four on the list. Keith clicked on it and saw the photo of himself, Robbie, Aaron, and Martha Handler, all looking quite serious as they left the train station for the trip to Huntsville. The headline was "Kansas Minister Witnessed Drumm Execution." She covered the basics of the story and attributed several quotes to Keith. She, too, had witnessed an execution, years earlier, and was intrigued by how someone could be approved as a witness on such short notice. No one from the prison would comment. Evidently, she had contacted the Flak Law Firm for a word or two, but found no one willing to talk. A counselor at Anchor House said that Reverend Schroeder had stopped by at least twice the previous week looking for Boyette. He had signed the register. Boyette's parole officer was mum. About half the article dealt with Keith and Boyette and their mad rush to Texas to stop the execution. There was a smaller photo of Boyette taken when he addressed the reporters the previous Thursday. The second half of the report took a different turn and dwelled on Keith's potential legal problems. Could the minister be prosecuted for knowingly aiding a felon in his flight to violate parole? To get to the bottom of this, Ms. Keene called upon some experts. A law professor at the University of Houston was quoted: "It was an honorable thing to do, but a clear violation of the law. Now that Boyette is at large, I suspect the minister might want to consult with a lawyer."

Thanks, loudmouth, Keith said to himself. And the violation is anything but clear, according to my lawyer. Perhaps you should do a bit of research before popping off in the press.

A criminal defense lawyer in Houston said, "There may be a violation, but looking at the whole picture, I think the guy is a hero. I would love to defend him before a jury."

A jury? Elmo Laird was hoping for a quick, quiet little guilty plea with a slap on the wrist. That's what Keith remembered, anyway. And to cover all angles, Ms. Keene chatted with a former Texas prosecutor who was quoted as saying, "A crime is a crime, regardless of the circumstances. I would cut him no slack. The fact that he's a minister is of no significance."

The fifth article was a continuation of the ferocious investigation into what happened in the governor's office in the waning hours before the execution. So far, the team of journalists had been unable to smoke out anyone from inside the governor's office who would admit to having seen the video of Boyette making his confession. The e-mail was sent from the Flak Law Firm at 3:11 p.m., and Robbie certainly made his server records available. The governor's office did not. Nothing was forthcoming. His close aides, and dozens who were not so close, were marching in step and saying nothing. This would probably change. When the investigations began, and the subpoenas started flying, the finger-pointing would begin.

At 6:02 a.m., the phone rang. Caller ID showed it as "Unknown." Keith grabbed it before it woke up Dana and the boys. A man with a thick accent, possibly French, said he was looking for Reverend Keith Schroeder.

"And who are you?"

"My name is Antoine Didier; I'm with *Le Monde*, a newspaper in Paris. I would like to speak about the Drumm matter."

"I'm sorry, I have no comment." Keith hung up and waited for it to ring again. It did, he grabbed it, gave an abrupt "No comment, sir," then hung up again. There were four phones in the house, and he hurried through and punched "Do Not Disturb" on all of them. In the bedroom, Dana was coming to life. "Who is calling?" she asked, rubbing her eyes.

"The French."

"The who?"

"Get up. It might be a long day."

Lazarus Flint was the first black park ranger in East Texas. For over thirty years, he had supervised the maintenance of Rush Point along the Red River, and for the past nine years he and his two staff members had patiently cared for the sacred ground upon which the family and friends of Nicole Yarber made their treks and conducted their vigils. He had watched them for years. They showed up every now and then, and they would sit at the point near the makeshift cross. They would sit and cry and burn candles, all the while gazing into the river in the distance, as if the river had taken her away. As if they knew for certain that was her final resting place. And once a year, on the anniversary of her disappearance, her mother made her annual pilgrimage to Rush Point, always with cameras around her, always wailing and carrying on. They burned more candles, packed flowers around the cross, brought mementos and crude artwork and signs with messages. They would stay until dark, and always left with a prayer at the cross.

Lazarus was from Slone, and he had never believed Donté was guilty. One of his nephews was sent away for a burglary he had nothing to do with, and Lazarus, like most blacks in Slone, had never trusted the police. They got the wrong man, he'd said many times from a distance as he watched Nicole's family and friends carry on.

Early Tuesday, long before anyone arrived at Rush Point, Lazarus parked his pickup truck near the shrine and slowly, methodically began dismantling the junk. He yanked the cross from the ground—there had been several crosses over the years, each larger than the last. He lifted the wax-covered block of granite upon which they stuck the candles. There were four photos of Nicole, two laminated and two framed in glass. A very pretty girl, Lazarus thought as he placed the photos in his truck. A terrible death, but then so was Donté's. He gathered tiny porcelain figures of cheerleaders, clay tablets with printed messages, bronze works with no discernible meanings, baffling works of oil on canvas, and bunches of wilted flowers.

It was a load of trash, in his opinion.

What a waste, Lazarus said to himself as he drove away. Wasted effort, time, tears, emotions, hatred, hope, prayers. The girl had been more than five hours away, buried in the hills of Missouri by someone else. She had never been near Rush Point.

Paul Koffee entered the chambers of Judge Henry on Tuesday at 12:15. Though it was lunchtime, there was no food in sight. Judge Henry stayed behind his desk, and Koffee sat in a deep leather chair, one he knew well.

Koffee had not left his cabin since Friday night. On Monday, he had not called his office, and his staff knew nothing of his whereabouts. His two court appearances, both in front of Judge Henry, had been postponed. He looked gaunt, tired, pale, with even deeper circles under his eyes. His customary prosecutor's swagger had vanished.

"How are you doing these days, Paul?" the judge began pleasantly.

"I've been better."

"I'm sure you have. Are you and your staff still working on the theory that Drumm and Boyette were in cahoots?"

"We're giving that some thought," Koffee said while staring out a window to his left. Eye contact was difficult for Koffee, but not for Judge Henry.

"Perhaps I can help here, Paul. You and I, and the rest of the world at this moment, know full well that such a ridiculous theory is nothing but a sick, lame, desperate attempt to save your ass. Paul, listen to me, your ass cannot be saved. Nothing can save you. And if you trot out this co-defendant theory, you will be laughed out of town. Worse, it will only create more tension. It's not going to fly, Paul. Don't pursue it. Don't file anything, because if you do, I'll dismiss it immediately. Forget about it, Paul. Forget about everything in your office right now."

"Are you telling me to quit?"

"Yes. Immediately. Your career will end in disgrace; get it over with, Paul. Until you step down, the blacks will be in the streets."

"Suppose I don't want to resign?"

"I can't make you, but I can make you wish you had. I'm your judge, Paul, I rule on every motion in every case. I preside over every trial. As long as you are the district attorney, your office gets nothing out of me. Don't even file a motion, because I won't consider it. Don't indict anyone; I'll quash the indictments. Don't ask for a trial, because I'm busy that week. Nothing, Paul, nothing. You and your staff will be able to do nothing."

Koffee was breathing through his mouth, frowning at the judge, trying to digest what he'd just heard. "That's pretty severe, Judge."

"If that's what it takes to get you out of office."

"I could file a complaint."

Judge Henry laughed. "I'm eighty-one years old and retiring. I don't care."

Koffee slowly got to his feet and walked to a window. He spoke with his back to the judge. "I don't care either, Elias, to be honest. I just want to get outta here, take a break, run away. I'm only fifty-six, still young enough to do something else." A long pause as Koffee rubbed a pane of glass with a finger. "God, I can't believe this, Judge. How did this happen?"

"Everybody got careless. Bad police work. When there's no evidence, the easiest way to solve a crime is to get a confession."

Koffee turned around and took a few steps to the edge of the desk. His eyes were moist, his hands trembled. "I can't lie, Judge. I feel rotten."

"I understand. I'm sure I would too, under the circumstances."

Koffee stared at his feet for a long time. Finally, he said, "I'll quit, Elias, if that's what it takes. I guess that means a special election."

"Eventually, but I have a suggestion. When you resign, put Grimshaw in charge, he's the best of your assistants. Call in the grand jury and indict Boyette for the crime. The faster, the better. It's a wonderfully symbolic act—we, the judicial system, in effect admit our mistake, and we are now trying to rectify it by prosecuting the real killer. Our admission will do much to soothe feelings in Slone."

Koffee nodded and shook the judge's hand.

Keith's office at St. Mark's received numerous calls throughout the day. Charlotte Junger fielded them all, explaining that the reverend was unavailable for comment. Keith finally arrived, late in the afternoon. He had been hiding at the hospital all day, visiting the sick, far away from phones and nosy reporters.

At his request, Charlotte had kept a log of all callers, and Keith studied it in his office, door locked, phone unplugged. The reporters were from everywhere, from San Diego to Boston, Miami to Portland. Six of the thirty-nine were from European papers, eleven from Texas. One reporter said he was from Chile, though Charlotte wasn't sure because of the accent. Three members of St. Mark's had called to complain. They did not like the fact that their pastor was accused of violating the law; indeed, he seemed to be admitting it. Two members called to express their admiration and support. The story, though, had not yet made it to the Topeka morning paper. That would happen the next day, and Keith expected the same photo to be splashed all over his hometown.

Luke, the six-year-old, had a soccer game under the lights, and since it was Tuesday, the Schroeder family ate at their favorite pizza place. The boys were in bed by 9:30, Keith and Dana by 10:00. They debated whether to keep the phones silent, but in the end agreed to remove the "Do Not Disturb" hold and hope for the best. If one reporter called, they would silence the phones. At 11:12, the phone rang. Keith, still awake, grabbed it and said, "Hello."

"Pastor, Pastor, how are we?" It was Travis Boyette. In anticipation of this unlikely event, Keith had rigged a small recorder to his phone. He pushed "Record" and said, "Hello, Travis," and Dana came to life. She scrambled out of bed, flipped on a light switch, grabbed her cell phone, and began punching the number of a Detective Lang, a man they had met with twice.

"What are you doing these days?" Keith asked. Just a couple of old friends. Lang had told him to keep Boyette on the line as long as possible.

"Moving around, can't stay in one place too long." His tongue was thick, his words slow.

"Still in Missouri?"

"Naw, I left Missouri before you did, Pastor. I'm here and there."

"You forgot your cane, Travis. Left it on the bed. Why did you do that?"

"Don't need it, never did. I exaggerated a little bit, Pastor, please forgive me. I got a tumor, but it's been with me for a long time. Meningioma, not a glioblastoma. Grade one. Benign little fella. It acts up every now and then, but I doubt if it will kill me. The cane was a weapon, Pastor, something I used for self-defense. You live with a bunch of thugs in a halfway house, and you just never know when you might need a weapon." Country music was in the background; he was probably in a seedy lounge.

"But you had a limp."

"Well, come on, Pastor, if you're using a cane, you need a little limp, don't you think?"

"I wouldn't know, Travis. You got some folks looking for you."

"The story of my life. They'll never find me. Just like they never found Nicole. Have they buried her yet, Pastor?"

"No. Her funeral is Thursday. Donté's is tomorrow."

"I might sneak around and watch Nicole's, whatta you think about that, Pastor?"

Great idea. They would not only catch him but probably beat him. "I think you should, Travis. You're the reason for the funeral. Seems fitting."

"How's that cute little wife of yours, Pastor? Bet you guys are having fun. She's so fine."

"Knock it off, Travis." Keep him on the line. "You thought much about Donté Drumm?"

"Not really. We should've known those people down there wouldn't listen to us."

"They would have, Travis, if you had come forward earlier. If we had found the body first, the execution would not have happened."

"Still blaming me, huh?"

"Who else, Travis? I guess you're still the victim, right?"

"I don't know what I am. Tell you what, though, Pastor. I gotta find a woman, know what I mean?"

"Listen to me, Travis. Tell me where you are, and I'll come get you and bring you back to Topeka. I'll leave right now. We'll do another road trip, just the two of us. I don't care where you are. You'll be locked up here, and then they'll extradite you to Missouri. Do what's right for once, Travis, and nobody else will get hurt. Let's do it, pal."

"I don't like prison, Pastor. I've seen enough to know."

"But you're tired of hurting people, Travis. I know you are. You told me so."

"I guess. I gotta go, Pastor."

"Call me anytime, Travis. I'm not tracing these calls. I just want to talk to you."

The phone line was dead.

An hour later, Detective Lang was at the house, listening to the recording. They had been able to trace the call to the owner of a stolen cell phone in Lincoln, Nebraska.

40

The memorial service for Donté Drumm was to be held in the sanctuary of the Bethel African Methodist Church, regular capacity of 250. But if folding chairs were wedged into every possible crevice, and the choir loft was packed, and the elders and young men stood two deep along the walls, the capacity might reach 350. When it was announced late Tuesday night that classes would not resume, phone calls were made, plans were changed. The service was moved to the high school gymnasium, capacity of 2,000. The time was set at 1:00 p.m., with Donté's burial to follow immediately thereafter at the Greenwood Cemetery, next to his father.

By noon, there were at least two thousand people inside the gym and more waiting patiently to get in. Donté's casket was placed at one end, under a raised backboard and goal, and it was surrounded by a massive sea of beautiful flower arrangements. On a screen above his casket, his handsome smiling face greeted those who had come to say good-bye. His family sat in the front row, on folding chairs, and as the crowd moved in, they gamely held on, greeting friends, hugging strangers, trying to keep their composure. A choir from his church stood near the flowers, singing and humming soft, comforting spirituals. Miss Daphne Dellmore, a saintly spinster who had once tried quite unsuccessfully to teach Donté Drumm the basics of the piano, accompanied the choir on an old upright Baldwin. To the right of the casket was a small elevated stage with a podium and a microphone, and before it, in rows of folding chairs, the Slone Warriors sat together, every player present, along with their coaches and trainers. They proudly wore their blue home jerseys. Other than the football players, there were a few white faces sprinkled about, but not many.

The media had been put in a box, literally. Under the stern direction of Marvin Drumm, the reporters and their cameras were bunched into a tight pack at the opposite end of the building, under the opposing backboard, and they were sealed off by a row of chairs laced with yellow police tape. Large young black men in dark suits stood next to the tape, watching the reporters, who had been warned not to make a sound. Any violation would lead to expulsion, and quite possibly a broken leg out in the parking lot. The family was sick of reporters, as was most of the town.

Roberta had wisely decided to close the coffin. She did not want the last image of Donté to be that of a lifeless corpse. She understood that a lot of people would be watching, and she preferred a smiling Donté.

At twenty minutes after one, the gym was completely packed. The doors were closed. The choir stopped and the Reverend Johnny Canty stepped to the podium. "We are here to celebrate a life," he said, "not to mourn a death." It sounded good, and there were a lot of "Amens," but the mood was far from celebratory. The air was heavy with sadness, but not the sadness that comes from loss. This was a sadness born of anger and injustice.

The first prayer was offered by the Reverend Wilbur Woods, the white pastor of the First United Methodist Church of Slone. Cedric Drumm had called him with the invitation, which he readily accepted. He gave a lovely prayer, one that dwelled on love and forgiveness and, most important, justice. The oppressed shall not remain the oppressed. Those responsible for injustice must one day face justice themselves. Reverend Woods's voice was soft but strong, and his words calmed the crowd. The sight of a white pastor standing on the stage with his eyes closed, his arms uplifted, his soul bared for all to see, soothed a lot of raw feelings, if only for the moment.

Donté had never discussed his funeral. Therefore, his mother chose the music, the speakers, and the order of the service, and it would reflect the strong Christian faith of her family. Donté claimed to have given up his faith, but his mother had never believed it.

The choir sang "Just a Closer Walk with Thee," and the tears flowed. There were breakdowns, loud emotional bursts followed by sobbing and wailing. When things settled down, two eulogies followed. The first was by one of Donté's teammates, a young man who was now a doctor in Dallas. The second was by Robbie Flak. When Robbie walked to the podium, the crowd instantly stood and began a restrained applause. This was a church service; clapping and cheering were frowned on, but some things cannot be helped. Robbie stood for a long time on the stage, nodding at the crowd, wiping tears, acknowledging the admiration, wishing he didn't have to be there.

For a man who'd spent the past few days raging at the world and suing anyone who crossed his path, his comments were remarkably tame. He had never understood the love-and-forgiveness routine; retaliation was what drove him. But he sensed that, at least for this moment, he should tone down his pugilistic instincts and just try to be nice. It was difficult. He talked about Donté in prison, their many visits, and even managed to get a laugh when recounting Donté's description of the food on death row. He read from two of Donté's letters, and again found humor. He closed by describing his last few moments with Donté. He said, "Donté's last wish was that one day, when the truth was known, when Nicole's killer was identified, one day when he was exonerated and his name was forever cleared, his family and friends would meet at his grave in the cemetery, throw a party, and tell the world that Donté Drumm is an innocent man. Donté, we are planning the party!"

Cedric's fourteen-year-old son, Emmitt, read a letter from the family, a long, gut-wrenching farewell to Donté, and did so with a composure that was startling. There was another hymn, then Reverend Canty preached for an hour.

Keith and Dana watched the funeral live on cable from her mother's home in Lawrence, Kansas, the town of her youth. Dana's father was deceased, and her mother was a retired professor of accounting at the University of Kansas. After dropping the boys off at school, Keith and Dana decided to hit the road, to take a day trip and get out of town. Reporters were dropping by the church. The phones were ringing. The photo of him, Robbie, Martha, and Aaron was on the front page of the Topeka paper that morning, and Keith was weary of the attention, and the questions. Plus, Boyette was out there fantasizing about his wife, and Keith just wanted her close.

Billie, his mother-in-law, offered to fix lunch, and the offer was immediately accepted. As they watched the funeral, Billie kept saying, "I can't believe you were there, Keith."

"Neither can I. Neither can I." It was so far away and so long ago, yet Keith could close his eyes and smell the disinfectant used to clean the holding cell where Donté waited, and he could hear the gasps as the curtains flew open and the family saw him on the gurney, tubes already in his veins.

As he watched the funeral, his eyes moistened when he saw Robbie so warmly received, and he wept when Donté's nephew said good-bye. For the first time since leaving Texas, Keith had the urge to go back.

Donté was laid to rest on the side of a long, sloping hill in Greenwood Cemetery, where most of the blacks were buried in Slone. The afternoon had become overcast and chilly, and as his pallbearers strained to carry him the last fifty yards, a drum corps led the casket, step-by-step, its steady, perfect rhythm echoing through the damp air. The family followed the casket until it was carefully placed on top of the grave, then settled into velvet-covered chairs inches from the fresh dirt. The mourners gathered tightly around the purple funeral tent. Reverend Canty said a few words, read some scripture, then gave the final farewell to their fallen brother. Donté was lowered into the ground next to his father.

An hour passed and the crowd drifted away. Roberta and the family remained behind, under the tent, staring at the lowered casket and the dirt scattered on top of it. Robbie stayed with them, the only non–family member to do so.

At 7:00 p.m. on Wednesday, the Slone City Council met in an executive session to discuss the future of Detective Drew Kerber, who was made aware of the meeting but not invited. The door was locked; only the six councilmen, the mayor, the city attorney, and a clerk were present. The lone black councilman, Mr. Varner, began by demanding that Kerber be fired immediately and that the city unanimously adopt a resolution condemning itself for its handling of the Donté Drumm affair. It became readily apparent that nothing would be unanimous. With some difficulty, the council decided to postpone, if briefly, the passing of any resolutions. They would take these delicate matters one step at a time.

The city attorney cautioned against the immediate firing of Kerber. As everyone knew, Mr. Flak had filed a mammoth lawsuit against the city, and the firing of Kerber would be tantamount to an admission of liability.

"Can we offer him early retirement?"

"He's only been here sixteen years. Doesn't qualify."

"We can't keep him on the police force."

"Can we transfer him to Parks & Rec for a year or two?"

"That ignores what he did in the Drumm case."

"Yes, it does. He needs to be fired."

"And so I take it that we, the city, plan to contest the allegations of the lawsuit. Are we seriously going to claim we have no liability?"

"That's the initial position of our insurance lawyers."

"Then fire them and let's find some lawyers with good sense."

"The thing for us to do is to admit our police were wrong and settle this case. The sooner, the better."

"Why are you so sure our police were wrong?"

"Do you read newspapers? Do you own a television?"

"I don't think it's that clear."

"That's because you've never seen the obvious."

"I resent that."

"Resent all you want. If you think we should defend the city against the Drumm family, then you're incompetent and you should resign."

"I may resign anyway."

"Great, and take Drew Kerber with you."

"Kerber has a long record of bad behavior. He should've never been hired, and he should've been fired years ago. It's the city's fault he's still around, and I'm sure this will come out in court, right?"

"Oh yes."

"Court? Is anyone here in favor of going to court in this case? If so, then you need an IQ test."

The debate raged out of control for two hours. At times, all six seemed to be talking at once. There were threats, insults, lots of name-calling and flip-flopping, and no consensus, though it was generally felt that the city should do whatever possible to avoid a trial.

They finally voted—three to terminate Kerber, three to wait and see. As the tiebreaker, the mayor voted to get rid of him. Detectives Jim Morrissey and Nick Needham had taken part in the marathon interrogation that produced the fateful confession, but both had left Slone and moved on to police departments in bigger cities. Chief Joe Radford had been the assistant chief nine years earlier and, as such, had almost no involvement in the Yarber investigation. A motion was made to fire him too, and it failed for lack of a second.

Mr. Varner then raised the issue of the tear-gas assault in Civitan Park the previous Thursday night, and demanded that the city condemn its use. After another hour of hot debate, they decided to postpone further discussion.

The streets were clear and quiet late Wednesday night. After a week of gathering, protesting, partying, and in some cases breaking laws, the demonstrators, protesters, guerrillas, fighters—whatever they called themselves—were tired. They could burn the entire town and disrupt life for a year, but Donté would remain peacefully at rest in Greenwood Cemetery. A few gathered in Washington Park to drink beer and listen to music, but even they had lost interest in throwing rocks and cursing the police.

At midnight, the orders were given, and the National Guardsmen made a quick and silent exit from Slone.

41

The summons from the bishop came by e-mail early Thursday morning, and was confirmed by a brief phone conversation in which nothing of substance was discussed. By 9:00 a.m., Keith and Dana were once again on the road, this time headed southwest on Interstate 35 to Wichita. As he drove, Keith recalled the same journey only a week earlier, same car, same radio station, but with a very different passenger. He had finally convinced Dana that Boyette was crazy enough to stalk her. The man had been arrested innumerable times, so he wasn't the craftiest criminal on the prowl. Until he was caught, Keith would not let his wife out of his sight.

Keith was ignoring the office and the church. Dana's nonprofit work and jam-packed daily planners had been placed aside. Only the family mattered at the moment. If they had the flexibility, and the money, Keith and Dana would have loaded up the boys and taken a long trip. She was concerned about her husband. He had witnessed a uniquely disturbing event, a tragedy that would haunt him forever, and though he'd been thoroughly unable to stop it or intervene in any manner, he was nonetheless burdened by it. He had told her several times how dirty he felt when the execution was over, how he wanted to go somewhere and take a shower, to cleanse himself of the perspiration and grime and fatigue and complicity. He wasn't sleeping and he wasn't eating, and around the boys he worked hard to carry on the usual banter and games, but it was forced. Keith was detached, and as the days passed, she was beginning to realize that he was not snapping out of it. He seemed to have forgotten about the church. He had not mentioned a sermon or anything related to the upcoming Sunday. There was a pile of phone messages on his desk, all waiting to be returned. He'd corralled their assistant minister into presiding over the Wednesday night dinner, blaming it on a migraine. He'd never had a migraine, never faked being ill, and never asked someone to pinch-hit in any situation. When he wasn't reading about the Drumm case, or researching the death penalty, he was watching cable news, some of the same segments over and over. Something was brewing.

The bishop was a man named Simon Priester, a huge round ball of an old man who was married to the church and had absolutely nothing else to do but micromanage those under him. Though only in his early fifties, he looked and acted much older, with no hair except matching white patches above the ears, and a grotesque abdomen that bulged out and hung grossly over the hips. There had never been a wife to scold him about his weight, or make sure his socks matched, or do something about the stains on his shirt. He spoke in soft slow words, hands usually clasped in front of him, as if waiting for every word to come from above. Behind his back, he was known as the Monk, usually in an affectionate tone, though sometimes otherwise. Twice a year, on the second Sunday in March and the third Sunday in September, the Monk insisted on preaching at St. Mark's in Topeka. He was a crowd killer. The few who came to hear him were the hardiest of the flock, but even they had to be cajoled into attending by Keith, Dana, and the staff. Because of the slim crowds, the Monk was overly concerned about the health of St. Mark's. If you only knew, thought Keith, who couldn't imagine larger crowds at other churches on the Monk's tour.

The meeting was not urgent, though the initial e-mail began with "Dear Keith: I am deeply concerned..." Simon had suggested a possible lunch, his favorite pastime, sometime the following week, but Keith had little else to do. In truth, a quick trip to Wichita gave him an excuse to leave town and spend the day with Dana.

"I'm sure you've seen this," Simon said after they were properly arranged at a small table with coffee and frozen croissants. It was a copy of an editorial in the morning edition of the Topeka paper, something Keith had read three times before sunrise.

"I have," Keith said. With the Monk, it was always safer to use as few words as possible. He was brilliant in taking the loose ones, piecing them together, and tying them around your neck.

Hands clasped, after a bite of croissant that had not been fully consumed because a large crumb was stuck on his lower lip, the Monk said, "Don't get me wrong here, Keith, we are quite proud of you. What courage. You threw caution to the wind and raced off to a war zone to save a man's life. Dazzling, actually."

"Thank you, Simon, but I don't remember feeling that brave. I just reacted."

"Right, right. But you must've been terrified. What was it like, Keith? The violence, death row, being with Boyette? Must've been horrible."

The last thing Keith wanted to do was tell the story, but the Monk looked so eager. "Come on, Simon, you've read the papers," Keith tried to protest. "You know what happened."

"Keith, humor me. What really happened?"

So Keith bored himself while humoring the Monk, who added to the narrative every fifteen seconds with a bewildered "Unbelievable" or a clucking "My, my." Once, while he was shaking his head, the crumb was dislodged and fell into his coffee, but the Monk did not notice. In this rendition, Keith chose the chilling phone call from Boyette as the final chapter.

"My, my."

Typical of the Monk, they had begun with the unpleasant—the editorial—then switched to the enjoyable—Keith's brave journey south—and suddenly it was back to the real purpose of the meeting. The first two paragraphs of the editorial commended Keith on his courage, but that was just the warm-up. The remainder chastised him for knowingly violating the law, though the editors, like the lawyers, struggled to set forth the exact violation.

"I assume you're getting top-notch legal advice," the Monk said, obviously anxious to give his version of the necessary advice, if Keith would only ask.

"I have a good lawyer."

"And?"

"Come on, Simon. You understand the nature of confidential relationships."

The Monk's overloaded spine managed to stiffen.

Chastised, he plowed on. "Of course. I didn't mean to pry, but this does have our attention, Keith. There is the suggestion that there could be a criminal investigation, that you could be in hot water, so to speak, and so on. This is hardly private."

"I'm guilty of something, Simon. I did it, plain and simple. My lawyer thinks that I may one day find it necessary to plead guilty to some vague obstruction of justice charge. No jail. Small fine. Record to be expunged later. There."

The Monk ate the last of his croissant with one savage bite and chewed on matters for a while. He washed it down with a slug of coffee. He wiped his mouth with a paper napkin and, when everything was properly cleared, said, "Assume you plead guilty to something, Keith, what would you expect from the church?"

"Nothing."

"Nothing?"

"I had two choices, Simon. Play it safe, stay in Kansas, and hope for the best. Or I could do what I did. Imagine for a moment, Simon, if I had done otherwise, if I had known the truth about who killed the girl and I had been too timid to move. They execute the wrong man, they find the body, and for the rest of my life I carry the guilt of not trying to intervene. What would you have done, Simon?"

"We admire you, Keith, honestly," the Monk replied softly, completely ducking the question. "What concerns us, though, is the prospect of a prosecution, one of our ministers accused of a crime, and in a very public way."

The Monk often used the word "us" when driving home a point, as if all the important leaders in the

Christian world were focused on whatever pressing matter the Monk had on his agenda.

"And if I plead guilty?" Keith asked.

"That should be avoided, if at all possible."

"And if I'm forced to?"

The Monk shifted his sizable frame, yanked on the sagging lobe of his left ear, then re-clasped his hands, as if ready to pray. "Our synodical policies would require the initiating of a disciplinary procedure. Any criminal conviction would mandate this, Keith, I'm sure you understand. We can't have our ministers going to court with their lawyers, standing before judges, pleading guilty, getting sentenced, with the media stumbling all over themselves. Especially in a case like this. Think about the church, Keith."

"How would I be punished?"

"It's all premature, Keith. Let's worry about it later. I just wanted to have the first conversation, that's all."

"I want to get this straight, Simon. I stand a very good chance of being disciplined, whether suspended, placed on leave, perhaps defrocked, for doing something that you deem admirable and the church is very proud of. Right?"

"Right, Keith, but let's not jump the gun here. If you can avoid prosecution, the problem is averted."

"Happily ever after."

"Something like that. Just keep us in the loop. We prefer to hear the news from you, not the newspaper."

Keith nodded, his mind already drifting away.

Classes resumed without incident Thursday morning at the high school. When the students arrived, they were greeted by the football team, again wearing their home jerseys. The coaches and cheerleaders were there too, at the main entrance, smiling and shaking hands and trying to set a mood of reconciliation. Inside, in the lobby, Roberta, Cedric, Marvin, and Andrea chatted with the students and teachers.

Nicole Yarber was buried in a private ceremony at 4:00 on Thursday afternoon, almost exactly one week after the execution of Donté Drumm. There was no formal funeral or memorial service; Reeva simply wasn't up to it. She was advised by two close friends that a large, showy service would not be well attended, unless reporters were allowed. Besides, the First Baptist Church had no sanctuary, and the thought of borrowing one from a rival denomination was not appealing.

A strong police presence kept the cameras far away. Reeva was sick of those people. For the first time in nine years, she ran from publicity. She and Wallis invited close to a hundred family members and friends, and virtually all showed up. There were a few prominent no-shows. Nicole's father was excluded because he had not bothered to witness the execution, though, as Reeva was forced to admit to herself in hindsight, she wished that she had not witnessed it either. Things had become quite complicated in Reeva's world, and not inviting Cliff Yarber seemed appropriate at that moment. She would regret it later. She would not regret excluding Drew Kerber and Paul Koffee, two men she now loathed. They had misled her, betrayed her, and wounded her so deeply that she would never recover.

As the architects of the wrongful conviction, Kerber and Koffee had a list of victims that was growing steadily. Reeva and her family had been added.

Brother Ronnie, who was as weary of Reeva as he was of the media, presided with a subdued dignity that fitted the occasion. He spoke and read scripture, and as he did so, he noticed the perplexed and stunned faces of those in attendance. All were white, and all had been convinced beyond any doubt that the remains in the bronze coffin before them had been swept away by the Red River years earlier. If any had ever felt the slightest sympathy for Donté Drumm and his family, they had kept it from their pastor. They had relished the thought of retribution and execution, as had he. Brother Ronnie was trying to make peace with God and find forgiveness. He wondered how many of those present were doing the same. However, he did not wish to offend anyone, especially Reeva, so his message was on the lighter side. He had never known Nicole, but he managed to recount her life with stories shared by her friends. He assured everyone that Nicole had been with her Father in heaven all these years. In heaven, there is no sorrow, so she was oblivious to the suffering of the loved ones she left behind.

A hymn, a solo, another reading of scripture, and the service ended in less than an hour. Nicole Yarber finally received a proper burial.

Paul Koffee waited until after dark to slip into his office. He typed a terse letter of resignation and e-mailed it to Judge Henry, with a copy to the clerk of the court. He typed a slightly longer explanation to his staff and e-mailed it without bothering to check for typos. He hurriedly dumped the contents of his center desk drawer into a box, then grabbed whatever valuables he could carry. An hour later, he walked out of his office for the last time.

His car was packed and he was headed west, a long road trip with Alaska as the likely destination. He had no itinerary, no real plans, no desire to return to Slone in the near future. Ideally, he would never return, but with Flak breathing fire down his neck he knew that was not possible. He would be dragged back for all manner of abuse—an arduous deposition that would go on for days, a likely date with a disciplinary committee from the state bar, perhaps a punishing ordeal with federal investigators. His future would not be pretty. He was fairly certain he would not face the prospect of jail, but he also knew he could not survive financially and professionally.

Paul Koffee was ruined, and he knew it.

42

Every store in the mall closed at 9:00 p.m., and by 9:15 Lilly Reed had turned off the registers, punched the time clock, engaged the alarm system, and locked both doors of the ladies' boutique where she worked as an assistant manager. She left the mall through a service door and walked quickly to her car, a VW Beetle, which was parked in an area designated for employees. She was in a hurry, her boyfriend was waiting at a sports bar half a mile away. As she was opening the door to her car, she felt something move behind her and heard a footstep. Then a strange male voice said, "Hey, Lilly." In a split second, Lilly knew she was in trouble. She turned, got a glimpse of the black handgun, saw a face she would never forget, and tried to scream. With astonishing speed, he slapped a hand over her mouth, said, "Get in the car," and shoved her inside. He slammed the driver's door, slapped her hard across the face, then stuck the gun barrel in her left ear. "Not a sound," he hissed. "And get your head down." Almost too horrified to move, she did as she was told. He started the engine.

Enrico Munez had been napping on and off for half an hour as he waited for his wife to finish her shift at a family restaurant in the mall's food court. He was parked between two other cars in a row of empty vehicles. He was still half-asleep, and he was sitting low in the seat when he saw the attack. The man seemed to appear from nowhere and knew what he was doing. He displayed the gun, but didn't wave it around. He overwhelmed the girl, who was too stunned to react. As soon as the Beetle lurched forward, with the attacker at the wheel, Enrico reacted instinctively. He started the engine of his pickup truck, lunged into reverse, backed up, then sped forward. He caught the Beetle as it was turning at the end of the row and, understanding the gravity of the situation, did not hesitate to crash into it. He managed to avoid the passenger door, where the girl was, and plowed into the right front tire. Immediately upon impact, Enrico thought about the pistol and realized he had left his at home. He reached under his seat, grabbed a sawed-off baseball bat he kept just in case, jumped across the top of the Beetle, and as the man was getting out, Enrico slammed the bat into the back of his shiny slick head. He would later tell his friends it was like smashing a melon.

The man was flailing on the asphalt, and Enrico hit him again for good measure. The pistol was only a toy, but it looked authentic. Lilly was hysterical. The entire episode lasted less than a minute, but she was already bracing herself for a nightmare. She scrambled out of her car and began running. The commotion attracted others. Mall security arrived in minutes, then the police and an ambulance. Enrico relinquished his prisoner, who was still on the ground, and began telling what happened.

The attacker had no wallet, no identification, nothing in his pockets but $230 in cash. He refused to give his name. At the hospital, X-rays revealed a hairline crack of the skull, thanks to Enrico, and a brain tumor the size of an egg. He was treated and placed in a secured room. Investigators collected fingerprint samples, and detectives attempted to interrogate him. He was wounded and drugged and gave them nothing. Several policemen and detectives were in and out of the room, and one finally made the connection. "I think it's that Boyette character," he whispered, and suddenly everyone else thought so too. But the man denied it. Two hours later, the fingerprints were matched and his identity was confirmed.

Ten hours earlier, on the other side of the world, two Black Hawk helicopters collided over the desert near Fallujah in central Iraq, killing nineteen members of a Texas National Guard unit. The tragedy was just what Governor Newton needed. With Barry and Wayne in near-euphoric agreement, they decided the governor should dash off to Iraq and show real leadership in the war on terror. The trip would also push him onto a larger stage and provide great footage for future use. And, most important, it would get his ass out of Texas.

His staff worked frantically to rearrange schedules, get military clearance, make sure the press was properly alerted, and sweat the rest of the details for the trip. Early Friday morning, the governor, Wayne, and Barry met for a briefing.

"They caught Boyette last night," Wayne said, looking at his laptop. "He jumped a girl outside a mall in Overland Park, Kansas. No sexual assault. He's in custody."

"He was in Kansas?" the governor asked.

"Yep. Bright boy."

The governor shook his head in disbelief. "Fifty states, and he stays in Kansas. A moron. What's the latest from Slone?"

Barry said, "Guard's all gone. DA resigned last night. All bodies buried. Streets are quiet, no fires. Classes resumed yesterday without incident and the football team plays on the road tonight, against Lufkin. Go, Warriors."

The governor picked up a report. Barry was burning up his laptop. All three were haggard and spent, testy and slightly hungover. They gulped coffee, chewed their nails, and never thought they would be so excited about a trip to Iraq.

"We have an execution in twelve days, gentlemen," the governor said. "What's the plan?"

Wayne replied proudly, "Got it all worked out. I've had drinks with a senior law clerk at the court of appeals. Obviously, they'd prefer to postpone the next one for a while. I told him we are in no hurry either. Word is being routed to the lawyer for Drifty Tucker that he should file something, anything, just dream up some wild claim for relief and get it filed, preferably before 5:00 p.m. The court will show unusual interest in Mr. Tucker's case and issue an order, no opinion attached, but will stay the execution until some undetermined point in the future. They'll bury Tucker's case. One day he'll probably read our obituaries."

"I like it," the governor said, smiling. "And when is the next one?"

"Not until July, eight months away."

"Eight months. Wow."

"Yep. We got lucky."

The governor looked at Barry and said, "How are things this morning?"

"Here, or national?" Barry asked.

"Both."

"Here, the big story is, of course, the Black Hawks in Iraq, but Drumm is still front-page news. They buried the girl yesterday, front page on a dozen papers. More editorials, everybody wants a moratorium. The death-penalty folks are insane. They are expecting twenty-five thousand at a rally here on Sunday."

"Where?"

"At the Capitol, across the street. It'll be a zoo."

"And we'll be in lovely Fallujah," the governor said.

"I can't wait," Wayne said.

Barry continued: "On the national front, it's more of the same. Rants by the left, not much on the right. The governors of Ohio and Pennsylvania are talking openly about moratoriums until the death penalty can be studied some more."

"That's about right," Newton mumbled.

"A lot of noise from the abolitionists, but it's all beginning to sound the same. There's so much overkill that the screaming is becoming monotonous."

"What about the polls?"

Barry stood and stretched his legs. "I talked to Wilson early this morning. We've lost ten points on the issue, with 61 percent of the registered voters in Texas still in favor. Looks like I win the bet, boys. Pay up. The surprising numbers are on the issue of a moratorium. Sixty-one percent want the death penalty, but almost 50 percent favor a hiatus of some sort."

"That'll go down," Wayne said with authority. "Let the shock wear off. Wait till there's another home invasion with an innocent family murdered, and folks will forget about Drumm. They'll forget about a moratorium and remember why they favor the death penalty."

The governor stood and walked to his favorite window. There were protesters on the street below, holding signs and parading back and forth along the sidewalk. They were everywhere, it seemed. Outside the Governor's Mansion, on every lawn of the Capitol, and in front of the entrance to the court of appeals with signs that screamed, "WE CLOSE AT FIVE. GO TO HELL." From aging hippies to Students Against the Death Penalty, they crossed all ethnic and social lines. He loathed them; they were not his people.

"Gentlemen, I've made a decision," Newton said gravely. "I'm not in favor of a moratorium, and I'm not calling a special session of the legislature to deal with it. To do so would create a spectacle. We have enough facing us already. We don't need the legislature creating another circus."

"We need to inform the media," Barry said.

"Prepare a statement. Release it after we take off for Iraq."

Friday afternoon, Keith went to Elmo Laird's office for a short meeting. Dana was busy hauling kids and couldn't be there, not that she really wanted to be.

With Boyette in custody, Keith was willing to let go of her, and she needed a few hours away from her husband.

Boyette's final assault and subsequent arrest were being widely covered, and Keith was taking some shots. Lilly's father was quoted as saying, "Some of the blame lies with that Lutheran minister in Topeka," and that angle to the story had gained momentum. In light of Boyette's record, Lilly Reed's family was relieved that the assault had gone no further, but still angry that such a career rapist was free and able to traumatize their daughter. The early reports slanted the story to read as though Keith had busted Boyette out of prison and fled with him to Texas.

Elmo explained that he had talked to the DA, and while there were still no immediate plans to prosecute Keith, the situation was fluid. No decisions had been made. The DA was getting calls from reporters and taking some heat.

"What's your best guess?" Keith asked.

"Same plan, Keith. I'll keep chatting with the DA, and if he moves forward, we will work out a plea agreement, a fine, but no jail."

"If I plead guilty, I'll probably face some type of disciplinary action by the church."

"Anything serious?"

"Nothing is clear as of now."

They agreed to meet again in a few days. Keith drove to St. Mark's and locked himself in his office. He had no idea what his sermon would be on Sunday and was not in the mood to work on one. There was a pile of phone messages on his desk, most from reporters. The Monk had called an hour earlier, and

Keith felt obliged to see what he wanted. They talked for a few minutes, long enough for Keith to get the message. The church was deeply concerned about the publicity and the likelihood that one of its ministers would face charges. The conversation was brief and ended with the agreement that Keith would go to Wichita on the following Tuesday for another meeting with the Monk.

Later, as Keith was tidying up his desk and preparing to leave for the weekend, his secretary buzzed and said a man with Abolish Texas Executions was on the line. Keith sat down and picked up the phone. His name was Terry Mueller, the executive director of ATeXX, and he began by thanking Keith for joining the organization. They were delighted to have him on board, especially in light of his involvement in the Drumm case.

"So you were there when he died?" Mueller said, obviously intrigued and fishing for a few details. Keith hit the high points of the story in a quick summary and, to change subjects, asked about ATeXX and its current activities. As the conversation went on, Mueller mentioned that he was a member of the Unity Lutheran Church in Austin.

"It's an independent church, spun off from the Missouri Synod a decade ago," he explained. "Downtown, close to the Capitol, a very active congregation. We would love to have you come speak sometime."

"That's very kind," Keith replied. The idea that he would be sought as a speaker caught him off guard.

After they hung up, Keith went to the church's Web site and killed an hour. Unity Lutheran was well established, over four hundred members, and its imposing chapel was built of red Texas granite, same as the State Capitol building. It was politically and socially active, with workshops and lectures ranging from eliminating homelessness in Austin to fighting the persecution of Christians in Indonesia.

Its senior pastor was retiring.

43

The Schroeders celebrated Thanksgiving with Dana's mother in Lawrence. Early the following morning, Keith and Dana left the boys at their grandmother's and flew from Kansas City to Dallas, where they rented a car and drove three hours to Slone. They roamed around the town, looking for points of interest—the Baptist church, the football field with a new press box under construction, the charred remains of a few empty buildings, the courthouse, and Robbie's office at the old train station. Slone seemed very much at peace, with city crews stringing Christmas decorations back and forth over Main Street.

From his first visit two weeks earlier, Keith remembered little about the town itself. He described to Dana the ever-present smoke and the constant wail of sirens, but looking back, he had been in such a state of shock that everything had been a blur. At the time, the thought of returning never entered his mind. He was in charge of Boyette; there was an execution pending, a body to locate, reporters everywhere. It had been frantic chaos, and his senses could only handle so much. Now, driving the shaded streets of downtown, he found it difficult to believe that Slone had recently been occupied by the National Guard.

The feast began around five, and since the temperature was in the high sixties, they gathered beside the pool, where Robbie had rented tables and chairs for the occasion. His entire firm was there, with spouses and partners. Judge and Mrs. Henry arrived early. The entire Drumm clan, at least twenty in number, including small children, arrived in one wave.

Keith sat next to Roberta. Though they had been in the same witness room when Donté died, they had never actually met. What do you say? At first the conversation was awkward, but before long they were on the subject of her grandchildren. She smiled often, though it was obvious her thoughts were elsewhere. Two weeks after losing Donté, the family was still in mourning, but they worked hard to enjoy the moment. Robbie proposed a toast, a lengthy tribute to friendship, and a brief memorial to Donté. He was so grateful that Keith and Dana could join them, all the way from Kansas, and this brought light applause. Within the Drumm family, Keith's mad dash south in an effort to stop the execution was already a legend. When Robbie finally sat down, Judge Henry stood up and tapped his wineglass. His toast was to the courage of Roberta and her family, and he ended by saying that something good comes from every tragedy. When the speeches were over, the caterers began serving thick sirloins smothered in mushroom gravy with more sides than could possibly fit on a plate. They ate well into the night, and though Roberta drank only tea, the rest of the adults enjoyed the fine wine Robbie had shipped in for the occasion.

Keith and Dana slept in the guest room and left early the next morning to eat breakfast in a Main

Street café known for its pecan waffles. Then they drove again. Using Robbie's directions, they found the Greenwood Cemetery behind a church at the edge of town. "The grave will be easy to find," Robbie had said. "Just follow the path until you see fresh dirt." The footpath was grass that had been worn thin. Ahead, a group of ten or so pilgrims were holding hands around the grave and having a prayer. Keith and Dana pretended to look for other headstones until they cleared out.

Donté's grave was a neat pile of red dirt ringed by dozens of bouquets of flowers. His large headstone read: "Donté Lamar Drumm, born September 2, 1980. Wrongfully executed by the State of Texas on November 8, 2007. Here lies an INNOCENT MAN." In the center was an eight-by-ten engraved color photo of Donté in shoulder pads and blue jersey, all suited up and ready to play. Keith knelt by the headstone, closed his eyes, and offered a long prayer. Dana looked on. Her feelings were a mix of grief for the tragic loss, sympathy for her husband, and an ongoing confusion about what they were doing at that moment.

Before they left, Keith snapped a quick photo of the grave. He wanted a memento, something to keep on his desk.

The conference room at the train station hadn't changed. Robbie and Carlos were toiling away, on a Saturday morning, with files and stacks of paper scattered among plastic coffee cups and empty pastry wrappers. Robbie gave Dana the grand tour, complete with an overblown history that Keith had managed to avoid on his first visit.

Their first farewell had been deep in the woods at Roop's Mountain, and at the time they were not sure if they would ever see each other again. Now, two weeks later, when they embraced, they knew it would not be for the last time. Robbie thanked Keith again for his heroic effort. Keith demurred and said that Robbie was the real hero. Both agreed that they had not done enough, though they knew they had done everything possible.

The drive to Austin took seven hours.

On Sunday, Keith spoke to an overflow crowd at Unity Lutheran Church. He told the story of his improbable journey to Slone, and then to Huntsville, to the death chamber. He dwelled on the death penalty, attacked it on all fronts, and got the clear impression he was preaching to the choir.

Since it was an official trial sermon, the church covered all of the expenses for the trip. After the service, Keith and Dana lunched with the Pastor Search Committee and the Reverend Dr. Marcus Collins, the retiring senior minister and a much-revered leader. During lunch, it became obvious that the church was enamored of the Schroeders. Later, as the prolonged good-byes were under way, Dr. Collins whispered to Keith, "You'll find a wonderful home here."

EPILOGUE

On December 22, the Chester County grand jury, called in session for a rare Saturday meeting, indicted Travis Boyette for the abduction, sexual assault, and murder of Nicole Yarber. The interim DA, Mike Grimshaw, had assumed his responsibilities with strict orders from Judge Elias Henry to get the indictment.

The day had been carefully chosen by Judge Henry to coincide with the ninth anniversary of the arrest of Donté Drumm. At one o'clock that afternoon, a crowd gathered in his courtroom for an unusual hearing. Robbie had filed a motion to declare Donté not guilty and exonerated, and the state, acting through Grimshaw, was not contesting the motion. Judge Henry wanted the event covered and publicized, but he detested the notion of cameras in his courtroom. Several reporters were present, but none with cameras.

It was another Robbie Flak Show. For an hour, he went through the facts, as they were now known, and clicked off the mistakes, lies, cover-ups, and such. With the outcome of the hearing certain, he did not belabor any point. When he finished, Mike Grimshaw stood and announced, "Your Honor, the State of Texas does not dispute anything Mr. Flak has said."

Judge Henry then read a short order that he had obviously prepared long before the hearing. Its final sentence read: "This court hereby finds, by clear and convincing evidence, that the defendant, Donté L. Drumm, is not guilty of all charges, is absolutely innocent of all charges, and is hereby fully and completely exonerated. His conviction is hereby reversed and his record is expunged. On behalf of this court, and on behalf of the State of Texas, I offer a sincere and thoroughly inadequate apology to the Drumm family." With great drama, Judge Henry signed his order, then handed it down to Robbie. As scripted, Robbie walked to the bar and handed it to Roberta Drumm in the first row.

The Texas Court of Criminal Appeals was still in its bunker. A mole had begun whispering, and when news broke about the "duty judge," the story hit page one. Though the court did indeed close at 5:00 p.m., even on execution days, Chief Justice Prudlowe assigned one of the nine as a duty judge, who was actually inside the building and supposedly monitoring the last-minute appeals. In theory, a frantic lawyer could call the duty judge and get some type of response from the court. It was a reasonable idea and not unusual for courts weighing life and death. However, the story exploded when it was learned that death-penalty lawyers in Texas knew nothing about the court's use of duty judges. Their existence was kept quiet by the court itself. So when Cicely Avis arrived at the Texas Court of Criminal Appeals at 5:07 on the day of Donté's execution, one hand holding a box of papers and the other hand banging on the locked door, there was actually a justice upstairs in his office ostensibly on guard.

The court announced that it was adopting the electronic filing of all petitions and pleadings, but denied that this change in procedure was a result of the Drumm case.

A complaint against Prudlowe was filed by the State Commission on Judicial Conduct. Two years would pass before the commission ruled that while his conduct was unprofessional, he did not engage in serious wrongdoing and he should keep his job.

The petition that did not get filed included the affidavit signed by Joey Gamble, the only alleged eyewitness at the trial. Legal experts debated the significance of his last-minute recantation and what the court should have, or would have, done with it.

Joey left Slone, then Texas. He blamed himself for what happened to Donté, and found solace only in the bottle.

On December 28, the last Friday in 2007, Keith and Dana walked into an empty courtroom in Topeka, at 4:30 p.m., and were met by Elmo Laird. Matthew Burns showed up for moral support, though Keith needed none. A judge appeared, then an assistant prosecutor. In less than ten minutes, Keith pleaded guilty to one count of obstruction of justice. He was fined $1,000, given one year of probation and one year of unsupervised parole. Elmo Laird was confident that within three years, his record would be expunged.

When asked by the judge if he had anything to say, Keith replied, "Yes, Your Honor. I would do the same thing again, if presented with the opportunity." To which the judge said, "God bless you."

As expected, the Monk informed Keith that he was immediately being placed on a leave of absence. Keith said not to bother—he was resigning. On Sunday, Keith announced to his congregation at St. Mark's that he was leaving to become the senior minister at Unity Lutheran Church in Austin, Texas.

Travis Boyette now faced life in Kansas, death in Missouri, and death in Texas. For a year, the three states wrangled, often publicly, about what to do with him. When he told a Kansas judge that he strangled Nicole in Missouri, the judge ordered him transferred to Newton County. Since he had confessed repeatedly, he had no desire to defend himself in a trial. Sixteen months after his trip to Slone, he was sentenced to death by lethal injection and sent to the Potosi Correctional Center.

Paul Koffee was eventually disbarred by a state ethics panel. He left Slone and became a bail bondsman in Waco. Drew Kerber filed for bankruptcy and moved his family to Texas City, where he found a job on an offshore oil rig.

Martha Handler won the race to the printing press and published the first of what promised to be a flood of books about the Drumm case. Her book was on the best-seller lists for almost a year. Her relationship with Robbie and the Drumm family soured when they could not agree on splitting the money.

*   *   *

The indictment of Travis Boyette and the exoneration of Donté Drumm put even more pressure on Governor Gill Newton to summon the legislature to Austin to deal with the aftermath of the execution. The governor and his advisers had hoped the passage of time would erode interest in the matter, but that was not happening. Death-penalty opponents were ramping up their efforts and sharpening their tactics, and they were being cheered on by much of the national press. The Black Caucus, led by Senator Rodger Ebbs of Houston, had only grown louder. Their vow of closing down the state's government until a special session was held appeared more and more likely. And the poll numbers were not trending the governor's way. A clear majority of Texans wanted the state to take a hard look at its execution business. They still wanted the death penalty, and by a wide margin, but they wanted some assurance that its use would be limited to those who were actually guilty. The idea of a moratorium was so widely discussed that it was gaining support.

Finally, the poll numbers got the best of him, and Governor Newton called the 31 senators and 150 House members to the Capitol. Since he dictated the limits of what could be considered, the agenda would be (1) a resolution on Drumm, (2) a moratorium on executions, and (3) the creation of an innocence commission to study the problems. It took three days to pass the resolution, which upon final approval declared Donté exonerated of all guilt and awarded $1 million to his family. When filed, and every member of the Black Caucus was a co-sponsor, the bill called for an award of $20 million, but the legislative process had whittled away all but a million. The governor, a tightfisted fiscal hawk, at least on the campaign trail, expressed his usual concern over "excessive government spending." When the *Houston Chronicle* ran its front-page story, it included the fact that the governor and his staff had spent over $400,000 on their recent trip fighting terror in Fallujah.

The moratorium bill ignited a political war. Its original language sought a two-year stop on all executions, during which time the death penalty would be studied from all angles and by all manner of panels and experts. Committee hearings were televised. Witnesses included retired judges, radical activists, well-known researchers, even three men who had spent years on death row before being exonerated. Outside the Capitol, rowdy demonstrations were held virtually every day. Violence erupted on several occasions when death-penalty proponents got too close to its opponents. The very circus the governor feared had come to town.

Since the moratorium fight originated in the Senate, the House began work on what was initially known as the Donté Drumm Commission on Innocence. As conceived, it would be a full-time commission with nine members who would study the roots of wrongful convictions and work to correct the problems. At the time, Texas had seen thirty-three exonerations, most by DNA evidence, with an alarming number from Dallas County. Another series of committee hearings were held, with no shortage of enthusiastic witnesses.

After settling into their new home in late January, Keith and Dana went to the Capitol often to watch the proceedings. They were in the crowd during several protests, and they watched the legislature suffer through the tortured process of coming to grips with a major problem. They, along with most observers, soon had the impression that nothing was going to change.

As the special session dragged on, the name of Adam Flores began to appear in the news. After twenty-seven years on death row, Flores was to be executed on July 1. In another life, he had been a petty drug dealer who had killed another petty drug dealer during a bad night. His appeals were ancient history. He had no lawyer.

The legislature recessed in late March, then reconvened the first week in May. After months of bitter infighting, the obvious had become even more so. It was time to forget this little war and go home. On final passage, the moratorium failed in the Senate by a vote of twelve in favor and nineteen against, all votes along party lines. Two hours later, the House voted seventy-seven to seventy-three against the creation of the innocence commission.

On July 1, Adam Flores was escorted to Huntsville and met by Warden Ben Jeter. He was placed in the holding cell and counseled by the prison chaplain; he ate his last meal—fried catfish—and said his last prayer. At precisely 6:00 p.m., he made the short walk to the death chamber, and twenty minutes later he was pronounced dead. He had no witnesses, and there were none for his victim. There was no one to claim his body, so Adam Flores was buried in the prison cemetery, alongside dozens of other unclaimed death row inmates.

AUTHOR'S NOTE

My heartfelt thanks to David Dow of the Texas Defender Service for his time, advice, insights, and willingness to slog through my manuscript and offer suggestions. David is a noted death penalty litigator, but also a professor of law and acclaimed author. Without his assistance, I would have been forced to handle my own research, a prospect that still frightens me and should frighten my readers.

The Senior Warden at the Walls Unit in Huntsville is Mr. C. T. O'Reilly, a colorful Texan who showed me his prison and answered every question possible. Thanks to him and his trusted assistant, Michelle Lyons, for their hospitality and openness.

Thanks also to Neal Kassell, Tom Leland, Renee, Ty, and Gail.

Some overly observant readers may stumble across a fact or two that might appear to be in error. They may consider writing me letters to point out my shortcomings. They should conserve paper. There are mistakes in this book, as always, and as long as I continue to loathe research, while at the same time remaining perfectly content to occasionally dress up the facts, I'm afraid the mistakes will continue. My hope is that the errors are insignificant in nature.